PALANSHIA

PALANSHIA

BOOK 3 - THE CONVERGENCE

WILLIAM CHANCELLOR

WILLIAM CHANCELLOR PUBLISHING

BOOK THREE of the FOUR-PART PALANSHIA SERIES

Illustrator: Lady Vanessa Arden King
Cover art: Lady Vanessa Arden King & William Chancellor

ISBN: 978-1-952448-33-1 – Paperback
ISBN: 978-1-952448-34-8 – eBook
ISBN: 978-1-952448-35-5 - Hardback

WILLIAM CHANCELLOR PUBLISHING

WWW.PALANSHIA.COM

THE PALANSHIA BOOK SERIES:
PALANSHIA book one: THE GIFT
PALANSHIA book two: THE BECKONING
PALANSHIA book three: THE CONVERGENCE
PALANSHIA book four: THE END SONG (2026)

DEDICATION

TO MY INCREDIBLE FAMILY

AND WONDERFUL FRIENDS

WHO INSPIRE ME CONTINUOUSLY .

CONTENTS

ACKNOWLEDGEMENTS

My sincerest gratitude goes to:
– my wife and incredible family and many friends, who have fanned the fires within me and encouraged my passion for this story over the past 35 years,
– my amazing illustrator Vanessa Arden King, for her exquisite artwork which takes my stories to a higher level.
– Julia Keeling, for their mastery of words, editing skills and tireless dedication to this project,
– my sister, Sheila Chancellor, for her genius and plot analysis,
– the anonymous inspiration for Toman Foggling, who I watched grow up over twenty years and who became a treasured friend,
– Jonas Grauer (audiobook version) for his masterful compositions, giving incredible depth and atmosphere to Palanshia,

PROLOGUE

The iridescence of Eth flickered for a second time since creation.

Pulsing unseen in the ground, shimmering through the water, and rippling through high currents of the air, the power of Ber'eth surged out from the core of the world.

The Shift resonated through the foundations of the three lands – the magnificent Great Continent in the midst of the Olmish oceans, Urborn in the far south, and the dying Palanth-Orric archipelago in the north.

All of creation began to respond, as if waking from a dream.

The unstoppable Beckoning had begun.

The Shift penetrated deeper into the world.

The lights of iridescent Eth shimmered again in once dead stone.

Sensing the Beckoning's flow within the Shift, the Uccell – Firstborn of the Continent – took flight from their mountain eyries in the glacial expanses of Ydassum.

The remnants of once vast flocks of the Firstborn rejoiced. For the first time in centuries, their voices thundered in jubilation through their remote highlands.

Many of the Palanth-Orren on the Great Continent sensed the Beckoning, and wondered, waiting. Others ignored the call surging out from the core of the world.

Sorcerers of Athlonia, alerted by the Shift, became aware of the existence of their banished kinsmen surviving on the Great Continent. Filled with rage and aided by forbidden forces, they summoned the power of the Irrshen.

Through sudden cracks in her crystalline prison, the Wailing One became aware of the Shift and Ber'eth's Beckoning. Her fury enkindled, she began devising how to escape her entrapment, and to satisfy her insatiable appetite for power.

In the Urbonnic southlands, arcane primordial forces began to stir, longing to break free.

As the currents of Eth moved unseen through the world, hope awakened in a lost Orrenic tribe held in thralldom in the Skyllian Alldai.

The unstoppable Beckoning spread further through the world.

The Shift resounded deeper into creation.

The Wailing One slowly began to writhe out of the cracks in her crystalline prison, and escape her ancient confinement.

The Legacy walked among the Spectrals as ancient, once-dead stones quivered with new life.

The Temmerung began to pulse with new iridescence.

For the first time since creation, the Firstborn of the Continent lent aid to the Orren.

From the dying archipelago of Palanth-Orron, the sorcerer Lords of Athlonia set sail for war.

Arcane primordial forces emerged from their underground realms.

The deep sands of the Alldai desert shifted as subterranean bedrock cracked and heaved.

The ocean floor shook, lifting tidal waves that began to surge and pound on the southern shores of Urborn.

PALANSHIA

The Hlimman, trapped in thralldom, sought a way out of their centuries-long imprisonment.
The unstoppable Beckoning permeated the world in preparation for the Atonement.

1

Quickly Now

"Tomi..." The glowing image of the Greinen spoke. The ice in her gaze belied the sudden warmth in her tone. "Shepherd of Fahtu-Shan, I await you. Come to me."

Toman's Linger faltered and blinked out, and his nostrils filled with a sickeningly sweet odour, mingled with the stench of sorcery.

He fell to the floor. "Ber'eth help us."

"Why struggle?" She chuckled darkly. "You will be mine eventually." Her tone sharpened. "And you will worship me. All will worship me."

Her words blistered in Toman's mind.

"Never!" He barred the doors to his thoughts against

her words. "Get out!" She would not enter! He wouldn't allow her. He pressed his hands to his head.

Father of Heaven, help us! As he released the prayer, a soothing sense of calm came over him.

Light ignited in the bones of his hands, making them flare like brilliant torches. The orange hue burned to nearly white. In an instant his Linger formed again in front of him, pulsing more powerfully than ever.

Toman pushed himself up from the bloody floor, away from his master's seemingly lifeless body, and stood to face her.

He shaped his Linger into a double-edged sword and raised it above his head. But before he could thrust it towards the terrifying blue mist glowing around Trend, the image faded with an angry howl.

He probed the air around Trend. Reluctantly he accepted the sudden emptiness and her absence.

Toman dropped back to his knees and slid his arms under his master's limp body.

As Toman lifted him, His Grace groaned, coughing blood.

Thank Ber'eth, he's still alive!

"Take care of the sick and wounded." Palan addressed an officer. He then turned towards Toman. "The sickbay is up a few flights of stairs, on the top deck." Palan's boots thudded in the dark corridor as he led the way out of the brig towards the main deck.

How could this have happened? Trend was obviously under the Greinen's control, but he hadn't even moved. He couldn't have touched his master.

A blur of impressions stormed through Toman's mind. It had all taken place so quickly. The muffled crack of bone breaking. His Grace falling next to him, gasping, moaning in pain. His silver eyes closing. A pale blue mist forming. The glowing image of a sensuous woman.

Just like during the battle on the Great River, the Wailing One and Torghyll must have teamed up once more in their rabid thirst for dominance. The memory of being bound to the flagpole on the Solyssia swirled in his mind again... The ravening presence of two evil beings looming over the barges, pressing against his Linger barrier. And then, like now, a horrible smell that had filled the air, the clear evidence of sorcery.

The back of Toman's throat still burned with the acrid stench in the brig. But this time something had been different.

The smell had changed.

The smell of sorcery had been mingled with an almost pleasant odour. Sweet. Toman wouldn't call it perfume. Perfume was different. Gentler. This odour had been so strong as to be almost overpowering.

The Greinen? It had to be her.

Toman shook his head. But how were the Wailing One's plans interwoven with Torghyll's? Was he a puppet dancing on her strings? Or did Torghyll have his own motives for helping her?

One thing was becoming clear.

Druin's fear about her reaching beyond her prison, touching the world, was well-founded. And just like he said, the Wailing One seemed to be repeating her cycles of torment. But... but... Toman sucked air through his clenched teeth. But instead of her typical attack against the Méndrensynn family, she'd chosen a different person. His master...

Toman carefully shifted his master's weight in his arms.

Guilt assaulted him. Why hadn't he protected his

master? Why had he spread his Linger out only over Palan, and not both him and His Grace? How could he have been so careless?

Trend's hair, pure white, like a Storryn's, like Torghyll's, like Uri's matted locks, dripping with blood. And then hearing the student's pitiful sobs for help through the Linger connection, and his pleas to be released from his dark prison. His utter hopelessness, pain and torment still clung to Toman's heart.

Then the Greinen, a sensuous transparent outline of thin milky blue, and what had looked like wings spreading out behind her, thick black veins branching through them like massive antlers.

Her sultry voice still spread through Toman's mind like rancid butter.

How had she known his nickname? Only Yannu ever called him 'Tomi' or was she able to read Toman's memories, like she had Druin's? The sweat on his body seemed to turn to ice, and his stomach churned uncontrollably. He had never known this kind of crippling fear.

Alyena had always said that there were times when a sense of fear, an alertness to dangers, sharpened the mind. It helped to make good decisions, and protected you from harm. But this feeling paralysed his soul.

He looked quickly again at his master's pallid face.

"This way, Toman." Palan waved towards another flight of stairs.

Toman paused for a moment to catch his breath.

He looked up, blinking to clear the sting of tears.

The masts creaked under the pull of immense ballooning sails as something prickled on the back of his neck.

Despite his exhaustion, he launched his consciousness

high above the ship and continued climbing up the next set of stairs.

Powerful cooler currents of air were still strong out of the north. The storm hadn't passed, but the sky southwards felt clear, serene, promising calmer skies and seas.

His Grace's arms and legs stiffened. He made a gurgling noise. His eyelids flickered open.

A glimmer of hope shot through Toman as his master's eyes began to move.

Unfocused and bloodshot, they seemed to search for something. "Son?" He coughed and spittle stained with blood appeared on his lips. His face twisted in agony. He slowly closed his eyes again, and his body relaxed against Toman's chest.

Miserable memories of his mother's death flooded through him.

He joined Palan at the top of the stairs.

"This way." Palan indicated a set of intricately carved doors the other side of the small deck. "Physician Wanner should be in the sickbay. He's one of the best."

Toman's tongue stuck to the sudden dryness in his mouth. He forced a swallow. "Please, Palan, would you have someone call the Riddern Chieftains? The Lord Protector, as well as the Highborns, would wish it."

Palan's silence showed his obvious reservations.

"Please." Toman's words caught in his throat. The muscles in his arms began to quiver under his master's weight.

"Of course..." Palan nodded. Glancing at His Grace's bloody face, he looked quickly away and gestured for a servant to approach. "Call for the Urbonnic savages."

The servant's eyes widened. "Yes, Your Highness."

"Thank you." Toman nodded then tensed as His

Grace groaned again, gurgling from deep within his throat. More fine droplets of spittle and blood flew from his mouth.

Toman's guts twisted tighter.

Palan opened the entrance to a dimly lit corridor lined with smooth dark red wood panels and called out. "Wanner! Assistance required!"

A door at the end of the hallway flew open, and the physician hurried out. "Your Highness, are you ill?"

Palan stepped out of the way and waved Toman forward. "It's the Ydassumer Lord Protector."

The physician's hesitation lasted only seconds then he beckoned them to enter.

Toman eased into the room, ducking the lintel, straining to keep His Grace from scraping the door frame.

"Over there." Palan's physician pointed to a narrow bed built directly into the floor. "Quickly now!"

2

Darkness Knocks

Staring around at the luxurious cabin in the uneasy silence, Druin gripped the upholstered armrests of his chair. His heartbeat pulsed in his ears.

But Lord Dalbonn had insisted they wait in the officers' accommodation allotted to Banah and Maiden Lorann. Out of harm's way.

What was happening belowdecks?

The Gendarme Captain's words still sent chills through him. He tensed his body to keep from shuddering. '*The prisoner snapped the first two sets of chains clamped on him. Something unnatural about that young man... killed two of my men, and I still haven't understood how.'*

Druin found it alarming that the Barrostanian student had been brought on board in the first place. Maylin's murderer – Banah's own attempted killer – was in the belly of the ship, just a few levels below. And something was going wrong again.

But Banah appeared to have taken the news of Trend being on board better than he had.

Maiden Lorann stood near a Byrwood credenza, watching her mistress attentively. It was comforting that the young woman truly cared for his sister.

"The interrogation should answer some crucial questions." Nodding slowly to herself, Banah continued gazing at the intricate patterns of the floor carpet. Her cheeks were flushed, her breaths shallow and quicker than normal.

Druin shook his head slightly. "Back onboard the Solyssia, Master Dobbesser had seemed so harmless. Just a young enthusiastic scholar, zealous in his field of study." Some of the information he'd offered would be crucial to the search for other Crethingan portals. The question of whether the Holy Enclosure and the Temple were two different locations could alone have an impact on history itself.

Druin closed his eyes. He could almost see the unkempt youth making his way to his sleeping quarters on the Boaddan, book-filled satchels flapping at his sides. In the Temmerung, Arden's vision of him, an innocent-looking figure, had shifted suddenly, changing to a sinister vapour then the stealthy murderer.

By Ber'eth, what had they brought on board?

He stood and rubbed the perspiration on his palms against his pant legs.

Banah looked up at him. Thin lines across her forehead creased slightly. Her otherwise serene expression contradicted the turmoil she must be feeling.

"We are fortunate to have Lord Dalbonn and Toman on board with us. And the Riddern Chieftains." Just mentioning their names gave Druin a certain sense of security.

"We are indeed blessed." A taut smile appeared at the corners of Banah's mouth. "Fyrst Foggling and the Lord Protector are our greatest assets in safeguarding this journey."

Even though her tone was firm and without inflection, Druin wondered if she was attempting to convince herself of the veracity of her words. "From the captain's description, the Barrostanian student is also under the power of sorcery through the Beàl'Toht."

Maiden Lorann placed a tea pot on the highly polished white granite tabletop in front of Banah. With a shaky hand, she poured her mistress a cup.

Banah touched her Maiden's hand. "Ber'eth is with us. The Uccell Lords will guide us."

"Let it be so." Druin bowed his head slightly. The tightness in his arms and chest seemed to lessen as Maiden Lorann softly repeated his words.

He looked around. Obviously high-ranking officers' quarters, its grandeur bespoke luxury at the highest level. The elaborately carved and gilded furniture, the intricately painted ceiling, and sparkling Vlachonian crystal windowpanes, the room shimmered with pale amber opulence.

Through an open door, elegant beds swayed gently with the movement of the vessel. Suspended from the heavy rafters with thick spider-silk ropes, they should be more comfortable than cabin beds bolted into the walls.

Sudden inexplicable anxiety and pain shot through Druin. Sensations of crippling fear. He struggled for air, stumbling.

"Brother?" Banah stood quickly.

"The pain… it's intense." He pressed his palms against his temples to try and stop the piercing sensation.

Banah grasped his arm and helped him towards his chair. "Brother, please, sit." Her voice quivered with nervous concern.

"Druin!"

"It's Arden in my mind again." Keeping his hands pressed to his head, he dropped into the chair. "Something's happened. Something bad. I feel her calling out to me." She had seemed so close, as though she was trembling against his chest, and then she was gone. A sense of total helplessness overwhelmed him. "I can't sense her now." His voice cracked.

"Can you tell where she was?" Eyes fixed on his, Banah spoke slowly. "Reach out to her? Communicate with her somehow?"

He shook his head. "Not while I'm awake. I don't have her gift."

She clasped his hand. "May Ber'eth watch over and protect her."

"Let it be so." Once again, he confirmed her prayer, then lowered his head. Arden's well-being was crucial. "She was close, Banah. I could feel her, right beside me, right here! I could feel her embrace, almost smell the flowers of her perfume… And yet she's untouchable." He rubbed his face with his hands. How could someone fill his senses so completely?

Banah sat back down and motioned for Maiden Lorann to join them at the table. "Dear Brother, let us not lessen our faith, no matter how dire things may seem.

Ber'eth *will* make a way." She paused, her eyes smiling at him. The golden light cast by the oil lamps seemed to convey a sense of hope with her words.

He nodded. "Arden has this special ability to summon an entrance and send her consciousness into the World of Visions. I have only been able to enter there from deep sleep. And even then, the Temmerung drew me in. I did not seek entrance. I can do nothing to reach her."

His sister placed her hand softly on his arm. "We can trust in Ber'eth."

If only he had Banah's unwavering faith. Her trust in Ber'eth's protection had always been stronger than his, immoveable, unaffected by circumstance or tragedies.

More fearful sensations shot through him, stronger than before. He flinched, clenching his fists.

"Druin? Are you unwell? Should I call the Riddern?"

"I'm fine. It's still Arden. But something else is happening. She's calling out again." He closed his eyes and concentrated. It was as though she were somewhere within his skull. "She is in a dark place, and hurt."

Her voice cut off and deadly silence filled his mind.

He looked at Banah. "Something terrible is happening." He balled his hands into fists. He hated the helplessness, feeling useless at a time of such need.

Closing his eyes once more, he sought further sensations of Arden.

He waited.

Nothing.

He tried once more.

Only a dreadful stillness enveloped his mind.

He shook his head and opened his eyes. "She was terrified, then the impression was snuffed out, extinguished like a candle flame. Sister, what does it mean?"

Banah leaned closer and squeezed his arm gently.

He needed to keep trying to reach her. He shut his eyes one more time and hoped to sense traces of Arden. '

Why had she stepped through that portal in the chapel? He should have tried to stop her, even if the Crystalline Man wanted her to stay. Barrost was far too dangerous for her to remain. The terrifying images of the flames leaping from the rooftops of the city sent a new wave of fear through him.

"Why did I leave her behind? I would ask Palan to turn the ship around, but..." his voice cracked, "...but that would endanger the ship, everyone on board."

"You didn't leave her." Banah clasped his arm. "It was Arden's wish to remain behind."

The warmth from Banah's hand seemed to spread through his arm and chest.

Speaking in a low voice, she looked into his eyes. "My heart is with you, Brother. Remember the message from Ber'eth, the Uccell's words that we should continue our course."

A sharp knock came at the door. Maiden Lorann frowned as she quickly rose to open it.

One of Palan's liveried servants stood in the hallway, gasping for air. "Forgiveness... My Lady... My Lord. It's your Lord Dalbonn. He's been badly hurt... is being taken to the sickbay as I speak. His Highness fears the worst."

3

Not Only Broken Bone

"Palan..." Toman tried to swallow. His tongue was like a piece of dry leather stuck to the sides of his mouth. "Can you get his feet? We want to disturb him as little as possible." Muscles beginning to cramp, he carefully lowered His Grace's body onto the cot.

"Yes, of course." Palan gently lifted the Lord Protector's legs over the low frame of the cot, letting his boots come slowly to rest on the mattress.

Toman arranged His Grace's arms along his body, then slowly pulled off his master's blood-stained boots and placed them under the bedframe.

"What happened?" The physician spoke in a clipped

tone. He moved quickly to the opposite side of the bed, placing a white enamelled basin and jug of water on a small table.

"The student struck him, but I didn't see how." It was still hard to believe. It had happened so quickly. "I heard a crack like bone splintering. Then..." Toman couldn't stop his voice from quivering with emotion. "I felt His Grace fall to the floor. Next to me. When I looked at him, his eyes were blank, then he closed them. But he is still breathing."

The many shelves of corked glass bottles, the salty alcohol smell, even the low ceiling all reminded him of Arzat's infirmary back on the Solyssia.

"Most likely a punctured lung." Physician Wanner began quickly unbuttoning His Grace's rumpled jacket.

The dull sunlight in the room seemed to suddenly brighten.

Was the storm passing?

"Fyrst Toman." Breathless, Lady Banah hurried into the room. "How is he?" The smooth distant expression Toman had always known on her face was marred with lines of concern.

Druin entered behind her, also trying to catch his breath. "We came as soon as we heard." He looked anxiously at the Lord Protector. "The student's doing?"

Nodding, Toman tried to swallow again. "Yes. Trend Dobbesser. He's under the Beàl'Toht. He attacked His Grace."

Lady Banah looked at her brother as if she wanted to ask something. Or was it fear in her eyes?

Druin raised a fist. "Another attempt at murder!" The intensity of his words burned.

The physician pushed open his master's jacket and began unbuttoning the shirt.

Toman gasped.

A livid bruise the size of a fist glared from under the shirt. Sunken slightly inwards, his master's sternum had what looked like a pool of blood, putrid brown and black, just under the skin. Surely His Grace's heart didn't have enough room to pump, nor his lungs to breathe!

Lady Banah covered her open mouth. "I'm so sorry, Fyrst Foggling."

The physician motioned towards the door. "Now, if My Lords and Lady would clear the surgery, I have work to do."

Toman nodded in agreement, but for some reason his legs wouldn't move.

Icy nausea filled him. Every muscle in his body knotted. Squeezing his eyes shut, the hideous scald on Uri's chest appeared behind his closed lids, splaying out like forked antlers from the evil mark – like the webbed veins that had spread out around the Greinen.

His Grace coughed again, gurgling darkly.

Toman started and opened his eyes.

Fresh brilliant red glistened on his mentor's mouth, dripping down over his jaw and his neck.

Palan stiffened sharply and looked out of the window.

His master took a ragged, bubbly breath. The terrible sound tore at Toman's mind.

Was His Grace drowning in his own blood?

Wanner turned him on his side, propping him up with pillows, letting the blood flow onto the sheets.

His Grace didn't open his eyes with the movement.

The room grew suddenly distant and seemed to spin.Toman closed his eyes again as a memory came into view.

Alyena lay on her bed, her skin colourless. Her clothes

drenched in sweat. The sorrowful sound in his father's voice, telling him she was leaving them forever...

Forever? How long was forever?

Forever held no meaning for him as a child. Waiting for the next holiday from school had often seemed to take forever. The night before opening packages for Wintersong had taken forever.

But, over the years, Toman had come to grasp a sense of the word.

Forever had been made up of morning after morning waking to a familiar emptiness. Day after day spent with a sense of sadness and loss.

Still, for years there had been those fleeting moments, just as he'd open his eyes in the early morning, when she had still been alive. Singing downstairs. He had been certain that she'd called him. Even the wonderful smells of her fresh bread had wafted up the stairwell.

She'd been alive again. At least in his heart. If only just for those brief moments.

Then reality would return as the grogginess of sleep cleared. The emptiness would settle back in, and the reality she was not coming back.

Over the years forever had become clear in meaning.

But, His Grace? Gone, never to return?

It couldn't be.

Toman wasn't ready to part ways with the man who had changed his life and who had given him a place of unbelievable honour. His master had to survive to see Toman's children. He had to.

"Now, please, if all of you would withdraw from my surgery?" The physician pulled out a drawer in a desk. He paused and turned to them, glowering, then looking at the doorway. He lifted a tray of slender, sharp-looking tools and placed them on a shelf above the headboard.

"His life is in the balance and I must attend to him immediately. Now, if all of you would..."

"Toman?" Palan's nod towards the door seemed to wake Toman.

"Erm? Oh. Yes, of course. Forgive me." Turning around to leave, Toman braced himself against the doorframe. Was the room swaying because of the choppy sea? He staggered into the corridor, bumping against Druin. "Forgive me."

The Highborn placed a hand on Toman's shoulder and squeezed firmly. "It will turn out well, you'll see."

Toman nodded. But he wasn't so sure.

The door at the end of the corridor opened, and a gust of salty air blew in.

Dressed in simple leather tunics, the Riddern Chieftains glided rapidly towards him. They looked somehow less dangerous without their long cloaks of shimmering feathers.

Chieftess Beruhn carried one of their tooled medicine bags over her shoulder.

"My good Chieftains," Druin walked quickly in front of Toman and bowed to the Urbonnic healers. "The Prince's physician has asked all of us to remain outside while he tends to the Lord Protector."

Chieftain Ruhand stared at him, then at the open infirmary door, then nodded.

A hardness passed over Chieftess Beruhn's snake-like eyes. "We will honour your request." Gazing around the room, she turned towards Druin who quickly looked down at the floor. "But give the Prince's Healer these. They are for the Lord Mischul." Glass tinkled softly as she reached in her bag and withdrew three stoppered phials.

"These will not heal the bone, but they will aid in

the breathing and in the flow of blood. If the blood is healed, the broken bone will heal." Chieftain Ruhand's deep hissing voice rumbled in his throat. "He should drink three drops of each. Mornings and evenings."

"Thank you." Druin took the small glass bottles.

With that, both Riddern inclined their heads towards the Highborns, and swept back down the corridor.

Lady Banah held out her hands.

"Sister?" Druin tilted his head slightly.

Unblinking, she nodded towards the small glass bottles. "The phials. Please. I want to make sure the Chieftains' wishes are represented." The strength of her Linger seemed to change, glowing a slightly stronger pure yellow.

"All right." Eyebrows raised, he placed the Riddern medicines in her open hands.

Toman watched from the hallway as Lady Banah walked back over the threshold and into the room. "Good Sir, may I, for just a moment?"

Physician Wanner jerked his head up as he wrung blood out of a wet sponge. His face quickly darkened. "My Lady, I said—"

"Of course, you may." Palan's quick response came from a corner of the infirmary. Just like back in the Summit meeting, his words carried a sense of unquestionable authority.

A frown remained on the physician's forehead as he nodded. "As Your Highness wishes." Physician Wanner stared at the Highborn as she approached His Grace's bedside. "But do not get in my way, My Lady." He turned back to the basin and quickly dipped his sponge in the now rust-coloured water.

"Thank you." She nodded and laid the small glass bottles out on the physician's tray. "These are from our esteemed Master Healers, the Chieftains. They are tinctures to aid in the recovery of our landsman, Lord Protector Mischul Dalbonn. We would appreciate it if you would also administer them to him, along with your treatments. Three drops of each to be given mornings and evenings."

The physician's eyes widened for a moment, then his frown returned, deepening into a scowl as he wiped more blood from His Grace's neck and face.

"You will do as she says, Wanner." Palan's now resigned flat tone still sounded respectful.

Continuing to scowl, the physician didn't seem to be making any effort to mask his irritation. "As you will, Your Highness."

"My appreciation, Physician Wanner." Lady Banah lifted her head and looked directly at Palan. "Before we go, we would also like to make a supplication for Our Lord Protector. Would you permit us?"

Something inside Toman lightened. A prayer. A plea to Ber'eth for help. Of course! Fear seemed to have driven it from his thoughts. And Lady Banah had a healing Eth resonance. Surely her prayers would convey Ber'eth's power more purely than anyone Toman knew.

"Of course." Palan nodded.

Druin walked back into the room and up to his sister.

Toman stepped into the doorway and paused. He wanted to hear how the Highborns prayed. What words would they use to release Ber'eth's power?

The infirmary seemed to fill again with a pleasant brightness. A change in the weather, smoother sailing, would be welcome. The movement of the ship surely wasn't helping His Grace's condition.

At the foot of the bed, Lady Banah stretched out her arms over His Grace. Her Linger intensified even more and a bright halo of deep pure yellow shone all around her.

Such unbelievable brilliance and clarity of colour! Her Eth resonance was like living golden light. As though clear afternoon sunshine glowed inside and around her.

Toman glanced at the physician's hard expression.

Lady Banah turned her palms down over His Grace as her warm light flowed over him. Slowly, his body began to glow with her Eth colour. Then the entire room filled with her brilliant yellow resonance.

Hope filled Toman. Maybe she would heal His Grace!

Wanner's blank stare seemed to confirm that he could not see the wondrous sight.

She began speaking softly. A private prayer.

Holding his breath, he sent his consciousness towards her. Perhaps he could catch words the Highborn spoke to Ber'eth. Learn how to pray better.

His Grace remained perfectly still, barely breathing, and his eyes still closed.

Images of Alyena on her deathbed returned. That terrible yearning filled Toman again... *if she would only open her eyes and stand!*

But she never did.

Toman studied his master as dread filled him and Lady Banah continued her whispered prayers.

On an impulse, he stretched out his hands and kindled his Eth, trickling a small flow of Ber'eth's power to reinforce his consciousness.

Keeping his voice low, Toman added a prayer. "Strength to Lady Banah. Power to her healing."

The Highborn smiled but didn't look up, then placed a hand on His Grace's foot and continued her soft utterings.

Shimmering webs of colourful lights began to flow in

through the windows. Weaving together, they formed a thin curtain that glistened like fine glass. Sparkling within the Highborn's yellow Linger, they seemed like highlights within a clear golden crystal.

Palan gasped, shaking his head and mumbling something about Toman's Gebayt Bithen.

Wringing out another sponge full of blood, the physician continued examining His Grace's neck and chest.

Toman concentrated harder to catch Lady Banah's words.

She was interceding for the man who had changed his life. "Father of Lights, this man's purpose is yet unfulfilled. Please allow him to complete the course you planned for him and his life..."

The glowing colour around her was wondrous, filling the room with warmth.

Relief flooded Toman as Lord Dalbonn's laboured wheezing slowly ceased and a tightness in his face seemed to soften.

Did this mean His Grace would be healed now?

Toman studied the hideous indentation in his master's sternum.

But His Grace didn't move.

He didn't even seem to be breathing.

Images of his mother's lifeless body flickered in his sight again. Bitter cold coursed through his veins. *No, no! Please, Ber'eth, no! Not my master!*

His Grace suddenly made a ragged gasping sound. Then his chest began to move at a slow steady pace. The indentation in his sternum remained – a slight depression in the middle of his chest.

Druin grabbed Toman's arm and squeezed it firmly. "I'm sure all will be fine, my friend."

Lady Banah's shoulders seemed to lower and she exhaled a long breath.

Toman leaned against the wall as his legs seemed to lose their strength to hold him up.

Physician Wanner stepped back towards the windows, his mouth open. He finally seemed to notice the sparkling filaments of light as they disappeared. He had obviously seen the lights, but apparently he couldn't see the resonances of Eth.

It was difficult to believe that so few Orrenic peoples could see Linger colours.

He'd known them practically all his life. He had grown used to the different shades glowing around most people. Not all people, just certain ones.

After making comments at a village Shantab about the various colours, Alyena had responded that few Orren saw the Linger lights.

He had wanted to know why some people's were bright and others dark? Some clear and others drab?

His mother had just smiled at him in response and shrugged. She couldn't answer his questions, but she did ask him if he could see her Eth resonance.

Of course. Yellow. But not bright like daisy pollen. More like the soft traces of dawn's first light.

She'd smiled.

She had explained that the Akkoren's Lingers were a rare and special gift from Ber'eth. And that their gift helped them read other people's colours. But she had died before his own Linger had appeared. His was corporeal and clear, not green like theirs. So he couldn't be an Akkoren.

It probably wasn't a mystery that few Eth colours had shown up in Barrost. Toman had never been in a gathering of so many people and seen so few colours.

According to His Grace, some Eth wielders could see their own colours, but almost never anyone else's. His Grace had taught that only those of Limmanian blood who had transparent Lingers like Toman, or who had the gift of the Akkoren, could have the ability to see the colours of Eth in others.

The Highborns seemed to be exceptions.

So few Limmanians had survived both conflicts. But surely, of the other survivors of Limmanian heritage, he wasn't the only one with this ability. The way the Highborns and His Grace spoke, they thought he was.

One of the physician's instruments clattered onto the tray.

Toman looked up.

Lady Banah had started moving towards the door, then stopped and bowed low. "My sincerest appreciation, Physician Wanner."

The physician's nod was almost undetectable. "I wouldn't have believed it, if I hadn't seen it with my own eyes." He removed the pillows helping to prop up His Grace, and gently lowered him back to the mattress.

Palan stared at his ship physician for a moment, then followed Lady Banah into the corridor.

Raising her head slightly, Lady Banah clasped her hands together and looked at Palan then Druin and Toman. "Gentlemen, we need to talk to Trend. Together. Immediately, if possible. There is much more to this than I initially understood. The Lord Protector's wound is not only broken bone. A very dark force has touched him."

"No." The sudden tension in Palan's voice surprised Toman. "I cannot allow it. The danger is too great."

Lady Banah kept her eyes fixed on him. "Prince Palandred, this situation is under your jurisdiction now, on your ship and with us under your generous care, but I would ask that you please permit us this. Lord Dalbonn is our trusted friend."

"My Lady, your safety comes first. This Barrostanian student on board my vessel is seething with deadly malice." Palan looked down at his open palms and closed them. He then glanced at Toman, then Druin, as though seeking support. His breathing slowed as he seemed to study Lady Banah's face.

Her resolute expression hadn't changed.

"If I may..." Druin touched Palan on the shoulder. "...I also want to see this succubus spirit. I think I know who she is." He lowered his voice and spoke through gritted teeth. "The Greinen. She shall not have another sacrifice." He looked fixedly at Palan. "And this Master Dobbesser was also behind our younger sister's death, and the murder attempt on Lady Banah. Please, I also ask you, allow us this."

For a moment Palan seemed to wonder what to say, then bowed slightly. "As you wish." His thick sigh sounded like unwilling resignation.

"Fyrst Toman, would you accompany us?" Lady Banah gathered the hem of her dress, took a step then waited, looking at Toman then Palan.

Toman hesitated. "Yes, of course, My Lady, but it really isn't safe for you. The Beàl'Toht is very powerful in the student. When we see the injuries His Grace has... Please My Lady..."

"Thank you for your concern Fyrst Toman, but we need Lord Druin's Eth ability now to combine with mine, to ascertain more specific details perhaps locked in the student's memory."

"Yes, of course." Toman bowed, catching a last glimpse of His Grace's cot as the physician closed the door.

Palan gestured towards the corridor entrance. "Follow

me." Anxiety was palpable in his voice, but his confident gait showed no signs of fear.

4

OUT OF THE TEMMERUNG

Arms crossed and holding herself tightly, Arden struggled to calm the nervous spasm rippling through her. *Calm. Peace.* She tried to command her heartbeats to slow down. The noise of blood pounding in her ears numbed her ability to think. She needed to work this out.

Why hadn't the portal appeared when she'd called?

Why had Crethingan left her so abruptly, and with so little instruction?

There had to be a way back. She couldn't be trapped in the Temmerung!

Sir Crethingan had said she was *The Legacy*, the culmination of all the tribes of Palanth-Orron. And that the Temmerung was responding to her voice. Whatever that meant, she needed to discover a way out of the World of Visions.

Trying again to slow down her erratic breathing, she focused her will and mind. Keeping her eyes open as Toman had suggested, she spoke. "Return to my body."

Arden concentrated on her bedroom, willing the portal to come.

She waited, but only silence and the billowing sheets of luminosity.

Normally, her consciousness would re-enter her body within moments. First the transparent colours would flow around her, then her room and her physical form would come into view. Then she would become aware of her surroundings as though waking from a dream. Her room, the desk and chair would appear. Why wasn't it happening now?

Thoughts raced through her mind.

Crethingan speaking to her.

Toman's encouragement.

The translations of the inscription from Warningen House.

What did they all mean?

If, as Sir Crethingan had said, she was 'The Legacy' and her mother's line carried Bohdnian blood, could that mean that the hideous Greinen, a Bohdnian Wayfarer, was also somehow related to her?

No! Arden's throat tightened and she clenched her fists. No, she couldn't be of the same blood as the Wailing One.

Hoping to leave the Temmerung as soon as possible, she concentrated harder on her room. She had to get back to the Baronhold, then to the university for those maps. No time to waste!

Arden closed her eyes for a moment, trying to envision

the rooms of her suite. She waited a little longer. Aspects began to appear... her bedroom... her study... her desk... and the tall windows lining the balconies.

But something was terribly wrong – no matter how hard she tried, she couldn't visualise her body! Why? Why couldn't she see herself?

Terror spread through her like a crippling disease. She couldn't draw in enough air. Opening her eyes and panting, she battled the panic filling her.

It couldn't finish like this.

She couldn't be trapped in the Temmerung!

What detail was she missing? What was different?

Different? Of course! She clapped her hands together. How could she have forgotten so quickly? Crethingan had pulled her into the World of Visions directly from the entrance to the chapel. Of course she wasn't in her room. Relief spread through her, and she laughed. She couldn't return to her body because she was in her body! She was physically in the Temmerung.

The simplicity of it!

And now? She swallowed hard.

How was she supposed to get back out? Crethingan had drawn her in, he should be able to help her return to the chapel in the Baronhold. The maps Professor Gwenndon had of the architect's structures, surely they held the key to where other portals could be found.

Spinning around, she hoped to see a trace of the Crystalline Man, any sign. He must be able to sense her distress and would come to help her. "Sir Crethingan! Sir Crethingan, please, Sir, how do I get back? Sir Crethingan?"

Wouldn't he have prepared her, explained some crucial detail, if returning was so difficult?

Once again, Arden waited. The silence seemed to

press in more tightly. Her rapid heartbeats continued to throb like dull thunder in her ears.

She shook her head. Did she just need to focus harder?

Closing her eyes again, she attempted to wrap herself in thoughts and feelings of safety and calm. She imagined the door to her suite, firmly locked against the typical hubbub of the Baronhold. She imagined her father, walking alongside her, holding her hand as a child.

She extended her consciousness deep into the Temmerung. Cracks and fissures split still dark stones. Currents wisped around the openings in the walls and floor, but it wasn't air.

Delving deeper, she let her mind hear and see through the darkness.

Stillness enveloped her.

No sign of a portal of any kind.

She opened her eyes again. Was there no way back?

Icy tendrils shivered down her spine as the Greinen's shrill laughter suddenly cackled far above, a mirthless sound of hideous demented triumph. Arden's stomach convulsed with fear.

Could the evil creature sense her torment from beyond the barrier and somehow feed off her fear, as she had with Druin?

The Wayfarer's haughty ridiculing tone continued, piercing Arden's mind with a sense of deranged amusement and decay. A ravenous succubus being, draining life from wills and souls.

"Silence!" Anger shook Arden's voice. "You will remain banished from this sacred place."

The harsh laughter ceased abruptly.

The low rumble of boulder grinding on boulder groaned in the darkness above. Fine dust floated down around her as the musty scent of ancient dry rock filled her nostrils.

Try to remember, Arden.

Had she missed some simple detail Sir Crethingan had mentioned? What seemingly small aspect had he spoken about, that was obviously far more important than it had seemed?

She cleared her mind of the distant sounds of the Greinen's moans.

Oddly, the voice of Toman seemed to come to her mind.

The memory brought a thrill of hope. Of course – *Forth-telling!*

She had formed a passageway through the barrier in Druin's vision. The opening had simply come into existence as she spoke. And she and Sir Crethingan had created the domed shield above her, by speaking it into existence.

Steeling herself, she articulated the words. "Portal, open." The stones beneath her feet shook as she spoke. "I require passage back to the chapel in the Galdyssen Baronhold." She brought the image of the garden chapel to her mind's eye, the high walls of the Baronhold, and the gently swaying silvery trees.

Instead of the misty luminescent portal forming before her, the precise outline of the doorway took shape. Beyond the dully shimmering stones of the opening, the flagstones of the garden pathway appeared. In her peripheral vision, the simple seats of the chapel came into view, then unadorned grey walls and a window filled with light.

Relief and joy filled her.

The profound simplicity of Forth-telling.

How did her words have such power within the

Temmerung? One day she would have time to fully investigate the phenomenon, perhaps with Professor Gwenndon. Toman should also know the impact of his suggestion, if she ever saw him again.

Stepping towards the open door of the chapel, she smiled, thankful to feel the grit of the firm stone floor under her shoes.

A sudden deep groan rumbled underfoot. Sand and dust cascaded down the slender stone door jambs. The paving stones heaved, causing her to fall to her knees.

She waited a moment with bated breath.

Silence returned to the austere scene.

Shaken, she stood again, struggling to regain her balance. She peered through the thinning cloud of dust and her heart sank. Neither Druin nor Lady Banah stood on the garden path. And by the intensity of light, it must have been past midday already.

They had probably long departed.

Another tremor rocked the chapel, splintering glass panes of the windows.

Arden stumbled towards the doorway as the massive lintel moved above her.

The tympanum cracked loudly, slipping in its arched mouldings. Then the lintel gave way, falling at a sharp angle to the entrance steps.

Arden screamed, throwing her arms up to protect her head. Pain shot through her shoulder as she fell to the floor and the long stone pinned down the hem of her dress.

"Help!" Tears flowed down her face as she struggled to free herself. Dust choked her. "Druin..." she lost the strength to speak. He wouldn't be able to hear her anyway. She had bid him farewell. He wouldn't even know that she had come back and was in the garden.

Indistinct shadows descended around her like a thin black veil.

The shrill laughter of the Greinen filled her ears like the screech of a vulture.

No, please no.

Not here, not in this way. She couldn't die here.

Complete darkness filled her vision, and her eyes closed.

5

Guiltless Guilt

Toman followed Palan back outside into the cool salty air. He paused to let Druin and Lady Banah catch up, wanting to keep the space between them small in case he needed to extend his shield over them.

Palan seemed to read Toman's thoughts and lowed his pace.

The skin on his arms tingled.

Out of instinct, he sent his consciousness skywards and probed the currents. The north wind was still strong but growing weaker. And the heavy grey cloud cover had already given way to wide strips of brilliant white stretching across a pale blue background.

Something drew his attention higher and wider.

Even though the storm over Norssum was growing distant, powerful forces were still moving all around them. It was as though unseen gales were bearing down on them from all directions.

But these currents were something far greater than streams of air converging. They felt more like wild hounds, baying and circling around their prey.

Their magnitude made Toman shudder.

The wind weakened suddenly, and the giant sails relaxed slightly. The ship slowed and entered a gentle calm.

A chill ran up his spine.

The eye of the storm?

It was just like the message the Uccell had given Druin! Were they now entering the quiet zone of something vast and terrible?

A sensation drew his attention back to the ship and he withdrew his consciousness from the sky. Impressions of decay, misery, hunger, imprisonment, but also deep sorrow.

It was the Barrostanian student.

The evil that Trend had brought on board seemed to pulse through the planks of the deck and throb under the soles of Toman's boots.

How powerful must that evil be, to permeate the entire ship?

Toman sent his mind down towards the brig. He shivered as a distant echo repeated a desperate cry for help. Then a powerful sense of sadness passed through him.

Had Trend been enslaved and forced to do evil against his will? How many of his actions were of his own will? Could he actually be innocent?

Regardless, the Barrostanian appeared to be full of wickedness.

Rapid flashes of heart-wrenching images had assaulted Toman when his Linger closed around Trend...

...imprisonment under the terrifying power of sorcery

...the searing heat raging through the marrow of every bone...

...then the ravenous hunger and a sense of rotting decay at the same time...

...darkness and biting cold...

...the putrid nauseating stench stinging in Trend's nostrils...

...desperate screams for help as a white-haired sorcerer scalded him...

Torghyll's hands pressing against his chest as the Mark of the Irrshen, splaying out like the branched antlers of a stag, was burned into his skin.

Laughing darkly, the sultry form of the Greinen had taken shape around Trend's body as his fear had overwhelmed Toman and he'd fallen to his knees. She had wavered at first on the edge of the vision, but under her transparent blue skin, forms had wriggled like maggots in a rotting carcass.

Then she'd called him Tomi. 'The shepherd from Fahtu-Shan.'

Icy dread seized him again.

How could she be connected with the Irrshen? But he'd seen it with his own eyes – she'd appeared within the Mark of the Irrshen, black forked prongs of a giant elk spreading out behind her!

Look at what she'd done to Uri and the men imprisoned to her will in the village on the Folumpor, and now this horror inflicted on His Grace.

Toman gritted his teeth as fear throbbed in his chest.

The Greinen could not win!

She had to be stopped! But how?

He needed time to think, to bring his thoughts into balance and calm the troubled waters fear always churned up. As Alyena had taught, he called on good memories to balance the scales. His mother's words had always rung true, 'Be vigilant against evil, but do not fear it. In the end, good, even though seemingly small in comparison, will always be more powerful.' Good could take longer to act, even though its changes were always more lasting.

Palan paused at the steps that lead belowdecks. Turning, he offered Lady Banah his hand.

She inclined her head towards him as if to say thank you, but took her brother's arm instead.

Palan descended towards the brig, beginning to hurry. It appeared that he wanted to get this encounter quickly behind him. But the frown and shakes of his head... he probably regretted agreeing to take them to see the Barrostanian.

He was right, Trend was very dangerous. Toman would protect them and not make the mistake he'd made with His Grace.

His master... A knot formed in his stomach at the memory of the brig and His Grace falling, his eyes shutting as though death were closing them for the last time.

The bones in Toman's hands burst with light.

The Highborns had the right to interrogate the man suspected of murdering their sister and of attempting to kill Lady Banah herself.

Druin had mentioned that, in the World of Visions, he and Arden had seen Trend pouring what looked like poison into Lady Banah's slippers. He'd said that Arden saw their little sister dancing in them shortly before she died.

Then those same slippers had almost taken Lady Banah to the grave in Barrost.

That was enough proof to hang Trend.

But executing him without further investigation would be terribly wrong.

They needed to know more.

From the rush of impressions through Toman's Linger, Trend had been trapped against his own will, locked in a hideous unseen world. Forced to do someone else's bidding. He hadn't killed of his own will. But the Barrostanian had committed murder anyway, and had tried to do it a second time...

Sour bile burned in Toman's throat.

"Captain Westrum!" Palan called out as they drew close to the massive brig door. "Is the prisoner safely bound?"

A muffled answer came from the other side of the heavy door. "Yes, Your Highness." Then a small window flew open. "He is chained. And unconscious."

The Prince's dull reddish Linger intensified, changing to a clearer red, oddly like the colour he disliked so much.

Toman had never seen an Eth resonance actually change in hue. His Grace had said that it was rare, but that any Linger resonance could shift slightly as the person grew older and matured or experienced deep inward changes.

Palan turned his back to the door and faced them, his mouth opening as if to say something.

Lady Banah nodded and spoke in a whisper. "Please, Prince Palandred. This is important to us." The kind tone of her voice seemed to disarm him.

Palan lifted his chin sharply then nodded. "Open!"

Druin tensed as the brig door creaked open onto a terrible scene.

The hideous black marks dripping on the walls, and the dark pools on the floor, made him choke. More than one person had died for there to be so much gore.

The pungent metallic smell of coagulating blood mingled with the putridity of rotting flesh. Druin pulled out his handkerchief and covered his mouth.

Something very familiar about the stench. The strike to his head had diminished his capacity to smell for the past few days, but that reek was unforgettable...

Sorcery. The same fetor as on the river in Borinbranth!

As the guard had said, Master Dobbesser appeared to be asleep. Most likely knocked unconscious by one of the guards. Chained to a massive post, his head leaned forward against his bonds. He gurgled in short erratic breaths.

Strange though, he bore no marks or bruises. His colourless face was smooth and youthful. His now stringy white hair was streaked with drying blood and hung like a dirty veil over his face and onto the base of his neck.

Hands blazing with orange light, Toman stepped closer to Dobbesser. Staring at the floor in front of the chained prisoner, he swallowed hard. He looked back to Druin and pointed to his feet. "My master fell here."

Palan coughed. "The reek in here is overwhelming."

Glowering at Master Dobbesser, Toman twisted his face in obvious disgust. He held out a glowing hand as his Linger shimmered from his fingertips, flowing around the unconscious student. "Powers flowing through my Linger are greatly magnified. Back on the Suyan

Folumpor, when I shielded the Solyssia, the fire arrows passing through my Linger exploded into fireballs. So, your Eth resonances should also increase greatly."

The transparent form quickly encased the student.

Toman's body suddenly lurched and he gagged with dry heaves.

The student's eyes flew open. Opalescent milky blue, they blazed suddenly like a hot white fire. He bared his teeth and growled at Toman like a crouching animal just before it lunges towards its prey.

Trepidation grew in Druin as he watched.

Had they disregarded their own safety with overconfidence in Toman's ability to shield them? But they couldn't stop at this point.

Kindling his Eth, Druin focused his power towards Toman's barrier. He gasped as his Eth resonance, passing through the transparent Linger, suddenly intensified to a brilliant deep blue and filled the encasement Toman had created.

The shift in intensity of his colour filled him with a sense of awe. Never had he seen it so strong, so vibrant. The ability of Toman's Linger to magnify was astounding.

For the blink of an eye, Druin thought he could sense Toman shiver.

Druin's Linger had always given him a heightened awareness of truthfulness or dishonesty in others. Truth is what they needed from Dobbesser. And answers.

Pushing his Eth forward into the student's thoughts, Druin shuddered. For some reason his mind began filling with flashes of his own memories. His childhood. Him laughing as a toddler. Walking with his father through the cool dappled shade of the Lath Courts. Going on adventures in the garden mazes at Warningen House.

Attending school, carrying books, visiting tutors. He saw himself packing for expeditions. Discovering the Queen Summerbird. Joy filling him, then the crippling sorrow of Maylin's passing. Immediately after that image, the World of Visions flashed before him, the silent darkness suddenly illuminated with wondrous sparkling lights. The familiar melancholy gouging his old prison of sorrow. Arden disappearing through the portal into the Temmerung. Sadness wrapping around his heart.

He shook his head and the sensations faded.

Arden would be all right.

His Linger had never reacted like this before.

Blinking, Toman shot Druin a fleeting glance then looked away.

Dobbesser seemed to deflate for a moment, moaning and becoming limp against his chains. Bathed in the deep blue of Druin's Eth resonance, the Barrostanian student looked strangely like a corpse frozen in glacial ice.

By the look in Banah's wide-open eyes, she was also witnessing the effect Toman's Linger had on his Eth resonance. She stepped closer to Druin but addressed Toman. "You should be able to see my brother's Eth colour resonance."

He nodded.

She continued, "Lord Druin's hue possesses a high level of empathy, and a sensitivity to the motivation of others. He will soon find out the truth in Master Dobbesser's story, whether he be innocent or guilty."

"How could he not be guilty?" Palandred growled from the corner of the infirmary. "He's a murderer. He killed your sister and ...and poisoned you!"

Druin flinched at Palandred's words. *Murderer* and *killed*... Never had such words been such an immediate reality before.

"Prince Palandred, my brother's Eth resonance is spectral blue, a powerful gift. He can discern intentions etched in the depths of the mind."

Eyes narrowing, Palan's face paled. "An empath?" He seemed to hold his breath as his cheeks flushed. "You mean that he can read..." He touched his temple.

Banah shook her head. "Not omniscience, Your Highness. The gift does not read thoughts, but rather senses motivation and truthfulness."

"Be careful." Toman sounded almost breathless. "The Greinen may still be controlling him."

Druin nodded. "My Linger gift creates a kind of window in my mind's eye through which I have a view onto a landscape. I'm on one side, the person on the other. Your Linger connection is much more powerful. You described it once as being like standing in an open door during a gale."

Closing his eyes, Druin concentrated on the student and sent his Eth probing for impressions, like a fisherman's net trawling through murky waters.

Something started and quickly moved deeper into the darkness of the student's subconscious.

Anger swelled in Druin. If the Wailing One was still there, he'd almost welcome a confrontation with her.

Impressions drifted into his own consciousness... at first great sorrow and solitude, then pitiful remorse.

He gasped as strangling melancholy enveloped him, pressing hard on him. The old familiar torment. The presence of the Greinen gouged into his emotions.

"Brother, are you all right?" Hands outheld, Banah kindled her Eth and approached.

Her glowing yellow resonance moved towards the student and the heaviness of melancholy lessened. "Yes. Thank you."

He pressed deeper. What had been Dobbesser's motivation?

Druin strained to hear, to see, to feel... anything. Any concrete explanation of his horrific actions? Any specific connections that they could investigate?

More impressions came and Druin shook his head. "It is unbelievable, but I actually sense innocence. And unfathomable suffering." He exhaled slowly. "But true guiltlessness. I also felt the Greinen. Her strangling tentacles. However, she withdrew when you ignited your Eth."

Banah turned to Druin. "I want to try and send my Eth within Fyrst Toman's Linger shield as well. The discernment of your blue Eth and the healing of my yellow will create Akkoren green, the resonance of a Reader. We need a Reader's power to see the source of this evil, what is making him do its will."

"See the Greinen?" Toman seemed to wince. "My Lady, please." He shook his head, alarm flaring in his tone. "Please rethink that. The Greinen dwells in him. Touching his consciousness, her power could crush your mind."

"Your gift is very special and the rarest form of all Lingers," Banah sounded like an older sister instructing a younger brother, "but my Eth does not create empathy nor a link between our minds. There is no danger for me, Fyrst Toman, but thank you. Blended yellow and blue resonances form a Spirit Veil that helps to communicate with the person despite the condition of their bodies or minds. It becomes a tool of restoration spoken of by Eth masters. Some who are in great need are not capable of communicating, or even locating the source of their pain, their fever, discomfort. We can reach deeper into their hidden inner being in search of a key to release healing."

Druin moved closer to his sister.

"I can see and hear things in the minds of those who touch my Linger." Toman nodded towards the prisoner. "Just before he struck His Grace, Trend brushed against my Eth. I could sense he was desperately trying to breathe, but only death and decay were filling his lungs. Eating no longer satisfied his hunger, nor drinking his thirst."

Druin and Banah looked at each other. She was obviously as surprised as he was at Toman's statement. Perhaps now, with Toman's help, they would be able to gather all the details they needed.

His sister closed her eyes and pushed the glow of her pure yellow into Toman's shield. In the same way his resonance intensified, hers erupted in brilliance.

But, instead of a pure green glow, as had happened on previous occasions, their blue and yellow lights flowed like individual threads. Each transparent strand wove quickly around the student, forming a diaphanous veil within Toman's powerful Linger. But where the filaments interlaced, a clear green shone.

"Astonishing!" Druin looked quickly to Banah who opened her eyes. "The lights are not blending, but weaving around each other. Each keeping its own hue, but the transparency reveals the combined colour where they cross."

Palandred said something indistinct from the corner of the room.

"No! Stop!" The student's sudden gurgled coughs sounded as if he was choking. The veins in his neck and temples bulged. He jerked his head back and forth. "No, no, no! Stay out of my mind! She will kill us all! She will kill—"

"Stop!" Banah clapped her hands hard together, the force of the sound seemed to shatter an unseen barrier.

Dobbesser silenced his rant.

"You will not harm this man! You will harm no one here!"

Druin had never heard his sister speak with such sharp-edged intensity.

"Reveal the source of the affliction." She turned to Toman, her tone softening but firm. "Fyrst, please describe what you see and hear through your Linger."

"Yes, of course, My Lady." Toman looked fixedly at Dobbesser.

The student barked a coarse laugh. His eyes rolled back in their sockets. "You will die, Daughter of the Clouds." He began moving his mouth but a strange duel between a male and a female voice spoke. "I require blood sacrifice! Blood!" He screamed, struggling against the chains across his chest and throat.

Banah clapped her hands together again. The sharp sound seemed to permeate even the thick beams of the room. "Reveal the affliction. Show yourself." She spoke barely above a whisper. "Now."

Toman's body seemed to stiffen. "A form is moving around him, a weave of dark threads, like a cloth of shadow. It is brushing against my Linger." He sucked air between his teeth. "Sudden warmth, a gentle heat. His thoughts are groggy, something is slowly waking up but is still sleepy with fatigue."

"Continue please, Fyrst Toman." She and Druin kept their arms extended and their palms open.

From the shuffling of boots in the corner of the room, Palan was pacing.

Toman squeezed his eyes shut. "Regret, My Lady. Powerful sadness. Wait, I see a scene. Trend is standing on the Limman Quay in Turicum. He has books under one arm. In the other, a half-eaten pastry. A man walks up to him. It's Torghyll, the white sorcerer."

"In our own city?" Druin couldn't believe such evil had been so close.

Toman's eyes seemed to search for something behind his lids. "Trend is bound to a stone slab. Torghyll pressing his hands onto his chest. His bones are burning with intense pain as a power flows into the marrow of his bones. Over and over again he is screaming for help, but no one responds."

"She hears you." Dobbesser's cold snarl sent ice crackling through Druin's veins. The student's voice was harsh and animalistic, but his eyes were pleading like a lost child, glassy with tears.

Toman continued, "Torghyll is unrolling a map, but his voice is a woman's. The Greinen. She is speaking through him. He is placing the image of the map into Trend's brain, with specific instructions. Places to be. Times to carry out her orders. When to kill the Méndrensynn heir." Toman frowned. "He was severely punished for failure to complete his task."

Kill the Méndrensynn heir... Druin glared at Dobbesser and an involuntary tear ran down his cheek. The nightmares this evil thing had put the whole family through! Then imprisoning him in desperate melancholy in the Temmerung.

"Did you murder Maylin?" Druin carefully articulated each word.

Trend's mouth flew open wide, tears flowing down his face. Terror filled his eyes as he looked from Druin to Lady Banah and back. His mouth contorted as if trying to speak. He nodded sharply, just once, then screamed as though inflicted with sudden pain.

Palan gasped.

His guards recoiled, holding up their swords.

"She's in my mind." The words came hissing out of Trend's mouth then he let out another piercing scream.

"We know Torghyll's mission was to kill me, but poor Maylin paid the price." Banah looked at him, her expression remained steady, but her voice was full of rare emotion. "Why would this wraith from the World of Visions want my demise?"

"Sh...she..." Trend screamed again, shaking his head violently.

"What is the Greinen's connection to Athlonia?" Exhaustion seemed to press the air out Druin's lungs but he continued. "How did she bring a sorcerer from Palanth-Orren under her will?"

The Barrostanian student didn't reply but continued fighting against his chains.

"Who are you?" Banah's low voice sounded almost cold, steeled with determined calm.

Trend's head flipped back. His neck was marked with chafing from the raw metal of his chains. "I am Canthalida, Wayfarer and goddess." He laughed. "You cannot stop me. I will be free."

Palandred flinched then became rigid.

A bright white light seemed to explode in the room.

Dobbesser screamed. Dark veins appeared in his cheeks and spread across his face.

Sounds rushed in around them. Howling wind. A roaring beast. Distant shrieks echoing as though passing through vast cavernous spaces.

The student slumped against his bonds and began sobbing uncontrollably.

The movement in the air dissipated.

The guards struggled up from the floor.

Palandred rose from his knees and stood shakily. Dobbesser sniffed. “Wh... Where am I?”

6

Summerbird Dust

Holding her father's hand, Arden skipped along the path. The warmth of his hand against hers filled her with a sense of protection and joy.

The day was bright and warm. The sky, clear blue. Wildflowers dotted the meadow's edge, tiny bluebells and yellow daisies.

She began to sing. A simple song Papa had written for her.

He always loved it when she sang.

He smiled.

Birds seemed to pick up her melody, carrying her tune into the highest branches of the trees.

Arden tried to raise her hands towards them, but her arms didn't respond. Fatigue seemed to hold her down.

She needed rest, badly.

Perhaps she'd have a lie down. Yes.

She moaned. The mattress was horribly uncomfortable, cold, hard and gritty, almost as though it were made of stone. She felt for blankets as the bed trembled.

Why was Father shaking the bed? His deep voice was strangely distorted. She couldn't make out his words.

Her bed moved again, and sharp hard objects pressed into her back.

She opened her eyes and gasped for air. Her mouth filled with dust and she coughed.

She was still in the chapel doorway!

How long had she been unconscious? Hours? Days?

Another tremor vibrated through the ground, shaking the loose stones on the floor around her.

She pulled on the hem of her dress.

It wouldn't move. A large piece of the broken lintel was holding it down.

Grasping handfuls of cloth, she pulled again, this time hard. She frowned at the dry ripping sound as her hem tore. The jagged piece of broken stone pinning her was exceptionally heavy. Pushing against the weight with her feet, it moved, then she struggled to her knees.

Her temples throbbed. She placed her palm over a lump on the side of her head and winced, withdrawing her hand quickly. Good, no blood.

Her legs took some coaxing to carry her weight as she tried to stand.

How long had she been lying there? By the angle of the light through the trees, not long. A couple of hours perhaps?

The distant cackling howl of the Greinen pierced her mind.

Spinning around, Arden expected to see the creature approaching. She held her breath in anticipation.

Dust still lingered in the air. Bits and pieces of broken stone covered the floor of the empty chapel. Otherwise, nothing moved.

Relieved, she looked around the silent garden. She needed to get away from the crumbling chapel. Immediately. Stumbling forward along the pathway, she shook herself. Bits of dry grit and dust fell from her hair and dress.

The garden door was still ajar, its frame slightly askew.

Arden pushed the wooden door open as the deep earthy sound of another tremor rumbled through the corridor.

She hurried up the flight of stairs to her wing of the Baronhold.

Fine pale dust and shattered pieces of the plaster ceiling lay across the stone pavers. She looked up. Swathes of the once pristine sculptured pattern had fallen, exposing raw brickwork.

Her rooms weren't far away.

She just needed to get her research notes then distance herself as quickly as possible from the Galdyssen Baronhold, and somehow reach the university. And Professor Gwenndon.

Hopefully the Highborn's Lord Protector had returned the maps, because she urgently needed to investigate what Crethingan had said about another of his portals. The chapel had obviously been one. And, according to Crethingan, there must be another in the Sunken Garden on the university grounds.

Hurrying as carefully as she could over the debris, she

made her way down the corridor and entered her room, closing and locking the door.

She glanced in the mirror. It was clear that the hem and one sleeve of her dress were completely ruined. Pulling the garment off, she threw it on the bed then leant over and shook more fine sandy dust from her hair. Brushing out the last of the grit, the smell of dry stone seemed to bring the haunting presence of the Greinen directly into her room. But for some reason, thoughts of the evil Wayfarer didn't evoke terror anymore. The idea that she could be distantly related seemed to diminish the fear. But The Wailing One was still very dangerous.

Arden flung open the doors of her wardrobe and took out a simple dark brown dress. She would need only the bare minimum. Her research was far more important. And of course, the small crystalline vase from Papa.

She pulled the dress over her head and quickly buttoned up the neck.

Seizing the red leather travelling bag she'd brought from Borinbranth, she unbuckled the flap and carefully layered her parchments inside, then nestled the vase amongst them.

She pressed the bag against her chest as another tremor groaned through the Baronhold. Pings of falling plaster echoed outside in the corridor. But what was that odd metallic sound, like a key turning in a lock?

The urgency to run throbbed through every vein in her body. Panic confused her thoughts.

Escape! Get away from here. Straight away.

Instinctively stepping over to her desk, she raised a hand, concentrating on the gentle billowing iridescence. Shimmering in front of her, the familiar misty opening began to appear. She breathed deeply, calming her still spinning thoughts in preparation to send her consciousness into the –

"You!" A woman's screech jolted her.

Arden spun around.

The Steward's wife, Lady Soffian Galdyssen, stood in the doorway. Her red dress sparkled in the late afternoon light. Thin streaks of white shone in her hair. Was that the silken black rose of mourning on her wrist?

"Milady?" Arden closed the portal.

Soffian walked towards Arden and slapped her across the face, causing her to drop her bag. "I knew it! You little witch! You filthy little ssslut!" Dropping a key to the floor, she grabbed a fistful of Arden's hair. "Grovelling hussy!" She stumbled, almost losing her balance. "Not only have you bedded the men from Ydassum, you've slipped into the sheets with my Torghyll."

"Lady Soffian! What are you talking about!" Arden gripped the Lady Steward's wrists. "Let go of me!" She pried Soffian's fingers from her hair then raised her arms to block another blow.

"I tell you, you little schlamp, he's mine!" She staggered backwards, bumping into Arden's desk.

"You are mistaken, My Lady! No man has bedded me!

"Filthy liar!" Jabbing a finger towards Arden, Soffian tried to regain her balance.

Arden thrust her chair towards the Lady Steward and stepped backwards.

"Where elssse would you get these powersss?" Soffian waved her hand towards the spot Arden's Temmerung portal had begun to form. Her slurred words were thick with resentment. She blinked, seemingly to try and focus her bloodshot eyes. "*He* gave you these powers...." She brought one of Lady Banah's velvet sachets to her face and squeezed. She inhaled deeply. A powerful musky fragrance filled the room. Around her belt hung three more of the Highborn's velvet bags.

"My Lady, those petals are dangerous! Too much and—"

"Liar!" Soffian screamed, spittle flying from her burgundy painted lips.

In the doorway, two of her Ladies-in-Waiting raised their hands to their mouths, their eyes wide as if with horror, then steadied themselves as another tremor shook the building.

"The effect of the petals is dangerous. Where did you get so many sachets?"

"None of your business." The Baroness fell forward on the desk, knocking over Arden's pitcher of water from the kitchen. She wrinkled her nose in a disgusted expression. "Besides, those savages had no right to keep them from me."

"But, My Lady, they can kill you."

Soffian stared out of the windows as a flash of lightning flooded the room with sudden brilliance. She blinked and raised a hand to her face. Her swollen, blood-stained eyes looked ghoulish. She gritted her teeth. "If it weren't for my dear Caldere —"

Arden shivered. "My half-brother? What does he have to do with this?" She shuddered, but answers came to her instantly.

Since his youth, Caldere had been obsessed with the Galdyssens, something that had always made Arden ill at ease. And his insistence that their families celebrate every annual festival together, Wintersong, Summer Solstice and the Festival of Ashwond. And now the Baroness was referring to him?

A chill ran down her spine as the confusion cleared.

Soffian's two children... Their murky green eyes were

more like Caldere's than the Steward's. And their hair, the same dark brown as her brother's, not red blond like Lord and Lady Galdyssen's.

"Mm, yes, Caldere." A twisted smirk spread over Soffian's lips as she closed her eyes and chuckled. "He's been quite useful. And good. I'm surprised you didn't find that out yourself." Barking a coarse laugh, she looked around, seemingly disorientated. A thin film of fresh blood covered her unfocussed eyes. "Or, maybe you have already. You know how men are."

The Baronhold shuddered again, adding to the horror of Soffian's disgusting words.

The Lady Steward blinked and droplets of crimson slid down her pallid cheek. "We have a special event this evening now Lord Galdyssen has passed away." She chortled darkly, tapping a handkerchief to the blood, smearing it across her face.

"Dead?" How could that be? Arden's insides soured.

"Found dead." Sofian rolled her eyes back in her skull and giggled. "Dead, dead, dead." The corners of her mouth turned suddenly downwards and her lips trembled as though she was about to cry. She looked like a child caught misbehaving, fearing punishment.

Her erratic movements, her confused reactions... signs of the toxins from the Summerbird petals? Or intoxication from drink?

Soffian frowned then spoke in a low solemn tone, fondling the rose tied to her wrist. "Life is for the living. Death is for the grave, which is where the Steward sleeps tonight!"

The sudden shift in her voice made Arden's flesh crawl with disgust.

She had to escape this growing nightmare. To what extent would the Baroness go in her madness? But Arden somehow had to defuse her wrath before Soffian focused it again on her. "I'm very sorry, My Lady. Please accept my condolences. I didn't realise he had been so ill."

Frowning, the Lady Steward seemed to struggle once more to focus on Arden's face. Her forehead smoothed and her eyes widened as though surprised to see her standing there. "That's alright, my dear. Everything will work out." She patted her chest as if comforting herself. "Everything will work out fine." Her sudden peaceful smile looked out of place in all the tumult and madness. "Now, get ready. Your brother and I are expecting you at the announcement dinner. We're expecting the other families as well."

An explosion went off in Arden's mind. Caldere was in the Baronhold and wanted her at the dinner?

"A new Steward must be elected this evening. It's urgent." Blinking slowly, she frowned again. "These superstitious townsfolk are threatening the peace of our city. Anyway, I can't be bothered with you from tomorrow on." She turned and stepped awkwardly towards the door.

Elections? So soon?

No, no! Something was terribly wrong.

The Baroness stopped in the doorway and addressed her Ladies-in-Waiting. "Follow me. Much to do before the big event." She seemed to ignore the fact that her home was crumbling around her.

Their faces misshapen and reddened with what looked like anguish, her Ladies bowed quickly and did as they were told.

Arden could barely breathe. Her legs and arms wouldn't move. Her heartbeats pounded in her ears. Forcing her lungs to draw in air, she attempted to piece together Soffian's words.

The Lord Steward's sudden passing... and a new Steward, that evening already? And Soffian was not first going into mourning before calling the Assembly of the Vandrian Quaterni?

Already arranged?

That could only mean...

The urge to retch almost overwhelmed her as the room began to sway. She tried to collect herself. She could not faint! She stumbled towards the bed and sat, struggling to order her thoughts.

Baron Galdyssen had appeared to be in excellent health that morning. No accident had been spoken of that could have caused his sudden death. The kitchen staff would have known if his heart was failing him. And Arden's chambermaid Lily wouldn't have been able to stop herself from passing on the latest tittle-tattle.

Disgust filled her.

Soffian must have taken the White Sorcerer as a lover. Or maybe he had taken her. And, after her unbalanced outburst, she obviously didn't intend to keep the cloak of secrecy over their affair.

But her brother!

He had obviously also been her lover, and probably for years.

Father would need to know, if he didn't know already.

Arden's heart raced wildly.

Soffian had already summoned the four families! They would vote on a new Steward!

A month of formal mourning would have been Vandrian tradition. Then an official gathering of the families of the Kingship, which normally took weeks to organise. So why that very evening? Especially considering the chaos in the Baronhold and the upheavals among the Quaterni. Also the breach of the protective wall to the Lower City!

Dread seeped into her bones.

She stared around the bedroom, the balcony, her desk, these rooms had been a welcome refuge from the noisy pretentious life of the Baronhold. Now the same rooms seemed to press on her like a dank tomb.

She rolled her cloak tightly and tucked it in her travel to keep the vase safe. She didn't need to bring any more clothes.

A jagged streak of brilliant light roared down into the plaza below, exploding near the façade of the Baronhold. A deafening roar slammed against the window, rattling the panes.

Arden gasped.

For the blink of an eye, the bolt of lightning seemed to have a mind of its own, branching out through the streets, turning down alleyways... as if it were probing for something.

Rioters rampaged through the plaza, running for cover as a second blast erupted from the black sky. Small blades in their hands glinted in the light. Others carried clubs or long sharp poles. Were they already at the entrance of the Baronhold?

Pressing her travel bag to her chest again, her body wouldn't stop shaking. "Sir Crethingan? Can you hear me? Can you open a passageway again?" She ran to her favourite spot, the place where she had first discovered how to open a portal and send her consciousness into the Temmerung.

She closed her eyes. She had to focus her mind.

Shouts of the Baronhold gendarmerie outside and the clash of steel on steel sent waves of panic through her.

She had to conquer the storm raging in her thoughts.

She couldn't summon a portal if she couldn't clear her mind and concentrate.

More shouts and loud thuds came from the floors below. They must be at the entrance doors!

Terror ripped through her mind. "Sir Crethingan, please? If you can hear me, please help! Open a passageway again."

Nothing. Only chaos and crippling fear.

Urgency pressed on her. She needed to get out of there. At once!

The servants' passage! She needed to get to it as soon as possible.

She ran from her room as shouts from the stairwell echoed at the end of the corridor.

Moving quickly over the thin layer of dust on the floor, tiny pieces of the sculpted and gilt plaster ceiling ground under her slippers. In front of her, three sets of fresh footprints lead towards the stairway. Soffian and her Ladies making their way towards the meeting in the Great Hall downstairs.

Dread filled Arden. She had to go that same way, even though she ran the risk of being seen.

The entrance to the servants' passage was on the landing. It was Arden's only hope to keep from being seen. Most of the Galdyssen family and even their staff didn't know where the hidden doors were.

Arden ran towards the stairway at the end of the corridor.

She stopped just before the landing and listened.

The pounding of her heart blended with the indistinct sounds of angry voices outside. Clanking metal sent shivers through her bones. The rioters wouldn't have a chance against the Baronhold gendarmes. But with the unrest in the Lower City, it surely wouldn't be long before they –

Footsteps on the flight of stairs below jarred her.

The gruff voices of two men reached her. By the clanking of metal and thud of heavy boots, they were gendarme guards. "Lady Galdyssen just said to fetch the little wench. She's up here! Probably taking her time packing. She and Baron Caldere want her in the Great Hall now..." One of the men laughed darkly "...to sip some of the special wine she's prepared for tonight's occassion."

Baron Caldere?

She covered her mouth to muffle her cry.

7

IT MUST BE THE BECKONING

Banah's heart raced. "Is everyone all right?" She looked around the brig. What force had struck them?

Panting, her brother nodded. "Yes, but what just happened?"

"Where am I?" The Barrostanian student spluttered again through his sobs. "How did I get here?"

Fyrst Toman exhaled slowly then faced the student. "Trend Dobbesser, you were brought here as a prisoner. To be tried for the slaying of Lady Maylin Méndrensynn, and attempting to end the life of the Highborn Lady Méndrensynn of Ydassum."

Blinking, the student suddenly went silent. Strands of

saliva dripped from his open mouth. He lowered his head and tears fell from his eyes onto the floor. He released a pitiful heart-wrenching wail. "M...murder? How?" He sucked in a gulp of air then coughed on his own slaver. "How? How...?" His entire body began to convulse, shaking violently against his chains.

The student's sorrowful cry softened as he continued to struggle for air. "I suppose... death will be better for me... than her prison. Her prison..." He began to sob again as his body went limp, hanging half upright within the iron bonds.

Banah held back tears of pity. She turned to Fyrst Toman. "Unfetter him."

The Prince's posture seemed to become rigid. "Are you certain, My Lady?"

"Yes, Your Highness, if you would allow it."

Prince Palandred shook his head. "He doesn't look dangerous now, but we can't be certain."

"I can check." The Fyrst gazed intently at the student, his fingertips glimmering an even brighter orange.

Banah studied the young Fahtu-Shanner's face as his Eth resonance wrapped around the student. Fyrst Toman hung his head low, breathing slowly and deeply. After a brief silence, he looked up. "She is not there, My Lady. But she has left desolation in her wake."

He bent over and worked a heavy iron peg out of a link in the chain.

The metal clanked to the floor.

The student's body seemed to fold in on itself as he collapsed.

Prince Palandred looked at Banah. "Do you pronounce judgement on him? Shall I have him executed now?"

Druin and the Fyrst turned their heads quickly towards her, questioning expressions on their faces.

"No, Prince Palandred. My appreciation for your respect of my authority over him. But, not yet. We need to gather and consider all the details we just discovered." The idea of killing a man, of watching a man be killed, repulsed her.

"My Lady?" Standing slowly upright with the iron peg still in his hand, Fyrst Toman sounded exhausted. "My Lady, I think there is one more person that must be added to the fallen, to those killed by him."

Still on the floor with the chains around him, Dobbesser continued sobbing as the Fyrst proceeded with his observation. "When I was in his consciousness, I saw a dagger in his hand." Lines of tension spread out from his eyes and he glanced nervously from the Prince to herself. "The knife went to the Hussar's throat and..."

Banah couldn't hide her gasp.

Toman nodded. "It was Trend who killed him. Not Uri, like we'd thought. Or *she*, the Wailing One, had him killed through Trend. I saw images but did not feel the motivation."

Cold beads of perspiration broke out on her arms and face, then an unbearable heaviness descended on her. Riddern law would also have to be brought into the balance of her decision. She would have to negotiate with the Chieftains now as well. She looked at Druin. "Dear Brother, what did you sense?"

His face looked at first completely devoid of discernible expression. He then shook his head. "Innocence. I felt that he was not aware of what he was doing. He was only conscious of the pain and torment stabbing him from every direction, the presence of the Greinen. Hunger devoured him. Thirst made his skin stick to his bones. Sleep seemed to release even more intense torture..."

Banah raised her hand. "I understand." She turned to the Prince. "May the prisoner be kept in your brig, under your watch, until decisions have been made?"

"Yes, of course."

"Then, if I may, Your Highness, could we speak about this after a moment of repose? I need to pray and regain my strength before coming to a conclusion."

"My Lady?" The lines around Fyrst Toman's eyes deepened. The sadness in his tone of voice sounded profound.

A desire to soothe his obvious pain rose in her. "Yes, Fyrst Toman. What is it?"

"My Lady, I don't understand what happened in here this evening." His respectful frankness was always refreshing. "I mean, the burst of Eth light? Where did it come from?"

She wondered that herself. Where had the brilliant light originated?

She started to shake her head when her brother responded before her. "Toman, your Linger caused our resonances to interweave but not mix. I saw individual threads of Eth colours, each separate and intact, not like the blended lights I've witnessed when Lady Banah and I have interlinked our Lingers before. Your Linger bonded and strengthened our powers but did not meld them."

"I... I also sensed an incredible surge just before what felt like an explosion of power. It knocked me to my knees." Prince Palandred's astonished tone surprised her. "Do you feel it was caused by the Beckoning? It must have been." Normally he didn't hide his disdain for Eth nor his repugnance directed towards Ber'eth. Now he sounded almost convinced of the wonder.

Banah found it impossible to hide her own amazement. "We must look further into this phenomenon. But, when we are rested."

"Yes, of course." Palandred nodded. "At least you seem to have accomplished what you required. The Barrostanian student hadn't been in his own mind, but had been a puppet of the Greinen."

The Fyrst spoke in a breathy whisper. "Under the Beàl'Toht, like the men killed in the village on the Suyan Folumpor, ...like Uri. But the Chieftains' son. So innocent..." He put his hand to his forehead. "Poor Hussar Fadron."

Banah turned to the door.

Druin walked up to her and offered his arm.

Glancing back to the brig before stepping out into the corridor, Banah swallowed hard as a heavy lump formed in the back of her throat.

The Prince's guards were lifting the student's limp body onto a chair.

He hadn't stopped weeping.

8

She Needs Our Support

Toman's hands still shook as he reached the deck and filled his lungs with the fresh evening air. Sickening sweetness, and putrid rot, still reeked in his nostrils.

What would happen to the Barrostanian student now?

Where had the Greinen gone? Slithered down a deeper tunnel in Trend's soul?

Or had one of her far-reaching tentacles been cut off?

Whatever that burst of light had done, the Barrostanian had been released. That was obvious. But would the Greinen be back for what she considered her property?

He quickly climbed the stairs back towards Palan's

sickbay. He wanted to be near His Grace, even if his master wasn't awake.

Reaching the upper landing, he hurried down the dark hallway to Wanner's rooms and tapped on the thin wooden panelling of the door.

"Enter."

Toman pushed down on the door handle and walked into the room.

Standing near His Grace, Physician Wanner straightened to attention and nodded. "Your Highness."

"Good evening, Sir." Toman kept his voice at a whisper. He swallowed against the dryness in his mouth. "May I see the Lord Protector?"

The physician always seemed to frown when asked a question, but his rumpled forehead smoothed quickly and he stepped aside, bidding Toman approach the cot.

"Thank you, Sir."

Wanner had washed his master's face and changed the bloodied shirt. His Grace's trousers lay folded over the footboard, and a fresh white sheet was pulled up to his neck.

The Lord Protector looked like he was simply tired and asleep. Only resting peacefully. His Grace's breaths were barely detectable. But they were there. His skin was pale as if he'd had a fever, but the dark rings under his eyes troubled Toman.

They reminded him of Alyena's before she passed away.

No, Toman. Resting, that's all! He will recover.

Looking through the windows at the stars beginning to appear, a sense of dread passed through Toman. But it was almost time for bed anyway, so his master *should* be resting. This night could be the turning point. His master hung in a dangerous balance between recovering—coming back—or slipping towards death. The night would probably be his judge.

Tears began to sting Toman's eyes. He cleared his throat. "Sir, how is he? Please tell me he will be all right." He couldn't stop his voice from quivering, and he pinched his lower lip to keep it from trembling.

A strange look of compassion passed over the physician's face, or was it of puzzlement?

Toman quickly rubbed his eyes. "Physician Wanner, the Lord Protector is like a father to me."

Wanner turned towards His Grace. "The Lord's breathing is steady now, but still very weak. Whatever the Highborn Lady Méndrensynn and Your Highness did... the Lord Protector stabilised." The physician narrowed his eyes and shook his head. "But he is not out of danger, Your Highness."

Toman wanted to say *I'm not a Your Highness.* But it didn't matter any more how people addressed him. There were more important things at hand. "Then there is hope." Speaking the words made his chest feel less heavy.

Thoughts of life without His Grace were hard to keep harnessed. It wasn't his master's time. He had to wake up. And walk again. He just had to.

Toman wiped his eyes as cold memories passed through his mind.

Alyena had also lain in what looked like a peaceful sleep. But his mother had never awakened, never moved from the bed until she was carried away for her burial. Toman pushed the images aside and turned to the physician.

"Once again, thank you, Physician Wanner." Toman took his hand and shook it, then bowed and walked to the doorway. He stopped and turned back. "Please, Sir, may I come again tomorrow morning?"

"Yes, of course, Your Highness." The physician closed the door quietly behind Toman.

Standing in the sudden darkness of the corridor, he covered his face with his hands. His body shook with sorrow.

Please, Ber'eth. Please let His Grace return to us.

He flinched as a hand came down on his shoulder.

"You alright, Tomi?" Yannu's voice seemed to come from far away.

"Yep." Toman gulped and took a quivering breath, then quickly wiped his eyes with his sleeve. "I'm all right." He lied. He didn't want to talk about his feelings just then. He lowered his eyes. "I don't understand why His Grace isn't waking up. He's breathing, but not responding."

Yannu lit a small oil lamp and held it up to Toman's face, seemingly searching for something. No trace of Yannu's tell-tale grin showed. "He'll be fine, I'm sure, Tomi. I'm sure." But his friend's worried tone sounded as if he was also attempting to hide what he really felt.

"What if I'd never left Fahtu-Shan, Yannu? Never got on the Sondervay, never worked for Eckel? None of this would have happened. Right?"

"Maybe." Yannu let out a long breath. "But, Tomi... *What ifs* only ever leave you with *what ifs*. They don't change today, and certainly won't change yesterday, and not tomorrow. And they rob you of hope." He held the oil lamp up again.

Toman blinked against the harshness of the small flame then squeezed his eyes shut. The privacy of darkness felt more comforting.

"I understand that Lady Banah made the physician give the Lord Protector the Riddern medicines. Their medicines do wonders." Yannu's sudden lighter tone sounded forced.

Toman's gut twisted as the scene came back to mind with the Chieftains, and the Lord Protector unconscious on the cot.

The Chieftain had said that their medicines would only help with the blood. Not the bone. The blood, if healed, would bring healing to the bone. But Lady Banah's Eth power had got his lungs responding again. Surely a sign of healing?

But His Grace still hadn't moved.

Fear resurged and burned through his mind. He fought to calm his thoughts.

"They call them 'The Savages' onboard here." Yannu continued, with the same tension pulling at his voice. "Yup, they seem to be terrified of them, like they were poisonous serpents." A trace of his old smile appeared.

Toman wished Yannu would just be quiet.

Words were hard to understand right then. And they irritated.

"For all her fanciness and refinement, Lady Banah has a way of getting her point across though, doesn't she? A knockout fighter, she is." He punched the air, grinning.

Yannu's fist seemed to slam into Toman's heart. His friend's disrespectful tone hurt.

The Highborn was not a pit fighter, she was a noble Lady!

"Don't you realise that she carries a terrible weight on her shoulders? The responsibility of a nation? And people have been trying to kill her? She's impartial and honours everyone. Why don't people get that?"

"Tomi..." Yannu winced as if in pain.

"Lady Banah doesn't need criticism. Especially not

from us. She needs our support. Our honour and our protection!"

"I... I..." Yannu's shoulders sagged.

Holding his fists stiffly at his sides, Toman paced to the end of the corridor and stopped.

Yannu followed closely behind. "I...I didn't mean disrespect, Tomi. I'm sorry." He sighed deeply, then blew the lamp out and put it on a small table. Opening the door for Toman, Yannu waited, then walked slowly out onto the moonlit deck.

Toman's chest hurt. Grappling with the rage charging through him, he followed Yannu in silence. Something began to prick his heart.

Yannu didn't deserve his angry words, but Toman couldn't stop the anger.

It continued to boil unchecked.

But was he only scalding himself?

What had he been thinking to reprove his best friend? ...But Yannu should know better. And shouldn't Trend somehow have known better as well?

Toman thrust his consciousness high above the ship.

The wind was still blowing out of the northwest. The storm had sped them away from the Estuary of Barrost at remarkable speed. But now gentle ocean breezes moved the ship at a steady but slower pace.

The Wasp Nest of the Northern Horn already seemed like a bad dream from a world away.

Palan's vessel was full of the sounds of rigging and subtle creaks of wood. How different a great ship was from the Highborn's long flat barges or from the merchant vessels on the Great Inner Sea. And the pleasant salty taste on the back of his tongue reminded him that they were on the Olmish Mechen, the Great Western Ocean. The Olmish Mechen was very unlike the Great Inner Sea. An endless salty giant, it stretched further than anyone knew.

The glistening moonlight on the distant horizon looked magical. The gentle up and down of the deck was strangely comforting, like being held in someone's arms.

A sense of calm began to fill Toman. It was good that Prince Lytwon was travelling overland because the ship's movement would have made him sick.

Yannu stepped up to the railing in silence and rested his elbows on the smooth varnished wood.

Toman put his arm on his friend's shoulder. "Please forgive me. I'm really sorry. This is all a bit much for me."

Yannu rubbed his eyes. "Honest, Tomi, I mean I wasn't badmouthing." His friend's anxious frown pricked Toman's heart even deeper. It wasn't Yannu's nature to be critical, especially not of Lady Banah.

Sighing, Toman nodded. "I'm really sorry. My sense of honour keeps a tight rein on words. Words can release things, bring things into existence that weren't there before. We just need to be careful what we say."

"I didn't mean to—"

"I know," Toman squeezed Yannu's shoulder then pointed to the vast waters of the dark horizon. "You know, I never imagined it to be so huge. I hear that no one knows where it ends."

Yannu frowned slightly and swallowed a couple of times, as if trying to wet his tongue. The tension around his eyes softened.

"I'm really sorry." Toman bowed his head.

"And no ship that has every sailed west has returned." His friend sounded suddenly as if he were talking in his sleep.

"And how do you know that?

9

Not Demons

Sea monsters? Toman couldn't keep his eyes off the dark waters.

Glancing back at the deck, Yannu tapped him on the shoulder and grinned. "I haf a surprise for you, Sir Mister Foggling. Sumzing zat—"

"Stop that." Toman frowned. "I'm not in the mood for jokes."

"I vill, but not just yet." A stupid smile beamed on his face again. "But methinks zat ze Cook Marta vill be very happy to see you, Mister Sir Toman."

"Stop that! Wait." No sooner had Toman scolded his friend a second time than a familiar voice called out.

"Yuhuuu... Sir Toman?" Cook Marta's chirping sent a cold shiver through him. She was on board Palan's ship! "I haf two nice bottle of mead fer you. One fer you and one fer Mister Yannu. It vil help you sleep. After all you haf bin tsrew today."

"Erm, oh, thank you, Cook Marta. You are very kind."

"You're velkom, Sir Toman." She curtsied then smiled. Flaring her skirt, she turned and walked away, her hips swaying.

Heat flushed in Toman's face.

Yannu whispered as soon as she was out of earshot. "And she tells me she wants to be your personal cook, Mister Sir Toman Foggling, now that Prince Lytwon is gone and all."

Toman wanted to swipe the mischievous grin off his friend's face.

"Do I see your cheeks reddening?" Yannu chuckled. "Are there perhaps some mutual feelings in there somewhere?" He pointed to Toman's chest.

Toman punched him on the shoulder. "Get off."

"Ouch! That hurt." Yannu's theatrical tone matched the high arch of his eyebrows. "You want me to get off? Get off, you say?" He started looking around, still rubbing his shoulder. "Off where, My Lord? Ah, wait!" He peered over the railing then looked up at Toman with surprise. "Actually, I could get off anywhere, couldn't I? Then swim to the next tavern for a tankard or two. But, if you'd be so kind, My Lord, as to drop me off at the first one you see, it would save me of getting my clothes wet."

Toman's laugh escaped through his nose. "Your madness is getting worse."

"You just now figuring that out?" Yannu winked then pointed to the cook's bottled gifts. "Finish up, Milord, then I'll show you where you're sleeping on this big floating apple crate. I heard that your room has real feather down mattresses."

Toman exhaled as tension began to flow out of him.

His friend's light-heartedness had a way of piercing the thickest-skinned soul, lightening the darkest mood.

Toman opened his bottle and quickly finished mead. Good, but a touch of honey would have made it just right.

"Up there, over to the left." Yannu pointed to the highest of the three decks.

Toman followed his friend up the stairs as his mind drifted back to images of His Grace... his vacant face, pallid skin and sunken cheeks. His unresponsive body. His almost silent, shallow breaths...

But could his master still hear even though he couldn't speak? Could he feel it when Toman touched his arm? Was he, like Trend, trapped in a prison in his own body?

Yannu started up a second flight of stairs, paused and slowly looked around. "This ship is humongous, isn't it?"

Toman nodded.

Even though about the same length as the barges, the ship's dimensions were very different, much deeper, but not as wide. And with so many decks. Nothing like the couple of richer merchant vessels Toman and Yannu had worked on when with Eckel's crew. Even though elaborate in design, Palan's vessel gave the impression of a warship equipped more for battle than for comfort.

Yannu stopped at a glass-paned door flanked by two guards.

"Your Highness." One of Palan's men clicked his heels together hard then inclined his head in what Mendelonians probably considered a bow. Hand on the sword at his belt, he leaned forward and opened the door with a gloved hand.

Nodding, Yannu stood to one side and waved down the corridor. "This leads to your room. The first one on the right."

"Wait. What? My room? You not coming?"

"My bunk is aft, in the servants' quarters, with the crew."

"Oh." But surely his manservant could stay in his own quarters. Yannu's room had been in his own suite in the Baronhold, so...? "Come on. I'm sure it's allowed." Toman paused, trying to read if the guard's steely expression meant disapproval or approval. As the Fyrst of Ydassum, surely he could be allowed to have his manservant in his quarters. He turned to Yannu. "Come on. We'll find a place for you."

Yannu smiled. "You kind of like my company, huh?"

"Maybe." Toman snorted. "But just barely."

Yannu tapped him on the back as they stepped into the lamplit hallway. "Thanks, Tomi."

"Sure thing, mate."

After a few brisk steps, Yannu reached the cabin and swung the door open. He looked quickly around the room then pointed to a corner. "Good. Your luggage is already here."

Palan must have had the trunks brought up. Really kind of him. They weren't light. And all those stairs.

Toman smiled. "And there's a divan. So you won't have to sleep on the floor."

The moonlight streamed in through the windows, glowing in eerie bluish rays across the floor and walls.

Yannu lit the oil lamp hanging on a thin brass chain.

The light filled the room with a warm glow.

Pointing to the bed hanging from ropes bolted into the rafters, Yannu grinned. "Interesting invention, eh Tomi? Kind of like a hammock." He pushed on it. "Moves with the pitch of the ship." He punched the mattress. "Yup, it's feathers. Nothing but the best for the Fyrst of Ydassum."

The low ceiling with thick supporting beams reminded Toman of the heavy rafters of his attic bedroom at Upland. But the dark wooden interior of the cabin was deeply carved with all sorts of strange sea animals and wavy plants.

He sniffed. The air in the cabin was a bit stale. He unlatched a window, pushed against the panes and breathed in deeply.

Instead of the familiar cool moisture of an evening on Fahtu-Shan, the salty warmth of the ocean air filled his lungs. Not entirely unpleasant, but it wasn't like home.

Yannu knelt in front of one of the trunks and lifted the lid. Mumbling quietly, he seemed to be in a discussion with himself. He pulled out one of Toman's nightshirts and paused, examining the stitching on the collar. "Tomi..."

"What's up?"

"Do you think that Trend brought his demons with him? People in the crew say that he is filled with them, and that he set them free, onboard. A lot of people say that they could feel them moving through the ship. Some fear for the journey now." His friend stood and handed him his nightshirt. "Back home, they say that those who murder get filled with demons and then they spread them wherever they go."

Toman shuddered. "Not demons..." After all they had discovered, he had more compassion than disgust for the Barrostanian student. "He was taken prisoner by the Greinen. His mind was. And I'm not sure *what* she is. I don't know anything about demons. All I know is that she is evil." Yannu didn't need to know what Toman had seen and felt through his Linger connection. And about the Hussar. Trend's full story would surely terrify his friend.

"But it's true, Trend committed unthinkable evil, taking the life of a very precious person to the Highborns, their baby sister. And he tried to poison Lady Banah." Toman shook his head. "But, I don't know if he was even aware of what he did. Or if he was in control of anything he said or did for a while... Yes, the evidence against Trend is undeniable, but I can't shake the impression of innocence."

Yannu stared, open-mouthed then shook his head. "Innocent, Tomi?"

He couldn't defend Trend nor prove he was actually innocent. But *guilty* was supposed to be different from this. It was when you wanted to do wrong and did it. Trend's situation wasn't the same. The visions of him screaming for help, trying to escape but remaining trapped within the Greinen's transparent carcass still tormented Toman. "Anyway, Trend should be very different now. After the Highborn Lady's healing powers."

Yannu stared at him then nodded.

Toman pulled his boots off and undressed.

"Your clothes, My Lord." Holding out his arms, Yannu gave him his stern 'it's my job' look. He examined the trousers and jacket then laid them out carefully on a small table. Scraping something off one leg of the trousers, he grabbed the clothes brush and began rigorous sweeps over the cloth.

Toman sniffed under his arm. He really needed a long hot bath but it would feel good just to be able to freshen up. A small wrought-iron washstand stood in the corner, complete with pale blue porcelain bowl, soap, a sponge and a pitcher of water.

Yannu lay Toman's trousers over the back of a chair and picked up his jacket. "Tomi... did you actually connect with Trend's mind. You know, through your Ber'eth connection?"

"Yes." The muscles in his stomach tightened. He didn't feel like explaining any more than he had done. He responded with reluctance. Hopefully his friend wouldn't ask more.

Yannu shivered. "Horrible."

Toman dipped the sponge in the water then squeezed. Rubbing the bar of soap over it, he scrubbed his armpits first.

"You don't think he gave you a demon?"

"What? Of course not." Toman rubbed the sponge hard across his chest and down his legs, then towelled off.

Yannu waited, his eyes seemingly unfocused as he took Toman's wet towel and hung it on the washstand to dry. "Your nightshirt, Milord." A twisted grin appeared on his face. "Otherwise, going bare-buttocked, you look like the plucked boiled carcass of some long-legged Gahoin." He chuckled stupidly at his own joke.

Toman shook his head. "You have quite an imagination. And, besides, no one sees me but you."

"Just trying to keep you house-trained, My Lord. Don't want you going feral on us."

Toman slipped the nightshirt over his head then climbed up into the swaying bed. Laying down, he moaned with delight as the soft mattress moulded perfectly to his back. Definitely down-filled. Menne-Gootay! The pillow was as well. With all the thick padding around him, even the pitching of the boat felt cosy.

He sighed as tension in his body eased. Cook Marta was right, once he laid down, the effect of the mead was nice. More than nice. His arms and legs relaxed, and a sleepy fatigue spread through him. His body was definitely ready for rest, but his thoughts weren't ready to be banked in the hearth for the night.

"G'night, Tomi." Already in his nightshirt, Yannu blew out the oil lamp and stretched out on the divan. "Sweet dreams, mate." His immediate slow deep breathing meant he was probably already blessed with slumber.

Toman waited for the heaviness of fatigue to pull him into sleep as well, but unanswered questions filled him with anxiety.

Would His Grace be any better in the morning?

Would he even make it through the night?

What would life be without him?

Emotions filled him as tears burned in his eyes then slid down his cheeks.

Alyena would have told him to be strong, to have faith. Not to allow fear and worry to corrode his heart. She seemed to speak to him out of the walls of the ship, '*Faith pierces the world invisibly, but returns to the world in a visible form.*'

She never gave up, not even at the end.

Neither would he.

Slipping quietly out of the sheets, Toman stood and raised his hands.

Almost as if awaiting him, the familiar pinpoints of lights appeared and his lungs prickled with the familiar sweet heaviness of the Gebayt Bithen.

Keeping his eyes open, he followed His Grace's first

lesson and spoke into his fear. "Ber'eth, I plead for...for..." The words caught in the back of his throat. "For His Grace, for his life. Heavenly Father." Gentle spasms jerked at Toman's stomach as he struggled not to weep. Weeping often meant giving in, accepting the worst. He was not ready to give up.

The air began to shimmer. The room started to sparkle with threads of many-coloured lights. Toman's reflection appeared in his Gebayt Bithen as it rippled around him like a vertical sheet of liquid glass.

He focused on His Grace.

A vision of the infirmary appeared – the cot near a window, a pair of boots tucked underneath it, a thin sheet pulled up to his master's neck.

Stretching out his hands, Toman willed the power of his prayer towards his beloved master.

He whispered his request. "Lungs, be filled with air again. Muscle, be rewoven. Broken bones, mended. Health returned." As he released his prayer into the vision, he could almost see his words flutter from his hands like a bird freed from a cage. As Alyena had always instructed him, his plea was now moving in the unseen world. It would resurface. When, he didn't know.

He closed his eyes and bowed his head. "Let it be so."

"I always knew..." Yannu stirred in his sleep, a thin smile appearing on his face, "...you are a great man, Tomi."

10

Silver-blue Gaze

Grinning at his slumbering moonstruck friend, Toman shook his head and whispered, "Yannu, my dear silly manservant, you are incurable."

But something about his friend's words he couldn't shake off. His never-ending belief that Toman was to be a *great man*, and was to accomplish great things.

Such words, from someone who knew you so well, left a mark on your soul. Strangely, they gave Toman the feeling of being surrounded by a protective barrier.

His Linger was powerful. Maybe he was supposed to do great things. Over the past year and a half, being always in the presence of His Grace, the Highborns or

Prince Lytwon, something was definitely changing in Toman.

The old schoolyard taunts were growing distant.

Brun's harshness was almost silent now.

Toman could barely make out their voices anymore.

Laying back down on the swaying mattress, he smiled. As soon as he stretched out, the last traces of tension drained from his body, and his limbs grew heavy with exhaustion.

He yawned.

The warm air of the cabin lulled thoughts. What he wouldn't do for some of the freshness of the highland fogs.

He wiped a thin layer of sweat from his forehead. His nightclothes were too warm. Glancing at his sleeping friend, Toman shrugged and slid back out of the hammock bed and dragged his nightshirt back over his head. He folded it carefully and lay it at the foot of the bed then crawled back in.

He pulled the thin sheet up to his chest and grinned towards Yannu. He'd be up and dressed before his friend anyway.

The oncoming drowsiness felt wonderful. His mind emptied of thoughts as he welcomed sleep.

"Chores all done, Ma!" Toman stopped at the open door and kicked off his mucky stall boots. He slipped into his clean wooden clogs and entered the Molkey, where his mother was busy making their special cheese.

"How did it go, Little Man? Your first day in Letters School." Alyena's silvery blue eyes seemed to sparkle.

"All right." He didn't feel like telling the whole story, the voices he'd heard through solid walls.

The scene faded but another from his childhood came to him...

Toman hung the manure rake back up on its peg, then ran up the stone pathway to the back of the house. The smell of fresh honey scones reached his nose. Warm lamplight glowed in the kitchen windows. A thin trail of smoke rose from the chimney and disappeared in the early evening fogs.

He stopped at the threshold to kick off his boots and put on his house slippers.

"You spoil him." Brun's grumbling passed through the door. He sounded like a distant storm.

"He's special, and you know that." Toman could almost see Alyena's smile in the tone of her voice.

Why was Brun always so cross? Toman's mind went blank as his cheeks began to burn with heat. A gentle throbbing in his ears muffled the sound of his parents' voices.

"You're going to puff his head up with notions that he's somehow special when he isn't."

"He has the gift of seeing and hearing, Brun. He cannot go without instruction."

Toman wanted to knock, to let them know someone was listening. It was rude to eavesdrop. But his hands wouldn't respond.

"He has my mother's gift. I saw it in his aura today."

"That means that you want to teach him your Limmanian ways. This is Fahtu-Shan. We are different here. We do things differently."

"He's Orrenic, Brun. But it's in his blood. Two Palanth-Orric tribes. Fahtu-Shanner and Limmanian."

Trembling, Toman mustered the courage and knocked, then opened the door.

Alyena smiled. "Evening, Tomi."

"Evening, Father." He nodded at his mother as he greeted Brun. A child was always supposed to greet his father first when entering a room. "Evening, Ma."

Brun grumbled something.

Toman took it as the return greeting.

His whole body shivered. The back of his head seared with pain. "Ah!" He grabbed the nape of his neck.

Someone touched his arm. "Son?" Alyena's voice sounded distant.

"My head." The burning went from the back of his head, down his arms and into his hands. "Mama, it's like fire!" He fell to the floor.

Her arms wrapped around him. "Brun, I told you. It's happening"

The dream grew distant then came back into view. He was older...

"Tomi!" Alyena called from the Molkey, "Could you bring me another ladle from the kitchen?" The music of her joyful voice filled his mind.

For an instant, childlike giggles bubbled over inside him and he skipped down the stone steps.

Holding her ladle up, he reached for the door handle but stopped before opening it.

This wasn't real.

He wasn't a child any more.

And his mother wasn't in the Molkey.

Alyena was gone. Forever.

Sobs quivered through him.

The scene changed again...

The boys from Eckel's old crew reached Turicum and made their way back to the barracks. Ando and Villi bickered with each other. "I dun wanna sleep on the top bunk! A murderer slept on that mattress."

"Shh! Keep your voices down. You never know where Eckel left contacts, his secret ears and eyes..."

The doors of the Blue-Eyed Ram came into view, swinging open as a wave of music poured out onto the street. Hammer dulcimers pinged like light-footed dancers, flutes warbled and beautiful voices harmonised an old folksong. The air felt alive with anticipation like the beginning of a fairy tale.

A shiver of joy ran up Toman's spine to the back of his skull. Certain music felt like it could trigger his Eth.

In a distant corner near a window, Uri and Shann guffawed at some joke, their tankards clanking in toasts.

Shann stood and walked to the counter, his coin purse jingling in his palm. Out of the shadowy edges of the scene, the white hair and pale skin of a Storryn emerged into the lamplight. The blind man drew closer to Uri and laid a hand on his head.

Uri grimaced, white hair streaking from his temples, as he shivered violently. He snarled, exposing jagged teeth.

Toman ignited his Eth and formed his Linger.

A sudden warm sensation enveloped his hand.

He pulled it out from deep within Uri's chest, blood dripping from his glowing fingers.

Uri gurgled hoarsely then collapsed, his body twitching. His milky eyes rolled back in his head.

Toman's skull seemed to explode with anguish.

The image of Brun kneeling in the garden slowly appeared. He was tilling the small patch of earth in Alyena's old garden. Odilia approached, a wicker basket on her arm, a flask of Linden flower cordial in the other. Brun looked up and smiled, kissing his daughter's very large belly.

Twins?

Lorann called from the cottage window, their infant son in her arms. "Wave to Papa." She had cut her long golden brown hair. "Wave" Smiling, she held up their son's hand in hers.

Toman woke with a start.

No. This is a dream!

Stop, Tomi. She is not yours.

He drifted back to sleep.

A deep longing filled him. She was not his... but who was? He wanted to belong to someone special...

Three very fair-skinned women with white-blonde hair, walked in a procession, their long dark green cloaks flowing behind them.

Their garments stood out in sharp contrast to the throngs of deep orange and blood-red capes lining the streets.

Did he know them? They looked familiar somehow.

He concentrated on their faces.

Their braided and rolled hair was fixed tightly at the back of their heads.

Etched into the skin on the napes of their necks, dark red tattoos in the shape of strange beetle-like insects seemed to move. With long feelers and segmented bodies, they looked a bit like wasps.

One woman, the youngest-looking, held the hand of a small child at her side.

Toman couldn't be sure, but hadn't he seen her with a suckling babe in another dream?

The child's clothes were of the same shimmering dark green fabric as the three women. His light wheaten hair was the same shade as his mother's.

The three women and the child walked in the shade of a black cloth held up on poles by four tall swarthy men.

The child's mother glanced towards Toman. She seemed to look directly into his eyes, her piercing silver-blue gaze filled with deep torment. As she proceeded, she lifted her chin slowly. Her expression hardened from misery to determination.

A warm wind blew. Fine white sand swirled in the air.

The scene shifted.

Two of the pale-skinned women stood on the deck of a ship, arms raised and palms open.

Huge crimson sails shimmered like spider silk in the sunlight.

High above, a huge blood-red sphere floated. Within its transparent shell, long tendrils of smoke writhed like tormented serpents.

The young mother appeared on deck and took a place between the other two women. This time her hair was down, blowing around her like a halo. At the back of her head, her neck and hair were stained with blood.

She raised her bloody hands, her piercing eyes reminded him of Alyena's, but this woman's were blazing with rage.

Toman started. It was just the world of dreams. Not real.

Or was it?

11

Come In, Come In

"*Baron* Caldere!" Arden cried out then clapped a hand over her mouth.

Hopefully the guards hadn't heard her.

She froze at the end of the corridor, quickly scanning the flight of stairs that led up to the landing.

Her heart pounded. There wasn't much time!

The servants' entrance should be somewhere in the wall on the other side of the landing. With Soffian's guards already on their way up, those passageways were her only escape.

Lily and the other servants had always been obliged to use the hidden passages within the massive walls because the Lady Steward detested seeing them about in the Baronhold.

They were not to be seen, nor heard.

Lily had said that behind the Baronhold walls was a warren of such secret passageways, and that the hidden corridors were full of peep holes. There were opportunities for spying throughout the Galdyssen residence.

No wonder the downstairs staff knew so much! A hive of gossip, the kitchens stirred up far more than good meals. But Arden had grown to cherish the kitchen staff's frankness.

Heavy footfall, now just one flight below.

Another slight tremor passed through the building, and more pieces of ornate moulding fell.

Renewed fear shuddered through her.

Trembling, Arden ran across the landing and blew out the wall lamps. The shadows should help hide her while she searched for the latch.

Running a hand frantically over the murals, she fought to keep panic from overwhelming her. Where was the door? She was certain the entrance was somewhere around this spot. Lily had stunned her one day, seemingly stepping through the solid wall with a pitcher of water.

Where was that opening now?

"Actually, I feel sorry for the lass. I didn't think she was supposed to be downstairs tonight." A deep familiar voice sounded as if it was close. Then two helmets appeared coming up the stairwell. "What has she ever done to conjure the wrath of the Lady Steward? Lady Shannorn's always been a gentle and quiet lass."

Arden recognised the voice. Samual of the Gendarme Guard. Lily's fiancé!

"Not our business!" The other guard's hoarse retort sent shivers through her. "You mess with Lady Galdyssen's orders, and you take your life in your hands."

Samual grunted something in response.

Pulling her sleeves over the tiny lights in her forearms, Arden pressed her body further against the wall. She held her breath. Was her life to end like the Steward's? What would Papa and Mama think?

"Her quarters are down this hall." Samual glanced in her direction then looked away quickly. Had he seen her? "She'll be down there, if anywhere." Relief filled her as Samual pointed down the corridor and headed towards her suite.

But he must have seen her! She only had moments before they would discover she wasn't in her rooms!

Spinning around to face the mural, small chips of dusty plaster trickled down around her. Frantic with panic, she kept her bag clutched in one hand and ran the other over the wall. Where was the slot Lily had used?

She found a slight indentation!

Her anxiety subsided as she slipped her fingertips into the slot and pulled. A door opened silently.

To Arden's surprise, Lily rushed through, breathless.

"Oh, Milady!" Her chambermaid's shrill reaction drew the guards' attention.

"There she is!" Shouting, Samual's fellow guard pointed at her.

"I was comin' to look for you—"

"Here, take this, Lily." Arden pushed her travelling bag towards her. "Protect it with your life! I will get it later, somehow."

Shaking, Lily took the bag and slipped it behind her skirts. "Yes, Milady."

The two guards reached them within seconds.

Samual glanced at Lily and his eyebrows rose.

"Evenin' gentlmun." Lily responded quickly but with surprising confidence. She curtsied, smiling at Samual. "You gents look to be busy, so if you won't be needing me now...?" She nodded back to the open servants' door.

Samual's eye widened slightly then he shook his head. "No, Milady."

The other guard looked at the two of them. "We need to escort the Lady Shannorn to an important meeting with the Baron Caldere."

"Well then." Her voice quivered. "A pleasant evenin' to you, gentlmun." Lily nodded, then curtsied to Arden, tears glistening in her eyes. "Milady." Lily turned, holding tightly to Arden's case, and slipped back into the servants' passage.

The door closed, leaving practically no trace of its existence in the ornate mural.

Arden lifted her chin. "Good evening. You were looking for me?" She couldn't hide irritation from her voice. But these guards were only doing Soffian's bidding.

"Erm, My Lady." Samual's voice suddenly tensed. "The Lady Steward and Baron Shannorn have requested an audience with your person. Downstairs, in the Crystal Parlour. Now."

Angry shouts echoed up the vast stairwell. The rioters were surely already at the Baronhold doors, and yet these guards were calmly carrying out orders from... a sorcerer and his deranged lover? And her own brother?

Which powers were at play here?

Some Athlonian sorcerer's?

The nightmarish Greinen's?

Maybe Ber'eth's... through The Shift?

Or all three at once?

Word had it that many in the Lower City had embraced reports of a prophetic dream, a Glortrom from distant Landsend. Lily felt that Ber'eth had sent a warning of dire happenings.

Hundreds had believed. Then thousands.

The Quaterni had scoffed.

The message was that the city was to prepare for attack, to protect its people. But the Vandrian Kingship's repugnance towards the pleas of its own citizens had become bellows fanning already smouldering coals. Now the fires raged.

Until yesterday, Arden had thought the likelihood of such widespread unrest had somehow still been remote. A storm looming only on the distant horizon. But it was now upon them! The unnatural weather seemed to produce strikes of lightning driven by some evil sentience.

And the tremors were increasing.

Now Lady Soffian had murdered her husband, of that Arden was certain. The Lady Steward's cryptic account of his death could mean nothing else. And she'd already called for a vote on a new Steward of the Kingship!

Arden followed the guards.

Arriving at the base of the stairs, she scanned the strange activity in the foyer. Servants hurried silently about, lighting deep blue candles, customary signs of a household in mourning.

A bright flash of light cast immense shadows across the floor mosaics. A moment later thunder erupted, shaking the remaining panes in the high mullioned windows.

Partially open, the grand entrance doors were filled with black-clothed figures filing in, heading into the dimly lit Great Hall. On the plush dark cloth of their garments, jewels blazed in vivid contrast.

Arden paused to study their faces. She had never seen the Quaterni looking so nervous. And why would they bring their children to an evening assembly?

The scene was all wrong!

Had Soffian called for a full Vandrian gathering to vote that very evening?

No Steward had ever been elected without the official time of mourning. Soffian wasn't showing even a modicum of grief for her husband before wanting to replace him. But with whom? Had she actually already selected someone as the next ruler of the Quaterni? Ber'eth forbid if it was supposed to be Caldere!

"The Crystal Parlour, My Lady." With downcast eyes, Samual waved her to the antechamber of the Great Hall. "Baron Caldere and Baroness Soffian are waiting."

She nodded and walked towards the side room as the nobles entered the adjacent Great Hall.

Obviously compelled to attend Soffian's gathering, their taut and fearful faces made them look more like prisoners than sorrowful guests.

This was so wrong. So horribly wrong.

Arden's insides began to writhe. She needed to get away from Soffian and Caldere at the very first opportunity. But she couldn't leave the Baronhold without her research parchments.

And how could she make her way to the Professor with these riots and in this storm, to see if he was safe?

Sir Crethingan had mentioned her needing to find another of his portals, in the Sunken Gardens on the university grounds. But how could she retrieve her case and try to reach the Professor without being killed?

Arden glanced through the doors of the Great Hall as something deep red sparkled in the candlelit dimness.

Soffian stepped towards the central table.

The candlelight danced off her dress in glaring ostentation. The dullness of the black cloth rose on her wrist seemed to absorb light. Calm and fashionable as usual, all traces of the blood smears were gone from her face. She assumed her place at the head of the table as the widow of the Lord Steward.

A huge bolt of jagged light roared down into the garden behind the hall, filling the wide back terrace with blue-white brilliance.

Many guests screamed in fear.

In the sudden illumination, it became apparent that Soffian's guards stood just behind each of the seated nobles.

Soffian waved a hand, and the doors were closed and bolted.

Anxious cries rose within the Hall.

"Sister! Welcome" Caldere stood in the doorway to the Crystal Parlour. His dull eyes seemed lifeless. "Come in. Come in. My Lady will join us here shortly."

12

King of Barrostania

Arden followed her half-brother into the Crystal Parlour, pressing her shaking hands against her bodice.

"Your Highness, the Lady Shannorn, as you requested." Samual bowed. His voice low, he sounded mournful.

"Leave her here. One of you stand guard outside the door."

"Yes, Your Highness." Samual bowed to Caldere then to Arden. Stepping back into the foyer, he closed the door carefully behind him.

Caldere turned and faced her, his stiff smile changed rapidly to a smug expression. He stood in front of a gilt table upon which an intricately patterned decanter of wine had been set out with three short-stemmed goblets.

The walls of the parlour were lined with glass cases displaying the Baronhold's vast collection of goblets, pitchers and platters, all arranged in order and ready for the servants who would wait on visitors in the adjacent Great Hall.

The muted sounds of people speaking, and chairs being moved came from the door to Arden's right.

The Quaterni were probably being seated for Soffian's untimely gathering.

Arden's entire body stiffened with trepidation. Seeing Caldere gloating so proudly, she struggled not to let her rage consume her. She wanted to scream at him, to demand he tell her what he'd done, and was planning to do.

But she held her tongue instead and glared back at him.

What shame had he already brought on their father's name?

Caldere's wicked rictus seemed to untwist, and a condescending smirk appeared. "Welcome, Sister."

It had been years since she'd stood this close to him. As a little girl, she used to dread being in the same room with him. Back then, he had towered menacingly over her. Her childhood had been filled with his heartless jeers and dark accusations. He had seemed incredibly strong, practically invincible.

Not any longer. Not the pathetic puppet who stood before her.

She was surprised how short he was compared to herself now. He seemed to have become almost diminutive in stature, barely taller than her chin. The only thing Arden feared about him at that moment was the cold-hearted authority he could wield against her.

Caldere walked around the back of the table and poured himself a goblet of wine from the decanter. Wrapping his heavily ringed fingers around the ornate drinking vessel, he raised it towards her, sneering. "We have you to thank for today, little sister." He lifted his goblet higher in a mock toast. "She will soon be free, thanks to you."

A frigid sensation prickled down her spine.

She? Who was he talking about?

Arden's mind raced. Would Soffian be finally freed to accomplish more atrocities? Is that what he meant? Or someone, or something, far more sinister.

Soffian's voice carried through the side door. Her finely articulated words permeated the Parlour. "Lords and Ladies, Barons and Baronesses, it is on this very sad occasion that I have summoned you this evening. My *beloved* husband, the Vandrian Steward, has passed away."

A few of what sounded like sympathetic reactions rumbled indistinctly.

Arden frowned. How dare Soffian pretend to mourn the Lord Steward? She'd obviously just had him killed – surely she wouldn't have done the deed with her own hands – and now she wanted others to join her in mourning him?

"We mourn his untimely passing as unrest threatens our Kingship. Peasants dare to affront our way of life, threatening to unravel the very fabric of our society. The need for strong leadership in Norssum is utterly paramount. A new Vandrian leader must immediately rise up in this time of chaos."

Arden gasped.

Soffian really was calling for an election? Hopefully at least some of the Quaterni would see through her bogus emotional facade!

Caldere stared blankly at his goblet then his lips twisted wryly. “King of Barrostania.” Barely audible, he sounded as though he was conversing with himself. “Yes, My Lady...” He chuckled darkly then filled his mouth with the wine and swallowed.

Soffian’s continuing discourse floated back into the room. “Now, fellow members of the Quaterni of the Great Houses of the great Vandrian Kingship, let us lift our glasses, first in remembrance of the Baron Lornz Galdyssen, and then again to call for a vote on the new Steward of Barrost.”

Agitated murmurs rumbled in the Great Hall.

“Come now, one and all. Lift your glasses with me in the very sweet memory of my beloved deceased husband. I insist.”

“Yes, My Dear.” Caldere seemed to address her directly. He poured himself another glass of wine then he lifted it back up to his open mouth. He looked fixedly at the door.

Was he waiting for someone?

A gurgled scream shot through in the Great Hall. Then someone else cried out.

Caldere smiled again.

Arden glowered at her half-brother. “What are you two doing?”

He blinked. “Dear Sister, we couldn’t have done it without you.”

Soffian’s now frantic tone seemed to penetrate the walls of the entire Baronhold. “From this historic day forward, there will be only *one* Vandrian to claim the Kingship. There will be only *one* king to rule over all the lands previously called Norssum. The country of Norssum is now the Kingdom of Barrostania, properly renamed for our illustrious forefather."

"You traitor!" Someone shouted.

The intensity of the sudden uproar in the Great Hall gave Arden shivers.

Caldere nodded as Soffian raised her voice again. "Drink, I say!" A moment of terrible silence filled the room. "Guards, please assist them!"

A woman cried out "Murderess!".

Another voice rose in terror. "Despicable treachery!"

Arden found it difficult to breathe.

The horrific irony. Having called the Vandrian assembly under the pretence of voting for their future, the plan was actually to end their lives.

"You see, dear little bastard sister, everything is falling into place. The old Kingship was so involved in prying power from each other that they didn't see the warning signs of impending invasion from our allies to the North.

The Glortrom from Landsend nearly upset our plans, but Soffian and I were able to convince the Lord Steward it was nothing but superstition, and that he'd be branded a fool if he took any action based on that prophetic dream.

We are happy to confirm that the Athlonian fleet is on time and is just north of the Bay of Barrost. Too bad the poor Steward didn't pay attention to the Glortrom." The corners of Caldere's mouth turned down and he shook his head in fake sympathy. He laughed then frowned. "That superstitious Glortrom nearly ruined everything."

Arden's jaw tightened in restraint. But she could no longer hold her tongue. "The Athlonians? Are you insane? And why me? What do I have to do with anything you are planning?"

Caldere laughed again. "Initially, I told father to send you here because of Soffian's indebtedness towards him. I wanted to keep you far from father's protection so you could join the closure of an epic chapter in Norssum history." He stared again at the door to the Great Hall. "Our first plan was to have you drink of the special wine tonight. Or have a knife dragged over your throat if you'd resisted." His chuckle sounded more like the hoarse cough of a diseased dog. "But Soffie and I felt that you were still useful. Very useful in fact. Something about your presence is releasing Canthalida, and her power is growing stronger."

Arden's skin crawled as strands of his hair escaped his coronet. Locks of pure white. Just like Torghyll, the sorcerer who had appeared on her balcony.

This couldn't be real. This couldn't be happening. Her entire body quivered with fear. How could she escape this madness?

Caldere shook his head. "Your Eth-Wielding friends almost ruined things, trying to preach that a Shift, a Beckoning was upon the world. They will be dealt with soon enough. At least we were able to snuff out the fires of doubt the Ydassumers kept trying to set among the Vandrian Houses."

The growing tumult from the Great Hall sickened Arden. Screams cut off with gurgling sounds. Chairs being thrown against the walls and floors. She thought she even heard the clang of steel on steel.

"You see, your Eth Wielder stopped Torghyll's plans in Borinbranth, but we were only taken temporarily by surprise. His downfall is planned, soon he will also bow to her. Someone is on board Prince Palandred's ship who will see to that."

Another tremor shook the Baronhold, but more

violently than before. More glass windows shattered in the distance.

"And if Syngordia doesn't accept our offer, we are amassing troops from Borinbranth along the border with the Double Crown Kingdom itself. War would be inevitable."

Something dark began seeping under the door.

Arden's heart almost stopped. It was blood!

A coarse shout came from the Great Hall. "Behold your King! Formerly Lady Steward Galdyssen of House Vandran. Bow now before King Soffian Vandran!" Probably one of her minion soldiers.

"Hail King of Barrostania!" Another deep voice proclaimed.

Soffian's voice rose again over the groans and sobs of people obviously dying. "My dear fellow Quaterni, let us bid adieu to the Vandrian Kingship and usher in the rebirth of House Vandran."

"All hail the King of Barrostania!" Many male voices now cried out in unison.

Soffian, King? Arden's stomach lurched and she shook violently. She vomited into the powdery dust on the floor. "Ber'eth keep us safe."

13

Into the Kitchens

Stepping quickly back from the table, Arden pulled out a handkerchief and wiped her mouth. She had to calm her nerves before nausea overtook her again.

Had Soffian completely lost her mind?

The Baronhold had become a madhouse!

The walls and floor moaned, shaking more strongly than before.

Thousands of pieces of cut crystal shook in the showcases. Tinkling and pinging over the low rumble of the earthquake, they sounded like eerie chimes.

Reaching into a pocket of his waistcoat, Caldere

retrieved one of Lady Méndrensynn's sachets and brought it to his nose.

He breathed in slowly, then exhaled, and seemed to relax. "The Trade Summit would have been the perfect setting for our performance." His laugh was strangely gentler than before. "But these tremors frightened the soft-hearted Steward, and he sent the delegates away too early for today's historic event." Caldere stared towards the Great Hall. "But even though we couldn't present Soffian as king at the gala, the last of the delegates will be scurrying home soon and will spread the story of a true King over Vandrian Barrost, an historic King with legendary Athlonian warriors and sorcerers at her side."

Arden shuddered.

Athlonian allies?

When did her half-brother begin this depraved collaboration?

Druin had mentioned his sister's Glortrom of Athlonian lords, and modern maps of Barrost!

Caldere sniffed at the velvet sachet and closed his eyes, his eyelids twitching. He opened them again and waved the bag towards Arden. "Soffie says this fragrance helps to quieten the terrible voices in our heads." A small drop of blood appeared on his upper lip. He nodded. "She's right."

Arden took another step backwards, closer to the entrance.

The side door to the Great Hall flew open. Another flash of lightning blazed behind the Baronhold, silhouetting Soffian's form.

She entered the Parlour, guards at her side.

Another dazzling streak of lightning erupted somewhere beyond the terrace, illuminating her sparkling gown. But her dress wasn't glistening only with deep red jewels! Blood dripped from her sleeves and hands.

The Baronhold shook again. Behind Soffian, large fissures zigzagged like drunken snakes through the wall of portraits.

Case after glass case in the Crystal Parlour cracked then shattered. The cut crystal tumbled to the floor, seeming to explode as sparkling shards flew everywhere.

Soffian cried out, covering her face.

Caldere stared at her with a blank expression.

A wide strip of the ornate ceiling stucco fell, filling the room with choking dust.

It was now or never!

Arden ran. She pushed the door open, revealing the vast foyer covered in pieces of plaster and thick grey dust.

Shouting, people ran about in the dark with lanterns and candles.

A powerful hand grabbed her wrist.

Arden screamed.

"Shh! My Lady!" Samual pulled her to the side. "Quickly now. Lily is ready for you down in the kitchens. He pointed to a dark corner of the foyer. "Over there, a servants' passage. Run, please My Lady, run!" He nodded stiffly to her, then resumed his place at attention.

"Thank you!" She dashed towards the wall Samual had indicated.

The panic throbbing in her ears deadened her senses. The loud voices echoing throughout the Baronhold seemed to diminish and the deep rumbling of the tremors somehow quietened.

She reached the wall and ran her hands frantically over the mural.

The latch!

She slipped a finger in the hole and pulled. Jumping into the passageway, she shut the small door quickly.

Total blackness enveloped her.

She stretched out her arms, brushing against the dusty stone with her fingertips. Groping her way along the wall she tried to get away from the madness as quickly as she could.

Straining to hear if anyone else entered the passage behind her, she stumbled over something on the floor. She paused for a moment, trying to catch her breath.

Had Soffian just murdered the entire hereditary lineage of the Vandrian Kingship? The Quaterni, the heads of the four Great Houses, all dead in one evening? Genocide of an entire bloodline, leaving only herself and her children?

Images plagued Arden's imagination... corpses strewn over the once elegant, grand meeting hall of the Baronhold. Dark pools glistening on the floor.

Tears began to fall as she continued down the passageway.

Soffian declared herself King?

King?

Why not Queen? But then, the insecurity the Quaterni had always displayed towards the kingdoms of Syngordia and Mendelon, and the fact that it had become a common proverbial saying on the Northern Horn that *no king had ever existed in Barrost and never would...* It seemed to explain Soffian's choice of styling herself as the one type of ruler a Vandrian could never be.

A sigh quivered through Arden.

If only Druin were there. To be shielded again in his arms, the way he'd held her when the Lord Protector and

Toman searched her apartment for Torghyll. She longed for that sense of security.

Soffian and Caldere would probably find her soon, and have her killed now because she'd run away.

Should she have stayed?

Her half-brother had said that she was still useful.

Useful?

He wanted her because she was somehow releasing the power of the Greinen?

That couldn't be possible! Or could it?

Arden's blood ran cold.

Crethingan had said that she was the *Legacy*, and that parts of the Temmerung were being restored each time she entered that mysterious world.

On her first arrival there, traces of multi-coloured lights had suddenly shimmered within the stones, but Crethingan said that cracks had also appeared. The Greinen's prison wasn't holding her power back any more.

But surely Arden couldn't be the reason for evil being released on the Horn! There were so many things to consider and even though many answers were falling into place, they didn't give any direction on where to go, or what to do now!

A flicker of golden candlelight danced ahead in the darkness.

Arden's body went rigid with fear.

The light undulated towards her at an alarming pace.

She crouched down, covering her head with her hands.

"Milady? Milady, is that you?"

"Lily Farnham!" Arden wanted to shout for joy. "You gave me such a fright! But I'm so relieved to see you."

"Please forgive me, Milady." Lily lifted her candlestick.

Her chambermaid's face looked as though she'd aged years since this morning. "We all knew something was terrible amiss, but when I heard the noise from the Great Hall... I was so afraid for you. I spoke with Samual."

"He helped me. Thank you both so much."

The rumbling of the quakes subsided. The sudden silence was more frightening than peaceful.

"I'm, I'm so glad I found you." Lily's voice cracked. "But we really must hurry, Milady. The stairs are jus' ahead."

"Th.. thank you. But is it safe?" Arden tried to keep up with Lily's pace. "Isn't the whole Baronhold crumbling?"

"No. Downstairs is under the big arches of the foundations. Nothing moves those stones. You'll be safe with us down there, Milady." Lily's concern was soothing. Having a friend by one's side brought an indescribable sense of comfort.

But would Arden ever be safe again with Caldere and Soffian wanting her for their plans?

Lily pointed to a spiral staircase. The aroma of fresh bread wafted up from below. "Quickly now, Milady. This comes out in the kitchen." Lily held up the candle and bade her follow. "Careful now. The steps are steep and worn."

Arden nodded.

Generations of servants had been obliged to walk these hidden passageways. Forever out of sight but always bound to their masters, the servants of the Baronhold reminded Arden more of slaves imprisoned within these walls.

Stepping out of the stairwell, Arden blinked to let her eyes adjust to the warm blaze from the wide hearths. Loaves of bread were out on the central table.

"Lady Arden!" Cook Ysbal threw her arms around her and gave her a motherly squeeze.

Arden hugged back, almost collapsing with relief, as fresh tears streamed down her face.

"Now, now, My Lady. Everthing will work out, you'll see." Cook pulled a handkerchief from her apron and dabbed at Arden's cheeks,. "Here ya go, My Lady. Please don't cry. It will all work..." Cook's voice trailed off, quivering as she pulled out another cloth from her apron and dried her own eyes.

"Lady Soffian..." Sobs choked Arden's words. "...she... she..." Just trying to speak of the atrocity brought the sounds and images back, people screaming, blood dripping from Soffian's hands.

"Now, now." Cook Ysbal patted her on the arm.

Arden needed to gather her wits if she was going to survive. "I need to get to the university. I have to talk with Professor Gwenndon." She looked quickly around. "My case? It's very important."

Professor Gwenndon needed to know what she'd discovered about Crethingan, about Caldere and Soffian. Hopefully the violence hadn't spread that far into the Upper City.

"University? Oh, yes, of course." Cook Ysbal rubbed her hands on her sleeves. "That's where you spend most of your time."

"Here you go, Milady." Lily opened a cupboard door.

Arden sighed with relief as her chambermaid held out the case.

The Cook's brow creased. "Now, Lily, go and tell the footman, Fram, we're ready. And where is that Bligger? And Jon? Always shirking when work is to be done. Where are those young men when you need them?"

"I'll check on them. We don't have much time!" Lily rushed out of the room.

Cook put her fists on her hips as she eyed Arden from head to toe. "My Lady, you look too fancy to be out in the Lower City. You'll need plainer clothes. Follow me." She turned down the short hallway towards the scullery maids' rooms.

"Thank you." Arden's head ached with pressure.

"In here, prompt." Cook walked into one of the rooms, turned and faced her. "Now, My Lady, you need to give those garments to me. Quickly."

Setting her case down on the floor, Arden unbuttoned her bodice and worked her dress up over her head then handed them to Cook.

"These will work better." Cook held out an armful of clothes and a cloak.

Tears wouldn't stop coming as the magnitude of the evening's events continued to press on her. "Caldere, Caldere...what have you done? Papa's name will forever be mentioned with murderers..."

Cook touched Arden's cheek. "Now, My Lady, everything will work out, you'll see." Helping her into the scullery maid's outfit, she grabbed the handle of a dustpan. "Please forgive me, but you look too clean. It's important you don't stand out, My Lady." Scooping up a handful of the floor sweepings, Cook sprinkled fine dirt over her skirt and cloak. "Now, please tuck your beautiful hair into your collar and rub some of this on your cheeks."

Arden nodded, dipping her fingers into the fine dirt.

Cook Ysbal neatly folded Arden's bodice and dress.

"Guards! I hear guards in the corridor!" Lily half-shouted as she came back into the kitchen.

"Quickly, My Lady, hold this!" Cook pushed the

dustpan into Arden's hands, turned and grabbed a broom. "And this. We're going to have to hide you right in front of them. But please keep your head down, My Lady, and go directly to the hearth and start sweeping it."

Arden nodded. Sickening fear gripped her, but she managed to keep her breathing controlled.

"Follow right behind me, My Lady. Closely." Cook's whisper changed abruptly to a shout. "I'll need that hearth spotless, you hear me? Spotless!"

They walked back into the main kitchen.

Cook seemed to suddenly bristle like a cornered cat. Her voice rose like a siren. "*What* are you doing in my kitchen?" She half turned to Arden. "Now, like I told you girl, get over there and finish cleaning that!" She pointed to the hearth. "And pull up your hood so you don't get soot on your head. You don't have bath day again for another week."

Then she stepped in between Arden and the guards, facing the two gendarmes. "And what do you think you are doing bringing swords in here? Samual, I'm surprised at you." Her shrill tone softened slightly.

Arden pulled up the hood of the cloak, keeping her head down low. She started rigorously sweeping the already spotless brickwork.

But, out of the corner of her eye, Cook looked formidable with her hands planted squarely on her hips.

"Is Lady Arden Shannorn in here?" The other gendarme spoke. "Her Highness, King Soffian, requires her presence. Immediately."

"Well?" Cook's voice rose again in pitch. "Do you see her? Ber'eth gave you eyeballs to see, no? Goggle with them, won't ya?" She unhooked a pan hanging above the hearth. "I have work to do, gentlemen." Her voice grew calmer but darker. "With all the Baroness' wishes and orders, don't you know. Got my hands full, without the likes of you underfoot."

Behind Arden, the rapid shuffle of soft shoes meant that Lily had returned. "Good evening, sirs." She paused. "Oh. Samual. Good evening."

"And those clothes in your hands, Mistress Cook? Who are they for?" The gendarme's words remained sharp but their intensity seemed to deflate.

"You can come bargin' in my kitchen and disruptin' my cookin' schedule, but you ain' gonna go looking through the Baroness' undergarments. Not if my life depends on it! *Her Highness the King* will hear about it, I'm warning you. She might call herself by a man's title, but she's still a woman and I think that if she hears of you looking through her underclothes... Well, she won't take a liking to it!"

"Listen. She's obviously not here." Samual's rich calm voice contrasted with the other gendarme's. "Let's go."

"Alright! Alright! But if you hear of Lady Shannorn's whereabouts, you are under obligation to report it."

"If it doesn't disrupt my schedule! Lady Galdyssen, erm, Her Highness the King likes her meals served punctually. Do you want to be responsible for her eating late?"

Indistinct mumbling sounded more like a whimper than a response.

"Now, get out of my kitchen!"

The heavy thud of their boots faded back down the corridor.

Arden stood and adjusted her cloak. Her sleeves slipped down her arms, exposing the moving pinpricks of light in her skin.

Cook and Lily's eyes widened.

"I'll explain later." Opening her case to double check

its contents, Arden gasped. The smooth milky stone of her father's vase began to sparkle with the same iridescent lights as in her arms.

Lily covered her gaping mouth.

"I don't have answers. I hope the Professor will."

"My Lady? If I may ask..." The Cook's eyes seemed to sag. "I thought the Baroness was friendly towards you. Taking you in to help you with your studies. What changed?"

"My half-brother, Caldere." Arden shook her head, still in disbelief. "I will tell you all about it when we meet again. Everything is changing. Look at the world around us. Please, keep safe. Don't anger Soffian. Or Caldere."

Lightning continued to strike somewhere outside. Blue-white light flashed through the small windows near the ceiling, followed by deep rumbling thunder.

"I must get to the Professor. He will know more."

Nodding, Cook pointed to the red case, then handed Arden her carefully folded garments. "You'll be needin' to pack your clothes in there too, My Lady."

Arden nodded, arranging them in her case. "They believed these were Lady Soffian's undergarments?"

Cook laughed, shaking her head. "A distraction, My Lady. Anything to keep them from noticing you, maybe finding out who you are."

Arden smiled. Cook's quick-witted joke was brilliant.

Shaking a finger toward the hallway where the gendarmes exited, Cook frowned. "Those are unmarried men. They don't know the difference. Probably never looked carefully at a women's underpants, except maybe when taking them off in the dark and in a frenzy." She blushed. "Well, you know what I mean."

Lily chuckled. "Fram is coming but I still haven't

found the other boys. You'll need all the protection we can find. I'll have another quick look."

"You do that." Cook nodded.

"Thank you, dear Ysbal," Arden clasped the Cook's hands and kissed them. "Thank you."

Lily screamed from the wine cellar.

Panic filled Arden and she grabbed her travel bag. Where was the door out?

Lily ran into the room.

"Cook! Oh Cook, Bligger and Jon are dead!" Gasping for breath, she choked. "Awful. Awful! I tell you, awful!" Her whole body shook as she sobbed. "I think they drank some of that wine for upstairs. Awful!" She wiped her eyes with trembling hands. "They were all purple-faced. They'd spewed all over themselves!"

"Oh my, oh my, this is going from bad to worse." Cook shook her head. "Poor souls, they'll be going home in a box now."

Arden pulled the hood up from her neck. The coarse dark brown cloth scratched against her skin.

"It'll keep the rain off you, My Lady." Straightening the cloak, Cook's eyes filled with tears. She reached up and placed an open palm on Arden's cheek."

Lily pushed open the door onto the courtyard. "This way, Milady. Fram is bringin' the cart round now."

14

Miasma

Hurrying out of the kitchen, Arden coughed. An acrid stench bit the back of her throat. Her eyes burned.

"My Lady," the young driver of a rickety cart patted the wooden seat next to him. "I think it bes' if you're sat next to me." His thick-jawed smile revealed two rows of small pale yellow teeth.

"I beg your pardon?" Arden frowned at his seeming forwardness.

He continued patting the seat, but his voice suddenly faltered. "My Lady, it will look like... well... like we be spoken for each other." He lowered his eyes and spoke nervously. "We'd 'ave fewer problems in the street, if you know what I mean."

"Now, be off before something worse happens. Or Her Ladyship the *King* shows up." Cook turned and sneered in disgust at the grand house Arden had grown to accept as her second home. But with Caldere's involvement in Soffian's horrific deeds, neither Borinbranth nor Barrost were home any longer.

Cook moved quickly to the cart. "This is Fram, My Lady. He's offered to drive you up to the university."

Arden exhaled sharply, then nodded. "I understand. Thank you, Fram." She climbed up, pushing her travelling case neatly under her legs. Important not to draw any attention to the noticeable colour, so she spread out her cloak carefully.

"Bye, bye, sweet Lady." With one hand Cook dabbed at her eyes with her apron, and waved with the other.

Lily leaned her head on Cook's shoulder. "May Ber'eth be with you and protect you." Covering her mouth, Lily's body began shaking.

"And with both of you. We shall meet again." Arden waved. Hopefully they would fare well and she'd see them once more.

Fram flicked the reins and the cart jerked forward.

Arden glanced back.

Samual appeared on the steps to the kitchens and Lily ran to him.

The old wheels creaked as Fram drove through the small servants' courtyard towards the open plaza and the entrance gates. For a few moments, the clicking of the horned-beast's hooves was the only sound penetrating her mind.

They entered the large plaza.

"Look at what those strange lightnin' bolts 'ave done!"

Fram manoeuvred around huge cracks and scorched marks in the paving stones. "That there ooze is vicious, My Lady." He pointed to a thick black liquid seeping through the fissures. "It be poisonous." He shot a furtive glance at her then looked back towards his horned-beast.

"Poison coming up from underneath the city?" She shuddered. Scenes of death flashed through her mind. Lords and Ladies, choking on poison, their hands held up to their mouths, gurgling blood.

Fram grunted and nodded. "We gotta be careful not to breathe too close or touch it. Word 'as it that certain folks die a nasty death if they do."

"*Certain* folks?" Arden glared at the glistening black substance.

"Yes, but it be very strange, My Lady." He lowered his voice. "Word 'as it that only Quaterni people, and their like from the Upper City, are dying." He pointed in the direction of the hills of Upper Barrost. "Only those livin' in them castles and fancy 'ouses be killed. Nobody else."

His nervous glances at her hands and face were unsettling. But he must be trustworthy, if Cook had recommended him. "That's terrible, Fram."

"Jus' a little while ago, some of their carriages were movin' through the Lower City. Now the drivers an' passengers be just a pile a bones, covered in black goo. As if they melted."

"That's dreadful!"

"People is locking themselves in their 'omes for fear." He kept staring nervously at her hands then her face and back again. "Folks are sayin' it's a curse just on the nobility. It's in their blood.

Panic tightened in Arden's chest. "Their bl...blood?"

"Yes My Lady. That's what they're sayin'."

What would kill only one select group of a

population? It didn't make sense. Her father and mother were of ruling Palanshen families, but not Barrostanian. She was of noble blood... would she die soon too?

"People is sayin' that it's the wrath of Ber'eth bein' drenched on them because they didn' heed the Glortrom."

"The Glortrom?"

He nodded sharply but kept his wandering eyes now on the reins. "Ber'eth sent a message but the Quaterni ignored it." He scowled, blinking nervously. "They don' care 'bout us."

The cloud cover was a low grey ceiling over the Baronhold. No telling when another bolt of lightning would strike.

Wide charred streaks across the plaza led up to the memorial statue of Barrùs. Smoke rose around the now twisted and grotesque metal effigy.

Arden's eyes watered as the acrid reek stung in her nostrils.

The back of her mouth burned as though on fire. She coughed uncontrollably. Was it killing her already? Her body shook with fear. She rubbed her cheeks. Were they going to start melting? "Fram? How...How long do I have... to die?"

He turned his head and looked her straight in the eyes. The corners of his mouth turned downwards as he spoke at a whisper. "My Lady, I think you'd be dead already, if you was gonna die." He swallowed. "When Miss Lily told me of your need, I was 'fraid for you. I heard the nobles started melting as soon as the reek got in their noses."

Arden covered her face as a sob erupted from deep within her.

She held her breath and tried to calm her thoughts.

Arden, do not fear. Do not fear. She repeated to herself.

Death wouldn't come to her on a wooden cart, with a complete stranger.

"My Lady, I think you'll be alright." The compassion in Fram's voice was soothing. He gently patted her arm.

She nodded, trying to slowly fill her lungs again without choking.

Distant shouts echoed in the darkness. Judging by the sound, the riots seemed to be withdrawing from the Bazaar Districts along the Baronhold walls.

Fram steered towards the side gate used for tradesmen. "Please, My Lady, cover your face and put your 'ed on me shoulder. I jus' want to tell the guards you be Miss Lily and not be feelin' well this evenin'. That I'd be personally takin' you 'ome."

Arden nodded. She pulled the hood up and lay her head on his shoulder. She wiped the tears from her cheeks then fixed a stare on the hind quarters of the horned-beast.

A guard stepped towards them.

"Halt!"

Fram's shoulder tensed as he pulled on the reins and the cart slowed to a stop.

She squeezed on his arm.

Moaning in the darkness above them, the wind began to pick up.

"You shouldn't be out this evening, Fram. You know what's happening in the Lower City." The man's voice was tense, almost angry. "And it looks like a terrible storm is blowing in."

Fram nodded. "Yes, I know." He cleared his throat. "But I need to be goin'. Miss Lily's been feelin' poorly this evenin'. I was takin' 'er to 'er folks."

"Well then." The guard spoke in an anxious tone as the iron gate creaked. "Good boy, Fram. But take the road around the Bazaar Districts. And be careful. Steer clear of the black slime. It's coming up all over. People are saying that a *miasma* is killing people."

Out of the corner of her eye, Arden caught the guard gesturing back towards the ooze in the plaza.

"But it don't seem to affect us, only the Upper City folk. You and Miss Lily should be safe."

"Will do. Thanks." Fram flicked the reins. "May good be on ya."

"And on you. You, too, Miss Lily."

Arden nodded under her hood.

The iron gate creaked further open and their cart moved into the darkness of the narrow street.

In the dim light of the streetlamps, she could make out patches of blackened cobblestones and cracks with the tar-like substance oozing out.

"It'd be safe now to look up again, My Lady."

She raised her head slowly as Fram turned into Highstreet, leading up to the university grounds.

In the distance, somewhere further down the sea wall, flames leapt into the sky, dancing up through columns of thick grey smoke. Two of the Quaterni Baronholds were burning.

Had Soffian set fire to them? Or had the lightning strikes sought them out.

Shivering, Arden clasped her cloak tighter.

Frightened people moved through the streets, mothers clutching small children, men guiding carts packed with what looked like all they owned. Others shouted slogans about death to the Vandrian houses, others begged Ber'eth to have mercy.

The eerie howling of the wind seemed to amplify their voices as powerful gusts bore down between the buildings.

A shrill sound penetrated the roar of the wind. The squawking of seabirds?

"My Lady!" Fram whispered sharply. "Keep your 'ed down. Somethin' terrible is 'appenin'."

"Please, stop addressing me as Lady! I mustn't be recognised." Her words came out more like a hiss than a whisper. She calmed her anxiety. "Call me Lily, if need be."

He blinked and lowered his head. "Please forgive me."

A powerful wind whipped her cloak wildly.

Arden grabbed at the cloth and clutched it to her chest, trying not to expose the lights in her forearms.

Just above the dull glow of smoky street lamps, thousands of white birds appeared. Gulls! They flew in and out between the buildings as though trying to avoid the open sky. Their unusual piercing shrieks sent shivers through her.

Were the birds frightened only by the storm, or was it something else?

Arden cried out as bolts of lightning arched just above the rooftops, spreading out like the roots of a tree. The searing blue flashes laced back and forth through the flock, as though searching. Small charred carcasses dropped to the cobblestones as the choking stench of burnt feathers and flesh filled the air.

"That be no natural lightnin'!" Fram slapped the reins against the rump of the horned-beast. "Come on girl, come on! We gotta get out of 'ere!"

His beast bleated fearfully then lowered its head as if in challenge as a barrage of flapping wings swooped towards them.

Arden screamed, pulling the hood down over her face and leaning against Fram. He threw his arms around her shoulders and pressed her head to his chest.

His bravery touched her. He had no hood on his cloak.

Shrill screeches deafened her. Sharp beaks and flapping wing tips assailed them. Small webbed feet clawed at her cloak.

Fram flinched as he pulled her tighter against his chest.

But then, almost as soon as they had come, the flock disappeared.

Fram let go of her and jumped down from the cart. "It's alright, girl." He caressed the horn-beast's head. "It's alright. Now, now. We be fine, girl."

A heavy drop of ashen rain splashed onto the cobbles near his feet.

Eyes wide open, he looked back and forth through the low clouds.

More droplets began pelting down. Each more grey mud than water.

Arden brought her rain-dampened sleeve to her nose and sniffed. That smell...brimstone?

A thunderous roar boomed through the darkness above.

"Ber'eth save us!" Fram's voice quivered. Another flash of lightning illuminated his face. Blood glistened from thin lacerations on his forehead and arms.

"You're hurt, Fram!"

"I be alright, My Lady. Jus' scratches."

Reaching to help him back up to the seat, her sleeve slipped. She quickly pulled it back over her wrist.

The lights would certainly frighten him even more.

Yet another odour saturated the air, this time a strange oily stench, like rancid putrefaction. Terror seized her. Sorcery, the same as on her balcony?

Another bolt of lightning roared down through the inky clouds, branching like luminescent bony fingers.

Fram gasped as the streams of blinding light began

creeping across the rooftops. Then the skeletal claws of light ripped downwards, exploding as they touched different parts of the city.

Had she made the right decision to seek out the Professor? Would she die trying to get to him? "Sir Crethingan, can you hear me?" She kept her voice at a whisper.

Fram must have heard her because he looked intently at her mouth then settled back on the cart.

She was relieved he didn't ask what she had meant.

The ancient architect had left her with so many questions.

He'd spoken of his portals... Why couldn't she also summon a portal and step through on her own?

His words came back to her. *I brought you here in your physical form. However, to return here in this form, you must go to another of my portals.*

He had pulled her physically into Temmerung. She could exit at will. But to enter in corporeal form, she had to enter through '*another of his portals*'?

Why hadn't he explained more?

Could she create a portal and enter or exit the Temmerung at will? Or had Crethingan meant only his architectural constructs of stone?

Why hadn't he explained more?

Sudden realisation overcame her.

Of course, Arden! Her face flushed with embarrassment.

Crethingan had obviously imbued specific structures with the ability to transform into a Temmerung portal. He hadn't created a physical portal out of thin air. He wasn't a magician, conjuring things out of nothing.

His Eth powers were obviously connected to stone.

As hers were.

Fram navigated around a carriage at the side of the

street. Its oil lamps burned brightly in their small glass cylinders. Its beast, still tied to the harness, pawed at the ground in agitation. The door was open. A jumbled heap of fine clothing looked as if had spilled from the seat onto the paving stones.

Arden screamed.

Bones protruded from underneath the cloaks and out through sleeves. They had once been people! A black gel dripped from the hollow sockets in the skulls.

"They look all melted, like candles that got too close to the fire!" Fram prodded his reluctant horned-beast. "Come on, girl! come on!"

Shaking, Arden looked up towards the university on the hill. With all this commotion, perhaps Professor Gwenndon had already fled.

Please, Ber'eth, let him have escaped!

As Fram turned the cart into another narrow street, shouts about a lightning monster rang out. Terror swelled in the Upper City.

She needed to speak with Crethingan! Could she reach out to him there and then? Calm had always facilitated the access, but she didn't have that luxury! She steeled herself, searching for the quietude of pleasant memories. Her mind needed to focus before the entrance would appear.

Walks with her father...

Singing below the trees in the garden...

"Sir Crethingan..." she whispered again.

The shimmer of a portal began to glow as foggy iridescence gathered ahead of them.

"On me Granma's grave!" Fram shouted, recoiling.

"Don't be frightened."

He swallowed hard, his eyes darting from her to the street and back. "But this mus' be sorcery."

"It's not. Please trust me." The soft flickering lights swirled. She sent her consciousness into the World of Visions. "Sir Crethingan? Can you hear me?"

Cries through the city disrupted her concentration. Bumps in the poorly paved cobbled street sent jolts through the cart seat. It was almost impossible to focus.

Blinding white lightning struck the street behind them. Exploding with a deafening roar, pebbles and sand flew through the air.

A sharp pain shot through the back of her head, and she fell forward.

15

Secret Meetings

Perspiration stuck Druin's nightshirt to his back and chest. He shifted his position on the mattress, awaiting the gentle descent into slumber. But it wasn't coming, even though the warm night air and gently swaying movement of the hammock bed should easily lull him to sleep.

Perhaps a more comfortable position would help.

Pushing the sheet off, he turned on his side, closed his eyes again and waited.

No good.

Not while the lingering sensation of Arden in danger remained on the edge of his thoughts.

Something prickled in his Ber'eth Appendage.

Was she calling out to him again?

Impressions of great anxiety, anguish and sorrow still pulsated through him.

She needed him, but he could do nothing to help her.

Moaning, he turned over again.

She seemed so close and yet completely unreachable.

If only he could enter the Temmerung at will, as she did. He had always entered the World of Visions in deep sleep, never of his own volition. A force had always drawn him in.

Arden agreed with him that it could only have been Ber'eth himself.

Druin would simply find himself in the same place in the Turicum palace, alongside Maylin as she took her last breaths. The bewilderment of his little sister's final thoughts would remain, piercing his heart long after he'd awakened.

He could never have imagined actually *asking* Ber'eth to go back into the World of Visions. For months he'd loathed the approach of evening, fearing that dreaded pull into the cycle of torment awaiting him in the Temmerung.

Arden had changed all that. She had broken the Greinen's crippling melancholy. And the atmosphere in the World of Visions had shifted. No longer a chamber of torture, it now intrigued him. It beckoned him and promised solace.

But the treacherous Wailing One still remained somewhere above the billowing sheets of iridescence.

Druin turned again on the bed and shivered slightly.

Was the air cooling down?

Images flashed of Arden in the Temmerung, of her recounting what she saw and how Maylin had been killed, and Banah had come so near death. And how the Barrostanian student had poured poison into Banah's slippers!

Rage still burned hot in him but, with all they had learned, pity was slowly replacing his anger. So much more about Trend had been revealed through the Spirit Veil of his and Banah's combined resonances, and the connection with Toman's Linger.

The Barrostanian student's imprisonment...

His nightmarish torment...

His unheard cries for help...

Druin longed to talk to Arden.

Could she possibly sense him, the way he could sense her?

"Arden, where are you?"

In the back of his thoughts, her soft musical voice was almost audible. He could visualise her gesticulating energetically as she engaged in analyses of language and history.

He smiled.

Tall and elegant, he found her breathtaking. Her turquoise eyes and long red-blonde hair cascading over her shoulders. Her innocence. Her smile. Everything about her was beautiful.

Tingling warmth spread through his chest.

His thoughts calmed and peace overcame him. Exhaustion permeated his body and sleep blanketed his mind.

Gentle morning mists rose over the precipitous crags of the mountain's backbone. Flowing upland with the warming air currents from the lower valleys, the thin wisps danced over the dense highland jungles.

Chattering like excited children at play, a small flock of brightly coloured Swordbills alighted on the branches of a majestic Loorwood. Their long tail feathers twirled in the wind like silken black ribbons.

A sense of calm lay over the valley. A sense of balance. Of harmony.

The fragrance of the warm moist earth pervaded Druin's senses.

The forest was a sacred place of solitude and wonder.

He loved and feared it.

High in the canopy, a deep piercing howl rent the quietude.

In the distance, the deep rumbling... of thunder? No, it couldn't be. The cloudless sky was clear brilliant blue.

The crown of a towering ancient tree suddenly shook violently, setting a flock of complaining birds to flight.

Throughout the forest canopy, the powerful calls of some dreadful animal picked up the birds' squawking, echoing off the sheer rock faces of the valley.

The ground shook.

Throwing his rucksack onto his shoulder, Druin sprinted towards the path.

Savage howls rose again. Howl after howl, a dreadful chorus resounded all around him.

The ground seemed to respond, shaking.

Standing became difficult.

Huge tree ferns cast pale green light all around.

He slipped on wet patches of lichens and thick mosses.

Dangling from rock outcrops, the glistening white fimbria of giant pitcher plants reminded him of the sharp-toothed snarls of his childhood nightmare. The Huddu-Han.

The snout-faced White Apes of the Cloud Forests.

But what had driven them down from the dense upland forests?

The air and ground began to reverberate. The cliffs around the valley shook with fury as a deluge roared down from the upper valley. Huge boulders spun through the air like balls tossed in a game.

A wave of water hit him like a wall of stone. His lungs filled with coolness as death cast deep shadows over his sight.

"No!" Druin awoke with a jolt, throwing his hands up. Panting, he pulled himself upright on the ropes of the bed.

He breathed deeply. Good. No water in his lungs!

Just a bad dream. It had seemed so real.

He fell back on his pillow and exhaustion returned more heavily than before. He forced himself to release the tension in his body. His heart slowed its frantic pace. Welcoming the returning drowsiness, he slipped towards slumber again.

He found a prayer swelling in him like a rush of emotions, a plea for something he had never desired before. "Ber'eth, I ask you to pull me into the World of Visions. And draw Arden in at this moment as well."

A wave of gentle heat passed through him.

Had he fallen back to sleep?

Or was it swirling currents of warm air?

His body seemed to sink through layers of mist, then he found himself standing in front of a luminescent portal.

Peace seemed to radiate from the opening. Joy filled him. An entrance to the World of Visions!

Smiling, he passed into that strange realm.

Peace continued. Calm silence.

Never had he entered without first being overwhelmed with sorrow. Once a dreaded world only of suffocating torment, always pulled into the last moments of Maylin's consciousness, forced to relive her death over and over again...

But now, thanks to Arden's bravery, that cycle of anguish had ended.

She had risked everything for him.

Druin peered at the luminous shapes billowing around him. "Arden?" He called out. "Are you here?"

Sudden anxiety passed through him, then severe pain shot across the back of his skull.

Stones around him flickered with iridescence.

"Arden? Is that you?"

"Druin?" Her voice quivered.

He turned towards the voice.

An arm's length from him, she appeared to be seated, hunched over something. Then she stood upright holding a red case, shimmering like a heat mirage. A dull-coloured cloak was draped over her shoulders. She seemed to be trembling.

"Arden? Are you all right?"

She burst into tears.

Druin drew closer. How he longed to take her into his arms! He could almost feel her breath against his face.

But they were in two different worlds.

The vision began to clear.

Tears beaded on her eyelashes and dripped onto her cheeks.

Her anguish stabbed at his mind. Spasms racked her body as she sobbed. "Druin, terrible things are happening. So many are dead. A horrible miasma in the city. People are melting in the streets."

Druin's muscles tightened with alarm. "Arden, are you safe? Have you been hurt?"

"No. I'm all right." She touched the back of her head gingerly.

But Druin could feel the throbbing pain on her skull. "Are you sure?"

She nodded as she began to cry again. "The Quaterni, all the Houses of the Kingship. Soffian murdered them, murdered every member of the Great Houses." She gasped for air. "I think she poisoned the wine to toast the death of her husband. Those that didn't drink, she..." Arden's lips quivered. "...she had killed! I was in the Crystal Parlour and heard her in the Great Hall."

High above them, the Greinen began a deep, almost cheerful, chant.

Druin and Arden looked up at the same time.

He could feel her shiver and the muscles in her stomach constrict. He wanted to retch, sensing her torment. "Are you sure you're safe in the city?"

"I don't know." Trying to catch her breath, she whispered, "I need to find the Professor."

Cradling her travelling case in her arms, she rocked gently back and forth. Agony shaded her fragile beauty like a dark funeral shroud. Her rapid short breaths frightened Druin. She could black out.

Looking on in wretched pity, he waited for her breathing to slow before asking another question.

"Arden, are you able to tell me more? Where are you?"

"I'm in a cart somewhere in the Lower City but I don't remember how I got through the portal." Confusion filled her thoughts. A lump on her head throbbed. Maybe debris from the last explosion of lightning had struck her.

"The Lady Steward." Wiping her face with a sleeve, Arden rose slowly. "Soffian murdered her husband and has declared herself King. She has renamed Norssum Barrostania and herself the King of Barrostania."

"King?" A bitter cold sensation ran up Druin's spine.

"And my half-brother, Caldere, is styling himself as Baron now! He is her consort and lover."

"Her lover?" Disgust swelled in him but he kept his face stern. How dreadful it must have been for Arden to discover that.

Arden nodded. "Caldere had one of your sister's sachets. I saw blood drip from his nose." She slowly lowered her case. "Caldere spoke of a collaboration with the Greinen and with Athlonia. About soldiers at the border with Syngordia."

High above, hideous laughter seemed to splinter and crackle through the air.

The back of Druin's throat quivered with emotion.

He quickly regained control over his feelings. "I'm so sorry. Arden, I'm so sorry we left you behind. It wasn't right, no matter what the Crystalline Man said!"

Her shoulders shaking with sobs, Arden looked up and spoke in a flat tone. "Canthalida, Ber'eth's plans shall come to pass. You can do nothing to stop him."

The Greinen's chant ceased.

Arden's cloak moved abruptly. Her hood flipped back onto her shoulders.

She gasped, "He put someone aboard your—" She vanished.

"Arden! Arden!" Druin awoke trembling, his nightclothes now drenched in sweat. "No!"

16

NIGHTMARES

The hard shaking surface under Arden bumped to a stop.

Her cloak moved suddenly around her. The hood pulled back.

"Please, please don' be dead."

Who spoke? Where was Druin?

A rough hand grasped her forearm, gently shaking her.

"Oh, please, My Lady!" The man's voice sounded tense. "I mean, Miss Lily! We're 'ere, Miss Lily. We made it."

"Fram?" Her head throbbed.

"You were knocked out for a bit there."

Cool misty rain fell on her face and neck. She touched her head and winced. "What happened?" She lowered her shaking hand. Luckily, the lump was small.

"Oh, Miss Lily..." Fram's voice quivered. He blinked rapidly then frowned. "Lightnin' exploded again. Rubble flyin' everywhere. You was hit and I thought you was dead. But I pulled you into the back of the cart. You kept talkin' to someone..." Kneeling next to her, Fram continued nervously. By the swollen redness of his eyes, he'd been crying. "...to a Mister Drew? And something about a Kantalinda?"

"Canthalida." She nodded. "And Lord Druin Méndrensynn." At least she hadn't dreamt it. Somehow she'd passed through the portal just as she was hit on the head. "How long was I – ?"

"Please forgive me, My Lady, I didn' mean to listen in. But you was talkin' a lot." His face twisted with an expression of anguish. "An' sobbin'." He dragged his sleeve over his eyes and sniffed. "Is it true, My Lady? The Quaterni? The whole families? Dead?"

She nodded slowly.

Fram shuddered, lowering his head. "Ber'eth help us!" He pointed above their heads. "We're 'ere, My Lady. At the university."

The massive entrance to the university campus arched into the darkness above them.

Relief. She'd made it this far, now she needed to find Professor Gwenndon. "Thank you, Fram."

"You really shouldn' be movin' yet, but we can't stay 'ere another minute, My Lady." Fram looked up, his eyes scanning the skies. He shook his head. "I don' see it now, but terrible things are 'appenin'..." He lowered his gaze towards the bottom of the hill. "An' strange ships with big white sails are comin' into the Firth."

"Oh my. I need to get across campus to the Professor right away." She quickly unlatched her case and felt for the pocket in her folded dress. Finding her small money bag, she retrieved a few coins. "Here. For you, Fram."

A look of surprise lit up his face. "Much obliged, My Lady." He helped her sit up, then jumped down and held out a hand for her.

Moving to the edge of the cart bed, she dropped her feet to the gravel.

It was easier to stand than she expected.

Wringing his hands, he bit his lower lip. "My Lady, if you would allow me now. Now that you're here at the university... My family... They be back in the Lower City. They may be in need of me."

"Of course, Fram! Thank you most sincerely."

He lowered his head. "No matter, My Lady. It was my duty." Climbing back up on the cart he handed Arden her red travel bag. He grabbed the reins and looked at her. "Please say a prayer for me, My Lady." His eyes were taut with worry.

"I will." He didn't even know her – and yet, what he'd risked for her... "Thank you again, Fram. Take heed. The storm upon us isn't over yet."

He nodded then slapped the reins against the beast's rump. "Come on, girl." The rickety cart creaked back down the street.

Arden turned and hurried through the archway. Hopefully the professor was still there.

Another streak of blue-white lightning seared through the sky, exploding on the hillside above the university. In the sudden light something vast moved through the clouds over the city. The giant black branches of a hideous moving tree?

She looked on as her stomach spasmed in fear.

No, it couldn't be...

She pulled the hood of her cloak back over her head and held on to her case tightly. The School of Eth Studies and Professor Gwenndon's office weren't far.

Each footfall sent pain shooting across the back of her head.

Relieved that the streets between the university buildings were almost empty, she hurried onward.

Not much further.

But what if the Professor wasn't even there? What if this whole trip had been ill-fated from the start? Fram risked his life for her, and was risking it again to get back to his family down in the Lower City!

But she had to get to Gwenndon. He had been like a second father. Where would she have been if not for his help? Sent back to Borinbranth? Dread filled her at the thought. Caldere's treachery was beyond belief.

Hopefully, their parents were safe. Surely her half-brother's demented plans would not have included them. Not them!

Toman's advice returned to her and she spoke her supplication out loud, "Please Ber'eth, not Papa and Mama. I forth-tell protection over them. And over Fram and his family."

A sense of hope came as the steps to the School of Eth Studies came into view, illuminated by the university's ornate gas lamps. Heart racing, she hastened to the main doors and pushed.

Locked!

No! She pushed again.

Turning and looking back to the campus, dim silhouettes ran through the drizzle.

Out of the deep shadows... a man moved quickly towards her.

Terror seized her.

"Lady Arden!" A familiar voice shouted. "What are you doing here?" Professor Gwenndon appeared in the soft golden light of the lamps. His face was flushed. Sweat slicked his hair across his eyes. "We are not safe here, My Lady." He fumbled with keys then pushed one into the door lock.

They ran down the dark corridor.

Doors to many of the lecture rooms had been left wide open. Papers were strewn over the floors. Desks askew. It seemed that evening classes had been in session as the disaster struck.

"You risked your life coming here, My Lady." He reached into his pockets as they arrived at his office door. He stared at her. "Why?"

"So much to tell. And I had to see if you were safe."

He blinked, shaking his head slightly. "My Lady?"

"I couldn't leave without knowing you were out of danger... and to tell you that I've met Crethingan in person."

His eyes widened as he searched through his bundle of keys again.

"Please, Professor, let me help you." She selected the key to his door.

"Sir Han Crethingan? The legendary architect?" He still had a look of disbelief on his face as she unlocked his office door and pushed it open.

"In the Temmerung. He drew me in physically. He said that there was another of his portals here in the university grounds."

"By Ber'eth, My Lady, you are changing history around us. But we don't have time now." Hurrying to his desk, he lit an oil lamp then began filling a satchel with papers.

"Professor, the Steward has been murdered." Arden paused. It was difficult to think about, let alone talk about again. "Lady Galdyssen murdered him this morning. Then she called all the families of the Quaterni to an evening assembly."

Gwenndon stopped and stared. "Murder! I'd heard only about his death, and the meeting."

Emotions welled up, constricting her throat. "All of them are dead now, too." She swallowed hard, struggling to keep her composure. "She declared herself King of Barrostania."

The Professor's mouth fell open. Shaking his head, he dropped into his chair, muttering. "When I heard the special meeting had been convened..." His voice trailed off as he stared out of the windows. "I thought it was for the emergency at hand. What is happening to this city?"

She followed Gwenndon's gaze through the windows. Blown by the sea breezes, low dark clouds of smoke writhed over the city. High above, streams of white lightning branched through the sky.

"Professor, there is a deadly miasma in the Lower City. Many people are dying, their skin melting off their bones."

"What?" Gwenndon stood abruptly. Packing more rolled parchments into his bag, he looked at her.

"And tremors have rocked the seafront." She added.

"Also here." He shuffled through other papers on his desk, his breaths coming in sharp gasps.

"Then the lightning. It seems to possess sentience, have a mind of its own, flowing through alleyways, ripping up paving stones. Then a deadly black tar oozes from the cracks." She shuddered again at the hideous memory of bones protruding from clothing. The burning in her throat and nose. The horrific acrid stench. It reminded her of the slight smell of the servants' unfiltered water that she'd drunk herself. "Anyone from the Upper City near it dies, but it looks as if no-one from the Lower City does though." How had she been saved?

He froze. "My Lady, I fear returning here will be your undoing." He studied her face. "You shouldn't have come."

She looked away. "I had to, Professor." She stepped closer to the window. "We really need to find the portal to the Temmerung that Crethingan mentioned. It's somewhere in the Sunken Garden."

Thick milky grey smoke lay over the blue glazed roofs of the waterfront. Red and orange spots of light glowed where fires were obviously burning.

Flames leapt suddenly from the roofs of the Galdyssen and Armgolt Baronholds as a gust of wind blew in from the Estuary. A view cleared of the ominous scene, like a terrible window.

Arden gasped. "Professor!"

Crowding the harbour just beyond the sea wall, a forest of tall white sails flickered in the eerie light of burning buildings. Emblems like the forked antlers of great stags spread over their white cloth.

High above the narrow streets of the Lower City, the branching horns of what looked like a gargantuan beast moved through the clouds. Its eyes, giant glowing sapphire spheres, moved back and forth as if searching. Explosions down near the waterfront shook the street.

"The Irrshen!" Arden pressed her travelling bag to her chest. Her mind reeled in terror.

"I see it. I see it..." The Professor's voice rose as he

rifled through bookshelves, packing more manuscripts into his satchel. "Athlonians, sorcery, the Sign of the Irrshen in the sky! Are all of our nightmares coming true at once?"

Pressing a hand against a windowpane, Arden covered her mouth to muffle her cry.

Below, on the avenue leading to the School of Eth, gendarme guards with raised swords!

Marching in front of them... Caldere!

17

Duty and Honour

Palandred's thoughts swirled as he climbed the stairs towards his cabin suite.

Images and impressions of the day's events shot through his mind. Too many to comprehend. It was hard to believe that so much had happened so quickly. The trembling in his hands had settled into his stomach.

He needed a glass of brandy. Or two.

Fatigue began to weigh on every part of his being.

Rapid footfall sounded on the steps behind him.

Captain Westrum hurried to his side. "Your Highness, the student has been secured. After whatever the

Ydassum visitors performed, he does not seem to pose a threat any longer."

Palandred started at the sound of powerful wings flapping just above them. Pushing his hair away from his face, he studied the starlit sky as black silhouettes of the Uccell slipped quickly out of sight.

Out of the shadows, Druin appeared on the deck above, folding a piece of parchment into his shirt. He quickly disappeared down the corridor to his cabin.

Westrum frowned slightly. "The Highborns have a very unusual choice of travelling companions."

Palandred smiled. "That's an understatement." The Uccell... the Firstborn of the Great Continent. They had touched him and had imparted into his mind their vast breath-taking history. He'd seen the land still untouched by the Orrenic Migrations, witnessed the horrific massacres of the Uran Draigana. And rivers of their blood.

He suppressed a shudder.

And, even if only in a vision, he'd been airborne with them, his own massive wings beating in time with theirs! The exhilaration of flight still prickled on his skin!

He sighed. If only the day had stopped there.

"What happened in the brig... did you see where the brilliant light came from?" Like the shock wave from a volcanic explosion, it had knocked him and others to the floor.

Westrum shook his head. "No, Your Highness, the light just seemed to explode around the Fyrst of Ydassum. It looked like a sheet of glass though. I've heard of Eth, but never of this particular phenomenon."

And how was it that Toman, Druin and Lady Banah could conduct Eth so effortlessly? Palandred's own experiences with Eth were full of misery. Even now, traces of the searing sensation remained in his palms. He rubbed his hands against his trousers.

And the Wailing One? A being out of children's stories? Had she really been controlling the Barrostanian student? Speaking through him?

Palandred's skin went cold at the memory.

And the unfortunate Lord Dalbonn... compassion came over Palandred as glimpses flashed again of the Highborns' Lord Protector lying mortally wounded in the sickbay. Lord Dalbonn meant so much to Lady Banah and Druin, and even more to Toman.

Palandred feared there was little hope that he would heal.

Chilling memories continued to fill his mind... the student's gut-wrenching sobs... Palandred had never heard a man make such sounds before. How had Toman and the Ydassumer Highborns released the student from the demon?

Could they free him as well?

He stumbled.

"Your Highness?" Holding out a gloved hand, Captain Westrum looked attentively at Palandred's feet.

"I'm fine." He lied, straightening up again. "I missed that last step."

He really needed that glass of brandy!

Even though the Barrostanian student had somehow returned to his right mind, how would his actions affect Palandred's relationship with the Highborns? Despite the fact that he had verbally authorised Druin and Lady Banah to judge the student's case, the young Barrostanian had taken that choice out of Palandred's hands when he'd murdered Mendelonian guards while onboard a royal Mendelonian vessel.

Judgement now fell back under Palandred's jurisdiction.

He cringed inwardly.

Normally his word was his honour, and he had intended to uphold it. But the situation had changed irrevocably.

"Thank you, Westrum. Keep me informed of any developments." Palandred dismissed the captain and entered the corridor leading to his rooms.

Dread weighed on his chest. Hopefully the situation wouldn't create discord between Lady Banah and himself. From what Palandred now knew about Druin's sister, she would be greatly distressed by the execution of the prisoner.

The walk to his door never seemed so long.

As he entered his stateroom, his valet Dreym stood quickly from one of the window seats and bowed. "Good evening, Your Highness."

"Evening, Dreym." Palandred closed the door behind him. "I need to get out of these clothes." They reeked of the brig.

"I thought you may be exhausted." Dreym motioned towards the bed. His voice sounded unusually tense. "Your nightclothes are ready for you, Your Highness."

His valet always gave him a sense of being home, back in Horróglоryn. He turned for Dreym to undress him.

Dreym's hands shook as he slipped Palandred's jacket off his shoulders. "Word has it, Your Highness, that something terrible is on board this ship." His valet's voice faltered. "A demon of untold power."

Palandred grimaced. "There was, but I think she's gone now. At least I hope so. She is called 'the Greinen' but she is the same *Wailing One* of nursery rhymes."

"Your Highness?" Dreym's outstretched arms stiffened

holding Palandred's jacket. "The W-Wai-Wailing One? "He stuttered. "Are nightmares coming true? The whole world seems to be going mad."

Palandred turned towards his valet. "It would seem so. It's insane to think that the whole world is responding to some force far greater than itself. But lately..." he paused, "...despite the strange events happening around us, it would seem that we're all following some kind of hidden script. The Ydassumer Highborns are calling it *the Shift*, a Beckoning that is being transmitted throughout the whole world by the power of Eth."

"A Beckoning?" Dreym tilted his head slightly and pointed to Palandred's neck. "Your collar, Your Highness?"

"Yes, of course." Palandred turned around.

Dreym unbuttoned the back of the starched band and slipped it off, then began undoing the cuffs of Palandred's shirt. "Word from your men, Your Highness, is that the Ydassumer Highborns also possess high levels of magic, and that they are protecting the ship with it."

"Not magic." Palandred shook his head. Images of Lady Banah passed through his mind. Her radiant presence, her unwavering sense of decorum and justice. Her beautiful smile. "Not magic," he repeated. "They are devout followers of Ber'eth. Their power is Eth."

"Eth." Dreym nodded as he hung up the jacket and slipped the collar into the pocket. He looked up quickly. "Your Highness, there's something in here. A sealed letter."

"Pardon?" Who could have slipped him a letter? Lady Banah perhaps? He found his cheeks warming at the thought.

Dreym handed him the folded vellum.

Fillip's large wax seal filled Palandred with irritation.

Of course. It was the note to the Vlachonian governor. He'd forgotten to include it with the chest he'd sent through the Ferend Service.

His valet pointed to Palandred's trousers.

Palandred nodded, slipping off his shoes and handing him the trousers. "Thank you, Dreym."

Eyes wide, his valet froze for an instant.

The shadows cast by the oil lamp swaying on its chain seemed to dance along the panelled walls.

"I don't think I ever really thanked you for your service." Palandred looked quickly down. The colours of the carpet seemed exceptionally rich in the golden lamplight.

Druin, Lady Banah and their whole entourage expressed thanks as an integral part of their culture. Why should it be so difficult for a dynast to express gratitude and appreciation? It wasn't a sign of weakness as he had been brought up to think. With Druin and his sister, it seemed to greatly augment their sense of dignity and decorum.

"I'm grateful. You do an excellent job." Now that he himself had expressed gratitude to an inferior, something inside him felt oddly stronger.

Dreym seemed reduced to a complete nonplus. He held out Palandred's nightshirt. "Your Highness, thanks are not necessary. It is my duty and my honour."

18

BIRTHRIGHT

Palandred took the nightshirt from Dreym. “Thank you.”

“Will that be all, Your Highness?” His valet walked over to the door and stood to attention.

“Yes. I am exhausted. I will retire now.”

“As you wish, Your Highness.” Dreym bowed, closing the door behind him.

Palandred glanced around the empty room and let out a long sigh of relief.

Finally, alone. Time to think through everything that was happening.

He opened the brandy cabinet and picked up the bottle of his favourite distillation then sat down at the table.

He finished his first glass quickly and poured himself a second.

Closing his eyes, he eased back into his upholstered chair, but his mind was still ablaze with impressions and questions...

...first, in the infirmary. Obviously, Toman and the Méndrensynns had engaged Eth. Had there been hints of blue and yellow, and then green?

And Toman's completely transparent form! It had resembled molten glass with flickering embers of light enclosed within its shimmering surface.

But it didn't make sense, because none of them seem to have suffered any ill effects from allowing Ber'eth to use them.

...then in the brig with the Barrostanian student. The criminal growling like a violent animal, then suddenly cooing like a courtesan! Was she really the ancient Wailing One of old myths? Her enticing voice had filled the room then slithered into his skull. She seemed to speak from within his thoughts!

He shuddered at the memory.

Then the Eth lights around Lady Banah and Druin. And the explosion? The blinding light? Where had they come from? Light had no physical properties, so what force had knocked them down?

He lifted his goblet again, swirling the sweet dark liquid in front of the flickering lamplight. The bouquet was strong and sweet. The smooth film of heavy liquid clung beautifully to the sides of the glass. The viscosity was perfect.

All day, his dreaded Eth had threatened to engulf him,

as it had done at this same time every year since his mother's death. The detestable prickling in the back of his skull had flared when Lady Banah, Druin and Toman had gathered in the infirmary, and then again in the brig. Thankfully he'd been able to subdue the demonic surges from overtaking him as they had that day with his mother. Never would he allow the accursed Eth storm inside him to do its harm again, to anyone.

And yet, being in the presence of the Highborns kept challenging his conviction.

How had Lady Banah conducted her Eth and yet not suffered any apparent anguish? No signs of torment, nor anything destructive seemed to happen to her. Perhaps her exceptional purity or her inner fortitude counterbalanced the maleficence of Ber'eth's power.

Palandred opened and closed his hands.

The anxiety was beginning to subside.

Thankfully, there were no more traces of the crimson glow that had appeared around his palms in the brig. No physical traces, but still the constant awareness of forbidden powers flowing just below the skin.

Eth resonances...

His was an odious colour of blood, but he'd never seen any other hues before that day. He'd been instructed of their existence. Druin's bluish glow and Lady Banah's yellow were obviously connected to their Eth power.

But the green? An overlap of blue and yellow?

Toman as well. His resonance had acted like a magnifying glass to the Highborns' Lingers! How? And none of them seemed to have experienced discomfort or harm because they were wielding Eth.

Why had Ber'eth dealt differently with him?

Why had Ber'eth cursed *him*? Why? *Why!*

He squeezed his eyes shut as a door opened in his

thoughts. His hands began to quiver. His heart raced. Rage scalded his mind.

For a moment, his resolve faltered.

Childhood memories flooded into him.

Glimpses of the nursery with the governess… playing with Leahn, practicing their Eth Lingers. Giggles fluttered through the air. Innocence glowed golden around them.

Those were happier times, when his twin sister was still with him. When he still trusted the lessons their governess taught them about Ber'eth. Before he knew the truth. The muscles in his neck tightened and he clenched his hands into fists. How could he have allowed himself to trust anything to do with Ber'eth?

The door in his thoughts opened wider. A murky crimson cloud flowed through the opening.

His fingers prickled.

His gut wrenched.

He opened and closed his hands again as minute traces of the deep crimson light surfaced, trickling through the veins in his fingers.

Not again! That hideous red scarab was taunting him once more, threatening to resurface and ruin other lives.

"No you won't!" Palandred finished his glass and sighed deeply. Pushing his chair away from the table, he stood and stepped over to the windows. Unlatching a small pane within the mullions, he opened it wide, and a stream of fresh salty air blew against his face.

He took a few deep breaths of the ocean breeze as the brandy's soothing effects tingled through his limbs. The tension in his body began to ebb.

Calm yourself, Palandred. Concentrate!

That's it, concentrate.

You can stop seizures. You did it in Barrost.

Palandred leaned out of the window slightly and looked southward. Even though the storm over Barrost wasn't far behind, the wind had already diminished.

To the west, out over the glistening dark sea, a vast herd of Vahlen blew misty jets high above their backs. In the bright moonlight, their moist spray looked like a bank of eerie luminous fog arising in the middle of the ocean.

Far beyond the massive water beasts, flashes on the distant horizon bespoke another storm approaching.

Hopefully, they would reach the Bay of Limman before it hit.

Leaving the window open, he turned towards his bed.

A chill shivered through his bones. The last time he slept in here, terrifying visions had assailed him. Dark-skinned men had appeared through the walls. Ochre paint shimmered around their eyes. They had called each other 'brother' and declared that they'd found their inheritance, their birthright.

Nonsense, but something about their search made bile rise into Palandred's mouth.

If the vision had any truth, like these Glortroms the Highborns and the Landsenders reported, perhaps his had held some specific signs as well.

Palandred wasn't certain, but the tall warriors, their svelte, dark-skinned bodies, their exotically slanted and painted eyes... they fitted textbook descriptions of the ancient Skylle, the blood-thirsty murderous southern tribes.

Palandred couldn't stop the barrage of thoughts and images.

The Firstborn of the Continent had allowed him to see their own memories of their massacre. History books gave accounts of the innumerable dead Orren, their heads as ornaments atop long poles leading to the entrances of each major city they had conquered.

Terrible!

His stomach lurched.

Concentrate, Palandred!

He poured another brandy and took a sip to calm his nerves. He looked at the letter to the Vlachonian governor. A sudden chuckle in his throat surprised him. Fillip would be incensed that the letter hadn't accompanied the crate sent to the Vlachonian governor.

Palandred didn't care.

Disappointing his brother, the King, had somehow grown less daunting.

What did Fillip want with the governor of Vlachonia? For that matter, what had his brother been scheming for Barrost?

Palandred took another sip, lifting the letter in front of the lamp. The parchment was too thick to read what was written within. But something in his stomach bubbled acid and he put the parchment back down.

Where was his friend Danuel? It wasn't like him not to send word. And Dreym said that no message regarding Danuel had been received since they'd left Mendelon.

Palandred struggled not to let hope dissolve.

Danuel had gone to investigate Fillip's doings but hadn't been heard of since. Had he fallen into the vicious web Fillip was spinning? Dread congealed in Palandred's blood. Was Danuel even still alive?

Apprehension filled Palandred.

Fillip's crates. How much gold had his brother stolen from the crown's coffers to finance whatever he was doing now?

Finishing the sweet brandy in a few large gulps, he lowered himself onto the mattress and lay down.

Dread throbbed in his heart like a fistful of thunder. Something was terribly wrong, but what exactly? In his mind, a wide horizon began to fill with ships of war. Storms raged high above their red sails.

The room began to sway back and forth. Blackness cloaked his sight. The hull of his ship seemed to lurch with a large wave.

A strange but frightening familiarity penetrated the room.

Distant voices cried out from beyond the walls. His Glortrom was returning!

"The Child of Orren, brothers! We have found him!"

Terror struck again in Palandred's chest. He opened his eyes as the voices continued, filling the room.

"The thief of our birthright.
You can hide from us no longer."

Grabbing the headboard, Palandred forced himself upright.

"The power you stole, we will extract from you.
The Rubinstone and its power are our birthright."

The back of Palandred's skull flared with stinging pain. His fingertips filled with accursed light. All around him images moved like ghostly murals painted on luminous fog. The heavy beams of his quarters blended with the vast white granite entrance of the Winter Palace. Fillip stood before his throne, his two sons at his sides. The jewel mounted above his throne blazed.

Each scene blended with the previous one, indistinct then distinct, then fading.

"No, no, no!" He grabbed the empty brandy bottle and

threw it in the direction of the apparition. It shattered across the table.

"The power is our birthright."

"Birthright? Birthright!" *Stay calm, Palandred.*

Standing up shakily from the bed, he groped for the bell cord hanging from the ceiling and pulled hard. He wouldn't be able to sleep anyway.

A moment later Dreym entered the cabin, still in his nightshirt, rubbing his eyes. Holding up his lamp, he blinked hard.

The voices returned. *"You can hide from us no longer."*

Palandred's hands ignited with searing pain. Lights glowed from within his bones. Rage mixed with fear surged within him. "Birthright? What birthright? Leave me alone!"

19

Please Stay

The boards of the floor creaked softly as Toman approached the infirmary.

He smiled for an instant. The entire corridor was well crafted from a fine-grained blond type of Byr tree wood.

There was something special about wood. It wasn't as durable as stone but could last for centuries if kept dry and properly treated.

He stopped in front of the door and listened. It was very late, but it had been impossible to sleep. He'd tried, but anxiety wouldn't let him close his eyes.

How was His Grace?

Toman wanted to try something.

He tapped a knuckle lightly on the panel, then held his breath, straining his ears for the faintest sounds of movement inside.

He knocked again, holding his ear close to the door.

Only the gentle creaking sounds of the vessel.

Perhaps Physician Wanner had retired to some other chambers?

Toman just needed to see his master again. He'd only take a moment.

Opening the door softly, he stepped over the threshold into the warm room. Moonlight glowed through the windows. The air inside was still and thick with the now familiar smells of medicinal salts and alcohols. His instinct was to open a window. But he'd better not. Not with his master in such a fragile state.

Palan's physician, Wanner, lay asleep on a narrow bed built into a corner of the room.

Careful not to thud his boots on the floor, Toman approached His Grace's bedside.

It was difficult to detect in the low light, but his master's chest rose and fell with thin breaths. Toman sighed with relief. At least His Grace was breathing without that hideous rattle of blood in his throat. Since the attack, his face had changed. Aged. It looked almost colourless. Even the patches of white hair on his temples had spread.

Despite the physician's reassurance, '*If the Lord Dalbonn continues at this rate, he should make it to Limmania, where there will be better facilities to aid his recovery*,' Toman wasn't certain.

Kneeling next to the cot, he leaned in close to his master. "Come back, Your Grace." He kept his voice low. "Please come back."

Wanner stirred. "Do not engage him in conversation."

His forced whisper hissed through the air. "His lungs would not take the exertion." The Physician's frown wasn't quite as deep as yesterday, but his tone was as sharp. Fully dressed, he peeled back the sheet and dropped his stocking feet off the edge of his cot. He slowly stood, rubbing his eyes.

"Of course, Good Sir. I won't make him speak. I mean, I won't ask him questions." There was another way of communicating that needed no words. His Linger. He carefully pushed back the crisp white sheet and opened the top of His Grace's shirt. Kindling his Eth, the tips of his fingers began to glow with the power of Ber'eth as he opened his palms over his master.

The physician's eyes bulged as he slipped into his boots. "What are you doing?"

"Please." Toman held up a glowing hand towards Physician Wanner. "I will honour your request, but I need to try and hear his consciousness. I will not engage him in speaking." Toman then placed a hand on his master's chest.

His fingers gave off more light as he formed a small disk under his palm. He pressed it gently against his master's skin. Blurred impressions rushed into his mind. Pain. Extreme fatigue. Loneliness.

He concentrated.

Slowly, sounds began to penetrate his mind.

Gentle melodies wove in and out. Songs about distant seashores. Hymns of a faraway homeland. Sweet bedtime lullabies. Voices invoking Ber'eth's blessing.

Images came into view.

A refugee camp. Smoke rising from smouldering fires. Vague silhouettes of soldiers standing guard over children queueing in front of a boiling cookpot. Many pale blond toddlers, each holding an empty bowl. So many silver eyes, like those of his mother and Lord Dalbonn himself.

Sorrow hung darkly over the camp like a widow's mourning shroud.

Two children ran across Toman's vision. An odd glow enveloped them. Barely three or four years old, a blonde girl and an older boy with darker hair. Their laughter tinkled around them as they played.

Toman focused on the two... something was familiar about them.

"It's time for you to go." Physician Wanner stepped closer to Toman, his frown darkening to a scowl.

Toman nodded, withdrawing the power. His Linger blinked out under his hand. A sense of emptiness filled his consciousness, then hollow sadness.

He had wanted to stay longer, perhaps even talk with his master through the Eth link.

Standing upright Toman turned to the physician and bowed. "My sincerest gratitude, Good Sir."

"My Lord." Despite a clear tone of irritation, the physician inclined his head respectfully. "Good evening, Your Highness."

Toman turned to leave.

He stopped suddenly as an anguished shout came from the cabin next to the infirmary.

"No, no, no!"

Those were Prince Palandred's rooms!

A loud thud vibrated through the wall, then glass shattering.

Alarm jolted through Toman and he pointed towards the sounds. "Physician, it's Palan! Should I help him?"

The physician frowned towards the wall, shaking his head and mumbling to himself. "Not again." He turned away and started inspecting the contents of a drawer. "No one can help him."

Toman's mouth dropped open.

The physician's apparent indifference stunned him.

Did Palan often have fits of rage? The Prince's behaviour had always been subdued, if a bit sad at times, but with no trace of such aggression.

Opening the door to leave, Toman bowed. "Good day, Physician Wanner. And thank you again."

Toman closed the door slowly behind him then stood for a moment, squeezing his eyes shut.

Palan's suite had fallen back into silence. Had it been a nightmare? Hopefully he was feeling better, or had got over his moment of fury.

Toman rubbed his face with his hands. He needed to gather his thoughts. His Linger connection to his master's mind had revealed some puzzling things.

With all the tents and campfires, His Grace must have been reliving memories of the civil war in Bnornum. But the two children playing? The impression they'd left had been particularly clear and strong. The purity of their joy had appeared completely immune to the bleak hardship of the camp around them.

Such were the powerful and yet fragile hearts of children. Powerful enough to rebuild from the rubble of sorrow, but so fragile that they could be crushed by solitude.

The two children somehow reminded Toman of His Grace and his mother Alyena. How strange!

Had His Grace and his mother actually known each other?

Toman recoiled at Palan's renewed growls.

"Birthright! Birthright?"

The wooden walls muffled the Prince's voice but not the searing edge of his rage.

The shrill ping of a small bell sent a shiver through the base of Toman's skull.

He started walking towards the entrance of the corridor. Maybe he could pass Palan's cabin suite, and reach the end of the hall unnoticed.

A door flung open beside him.

A man in a nightgown walked quickly across the corridor and entered Palan's suite without knocking, leaving the door open. Probably his valet.

The fruity scent of brandy wafted toward Toman.

Strange male voices spilled from Palan's rooms. "*You can hide from us no longer! It is our birthright!*"

Scowling, the Prince stood stiffly near a table, his brilliant crimson resonance flaring from his hands and face, dancing like flames around a cookpot.

Had his Eth colour changed? It seemed a clearer red.

Palan roared again, "Birthright? What birthright?" He gulped for air. "Leave me alone!"

The valet gaped at Palan, then shook his head, frowning.

Toman quickly took a step backwards, away from the light. Hopefully Palan hadn't seen him.

But Toman froze as Palan fixed his eyes on him.

The Prince stood in a calf-length nightshirt, his eyes unblinking, staring at Toman.

For an instant, heat flared in Toman's cheeks.

Palan probably didn't appreciate being overheard at that moment.

"Toman?" Panting, Palan shook his head as though confused. His tone shifted between anger and surprise. He seemed to swell, filling the doorway. "What—?"

"I was just visiting Lord Dalbonn." Toman pointed towards the infirmary.

"Sickbay?" Confusion filled Palandred's eyes. Then his expression lightened slightly. "Ah, right." He cleared his throat. "What, what did you just hear?"

"Please forgive me." Normally Toman would have found himself stuttering in embarrassment, begging for forgiveness, or his face and ears blazing with shame. "I didn't mean to eavesdrop, but it was impossible not to overhear you."

Palan frowned.

"I heard strange voices. Men speaking." Unease made Toman hesitate. "Where did they come from? Are you safe?"

"You could hear them as well?" Beads of sweat dripped down Palan's forehead into his eyes. He blinked then rubbed them.

His frown smoothed.

His Eth resonance began to flicker more slowly but remained bright and clear. He leaned back against the door, exhaling slowly. Then he seemed to regain his composure quickly pushing his cabin door open wider. "Come in." He stood aside for Toman to enter. "Please. Come in."

"Thank you."

Palan quickly closed the door behind them.

Inside, the smell of sweet alcohol stung in Toman's nostrils.

Palan's servant carefully picked up glistening shards of glass, gathering them in a dustpan. He paused for a moment, looking sadly at Palan, then Toman. "Please forgive the inconvenience, Fyrst of Ydassum."

Toman stopped himself from explaining his position. "No inconvenience."

Palan opened another window, turned then dropped into a dark green upholstered chair. Weakly raising an arm, he pointed across the table to a sleek chair of some shiny black wood. “Please, Toman, have a seat.” He lowered his face into his slightly glowing hands. His clear red Linger still smouldered around him.

“Thank you.” Toman pulled out the chair and sat at the smooth table. Both were of superb craftsmanship, except for a single gash in the otherwise impeccable inlay of the table top.

“Toman…” Palan let out a sigh. “You heard the voices as well?” He glanced at his servant then continued. “I’m the only one who has ever heard them. But they are real. And this nightmare has to end.” He began mumbling so quietly, it became impossible to understand him.

Toman could only imagine Palan’s anguish. “I think a Glortrom just visited you. One visited My Lady before we left Turicum, and she had another in the Galdyssen Baronhold. The visions always contain important information from Ber’eth. Can you remember all you saw and heard?”

Palan looked up, his eyes bloodshot. Sweat pasted thin strands of hair to his forehead. “Toman, tell no one. Your word, Toman? Do I have your word?”

“Yes, of course.” Why would he not want Toman to speak of his Glortrom?

Palan studied Toman’s face as if scrutinising his truthfulness then he nodded as if satisfied with what he’d found. “Thank you.” His resonance flickered again, this time swirling, becoming brighter. He looked as if he stood in a crimson storm. But the shade of his colour was more intense, at least as strong as Lady Banah’s and Druin’s. Toman had never seen such a brilliant red.

"What you heard..." Palan went silent as he studied Toman's face. One of the Prince's eyelids twitched.

"Your Highness." The servant held the dustpan full of broken glass. "If I am no longer needed?"

"Of course. Thank you, Dreym." Palan waved towards the door. "That will be all for now."

Toman blinked. Impressions of profound darkness swelled around the Prince. They seemed to be deep red, but not the colour of his Eth resonance. Were there other forces involved?

"Perhaps I should go as well?" Toman stood. "But if there is anything I can do?"

"There is. Please stay for a moment. I'd like to talk."

20

Torment or Journey?

A sense of wonder and gratitude filled Palandred.

Not only had Toman somehow repelled the evil wraith in the brig, but he also had the ability to hear the waking nightmares of others.

Palandred had assumed that only he could hear or see the dark-skinned men.

How could an Ydassumer prince have heard the voices when none of his crew could?

Dreym had been baffled when Palandred mentioned them on the trip north to Barrost.

And Wanner had seemed to question Palandred's sanity when he'd tried to explain.

With the turmoil in Barrost, the dreadful memory had dimmed.

Until now.

Could it be true that Toman had heard them as well?

Palandred shuddered. "You say you heard the voices?"

"Yes." Nodding, Toman sat down again.

A strange weight seemed to lift off Palandred.

Unblinking, his guest fixed his eyes on him. "They sounded like the strange men who have haunted some of my dreams this past year."

"No one else heard them before. Before you."

Toman continued looking attentively at him. "You also received the Uccell's Touch – these men look like those who slaughtered the Firstborn of the Continent."

"The Skylle of the southern deserts."

"I've heard that name before." Toman scrutinised the shadows under the hammock bed. "Did you only hear their voices? You didn't see them?"

"No." Palandred shook his head. "Only voices this time."

"This time?"

"For years, I've had clusters of nightmares around the same time each year. Now they seem to be increasing." He shook his head. "But until now, they were never with apparitions or audible voices! On my voyage to the Barrostanian travesty they called a trade summit," he didn't try to hide his disdain for the contemptible waste of time, "my cabin faded in and out of a terrible vision." He waved a hand towards the starboard wall. His skin crawled at the memory. The story seemed to return more clearly as he spoke. "The Winter Palace in Mendelon City appeared through these walls, then strange voices and faces. Dark-skinned men, searching. Their eyes lined in dark yellow paint."

"Dark-skinned?" Toman leant forward and placed his hands on the table. "Gold around their slanted eyes?"

"Yes."

"And were they also very tall and lanky?"

Palandred nodded.

"Yes. Yes. Exactly like in my own dreams! But yours sounds like a true Glortrom! What did Ber'eth show you in it?"

Palandred searched his memory. "An attack on Mendelon. Destruction. Rivers of blood. Death."

Toman shivered.

"They are looking for something, a stone. They called it the Rubinstone. They want it, and its power, returned." Their gruff voices seemed to rumble back into Palandred's mind. He squeezed his eyes shut and recounted their words aloud,

"The Child of Orren, brothers.
The thief of our birthright.
You can hide from us no longer.
The power you stole, we will extract from you.
The Rubinstone and its power are our birthright."

Palandred's hands began to shake, but he continued. "They repeatedly stated, 'We have found him, and the Rubinstone. The Child of Orren. Thief of our birthright'."

"Menne Gootay." Toman rubbed his forehead. "I don't understand. *Thief*? Ruby Stone?"

"Rubinstone." Palandred corrected him. Fire seemed to explode in his skull. Of course! Ruby Stone, Rubinstone! Why hadn't he realised it before? Something so obvious! If only he had Toman's simple logic. He wanted to laugh but suddenly found it difficult to breath. Standing shakily, he rolled up the sleeves of his nightshirt and splashed some water into the wash basin. He cupped a handful and paused. "Of course!"

"Of course?"

Palandred lowered his face into his hands. Rubbing the fresh water onto his cheeks and temples, he looked up. "It's a long story and starts with my mother." His stomach tensed. His hands shook as he dried his face with a towel Dreym had laid out.

How had he not seen the connection?

He drew in and held a deep breath to help calm himself, then exhaled, dipped his comb into the water and pulled it back through his hair. It needed a trim. It was already down to his shoulders again.

He looked at Toman and put the comb down. "This grievous chain of events started with the Queen herself, my mother." Mentioning her sent another wave of anxiety through him.

Focus, Palandred. Focus.

"She accepted a jewel as bride price for my sister Isabella, a large invaluable ruby, a *gift* from the king of Syngordia. I discovered later that the jewel had been mentioned in the Treasury of Immen before it showed up in the coffers of the Double Crown Kingdom." He grasped the towel. "The demon stone must have been Skyllian, plundered during the Expulsion Wars, because no red gems of that size and brilliance had ever been mentioned in the north regions of the Great Continent. This jewel also had an unusual inner flaw, a crystalline structure that looked like a Scarab-Wasp – the devilish symbol the Skylle considered sacred." He released the towel, opening and closing his hands. He studied his palms. He wouldn't have been surprised to see the demon insect surface right through his skin at that very moment.

Toman looked intently at Palandred's open hands, then frowned slightly. "How do you think Immen, and then Syngordia, came by it?"

"I'm not certain. As I mentioned, no specific record exists. None that I've ever discovered. But it's clear that Immen has long been the repository of much more than just scrolls of learning. I am certain the Skylle left behind untold wealth that no treasury officially reported."

Tension seemed to drain from Palandred as he spoke. It was good to finally talk to someone about all this.

"Apparently, the Abbaths of *Holy* Immen do not refrain from bribing rulers of other countries if it serves their secretive purposes. Extracting political favours from the Double Crown Kingdom seems the least of their sins," he scoffed, shaking his head. "And a jewel of such worth would have tempted the insatiable appetite for power in that royal house."

Toman remained attentive, but his eyes appeared to focus on something beyond the room. "I knew that many Eth wielders were sheltered there, and that there are different and very complicated beliefs in Geholiogarth. But I didn't know they were so strong politically.

"The facades of Geholiogarth appear pristine and unblemished from the outside but within their elaborate crusts, the ruling Abbaths of Immen have always cultivated unscrupulous affairs."

"Do you think the House of Syngordia is also under the thumb of Immen?" Eyes widening, Toman sounded doubtful.

"I don't doubt it. I feel certain my mother thought so as well. She always despised the House of Syngordia, even though they are our closest relatives." Palandred shook his head. "But she was besotted with their jewels. Diamonds, emeralds, rubies, sapphires... She couldn't satiate her lust for them. I think Richarr knew he could buy his way deeper into our family with her desire for the Great Ruby, once she'd heard of its existence."

Memories flooded back and Palandred closed his eyes. "My sister, sold to the highest bidder."

Toman stirred. "That's appalling. I can't fathom a world in which your children are sold into marriages against their will."

"I agree. On the day my sister Isabella had hoped to present Danuel, the love of her life, to the Queen, Her Majesty struck them a devastating blow." Palandred found himself clutching his nightshirt. He released it and smoothed the cloth. "Isabella had already been sold to Richarr. Contracts already signed and paid. Two lives destroyed and hung as a pendant on strands of diamonds." Palandred didn't try to mask the loathing that seethed in him.

Toman frowned.

"She was more a tyrant than a mother." Palandred rolled his sleeves down and lowered himself back into the chair. "My closest friend, Danuel, never recovered from the trauma of what she'd done."

Not knowing Danuel's whereabouts still tormented him.

Her Majesty's horrific performance that day remained vividly in his mind. Like a haughty actor bowing in the lamplight on a stage, she glowered at them. A hideous sparkling toad glowing in reddish light. The huge jewel lay on her breast like a blood-stained trophy of her victory over Isabella and Danuel. "That's when..." The muscles in Palandred's jaw tightened. He paused, then continued, "That's when Ber'eth's curse erupted in me. It seared through my skull then struck the heart of the jewel. A gruesome crimson light emerged. The demon insect was released, and it killed her." Palan winced, raising his hands against the memories.

Sitting up straighter in his chair, Toman's frown appeared again. "Surely you're not speaking of your Eth?"

"I just wanted her to stop hurting Isabella, stop blighting Danuel's life." Palandred lowered his head. "I didn't mean to. The ruby. My brother was always certain Richarr knew of its curse, the demon inside. But I was the one who—"

"Palan, your resonance is powerful, the most powerful red I've ever seen." Toman rose from his chair.

"Pardon?"

"Your Eth. It's the most powerful red I've ever seen."

"You see Eth colours? Are you an Akkoren? But your Linger is transparent, not green."

"Yes. It seems that the Readers' green isn't the only resonance with the ability."

"And you see my Linger?" It disconcerted Palandred that Toman could perhaps see the demon force coursing through his body.

"Yes, and your Linger is powerful. Very powerful. And it's changing."

"Changing? What...what do you see, exactly?"

Once again, Toman's gaze seemed to focus past Palandred. "A blaze of red, dancing like the flames of a smithy's furnace around you. When you appeared in the Galdyssen Plaza in Barrost, it looked like the thin, dark red along the horizon at sunset. Today it became even brighter, clearer and many times more intense."

Palandred recoiled inwardly. Was the horror lurking in him preparing to resurface and kill again? "I don't understand." What he wouldn't do for another glass of brandy! Dreym could bring up another bottle and two glasses from the larder within minutes.

"The only others I've seen with such colour clarity and intensity are those of the Highborns, Lady Banah and Druin."

"You see this with your own eyes? I mean, it's not a vision or dream of some sort?"

Toman shook his head. "I see a lot of colours, like a forest of leaves each with different hues. There were many more colours back in Ydassum. As we travelled to Barrost, most of the people's Eth resonances dulled. They seemed to lose colour. But yours and those of the Highborns are standing out brighter."

Palandred stared at Toman as a sense of wonderment returned, but also anxiety. Was the scarab demon growing stronger? Could Toman sense it? But then, the Highborns' Eth lights were also increasing?

Could this be the beginning of another nightmare... or a journey of discovery? This time with Toman?

Something caught in Palandred's throat, and he swallowed. "Toman?"

Toman looked at him enquiringly. "Yes?"

"The jurisdiction I gave Lady Banah... over the Barrostanian student's case. It has fallen back onto me because he killed Mendelonians on Mendelonian territory. He must be executed."

His friend's face fell.

Palandred lowered his head. "I gave Lady Banah my word, but it wasn't my word to give. What will the Highborns think of me?"

He really needed another glass of brandy now. Reaching for the servant's cord, he pulled. The muffled ping of Dreym's bell sounded through the walls.

In the distance, a loud crack of lightning seemed to explode, then the boom of thunder washed over the ship.

21

War to Come

"This should be the dining room." Banah approached the deep blue painted door trimmed in gold leaf. "It is as Prince Palandred described it."

"Indeed." Lorann reached for the highly polished door handle.

Banah's health had improved greatly over the last few days. But at times she longed for the soothing effects of the Summerbird petals, their ethereal fragrance, their calming properties. Without them, the pressure of guilt was nearly crushing her.

Hopefully her Maiden wouldn't notice her inner struggles.

To have failed so abysmally in Barrost.

But there was too much still at stake to give in to the mental pain.

"The others should arrive soon." Banah entered the luxuriously furbished room.

Lorann followed her through the open door and gasped softly.

Standing in silence for a moment, they took in the colour and opulence of the low-ceilinged room. The intricately gilded posts and lintels throughout were carved with various motifs inspired by the sea. On the ceiling, undulating patterns of dark blue-green waves were inlaid with countless stars and small crowns carved from tiny seashells. In the centre of the ceiling, a large smoothly painted fresco displayed a fleet of mighty ships with billowing sails, the royal Mendelonian banners unfurled atop countless masts. The mighty armada of the most ancient dynastic house of the Northern Horn.

Burnished gold leaf shimmered everywhere on moulding and trim.

The windows were no less showy. Their mullioned forms were filled with roundels of Vlachonian amber glass which diffused the morning light into pleasant, gentle luminosity. The room exuded a kind of masculine confidence and strength, but also somehow had an inviting, protective atmosphere.

Lorann studied the table in the centre of the room, then turned towards Banah. "My Lady, it looks as though His Highness' servants have already prepared the settings. Shall I go to the kitchens and assist the Prince's staff with serving?"

"Thank you, but I'd like you to be with us this morning, next to me."

Her Maiden's cheeks flushed slightly.

"Dearest Lorann, where would I be now if it weren't for you?" Banah looked her directly in the eyes. "Your presence is a great joy and comfort. Your clear-minded judgment, and your keen ability to appraise situations, have been invaluable to me. I think it's time to give you the opportunity to observe more closely the different cultures we are visiting, to have a window into the functioning of governments on the Northern Horn."

Lorann lowered her head, nervously smoothing the sleeves of her dress.

Banah touched Lorann's cuff. "I feel these meetings will be beneficial for your future, regardless of the path you choose for your life."

Pulling out a handkerchief, Lorann dabbed the corners of her eyes. "My Lady, the honour is overwhelming."

"My dear Lorann, I think the time is right." Seeing her Maiden's discomfort, Banah quickly pointed towards the table and continued with a different topic. "The embroidery on the hem of the silken tablecloth is exquisite, don't you think? Such fascinating patterns of the sea. Leaping winged fish. And I believe the blue motifs that look like blossoms are the tentacled arms of squid."

"Squids?" Smiling weakly, Lorann lowered her hand and looked up. "We don't have the custom of such decoration in Ydassum." She swallowed and tucked her handkerchief away. "The pale-yellow porcelain looks translucent, almost like milk glass."

"Mm," Banah agreed. "Exceptional quality, from an exceptional ancient dynastic house." She approached the table and began walking around the chairs. On every piece of porcelain, the deep blue, yellow and red floral motif of the House of Mendelon glinted.

Lorann followed, inspecting the settings. "But a little overly decorated though, don't you think?"

Banah frowned. "Each culture nurtures its own sense of beauty and balance. Each has individual tastes and its own sense of aesthetics."

Face flaring red, Lorann clasped her hands together on her stomach. "Please forgive the criticism, My L—"

"Personally, I see a great fondness for the sea in their designs. And a profound appreciation for the showiest of flowers, the Ember Lily, the official emblem of Mendelon." She waved her hand toward the ceiling and beams. "I also get the impression, that men decorated everything in here."

Lorann looked up, biting her lip. "I agree with you, My Lady."

Banah listened for footfall in the corridor. "I wonder what is keeping the others?" Hopefully she would be successful at hiding the crushing weight pressing on her.

Fortunately, Lorann hadn't seemed to notice. Or perhaps she had and hadn't drawn attention to it. Her discernment was astute. She had become aware of Banah's addiction to the Queen Summerbird petals long before Druin had suspected anything. She had gently insisted that Banah rest more, take better care of herself.

Banah hadn't followed her advice, and only later realised the true state of her health and her failings at important duties. Holding back a sigh of remorse swelling in her, she needed to keep her emotions calm.

Druin would notice her state of mind.

How much of her plans had she ruined by her inadequacies? She would soon have to face the Limmanian people with empty hands and words. She had hoped for so long to aid them in their plight under the old Mendelonian War Treaty. She had imagined speaking out for their cause in front of the dignitaries gathered in Barrost, the city that had first brought accusations of treason, and that had summoned the tribunal of Mendelon against them. The dream of bringing the good news of at least the beginnings of change, a shift of policies finally in their favour, was gone.

Her failure to speak out for the Limmanian cause at the Trade Summit soured in her. Perhaps the greatest opportunity of her lifetime to help—lost while she lay unconscious. Years of planning wasted. She hadn't even been able to present the proofs of the Riparian League abuses on the River Folumpor.

What validity would her arguments have now with the utter turmoil in Norssum? The city was in chaos. How would things be in its future?

But now, with each passing league that they distanced themselves from Barrost and drew closer to their imminent arrival in Limmania, the torment grew stronger.

Frightening images of the unnatural storm over Barrost returned to her mind. Icy chills swept through her. She fought against feelings of utter failure, attempting to smooth her face of expression. She couldn't show weakness.

Lorann stepped to the open door and glanced down the corridor. Looking back at Banah, she shook her head. "No sign of Prince Palandred. Nor Lord Druin, or Toman."

It was highly uncustomary that their host wouldn't be there to greet them already. But the terror-filled departure yesterday had been exhausting... And then the horrors that had followed them onto the ship, trapped inside Professor Gwenndon's student. Utter fatigue must have hindered the others rising in time. Nevertheless, an official meeting—"

"My Lady, someone is coming now."

Banah turned towards the doorway to greet the Prince but her brother appeared, walking alone.

"Morning, Sister. Maiden Lorann" Glancing at Banah, he quickly looked away and moved to the opposite side of the room.

"Good morning, Brother."

"My Lord." Lorann bowed.

Keeping his head down, he clasped his hands together. His lips moved but he made no sound.

A sense of alarm flashed through Banah. "Dear Brother? Is something amiss?"

He raised his head slowly. His eyes seemed unfocused. His dark expression filled her with apprehension. "I spoke with Arden last night. She hadn't made it out of Barrost."

Anxiety prickled through Banah's chest. "She didn't escape before the Athlonian fleet made landfall?"

He shook his head, swallowing hard.

Banah grasped the sides of her dress with both hands. "Has she come to harm?"

"No, she was alive, and was safe, but I don't know for how long." He spoke as though out of breath. "But, Banah, the Athlonians weren't the only plague on the city."

The anguish in his tone filled her with foreboding.

"The four houses of the Vandrian Kingship are dead. Slaughtered, not by the invaders, but by Lady Galdyssen."

"Oh no." Lorann pressed a hand over her mouth.

"What?" Banah shook her head. She shuddered as nausea filled her. "How? When?"

"Yesterday, not long after we departed," Druin's pale face lost all expression as he spoke, "before the ships arrived. The Lady Steward murdered her husband, then evoked an emergency assembly of the Quaterni for an immediate vote to replace the dead Steward. Then she killed them all, too."

"What poor Lady Arden must have gone through!" Banah didn't want to imagine the horror of such a thing. Her mouth drained of moisture. She struggled to swallow. "But you say she is safe?"

"I don't know." Druin answered sharply. "I don't know..." His tone softened. "It must have been devastating. She heard everything from the Crystal Parlour next to the Great Hall." He took a deep breath. "The Steward's wife had announced the urgent meeting of the Quaterni. There she poisoned them all. Or had her guards cut them down. A massacre. Arden's half-brother, Duke Caldere, was at Lady Soffian's side." He paused, rubbing his temples. His tired eyes filled with tears. "Arden heard it all. The Great Houses of the Quaterni are dead. And Soffian has declared herself King of Barrost."

A subtle groan came from the doorway behind her.

Banah started, turning quickly towards the sound. "Oh, Fyrst Toman." She hadn't heard his approach.

"Please forgive the interruption, My Lady." The Fyrst's eyes seemed to reflect the shock in the room. "Druin, you said Lady Arden was safe when you last contacted her?"

"Yes, she spoke to me in the Temmerung. She was in some kind of cart, heading towards the university, I think." He raised his head as he spoke. "She was terrified. There was some kind of miasma devastating the Lower City. People were dissolving in the streets."

Toman shuffled his feet, speaking breathily. "Just like

in Lord Dalbonn's history books. The Plagues of Barrost at the end of the Skyllian occupation."

Druin nodded. "Then something happened and she faded from the vision. I thought I saw a hand appear and pull her from view." His body slumped.

"Perhaps she's safe with Professor Gwenndon. I pray she is." Banah hurried to her brother's side and clasped his hand in hers. "Dear Brother, what else do you sense in your heart? Can you perceive her state of mind?"

He closed his eyes. After a few moments, he nodded. "She is focused. Her courage is resolute. But she is very afraid."

A tense silence filled the room.

"Please forgive my bad manners." Toman drew closer to the table and bowed, one arm behind his back, the other pressed to his stomach. "Good morning, My Lady and Maiden Lorann. Druin. I hope you slept well despite the events of yesterday." He sounded fatigued, and his smile a little forced, nonetheless polite. It was good to see him wearing the blue sash.

The Fyrst's suffering must have been great. His beloved mentor was lying unconscious in the infirmary with severe and inexplicable wounds to the chest.

"How is your Master this morning, Fyrst Foggling?"

The Prince's physician had reported that Lord Dalbonn's condition was stabilising and that the Riddern tinctures had eased his breathing. He seemed to be sleeping more peacefully, but the indentation in his sternum still presented an urgency to get him to a proper facility in Limmania.

"He is stable, My Lady. But His Grace still couldn't speak this morning." He looked at her, the expression in his grey-blue eyes reminded her of a lost child's. "I am hopeful. And grateful for the Riddern's medicine and

Physician Wanner's care." The pained expression on Fyrst Toman's face softened as he spoke. Chin held firm and high, he turned towards the window. His regal bearing reminded her more of the Lord Protector every day.

She was glad her impressions of the gifted young man had been accurate. The promotion to Fyrst in a public ceremony had created a noble atmosphere around him. It had opened opportunities in the complex Barrostanian society that drew out his strengths, and perhaps revealed to him some of his weaknesses.

She smiled inwardly. The influence the status had given him had shown even more of his impeccable character.

He had done well, exceptionally well.

Fyrst Toman turned back towards them, pointing to the open door. "Palan will be arriving shortly. He rang for his valet to dress him as I came from the infirmary just now."

Banah smiled in astonishment. The Fyrst calling Prince Palandred by his first name? Fyrst Foggling knew that only family or close friends of the dynast could address him in such an informal manner, or someone with express permission of the Prince himself. Dalbonn's lieutenant appeared to be in Prince Palandred's confidence already.

A sense of intrigue filled her as Fyrst Toman walked further into the room. He was a constantly unfolding mystery.

Silence fell again as they all remained standing next to chairs around the table, waiting for their host.

The moments alone with her landsmen gave Banah courage to speak openly, honestly. "When we have another chance to speak privately, I would like to address a few issues encountered in Barrost." She couldn't hide her tone of regret. "As we enter the next part of our journey, I cannot help but feel remorse that I did not achieve what I had set out to do for Limmania. So many of my plans came to naught."

Fyrst Toman suddenly cleared his throat. "My Lady? Pardon me please, but no fault can be found with you. With the growing violence, our plans had to change. And the riots surrounding the Baronhold looked like they were spreading into the upper city. And, My Lady," his voice filled with sympathy, "you were almost killed, twice. We're very grateful that you are still with us, My Lady." His smile seemed natural now.

Druin looked up at him, a gentle expression on his face.

"Thank you, Fyrst Foggling." Even if not according to protocol at times, the Fahtu-Shanner's sincerity and lack of fear to speak his mind were endearing. "As all of you know, the Summit would have been the perfect platform to draw renewed attention to the Limmanian plight. It could have afforded me an opportunity to bring to light their suffering under the antiquated ordinances designed specifically to thwart their recovery from the wars. The Limmanian people have suffered enough." Of course, the Summit would not have been the final occasion for discussing the current complex political situation, but it could have been the beginning.

Crossing his arms over his chest, Fyrst Foggling's eyebrows rose, then he frowned. "Weren't those laws made over a hundred and fifty years ago? The historic Mendelonian peace talks after the Skylle were thrown out?" A sparkle suddenly lit up his eyes. "Perhaps you'll still have a chance, My Lady! Palan could do something, I'm sure. You should ask him."

Staring at Fyrst Foggling, Druin's mouth fell slightly open.

Banah tried to keep her embarrassment hidden. Once again, the Fyrst's frankness went to the heart of the matter. He had stated the obvious, but his straightforward delivery made her smile.

The idea of approaching the Prince with these issues had passed through her thoughts, but she wasn't ready for any probable confrontation. Not with him as their host. Yes, Prince Palandred was a representative of the House of Mendelon, the dynastic house that had propagandised the accusations, but he had not scripted the laws against Limmania. His ancestors had. And... with his seeming detachment from his ruling brother, would he even be the person to address regarding this situation?

And yet, Fyrst Toman had ignited the idea. Perhaps she should take advantage of the Prince's proximity.

Standing near the still open door, Lorann's posture stiffened as she mouthed, *he's coming*.

"Good morning." Speaking in a low voice, Prince Palandred looked around the room. His bloodshot gaze confirmed that he, too, had spent a restless night. "Please forgive my tardiness."

The pleasant soft glow of sunlight filling the room seemed to brighten. Some clouds must have thinned.

"Good morning, Your Highness." Banah and Lorann bowed together.

A few steps behind him, a small group of servants silently entered the dining room, carrying trays.

A servant pulled out a chair for the Prince, who waved a hand towards the other chairs. "Please, everyone, be seated." His face looked ashen and drawn, as though he'd aged noticeably since yesterday.

"Thank you, Prince Palandred." As Banah sat down on the beautifully embroidered cushion, she motioned to Lorann to take the chair next to hers.

Lorann smiled nervously at the Prince as she took her seat.

"I have a message..." A servant announced from the doorway. Pulling a note from his pocket, he read aloud, "...for Sir Mister Foggling."

The Fyrst jerked his head up, his eyes wide open.

The servant read aloud, "From Cook Marta: *Dear Sir Mister Foggling, I made some special things for you.*" He set down a plate of five folded pastries in front of Fyrst Toman. "*Eat up. All you wants. You needs your strength.*" With an amused but strained expression, the servant tucked the note back in his pocket.

The Fyrst's nervous laugh made Banah smile.

Lorann hid a chuckle well behind her hand.

But hearing of Cook Marta reminded Banah of Uncle Lytwon. How was he faring? Where was he on his journey to his homeland?

The servants poured steaming tea into the cups. Selecting long silver tongs, one of them placed a group of different pastries in front of Prince Palandred. "Especially for His Highness."

They finished by serving an individual selection of other pastries to each person, then looked over the settings and glided silently back out into the hall.

An odd, rather tense silence returned.

Banah glanced at the group gathered at the table.

Everyone seemed pensive, in distant thoughts.

Druin's eyes were fixed on his cup. Probably worried about Lady Arden.

Prince Palandred's brow furrowed as he studied his folded hands.

Fyrst Foggling stared out of the window. The corners of his mouth sagged slightly, accentuating the deep sorrow in his eyes. He blinked, slowly looking at everyone in turn, his gaze stopped on Banah.

Compassion for his situation wrapped around her heart.

"Your Highness, I think we have some very important news you should be privy to." Banah looked at Druin. "Things revealed to my brother through the Temmerung."

Looking intently at Druin, Prince Palandred leaned slightly forward onto his elbows.

"Last night I spoke with Lady Arden." Druin straightened in his chair and inhaled slowly. "Something horrific has happened in Barrost, besides the attack we saw. Lady Soffian has murdered her husband, killed all the members of the houses of the Quaterni and now declares herself King of Barrostania – not Norssum."

Prince Palandred's face twisted in disgust. "She is calling herself a king..." His voice trailed off. "A king!" He growled under his breath.

"Her chosen consort is the Duke of Borinbranth's son, Caldere."

"War will be unavoidable." The Prince's angry tone seethed despite his whispered speech.

22

Threads

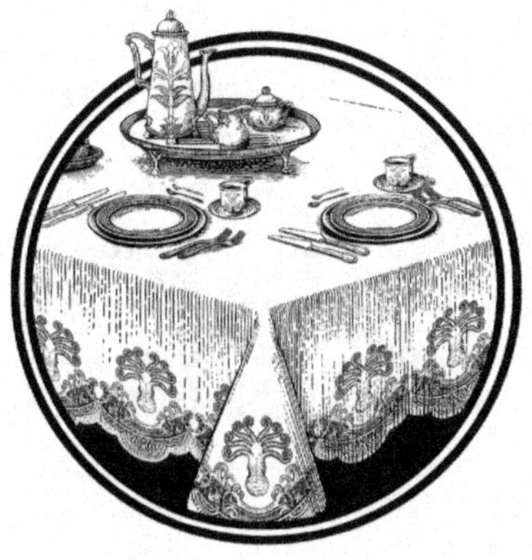

Toman looked from Palan to Lady Banah as a sense of urgency filled him. "There is more, My Lady. I've had strange repeating dreams, and I feel they are important for all of us."

Druin quickly raised his head and stared at Toman. "Repeating dreams?"

Goosebumps prickled up Toman's arms.

Of course. The Highborn's repeating nightmares in the Temmerung. The death of his sister, and the curse of '*The Greinen's Reach*' as he'd called it.

They had to relate to Toman's own dreams, and somehow to Palan's Glortrom.

But what was the connection? What was the cloth all these fibres were creating? "Ber'eth is revealing that there are many currents surging in this storm. My dreams, and more Glortroms." Toman tried to read Palan's expression.

Clasping her hands together, Lady Banah looked at Palan, then back to Toman. "Please proceed, Fyrst Foggling."

"Yes, please do." Druin held his spoon motionless over his steaming cup as the honey on it began to drip into his tea.

Toman nodded. "I've had strange dreams, some repeat over and over again. Others I've only dreamt once. They began before I left Fahtu-Shan." He nodded again then closed his eyes. "In one dream there is a fleet of ships with transparent hulls that look like crystal glass. Three very pale-skinned women stand on the main deck of the first ship. Their hands are held high, and their hair glows around them like golden manes. High above them, a strange dark globe floats. It looks like the crystal glass of the ships' hulls, but inside it a fierce storm is raging. Long shapes, like snakes of dark red smoke, twist and squirm. As though they want to break free. Then dark-skinned men shout a war cry and begin running up a shoreline after me." Toman paused, surprised that his heartbeat had begun to race.

"And you feel that this was a Glortrom, Fyrst Toman?" Lady Banah spoke in a controlled, but almost anxious tone.

He shook his head. "I don't think so, My Lady. It was a normal dream in the sense that it ended the moment I awoke. Not like yours and—" He stopped himself and looked at Palan. "But I wonder... The same three women keep appearing in the dreams with the ships. At first there were only the women, but later one of them had a child. At first it was a small baby, then in the next dream, it was older, perhaps by two or three years. She's the same woman though, I'm sure. There had only been weeks between dreams, and yet the child had aged years." Toman studied Lady Banah's face. "My Lady, they feel like dreams that are messages from Ber'eth, but not Glortroms."

Palan looked at Toman, his eyes narrowed. "Toman, what is your definition of a Glortrom?"

"It's like a living prophetic dream, a vision that reveals things that we are not capable of knowing, not on our own. What I've heard about the Glortrom from Landsend and from My Lady Méndrensynn, Glortrom visions also continue after you wake up, as though the world all around you becomes less corporeal, and almost transparent, and another world becomes more real than the real world. But it's not always clear what the Glortroms mean. Things of the future are mixed with things from the past. Or from the present. But it's always a powerful message of events that we should prepare ourselves for, sent to us from the mind of Ber'eth."

Palan looked to Lady Banah as if searching for confirmation of Toman's words.

"The Fyrst described it well." Lady Banah nodded then turned towards Maiden Lorann. "Have you also had any meaningful dreams?"

"No, My Lady." Maiden Lorann shook her head.

"Nightmares come true all the time." Palan's forehead creased slightly. "Without calling them prophetic dreams."

"However they are named, Glortroms are historical phenomena, and are to be studied carefully." The

Highborn Lady looked back to Toman and nodded. “Please recount every detail you can remember.”

“In other dreams, these three women – I think they are the same ones – are walking in what looks like a parade or ceremony. There are musicians and many dancers, but the atmosphere isn’t joyful. It’s almost fearful. On the backs of their necks, here where the Eth Lobe is,” he tapped on the base of his skull, “there are reddish black tattoos of some kind of insect. Perhaps a beetle. Or a wasp.”

“The Scarab-Wasp. Like the one in the Rubinstone.” Palan hissed through his teeth, locking eyes with Toman. “The Skylle.” He spoke under his breath. “Their sacred symbol.”

“The emblem of their desert race...” Toman couldn’t stop the slight tremor in his voice.

For an instant, Lady Banah and Druin glanced nervously at each other. They both stiffened in their seats.

Lady Banah seemed to struggle for breath, but regained composure quickly. “Please continue with your dreams, Fyrst Foggling.”

“Yes, My Lady.” A storm of thoughts raged through Toman. Why was he being shown the Skyllian emblem in his dreams? It was a part of Palan’s childhood nightmare! Surely, they must be connected? How were they connected? What were Ber’eth’s plans?

Lady Banah cleared her throat, looking intently in his direction.

“Forgive me.” Where had he stopped in the story? Ah, yes... “The three women that appear in my dreams remind me of my Limmanian mother. The same pale golden hair. The same almost silver eyes. Many things were happening at the same time. There was a city on the coast under siege. It looked gleaming white, and had many towers. A large palace was at the end of a peninsula."

Palan stood quickly and walked over to a window.

"Prince Palandred?" Lady Banah stood from her place at the table.

Maiden Lorann followed the Highborn's actions then moved closer to her Lady.

Palan stared through the pale golden panes. "The city Toman just described... it sounds very similar to my capital city, Mendelon."

Toman also got up from his seat.

Druin's Eth resonance flared, filling the room with brilliant blue. "Palan, would you like to share more? Have you also been visited by a Glortrom?"

Shaking his head, the look in Palan's eyes seemed to harden. "I'm sorry for the Quaterni. No one should end that way, let alone a ruling family." The veins in his neck seemed to pulsate. "When power is taken by force, it must be maintained by force. The larger the kingdom, the greater the war."

Druin also stood slowly up, his eyes fixed on Palan. "If you have been visited by a Glortrom, we'd like to help you. You shouldn't carry the burden alone."

"Help me?" Palan's tone of disbelief sounded mixed with surprise.

Druin nodded. "Yes, of course, my friend. Glortroms are too heavy to carry alone." He pointed to his sister. "Banah's—"

Palan interrupted him, "I... I heard Skyllian voices."

"I heard them as well. I mean, I heard the voices speaking to him." Toman could now confirm this, without breaking Palan's trust.

Palan continued, "The voices are looking for what

they call their *Birthright,* and they think I have it." His hands trembled as he slipped them into his pockets.

Lady Banah took a step towards him.

Palan's face went blank. "Lady Banah." His voice quavered. "I made you a promise that I cannot keep."

Lady Banah stopped, frowning slightly. "Pardon, Your Highness?"

"The Barrostanian student. He killed Mendelonians on Mendelonian territory. The law forces the matter out of my hands. Please forgive me, I did not have the authority to give you jurisdiction over his fate."

Toman expected the Highborn Lady to voice a strong complaint, perhaps even reprimand him, but she just stood in silence, looking at him. That kind of look from Lady Banah would have made him cower, but Palan just looked back, unblinking.

"I understand, Your Highness." She folded her hands tightly over her stomach. "Thank you for informing me."

The tense stillness that filled the room felt as if a bolt of lightning was about to strike.

Toman had never seen Palan look so nervous, so meek.

"My Glortroms are about the Skylle searching for me..." Palan spoke quietly to Lady Banah. "...to extract a demonic power from me. They call me *The Child of Orren. The thief of their birthright.*"

Lady Banah gasped and reached for the back of her chair, then sat down slowly. "However we may help, please allow us."

Palan also sat back down. "Thank you, My Lady."

Druin faced his sister and pulled out what looked like a small ivory flute. "I should also inform Lord G'nallun of our conversation here this morning."

She nodded.

Palan's brow creased. "The Firstborn of the Continent?"

"They have been aiding me in the exchange of information." Druin's humble tone sounded almost like an apology.

"We are all part of the same story." Toman looked at the platters on the table. But somehow, his appetite had gone. "Perhaps we can unravel these threads together."

23

Memories and Mourning

Dalbonn tried to turn on the mattress. A sharp pain shot through his chest. Sweat drenched his face and arms.

Air. He needed air. He gulped mouthfuls but his lungs craved more.

"Here you go, sweet boy." Steam rose around the woman at the cookpot as she handed him a bowl.

"Thank you." Mischul accepted his portion of boiled watergrass seed. It would stop the ache in his tummy, at least for tonight. The grownups said many didn't even have food. That they should be grateful. These are hard times.

"Now, sweet boy, if you would continue walking." The

woman waved him on, a smile on her otherwise sad and wrinkly face. "Other children are waiting."

But that's just what he was doing, too. Waiting. For Paula. She was supposed to be in this queue.

But there were so many children. And more were arriving in Honstan every day.

The grownups said that the war had spread over into the borderlands in the north.

The North must not be very far away, because the grownups also said that the whole camp would be moving again soon. Maybe tomorrow morning. It was important to keep the children safe.

Mischul looked for Paula again down the row of children.

"Now, be a good boy. Don't loiter here."

"Yes, Ma'am." But he needed more time. He dropped his spoon and flicked it into the grass with his toe. That would give him a few more moments in case Paula came.

The cook lady pursed her lips and sighed at him. Shaking her head, she handed out other steaming bowls but let him stay where he was.

Mischul thought he saw her smile at him again.

Kneeling in the grass, he found his spoon and stood up, brushing off his breeches.

"Hello, Mischul Dalbonn." Paula's pretty smile made her face glow. Her kind eyes seemed to sparkle at him.

"Hello." He was suddenly not hungry anymore.

Her eyes, her voice... she reminded him so much of Toman.

Pain shot across his rib cage, but he tried to keep his moan low. Hopefully Paula hadn't noticed.

He glanced at his chest. Why did it hurt?

Where was he?

"Get in line, recruit!"

Mischul looked up. Paula was gone and so were the children. Bigger boys and young men stood to attention with him.

The training officer's sharp command sounded more like the bark of an angry dog.

Mischul kept his face rigid. "Yes Sir." He didn't mind the discipline. It would make a man of him.

Like his father.

Memories of his father flooded him with dangerous, unstable emotions.

The back of Mischul's throat swelled as images from his childhood flashed before him. A strong tall man. His father. His bright smiling eyes... and self-discipline. A protector of the family. But he died when the village burned down. Mama had said that he lived in the Bosom of Ber'eth now.

Old memories continued to surge through him.

Leaping flames roaring through the roof of their house.

People ran about, shouting.

Children were sobbing in the streets.

He forced his mind back to the present.

The training officer began speaking to all of them, the new boys and the young men alike. "Now, recruits, we have the privilege today of some special teachers."

Mischul looked up and gasped.

The teachers were huge, at least twice as tall as him. And dark skinned. They wore feather clothing. Their tattoos seemed to move.

"The Stagriders will be instructing you on the use of plant and animal toxins."

Dalbonn shuddered and opened his eyes. Blinking to clear his vision, he tried to focus. Where was he?

Dark carved beams overhead. Clear glass panels in the windows. The distant sound of gulls. The swaying movement and gentle creaking of wood.

Of course! Prince Palandred's ship. He was on the Prince's vessel.

The movement sent more pain through his sternum. He gasped then gritted his teeth. More pain than he'd ever experienced.

How gravely was he wounded? How had he even been wounded? He couldn't remember.

A familiar sweet taste on his tongue.

Dune Ginger. Normally used to stimulate blood flow.

But, combined with the bittersweet flavour on the back of his tongue... the Chieftains had probably also administered Sand Jasmine and Red Honey to induce profound sleep or to help the gentler passage to—

They must have expected his passing during the night.

The Riddern syllabus of Medicine Lore taught that the severely wounded, or those in very frail health, followed a dark path deep in the night, either towards death or recovery.

He wasn't ready for the Bosom of Ber'eth!

A shiver passed through him and, for an instant, the narrow bed pressed against his back and arms like a coffin. The dark sickbay looked like a morgue.

No! He wasn't ready for death! He tried to push away the thoughts of Druin reading a eulogy surrounded by Summerbird blossoms, Toman standing with his head bowed.

No, not death for him, not now!

But he couldn't move. His body wasn't responding. His heart was beating, so life was still in him. He was still alive!

But for how long? The back of his throat quivered with emotion as sleep engulfed him again.

More dreams. Sights. Sounds. A dirge was playing.

A familiar scene appeared.

The Lanfoths gathered slowly around a casket also draped with orchids.

But this wasn't his own funeral. Not his own passing.

An icy chill spread through Dalbonn as he approached the coffin.

He recognised the man!

A wave of guilt and unbearable sadness crushed Dalbonn.

But he would not cry.

Tears were not for the strong.

He was no longer an Apprentice.

He had to get through the ceremony.

"Lord Dalbonn, my deepest condolences," Lady Ahnya, the young Lanfothe Consort, bowed to him. "He will be missed by us all."

His eyes stung and he swallowed.

Showing emotion was for the weak. He was not weak. "Thank you, My Lady."

Lanfoth Steffen put a hand on his shoulder. "You didn't know, Lieutenant Dalbonn. You are innocent. Peace to your soul. And healing."

But he wasn't innocent.

He had killed his Master.

He had slid the poisoned blade between his Master's ribs and had enjoyed the sensation of watching him die, writhing in pain.

Dalbonn wanted to sob out loud. He must not. He must not show weakness!

But he couldn't stop the hot tears streaming down his cheeks.

He had never been able to mourn his Master.

Until now.

24

Through a Fog

Climbing the steps to the infirmary, Toman admired the passing coastline.

Such rugged, tranquil beauty.

He wished he could stop and enjoy the view. Soak in the sights and smells of his mother's homeland.

But he couldn't.

Any joy about finally being in this wondrous region of the Northern Horn was quenched by the anxiety gripping his heart.

Would His Grace pull through? Would he live? Be restored? Had he shown any signs of improvement since Toman's visit this morning?

And Trend would now be executed...

...where would the Greinen strike again?

Raindrops began to pelt the decks as Toman entered the hallway that led to Palan's rooms and the infirmary. Ahead, the physician's door stood slightly ajar. A thin beam of sunlight lay across the shadows like a gleaming sword blade. He reined his emotions in and continued.

The familiar salty alcohol smell permeated the still air.

Toman knocked once then pushed the door further open.

"Your Highness." Physician Wanner looked up from his chair. His face appeared pale and worried. He stood quickly, as though he'd been expecting someone. Moving to the bedside, he touched His Grace's forehead and turned to Toman. "The Lord Dalbonn is still steady in his breathing."

The hideous rasping sound was almost gone. Only faint gurgles could be detected as his chest rose and fell weakly.

Hopelessness clawed at Toman's heart. "Good Sir, has anything happened since I was here this morning?"

Wanner shook his head. "He shows no signs of healing, Your Highness, and I fear that stagnation could be causing him to gradually grow weaker."

Something in Toman cried out to give in, to collapse and fall into the gaping void opening up in front of him.

"But we're almost, in Limmania. You, and the Riddern Healers, have done much for my master. But we should be able to get him to even more help in the city."

Wanner exhaled as he shook his head again slowly. "He can't be moved, Your Highness. We'll have to find physicians and bring them on board."

"We can have that done! I'll ask Palan for help."

The doctor blinked at his words, lowering his eyes to

Toman's chest. "Er, yes, you could ask His Highness. But I would recommend asking your Highborns, if I were you."

"I don't understand."

Wanner's nostrils flared slightly. "You shall find out soon enough." He now fixed his eyes on something on the floor, then added, "Positive sentiments towards members of the House of Elstundreth of Mendelon do not run high in Limmania. A favour would be best requested through your Highborns, rather than by those who are resented."

Toman frowned. Why would his mother's people bear a grudge against Palan? Then again, as His Grace had said, the fame and wealth of a great House always drew resentment and bitterness from jealous people.

It was true. It had saddened Toman to learn that armed guards had to be posted at the Highborns' private Lath Gardens. The Méndrensynns had to post them at the entrances day and night, to safeguard their special plants from envious thieves.

He pointed towards His Grace. "Would you mind if I pray again?"

The physician's expression glazed over coldly. He glanced at the tools on a tray. "Mm."

Toman nodded. It wasn't a 'yes', but it wasn't a 'no' either.

"Thank you, Good Sir. Then, if you would, please allow me a moment alone with the Lord Protector?" A prayer was swelling up deep within Toman, but he preferred to pronounce it over his master in private.

"Whatever Your Lordship wishes." Wanner's tone was flat. "Just do not cause him to move, or to speak." He walked towards the hallway.

"Of course." Toman clicked the door shut as soon as the physician was over the threshold.

Facing His Grace, Toman raised his hands and focused on the most important person in his life. A mentor... more than a mentor. The Lord Protector was more like an architect of the soul, a man who had changed his life for ever.

Igniting his connection to Eth, Toman willed the flow towards His Grace.

The brilliant glow in his fingertips cast golden orange light over the pristine white sheets.

He gently opened his master's shirt and flinched.

The livid bruise across his sternum had changed to a sickly blackish-brown colour.

Toman placed his hand tenderly on the wound, extending his glassy Linger out from his palm.

The connection to His Grace's mind was immediate, but filtered somehow with what felt like a thick fog.

Whirlwinds of emotion hit Toman.

Fear. Confusion. Sorrow. Pain.

Toman's eyes began to sting. He dropped to his knees on the floor alongside the cot as the impressions pouring out from his master's mind overwhelmed him.

The torment of crippling loneliness.

Regret for unfinished business.

More stabbing pain, shooting from his chest throughout his whole body.

The wound under Toman's Linger seemed to burn under his glowing hand. Fighting against the crushing weight in His Grace's mind, he focused harder on his Gebayt Bithen. *The power of his prayer pitted against the power of his master's tormented thoughts.* "Dear Ber'eth, may your power flow into this remarkable man. Healing.

Healing into his body. Restoration of his bones, his muscles... his mind."

Toman welcomed the familiar glistening of his Gebayt Bithen. Transparent sheets of light undulated around them. Like thin curtains of molten glass, the watery reflections swirled though the room.

Impressions began to flow stronger through his Linger.

Fires burned in his master's blood, searing pain that penetrated the bone.

Toman couldn't perceive any images, but he had the sensation that His Grace was revisiting the events in the brig with Trend. But a thick putrid smoke, dark grey like that of burning carcasses, veiled Toman's vision.

The stench of decay lay thick in His Grace's nostrils.

Obviously, it had been Torghyll's Beàl'Toht within Trend.

Toman gritted his teeth in rage.

A deep rich voice rose through the fog in His Grace's mind. "Toman? Son?"

Toman gasped. "Your Grace? Can you hear me?"

A vague impression came back. "Yes."

Something inside Toman collapsed, and he wept. "Your Grace, I'm so sorry. I didn't protect you—"

New impressions flickered through the connection.

The smoky atmosphere thinned, and his master stood next to him in the brig. The Greinen's staghorn tendrils spread out before them.

His master cried out. Unbearable pain hit his chest, and he crumpled to the floor.

A sob choked in Toman's throat. "I'm so sorry."

The scene disappeared and the smoky veil closed back in.

"Your Grace!"

"Son?"

"Yes, master? Yes?"

His master's emotions trickled through the connection. Gratitude and deepest remorse at the same time. "I, I..."

Then his presence faded from Toman's mind.

An icy dark haze flowed into the connection.

Complete silence followed.

Toman couldn't sense a heartbeat, nor breath.

"No, no! No, please!"

He jumped to his feet, hot tears streaming down his cheeks.

He wouldn't give up. Keeping his eyes on the shimmering lights, he concentrated stronger on his Gebayt Bithen.

The floorboards vibrated as the ship lurched in the water.

New images flashed through the weakening connection.

Blood blackening. Muscles wasting away. Bones throbbing with pain.

"No!" Toman shouted. "Every trace of the Greinen's touch, leave his body!"

The door swung open. A loud gasp behind Toman told him the physician had returned.

Toman didn't turn around, but continued. "Recovery of what has been destroyed." The shimmering curtains of his prayer flowed from his glowing hands and forearms. They wove in and out around His Grace's cot, as though alive, searching.

A gentle wind blew through the infirmary.

"Restoration of his health, dear Father of Heaven."

"Did.. Did I hear the Lord Protector speak?" Wanner's

sharp words sounded peculiar, insecure, as though he spoke with a mouth wide open.

Toman ignored the interruption. He must hear what His Grace wanted to say!

"You need to leave." Wanner growled under his breath.

"Not now. In a moment, Good Sir." Toman pushed his mind through the lingering smoky haze. Terror ripped through him as a sudden emptiness filled the connection. Where was His Grace's consciousness? Toman needed to hear his master again! What did he want to tell him?

Death could not have come. It was surely not his time

The physician tapped Toman on the forearm. "Please remove your hand from the patient." He spoke through gritted teeth.

"Just a moment!" Toman glared at Wanner's slender, delicate-looking hand.

Wanner blinked and stumbled backwards. "Pardon, Your Highness."

"Please forgive me, Good Sir. Just please stand away." Hands trembling, Toman turned back to His Grace, concentrating on his plea and listening for any trace of a voice. "Healing, let healing flow into him."

Wanner dropped into his chair as Toman's Gebayt Bithen expanded even further and the sparkling pinpoints now illuminated the entire infirmary.

Toman let his consciousness come to rest in the growing silence in His Grace's mind.

The complete absence of impressions sent alarm through Toman.

Was this the mind of someone who had died?

"Please, please, no!" A sob convulsed deep in his throat.

No, he couldn't accept the absence of life in His Grace. He could feel his tears begin to drip off his chin.

No, Your Grace, you cannot leave me. I need you in my life...please come back.

Toman released his plea. "Let it be so." And the silken lights dissipated.

Something indistinct stirred through the Linger connection.

Joy washed over Toman.

A faint voice!

Feebly spoken words rose through the fog. "... love you, Son."

The sound of His Grace's voice took his breath away.

Gasping, Toman staggered past Wanner through the open door. His Linger connection broke. In the hallway, he stumbled, bracing himself against the panelling.

"Tomi?" The sound of Yannu's voice seemed to call to him from far away. "Are you all right?"

Still leaning against the wall, Toman tried to catch his breath.

"I was worried..." Yannu's voice was also breathy, as if he'd been running.

"What, what's the matter?" Toman stood upright.

His Grace's voice still filled his ears. Hope burned again in the hearth. His master wasn't dead.

"You haven't heard?" Yannu panted for air. "Two of the servants, they died this morning. Poisoned? Or just bad food maybe. The other servants say that they ate some of the pastries that weren't eaten from your morning tea." He swallowed hard. "I was worried about you."

25

Limmania

Palandred's mind reeled. "Unravel these threads together?" He walked again to the window, and spoke aloud. But more as a question to himself.

"Yes." Lady Banah joined him, looking at him intently. "And I am sorry you've had to bear your Glortrom alone." She sounded concerned. "These visions from Ber'eth are an immense burden to carry." Lifting her chin slightly, she then nodded. "But we shall help you in any way we can. I feel Ber'eth is drawing us all together for a purpose."

Ber'eth.

If only that name wasn't so prevalent in their conversations.

Palandred kept his opinions about the *omnipotent being* to himself.

Perhaps Ber'eth wasn't the maleficent spirit Palandred had always believed, but he wasn't willing to relinquish his view completely. Not yet, even though the Highborns and Toman seemed to suffer no ill effects from conducting Eth.

"And we shall have great need of each other during the Shift that is upon us." She looked him directly in the eyes again. "Of that I'm certain."

Her stare sent a shiver up his spine.

What an incredible woman! Everything about her bespoke strength. The determined way in which she stood, the firm set of her delicate chin, the manner in which she held her head high, not to mention her piercing blue gaze.

She stepped suddenly towards him.

For an instant, the urge to hide quivered through his body.

"Prince Palandred, I want to thank you again," Her inscrutable expression softened to one more of compassion, "for passage on your ship, and for all that you're doing for me and my landsmen, and for representing the Confederation of Ydassum at the Trade Summit. And for your good intentions regarding the fate of the Barrostanian student."

Palandred's tongue stuck to the roof of his mouth. He swallowed with some effort. "My pleasure, My Lady."

She blinked slowly and a gentle smile appeared on her lips. What a difference a smile made to her exceptional beauty.

"Please, call me Banah."

Something hit him in the chest. Or it felt as though it had! "Ba...Banah?" He repeated.

She inclined her head, continuing to smile.

The room seemed to fill with the thundering of Palandred's heart. "Thank you, My Lady." He reached to kiss her hand.

"My Lord." She bowed quickly, clasping her hands together in front of her.

Palandred glanced at his own outstretched hand, then lowered it.

But still, Lady Banah had asked him to use her first name!

He could call her Banah!

The ramifications were immense.

"Well then!" Druin's burst of energy startled him. His old school friend looked from his sister to Palandred, then added, "I think we should be drawing near the islands around the Bay of Limman. Shall we go out on deck to see them, and take some fresh air?"

"Excellent idea. We disembark soon." Banah looked at her servant then pointed towards the hallway. "Maiden Lorann and I shall join you shortly."

No one had touched the meal. Palandred didn't feel like eating either.

Toman opened the door and bowed for them all to exit.

Palandred waited for Banah and her servant to leave first, then he followed Toman and Druin down the steps to the main deck.

Striding out into the lingering morning freshness, Palandred's head still spun wildly. It was hard to believe a heartbeat could muffle all other sounds.

He walked quickly over to the balustrade and gripped the railing.

Breathing in deeply, then exhaling slowly, he attempted to calm himself.

The familiar taste of salt tingled on the back of his throat.

Focus.

He took another gulp of air and the tension in his body began to ebb.

A strange sense of belonging permeated him. Not being alone in such a time of need... having people close who weren't vying for favour from the House of Elstundreth, companions who seemed to genuinely want to help without pretence.

It was all difficult to take in.

And Banah had said he could call her by her first name!

His insides seemed to turn into the gelatinous bodies of sea creatures found on the beach after storms.

He rubbed his face and tucked his hair behind his ears.

Walking up to Palandred, Druin stared at him then gave him a boyish grin. "A lot to take in, isn't it?"

Toman leaned on the railing and looked sideways at him. "Palan, are you all right?"

Palandred nodded quickly. "But if the two of you wouldn't mind... I would like to have a moment alone? To think. Before Banah returns."

"Of course." The roguish gleam in Druin's eyes looked almost comical.

"Uh-huh." Toman tilted his head. "It would be a good time to see my master." Looking up at the sails, he added. "The air currents are changing. We could have another storm."

"Thank you." Palandred looked into the clear dark water.

Banah's words returned in a whirlwind. Had her

gesture also meant that there could be—? Shaking his head, he answered his own question.

No, that wasn't possible.

But could she and he...? He couldn't stop the flow of thoughts pouring through his mind.

It was probably premature to even think it could be possible... but her gesture, offering him her first name. He couldn't shake off its significance.

Banah. Such a gentle, old-fashioned, melancholic name. If he wasn't mistaken, Banah also had the connotation of 'fragility'.

He saw no weaknesses in her, especially now that the mind-fogging effects of the Summerbird petals had dissipated, but the idea of her needing protection made something in his chest grow warm.

The two of them together? She was of an old Orrenic culture, governed by the archaic Shantab system, not accustomed to the life of modern dynastic rule. Two worlds like that would never mix. They never had.

Besides, she'd never feel that way towards him.

He sighed. If he could just convince his still racing heart to align with those thoughts!

Warm breezes began to sweep over the decks. Something in the air already smelled more like home.

Home?

He shook his head. Mendelon didn't really feel like home any more. Not with Fillip's dark machinations casting shadows over Horróglоryn, and now they were extending all the way up the Horn. The real question for Palandred was how long would he even have a home to return to, if Toman's visions were also true. Horróglоryn North and South would not be exempt. The Twin Cities were only a short boat ride across the small bay from Mendelon City.

Despite all this, the oppressive weight of Fillip's control over his life was somehow growing lighter. Thoughts of Druin, Banah and Toman calmed Palandred's mind and he smiled.

Not feeling alone was a strange, but also an intimidating, sensation.

Comforting, and yet unusually frightening.

It was difficult for him to accept that people really existed who seemed sincerely concerned about his welfare, and who were not simply trying to take advantage of the wealth and power of his dynastic House.

But something almost wondrous was happening. It was undeniable. However, Palandred wouldn't attribute the Highborns' and Toman's offer of help, or Druin's unbelievable connection to the ancient Firstborn, to the influence of a supernatural being. Not Ber'eth.

No, that couldn't be.

Or... could it? The signs that Ber'eth was a benevolent being were accumulating. Even though Palandred lived with a demon inside his body due to the power of Ber'eth, none of the Ydassumers seemed to suffer any sort of ill effects after using their Eth resonances.

"It won't be long now, Palandred." Banah's voice was so close, it startled him.

He stopped himself from gasping at the unexpected sound, but his heart broke into a full gallop. "Long?" He turned towards her, warmth spreading rapidly in his face.

She bowed.

Just behind her, Banah's Maiden lowered her head then also bowed.

"Not long until we reach Limmania, and Druin hears back from the Uccell Lords." Banah rested on the highly polished wooden balustrade and looked out at the horizon.

How she radiated peace and strength, both at the same time, eluded Palandred!

Both Fillip and their mother ruled with formidable strength, but through fear and intimidation. There was nothing peaceful about their power.

"We need the help of the Firstborn. And I hope we will be able to gather more information when we arrive, from the Steward of Limmania..." Her voice trailed off, then she spoke with compelling emotion. "As you know, it is the homeland of many displaced persons who fled to my home country. Ydassum has long given succour to refugees from Limmania."

Palandred nodded.

Druin had often mentioned her affection for the impoverished vassals. And in Barrost she had wished to address the Quaterni regarding their predicament, although circumstances being as they were, she had not been able to do that. But her dedication to them was admirable. "You've obviously been to Limmania before?"

She blinked. "No. This will be my first time." Her eyes were practically identical to Druin's in shape and colour, but so different in expression. "And you?"

"Many times." The pleasant memories brought also a familiar and painful sense of sadness. "As a child, with my twin sister, Leahn." He lowered his voice. Speaking of Leahn was difficult. "I spent some time here. Holidays mostly. The Queen wanted to expose my sister, the one she considered least important of her offspring, to possible future marriage prospects. Peculiar though... previously she had selected only the most wealthy and powerful for marriage into our family. I still don't understand why she would choose anyone from

Limmania. Their highest-ranking class is only a Stewardship, which she considered far beneath her." He shook his head.

Banah's brow furrowed.

He stopped himself recoiling from her glare.

What had he said?

He changed the direction of the conversation. "Actually, the few visits we made to Limmania are very beautiful memories in an otherwise unremarkable childhood. You probably had a similar experience. Royal duties of a sovereign's children are mostly to be displayed like silent trophies, especially to visiting dignitaries. Most of my recollections of Limmania are from the years before Her Majesty's death. A few cheerful fragments remain."

Banah seemed to relax slightly, but her hands remained clasped tightly together, and her unwavering focus seemed to burn a hole in his skull.

"I have very fond images in my mind of playing with my twin sister in a labyrinth of hedges in a walled garden. It was full of secret paths. I remember lots of foliage of all shapes and colours." Then he shook his head. "I don't remember much of anything else, except the mountains encircling the city. They tower directly behind it like a dark grey curtain. They sometimes frightened me as a child."

Relief filled him as the thin lines on her forehead smoothed.

"But I'm sure you know how childhood memories are..." he shook his head slowly, "...they fade like old cloth, blanched with the events of life." His childhood had ended abruptly that horrific day when he'd caused his mother's demise.

"You should hold on to those good memories." Her

unexpected smile changed her features completely, as though a stone statue had suddenly come to life. "Protect them in your mind like treasures. They will become more valuable with time."

Her following silence felt unnatural.

"Maylin. Our little sister... She was a treasure." Banah raised her hand to her breast. "And still is – in here."

The frail sadness in her voice...

He wanted to embrace her.

A chill ran up his back. Her ordeal with her infant sister... how had he forgotten so quickly? The murderer was on board his own ship!

Druin approached them from the starboard side. He seemed hesitant to interrupt.

The vast rugged Limmanian coastline was now clearly visible. Countless thin waterfalls cascaded from the towering coastal ranges into small coves and rivulets that ran to the ocean. Above the escarpment, the splendid hue of the bright sky formed a brilliant backdrop to the pristine white clouds. Ahead, the small archipelago he knew so well stood at a short distance from the shoreline.

"My Lady, aren't they stunning?" Banah's maiden pointed to the steep, rocky, forest-covered slopes.

Palandred hid his disapproval. He would have reprimanded an underling for speaking uninvited, directly to her lady. Mendelonian servants were rarely to be seen and never to be heard. But Banah obviously had a friendship with her servant that he would respect.

"Yes, indeed, Lorann." She beamed at her servant. "The islands ahead mark the entrance to the protected waters of the Harbour of Limman. The brilliant white cliffs of Wyssmaur shine true to its name, *White Beacon*. Even from this distance, they beckon ships to enter the safety of their harbour. Tunfluh, Goyt and Gahdan,

Refuge, *Protected Hold* and *Granary* in Old Orrenic, rise from the water like sentinels cloaked in verdant mantles. Once heralds of a proud city and nation."

Her obvious high regard for the country struck him as unfounded.

The vassal state had never done anything historically important, except for the treachery against the Orrenic Alliance. But her knowledge of the geography was impressive. He hadn't known the names of the islands. "It's a shame that they ended an important epoch of Orrenic history by aiding the Skylle."

Taking a sharp breath, Banah tightened her lips. The tension around her was palpable.

Her maiden covered her mouth and stepped back.

Had he said something wrong again? An acrid feeling seeped into his stomach as she looked at him, her eyes locking with his. Their bright blue seemed to turn a stormy shade of grey.

He braced himself for her fury.

"Palandred." Her nostrils flared slightly. "Are you certain your historical account is completely accurate?"

Her gently-spoken response shook him. Of course, it was accurate.

Or was it?

"Yes... erm..."

His thoughts seemed to drain through a crack in the base of his skull.

"History recounts... My brother has always said—" He stopped himself. Now that he thought about it, Fillip had always been the source of his knowledge regarding the country.

He made another attempt at the conversation, "I mean, my brother has always said—" He stopped himself again.

Was he quoting Fillip once more? His controlling, scheming sibling?

An icy realisation dawned on Palandred. Fillip was a consummate manipulator. Was perhaps everything his brother had said about Limmania also just a part of his own distorted construction?

Banah observed him in silence.

His heart sank as uncertainty crumbled his convictions. "Excuse me, Banah..." Of course, he'd always based his opinion on Fillip's accounts. "I'm not sure anymore. I've always been taught—" He shook his head. Embarrassment seared through his face.

"I understand." The softness in her voice pervaded his mind.

The power of a gentle voice was unfathomable.

She addressed her servant. "Dear Lorann, could you leave us for a moment?" She nodded towards the stairs leading to their rooms.

"Certainly, My Lady." Her maiden bowed low then made her way towards the steps.

Banah squared her shoulders. "Are you aware that the allegations against the country were never officially verified before laws were ratified and sanctions imposed? And that Barrost launched the campaign against the shipbuilders of Limman before any wrongdoing had been established in the courts. And that the ruling members of the House of Mendelon joined that campaign without ever having an official enquiry by the Alliance?"

"No, I was not aware of these things." His face must have been dark red judging by the heat in his cheeks. For a moment, his stern childhood governess glared at him in the nursery. His mother directed another of her eternal tirades towards him and his siblings, all standing to attention for inspection.

Banah blinked as though waking from a dream. “Please forgive me, Palandred. I didn’t mean to...”

He nodded but struggled to focus. He wanted to look away but couldn’t. Head pounding like a storm, he swallowed. “I’ve... I’ve only ever been my brother’s puppet. His ministers always reported major losses where our family’s holdings in Inner Limmania were concerned.”

He frowned, shaking his head. The growing sense of guilt choked him. How much, if any, of Fillip’s intelligence was actually true. “My brother’s ministers always reported that the crown’s efforts to administrate Limmania’s untapped natural resources would benefit the impoverished country. That the native work ethic had foundered after the inquisitions.” He closed his eyes.

She spoke calmly. “Limmania has surely paid any conceivable debt, many times over.” She stared for a moment at his mouth, then deeply into his eyes again. “Isn’t it time to let them decide their own fate? Give them back the right to rule their own country?”

The depth of her concern for the nation was profoundly moving. Palandred had never seen any motive other than greed driving the relationships of monarchs. Her compassion for the people of Limmania was much more than simply soft-hearted idealistic affection.

For a moment, another slight expression of disapproval crossed her face, then disappeared. “And stop this ceaseless ignominy. Release them from the shame of dishonour and disgrace.” Her serene expression became intense, but he couldn’t tear his eyes away from hers. “The course of history can be changed.”

"Changed?" Palandred closed his eyes as a cavernous emptiness expanded in his chest. A darkness without end. So many years of dangling like a marionette from Fillip's tight strings! Hopelessness gave way to hot rage. Him, standing against his brother? A powerful sense of determination hardened within him. "Change."

The look of surprise in her eyes lit up her entire face. "Yes."

"I never know what His Royal Highness is planning. He has always endeavoured to keep me ignorant of his schemes. In the dark. Many in the palace are too afraid to report anything to me, let alone oppose anything he does."

Banah must have a hideous picture of the House of Elstundreth, of him.

He wished he could have made her acquaintance without Fillip's shadow over his life. He studied her face.

At least he was able to control the shaking in his hands.

He lowered his head when no more words would come.

"Palan?" How could the gentleness in a voice be so piercing? Her smooth calm expression was impossible to interpret.

He looked up.

She touched his arm. "We should get inside. It looks like rain."

26

ARRIVAL

Banah walked across the rain-drenched main deck. Careful not to wet her sleeves on the balustrade, she held on firmly and leant out further in order to better observe the huge water animals.

Below, gliding just beneath the surface of the limpid blue-green water, they appeared more like a vast flock of gargantuan underwater fowls than fish. Their every movement graceful and elegant, they performed a flawlessly choreographed dance.

Also peering down, Lorann held a hand to her chest. "What are they, My Lady? They're huge."

"Fughol." Palan responded, not looking at Banah's

maiden. "They often appear near the surface after it rains. The span of their fins can reach ten to fifteen paces across. Twenty in some that have been found. They are usually as peaceful as they seem now. But, if frightened, in the blink of an eye they can whip their tail tips like spearheads, and pierce even metal shields."

Lorann stepped back. "How frightening."

Fyrst Toman approached the balustrade and silently stared down at the creatures.

Master Yannu Elden accompanied him. Fatigue seemed to mask the usually cheerful countenance of the Fyrst's manservant.

"Fughol, you say?" The familiar-sounding word piqued Banah's interest. "Would that be a derivative of Old Orrenic, for 'winged'?" Her days spent with tutors and history lessons were a few years behind her, and the ancient languages of her Letters School curriculum had grown a little distant.

"Some dialects on Fahtu-Shan come close to Old Orrenic." Druin turned towards Fyrst Toman. "Correct, Toman? I thought I'd heard the word while visiting my family's estates there."

The Fyrst nodded.

Banah lowered her voice and addressed Lorann. "Our family has an estate on Fahtu-Shan. Druin is responsible for its maintenance and keeping in contact with the farmers who live there."

Fyrst Toman blinked slowly. His voice sounded distant. "My father's dialect still uses the word 'flughol' to describe wings or things with wings."

The expression in his eyes pierced Banah.

Distant. Forlorn.

Moments passed as the Fughol continued their silent

underwater flight, barely breaking the water's surface with the tips of their fins.

There must have been hundreds.

Perhaps thousands.

Toman longed for Fahtu-Shan and the solitude of the highland pastures. Just him and his flock. The bells of the lamblings tinkling in the cool fogs. The gentle chill of the morning dew on his face.

But he was here, in his mother's homeland, not on his father's island.

Toman's mind was a buzzing hive. Too many thoughts and feelings, too close to each other.

Why couldn't he simply trust in Ber'eth that all would turn out well? Discard the worry and appreciate this day? But a sense of dread kept stifling the joy of finally being in Limmania. Would someone else get hurt? The tingly anticipation of being on his mother's native soil... numbed by the fear that something else would go wrong.

Not only that, but their journey was in the midst of the Great Shift happening in the world. Ber'eth was calling out to his creation. Ominous Glortroms and powerful foretelling dreams were hinting at things to come. Unearthly powers were flowing through the air, the water, the soil.

He could feel them.

So could others.

The knowledge that Ber'eth was pouring out his power through the world should have been enough to calm Toman's anxiety. But it wasn't. Not completely.

The Greinen? Where was she now? Hopefully her disappearance from Trend's mind meant she'd been weakened somehow.

And how would His Grace fare?

His beloved master... The back of Toman's throat

swelled again with sorrow. Trying to ignore all the conflicting emotions, he kept his eyes on the entrance to the haven ahead.

"We're here. We're finally here." The joy was unmistakable in Lady Banah's soft voice as Palan's ship passed between the three islands at the mouth of the harbour.

Secluded, and almost entirely encircled by a craggy barrier, the Bay of Limman seemed to beckon them into its calm waters. Safe from ocean storms, the landscape reminded Toman of the Hohn Fennsor mountain ranges that protected Norssum from gales off the Olmish Aved.

Opposite the entrance to the bay, dark grey mountains towered behind buildings clustered not far from the water's edge. Chills prickled through Toman. They looked like immense stone fortifications.

To the north a great river had cut a deep valley into the mountains. If Toman remembered correctly, it was called the Limman Folumpor. Opening up to an estuary much smaller than the Suyan Folumpor's in Barrost, its nearside bank was cluttered with what appeared to be the ruins of old industrial buildings atop a massive stone embankment. And on the far bank were the tangled remains of what must have been the famous shipyards.

In front of the rubble piles, a long stone quay jutted out into the bay from a wide paved plaza where crowds were gathering.

Toman sighed deeply, trying to relieve the tension in his chest.

He was finally visiting Limman, the capital of his mother's ancestral home. He could hardly believe it!

She would have been so proud to know he'd made it.

Reaching instinctively into his shirt pocket for her herbs, he rubbed the leaves gently, then brought his fingertips to his nose. A warmth filled him. He could almost see Alyena standing over the hearth at Upland, stirring a pot of her delicious stew.

Palan's captain shouted orders to prepare for docking. Riggers dropped the sails, and the vessel slowly made her way towards the quay.

"Two dead, one still seriously ill." Yannu's tense voice startled Toman.

Toman faced him. "Pardon?"

"The bad food this morning. Cook Marta is beside herself. Won't stop sobbing. She says that she had nothing to do with it, that all her ingredients were from the ship's larders. Someone must have tampered with the pastries later. One of the servants?"

"That's terrible."

"Yes, but Trend is still a pathetic pile of mush at the moment, and he has been locked in the brig since he came on the ship. So it couldn't have been him again."

Toman nodded. "I think you're right." Who else on board would want them poisoned? Anxiety flared again in him. His Grace would have looked into it right away. But Toman was exhausted. And they were about to disembark. "The Prince will probably have someone investigate it."

Yannu stared blankly at Toman's chest and nodded. "Of course."

Deckhands began running about, throwing ropes ashore. Some jumped onto the quay.

Lady Banah and Druin walked a few paces behind Palan as he crossed the deck.

Toman made his way towards them.

Two small barges bearing Mendelonian colours navigated past, towards the entrance of the Bay. Such a small example of the trade that used to come and go on these waters.

Even from this distance, Limmania had a sense of goodness about it. Something humble and deep. Wholesome and special.

The towering backdrop of jagged mountains, the sparkling clear waters, the gentle breezes in the harbour... He could almost visualise the prosperous shipbuilding and trade centre it had been in historical times. But seeing the ruins reminded him of what he'd read in His Grace's books... *Limmania was forced to dismantle its shipyards under the pressure of terrible scandals.*

The new Palanshen rulers in old Noèsh, now Norssum, and Palan's ancestors in Mendelon, had accused the Limmanian shipwrights of taking bribes and aiding the last of the Skyllian overlords in their escape. Courts had condemned and beheaded two prominent captains after Skyllian gold had been found in one of the captains' chambers.

Toman shook his head. What would it have taken for the courts to reconsider their judgement before acting in such a way? Before killing people? Didn't they realise how easily it would have been for adversaries to plant accusatory evidence?

The reason for Lady Banah's anguish over the injustices done here was becoming ever clearer.

But His Grace had also told stories of great valour and bravery.

The Shiplorn, for example. The stories of captains and their families who had been taken captive and forced to transport fleeing Skylle to their homeland. Some accounts in His Grace's library said the brave captains had driven their ships against the crags around entrance to the bay, plunging themselves and all on board into the strong currents.

Of the fabled Shiplorn, none had ever returned. No survivors, not Skyllian, nor Limmanian. All had drowned, so the stories told.

Alyena had still sung poems mourning their loss over a century after their deaths.

Anger rose in him. Why had accounts of their heroic sacrifices not been considered when the Palanshen and Mendelonians had flung about accusations of treason and ruined the livelihood of an entire nation?

"We are here." Lady Banah exhaled long, a wistful smile appearing on her face.

Toman stared towards the plaza.

Goosebumps rose on his arms.

Festooned in bright blue and white, the entire waterfront was alive with banners and flags displaying the national colours of Ydassum, in honour of Lady Banah's State Visit. From windows, countless colourful kerchiefs waved as joyful shouts rose. Along the shoreline near the plaza, the emblems of each of the Ydassum provinces swayed from tall poles.

A pang of sorrow passed through Toman. His great pleasure to finally be there was locked in a cage of anxiety that His Grace would not recover and would soon depart from this life for Ber'eth's eternal realms. It was as though he was observing a festival from the barred windows of a prison cell.

But, he couldn't dwell on that impression. Glimmers of reassurance had given him the strength not to give up hope.

Lady Banah's prayer and his master's breathing becoming more regular...

The Riddern's medicines...

Physician Wanner's attentiveness...

Toman had to rein in his thoughts, and expect the best of results, not the worst. He had to convince himself. Expecting good always displaced fear and doubt, and made room for changes for the better.

But he'd never imagined arriving at the home of his mother's ancestors without His Grace at his side. This was his master's homeland, too.

Toman studied Lady Banah.

Her normally unreadable face was full of emotion. Did her lips tremble as she pressed a handkerchief to her mouth?

She lowered her head slightly.

A gentle breeze blew Lorann's loose glistening hair over her face. She tucked strands behind an ear, then lowered her hand and immediately reassumed the identical position to that of her Highborn Lady.

Toman looked away as the old pressure returned and squeezed around his heart.

"My goodness." The astonishment in Druin's voice was unmistakable. "Banah, what a reception!"

Palan turned away from the railing, mumbling to himself. "Never have I seen such a display in Limmania, not even for my mother."

"A gathering befitting you, Highborn of Ydassum." Chieftains Beruhn and Ruhand appeared beside them, the long feathers of their colourful headdresses swaying back and forth.

"Thank you, Chieftess." Banah bowed, her heart pounding wildly.

It was difficult to take in the jubilant sights and sounds of the crowds.

The air was alive with celebration. So many had come out to welcome them!

Their cheering filled her with awe, displacing the unusual blend of astonishment and shame coursing through her just a moment before.

"I think they love you, Dear Sister." The wonderment in Druin's face lifted her heart even further.

Lorann glanced towards her. Even her face seemed to be aglow with delight. "My Lady! Isn't it magnificent?" She pointed towards the plaza.

Banah kept her breaths deep and steady. It helped maintain the composure required of her and her office.

But the conflict within her still raged. The regret at not having spoken up at the Trade Summit was growing unendurable. Limmania desperately needed a voice amongst the ruling houses on the Horn. She was certain she could have been that voice. A voice to initiate change.

But she'd failed. Miserably.

Circumstances had been extremely difficult. The Queen Summerbird petals had confounded her ability to reason properly and had severely dulled her judgement. And then the Barrostanian student's terrible actions.

Banah shuddered inwardly at the memory of the burning sensation passing through her feet. The poison in her slippers that had also killed poor little Maylin. Regardless, she had prepared for so long to lift a torch in the name of Limmania, to plead for their release from unfair laws and sanctions. She'd hoped to see the beginnings of change on this State Visit.

The weight of her inaction was becoming very heavy to bear.

She shouldn't be so harsh on herself. The Steward of Limmania would not know of her failed plans. He wouldn't be disappointed.

But she knew.

A psalm from Friar Robbeth came suddenly to mind. Banah closed her eyes and concentrated on the words.

Criticise not, that you be not judged.

Do not seek faults in others.

Neither in yourself.

Forgiveness is a powerful flood with no specific direction.

Bathe in its waters and pour it out into the world around you.

The hair on her arms rose as though cold air flowed over her. How could she have forgotten such simple truths?

She'd never thought of herself in need of her *own* mercy, but she needed to allow Ber'eth's designs to reach into her deepest thoughts, even those she harboured against herself. Or perhaps, *especially* those she harboured against herself.

Those regrets seemed to be the most deeply rooted.

It had always been clear that she was obliged to forgive offenses against her. But, perhaps she should also forgive herself.

She could never have imagined how difficult that task would be.

At the end of the quay, the Lord Steward and a group of his councillors formed a half-circle. Their deep crimson robes set them vividly apart from the crowds behind them in the plaza.

Banah smiled. The half-circle as a formation of welcome reminded her of the Ydassum ceremony for the arrival of the Uccell Lords back in Turicum. But deep red was an unusual colour for the official garments of Orrenic rulers. Almost all countries on the Horn favoured variations of blue, white, yellow, or sometimes green.

After the Reformation Period, Limmania had chosen deep red as the background colour of their flag as well, to reflect the blood shed by so many of its people. In its centre two white hands were depicted, palms open as though in greeting.

Liveried attendants began to line both sides of the quay, raising slender arches wrapped in flowers.

Druin slipped an arm under hers and pulled her close. He whispered, "Dear Sister, try to calm your mind. I know you avoid such recognition, but you are a magnificent leader. Lord G'nallun said that we would enter the eye of the storm, and that it would be a place of tranquillity and of preparation. All will work out, for all of us." He kissed her temple.

Nodding slowly, she squeezed his arm then released it as the light-hearted sound of wooden flutes drifted towards them. Other wind instruments joined the flutes, then small drums and singers. The air began to fill with music.

Servants pulled an awning onto long poles and secured it into place over the gangway. Lorann indicated to Palandred's guards their correct positions for the disembarkation.

The Riddern Chieftains moved to the back of the deck. The stunning elegance of their glistening feather garments captured something of the untamed beauty of their native forests.

Druin clasped his hands together and looked at her, his eyes sparkling with youthful delight.

Palandred moved behind Druin.

Banah stopped herself from showing any displeasure. Palandred knew that international protocol required that higher ranking dignitaries precede those of lesser rank. His status was much higher than theirs. Highborns from Ydassum were not in the same category as a dynastic prince of Mendelon.

She stepped over to Palandred. “Prince Palandred...” It still felt too odd to call him by his first name. “Thank you for the honour, but we are your guests, on your vessel. Disembarkation protocol requires us to assume places behind you. I wouldn’t want to offend the Lord Steward.”

He seemed to stiffen. His lips thinned to a straight line, and the veins in his neck pulsed.

Nodding once, he stepped slowly past Banah and spoke to her in a low voice. “I hope I don’t ruin your visit.”

She frowned as the faint dissonant sound of a hiss rose from somewhere on the quay. A chill ran up her spine. Who would dare display such insolence?

“Fillip was right.” Palandred’s eyes were fixed on the gangway. “They hate me here.”

27

In Honour of Ydassum

Druin admired Banah as the two of them walked onto the petal-covered quay.

A few steps behind Palan, they walked together towards the Lord Steward Loraimen.

Attendants continued tossing white petals onto their path.

The air was suffused with an unusual but exquisite bouquet. The decorative arches held just over their heads were interwoven with many white blossoms Druin had never seen before. Sweet and light with a hint of spice, the refreshing smell was a pleasant change from the heady muskiness of the Queen Summerbird.

Banah glanced up at the flowers. Her nostrils flared slightly as her chest rose. A moment later a wide smile appeared on her lips. “Beautiful.”

She looked every bit a sovereign, walking on the carpet of petals under the floral canopy. Ydassum was not a country of kings or queens, but in this setting, following so closely behind Palan – a noble prince of the dynastic House of Mendelon — she was equally regal in bearing and countenance.

Druin smiled.

She was everything he wasn’t, and could never be.

This was her world.

Negotiations, protocols, policies of state and commerce, she excelled at every level of statesmanship. Soon to be crowned Lanfothe and hereditary ruler of Ydassum, she reminded him more of their father by the day.

A sense of pride swelled in Druin as the Limmanian Steward, still a few feet away, already bowed towards them.

Palan suddenly stopped and turned to Banah.

Was there a problem?

His sister seemed confused, looking nervously from Palan to Steward Loraimen.

Moving to one side, Palan bowed then raised an open palm towards her. He lifted his head and spoke clearly, “The Highborn Lady Banah Ahnya Eleor Méndrensynn, firstborn of the house of Méndrensynn.” He beckoned her to join him, rather than remain behind him as she’d wished.

Druin suppressed a chuckle at the awkwardness of Palan’s noncompliance with Banah’s express direction. His old friend hadn’t heeded her request. He had blatantly ignored it!

Perhaps he was made of much more resilient stuff than Druin had realised.

Palan obviously had his own sense of honour.

The irony was exquisite.

By Banah's own rules of formality and etiquette, she wouldn't dishonour Palan's public gesture. She would certainly feel obliged to comply in silence. But it would deeply upset her sense of international protocol.

Druin struggled to control the laughter bubbling up inside him. Telling himself not to laugh made it even more difficult to restrain.

Banah would surely realise she couldn't keep every situation neatly ordered, despite the accepted procedure. Frozen for a few more tense moments, staring at Palan, she finally acquiesced and stepped forward next to him.

Sighing with relief, Druin moved to a position behind his sister, but despite his effort to hold back his mirth, a short chuckle escaped through his nose.

The nervous twitch at the corner of his sister's mouth probably meant she'd heard him. He could imagine a strained but reserved expression on her face.

The shuffling of boots behind him drew his attention. He looked around.

Toman appeared under the floral bower, his face slightly red. He walked to his position in front of the Chieftains. Behind the Riddern, Banah's Maiden took her place.

Sympathy filled Druin. Had Toman been crying? Had something happened to Lord Dalbonn?

Apprehension quickly sobered any feeling of mirth.

A few paces away, the Lord Steward lifted his arms out wide. Behind him, the half-circle of dignitaries also raised their arms.

"Your Highness Prince Palandred Elstundreth-

Fathringen of Mendelon." Lord Loraimen spoke in a loud but rather shrill voice, bowing stiffly to Palan.

"Steward Loraimen." Palan inclined his head politely.

The Lord Steward then faced Banah and Druin and addressed them together. "Most honoured Highborns of Ydassum." His bow was both humble and extravagant.

The deep red cloaks of the dignitaries brushed the paving stones as they repeated the Steward's salutation.

"Limmania welcomes you." Steward Loraimen made a sweeping movement towards the people gathered in the vast waterfront plaza.

A deafening roar of jubilation erupted. A sea of blue and white banners, kerchiefs and ribbons undulated above the heads of the crowd.

Face flushing pink, Banah bowed. "Thank you, My Lord."

Druin followed suit. "Thank you."

Looking up at the Riddern Chieftains, the Lord Steward's eyes widened in what appeared to be fear and awe. "Welcome, Master Keepers of Healing Lore." He bowed to them briskly, then quickly looked away.

Lord Loraimen glanced at Palan as he turned back to Banah. The bitter disdain in his expression lasted only a moment, but was unmistakable.

Anxiety tightened in Druin's jaw. The ages-old animosity between dynastic overlords and vassal state was obviously still festering.

Hopefully Limmania's conflict with the House of Mendelon wouldn't have a detrimental effect on Banah's State Visit. So far, the atmosphere was spectacular. His sister needed such a reception, especially after Barrost and so many disappointments.

His conscience pricked him. Because of him, she'd come closed to death. His own ignorance was still beyond belief – even after Faydann's demise, he hadn't recognised the Queen Summerbird's toxic properties. Or perhaps he hadn't wanted to recognise them? Thankfully, the Riddern had intervened in time. Perhaps not all was lost with the discovery.

The Chieftains had cautioned about the dangers of the Queen Summerbird, but their encouraging words regarding the exceptional properties of the new orchid had renewed Druin's optimism. The species could still have outstanding positive qualities, perhaps used in minute quantities.

"This way, please, to the Grand Plaza." Steward Loraimen motioned towards the centre of the plaza and began walking under more floral arches, this time woven with the delicate blue flowers of Maiden Song. A beautiful symbol in the Language of Flowers, they befitted Banah as a sign of ultimate purity, as well as welcome.

The Steward slowed his pace and whispered to Banah. His face lost all expression for a moment. "The Ferend Service delivered a message this morning of your arrival a day early." He paused. "I am truly sorry about the events in Barrost."

Banah nodded slowly. "Lords of the Firstborn also delivered a message from Ber'eth to my brother, that we should stay on course."

"The Uccell, My Lady?" The Steward's eyes widened as his face seemed to drain of colour.

Banah nodded again.

"Then we shall continue with our planned celebrations."

Shouts of "Honour to the House of Méndrensynn" filled the air.

Thousands of people waved the national colours of Ydassum even higher. "Honour to the Cloud Kingdom!"

Throughout the crowds, many eyes lowered to the ground and expressions of anxiety appeared on faces as the Riddern walked past.

Emerging from the multitudes gathered, two lines formed, one of men and one of women, all in long flowing dark green garments. They parted the crowd then beckoned Banah and their party to follow in the procession.

The lines of men and women clapped their hands together over their heads and began spinning and chanting. "Rejoice, Limmania, Rejoice!". The shimmering fabric of their clothing spread open around them like the unfurling blossoms of Trumpet Flowers.

Shouts of jubilation continued around the dancers as the Lord Steward led them deeper into the plaza, towards a low stage festooned with green ribbons and more white flowers.

At the steps of the platform, the dancers scooped up armfuls of white petals from woven baskets and threw them into the air.

Druin took in the sight with great pleasure. Framing the spectacular celebrations, to the east, behind the city and all around the harbour, the massive mountains rose skyward like a natural stone amphitheatre. To the north, ancient ruins topped an immense embankment that flanked the river. By the height of the stone wall, the water course must flood at times.

Palan and Banah looked magnificent standing next to each other.

His sister held her chin firm and kept her brow smooth, but it was obvious that she was struggling to keep her emotions under control. Such attention would move her deeply. She preferred humbler entrances and never showed any fondness for pomp.

But he welcomed it for her.

He grinned. Even though it may unsettle her reserved nature at that moment, it would do her well to receive the praise of others.

She reached the steps and stopped. Turning back, she looked over the crowds and smiled.

She had never looked so noble.

Beside her, Palan stood motionless, staring at the ground in front of him.

Musicians gathered in ranks around them, continuing their intricate melody. Singers began a gentle, almost melancholic tune. Not a song of desperation, but one of distant hope and longing. Then, layer upon layer, strings joined in, building on the melody. Piping notes from wooden instruments followed, interweaving with the words, creating an ethereal sound.

A few of the green-clad dancers leapt up onto small pedestals at the edge of the platform. They began tapping rapid steps on the hollow wooden stands, adding precise beats to the song. The rest of the dancers joined the musicians in front of the stage, their long costumes flowing around them as they whirled.

Smiling broadly, Lord Loraimen positioned himself behind a podium at the top of the steps. He raised his hands and the music concluded with all the dancers bowing towards Banah and Palan.

"This is a great day for Limmania." The Lord Steward announced in his somewhat high-pitched voice, and silence fell on the crowds. He invited Banah and Palan to join him then held his hand out towards Druin.

They all climbed the steps as a small group approached bearing huge bouquets of more white blossoms.

Their arms were full of what looked like a stunning alba form of the Ember Lily. The species' typical black spotting stood out against the white petals and sepals.

Stunningly beautiful!

Druin had never heard of a pure white mutation of the known red violet form of the Ember Lily. But the other flowers entwined with them... Goosebumps rose on his arms. No, no it couldn't be! *Marchonensis candidus* – the White Spider Orchid? Its long twirling petals hung down like the loose curls of a maiden's hair.

He stared again at the surrounding mountains. What treasures their hidden forests must hold!

He'd never been on expeditions into southern high-altitude regions. Always following the routes his grandfather had taken, he had pressed ever higher into the Cloud Forests of eastern Ydassum and into the western reaches of the Thousand Rivers Districts of Auyana. Now a strong desire to explore the rainy interior of Limmania grew in him. However, he'd need a trained guide to circumnavigate any groups of Huddu-Han, the snout-faced White Apes.

"We have the immense honour of welcoming the Highborns of Ydassum, Lady Banah and Lord Druin Méndrensynn, on their first visit to our shores, and to our city." He didn't address Palan, but continued his speech.

Druin cringed inwardly. Even though this was Banah's official State Visit before her coronation, the presence of the Prince of Mendelon should have been recognised in the Lord Steward's official welcome.

Eyes still on Banah, Lord Loraimen's chest seemed to swell as he proceeded with his address. "But the presence of the House of Méndrensynn has been felt long before this historic day. Their kindness towards Limmania has been cherished for generations. This great family's generosity provided a new homeland for many of our exiled people, and their visit today marks a new chapter of this celebrated friendship."

The attendants arranged flowers around Banah. The powerful sweet scent must have been from the White Spider Orchid. The Ember Lily wasn't known for any notable fragrance.

Banah's eyes glistened with emotion.

Once again, a strong sense of pride for his sister filled him.

Despite the great distance between their countries, Banah's efforts and voice had kept alight the torch their great-grandfather had lit.

Steward Loraimen carried on, speaking over a silent crowd, "During the scourge of the Skylle and again in the horrors of the Expulsion Wars of the Urbonnic overlords, the great House of Méndrensynn has remained a beacon of hope, a source of inspiration. And especially so, Lady Banah Méndrensynn."

Renewed shouts of honour and blessing rang out.

Once again, flowers flew through the air and fragrant petals rained down around her.

Banah's shoulders began to quiver as she pulled out a handkerchief.

28

Where are the Children?

Toman couldn't agree more with the Steward's words.

Lady Banah was both a remarkable leader, and of a remarkable family.

Toman counted himself very fortunate to be among those whose lives had been blessed by the House of Méndrensynn.

The Lanfoths of Ydassum had been more than generous in response to the plight of his mother's people. Gifting the displaced Limmanians vast tracts of rich arable land in the northern province of Honstan, they had ensured the survival of Alyena's exiled ancestors.

The Skylle had expelled many coastal Orrenic tribes back then.

Thanks to Lady Banah, Toman belonged to something far greater than he could ever have imagined. He was *Lieutenant to the Lord Protector Mischul Dalbonn* and *Fyrst of Ydassum*.

He even had his own personal manservant!

But then, Yannu was much more than any servant. He was his best friend.

In addition to their generosity, the invitation to accompany Lady Banah on her State Visit was an unbelievable honour. In the beginning, he was to come as Apprentice to the Lord Protector, but now as Fyrst of Ydassum. After the state journey, he was also to participate in the coronation ceremony at Immen where she would assume the title and role of Lanfothe.

A shiver of gratitude ran through his entire body. The privilege to be in service to the Méndrensynn family... It was almost too good to be true.

But Lady Banah was much more than a benefactor caring for the needs of the unfortunate. She had also proved herself time and time again to be an insightful, wise leader. The inclusion of the Riddern and the Uccell as equals on the trip illustrated her integrity.

His Grace had mentioned that no other Palanth-Orric nation had ever treated the Urbonnic Riddern tribes of Ydassum or the Firstborn as fellow citizens of the Great Continent.

For many, they were simply tolerated outsiders.

Many in Barrost had still considered the Riddern to be nothing more than swarthy tattooed savages, and the Uccell as hideous winged monsters.

Alyena's praises of the ruling family came to mind. Before she passed away, his mother would speak highly of the Méndrensynns whenever a member of their family paid one of their regular visits to their lands in Fahtu-Shan.

Toman chuckled.

In recent years, that family member had probably been Druin!

To think that he, Toman Foggling, a farmer from Upland, was on first-name terms with the Highborn now! "Rueddan and Brun wouldn't believe it." He whispered to himself, smiling, it was so hard to grasp. "And Odilia would be so proud."

Looking from Lady Banah to the Steward, something inside Toman swelled with warmth.

"Lady Méndrensynn..." sympathy filled the Steward's speech as he continued, "...has also recently suffered grave hardships in order to reach our shores." He stopped abruptly, seeming to struggle with his emotions. "To bless our land!"

The crowds roared, waving their banners again. Their multicoloured Eth resonances flickered brightly. Never had Toman seen so many clear bright Eth colours all in one place.

Standing in Alyena's motherland, a powerful sense of belonging filled him. It was as if everything around him – the warm salty breeze, the sheer stone mountains, the sparkling waters of the Bay of Limman – were all a part of him, and he of them. They all seemed to welcome him.

As a child, he had often been told that he was like Alyena and nothing like Brun, even though he and his father were often mistaken for twin brothers when they'd brought livestock to the fairs.

Toman wasn't at all like his resolutely Orrenic father.

Not really.

He was definitely like his mother. And his mother's foreign ways had often irritated Brun. So had Toman's.

The dancers leapt down from their podiums and began singing a sweet but somehow sad melody.

The song surged through the crowd.

"Your homeland beckons you home.
Your homeland welcomes you home.
Fathers, rejoice!
Mothers, rejoice!
Your children will come home again!"

Standing on a carpet of white petals, Lady Banah looked like a princess out of a nursery rhyme.

Icy goosebumps shivered up Toman's arms.

The Eth resonances continued shimmering through the crowds, clear and bright. Quite different from the dull colours in Barrostanian crowds, these flickering lights reminded Toman of the colours of his Gebayt Bithen.

Since he'd left home, so much of his life had begun to feel like pages from a child's story. Like fables coming true.

Faces in the crowd looked strangely familiar. Strangely like family. His brother and sister, Rueddan and Odilia, would have blended in perfectly.

His mother's likeness was reflected in the faces of many women in the plaza. Her bright smile and pale grey-blue eyes were everywhere he looked. Her strong chin. Her thick pale blond hair. Even the bold and yet intricate needlework on many dress hems and cuffs of shirts reminded him of her. The same swirling leaves and vines Alyena used to stitch on what she'd called their 'fancy clothes'.

A sense of finally belonging, finally being a part of a

tribe, overwhelmed him. He may look perfectly Orrenic, but he felt Limmanian.

"And now a tour of our great city." The Steward waved a hand towards buildings on the opposite edge of the plaza, facing the Bay. Surrounded by a resonance of rich gold, he finished his greeting and stepped down from the podium.

Lady Banah, Druin and Palan joined him.

Lorann and Toman followed as they all started moving through the crowds towards the city gate.

The elegant presence of the Highborn's Maiden sent an old, familiar shiver through Toman.

The red-cloaked men followed behind.

The Steward made another sweeping gesture towards what looked like ancient storm walls stretching from the massive river embankment to the far side of the plaza.

A few uniformed men marched at the top of the embankment.

The Steward glanced sharply at them but continued his speech "This lower level of the city is called The Netherns or 'the Lower Village'. It dates back to the original Welsordian culture in the Orrenic settlement period. The houses and shops you see were carved into the original fortifications and sea wall."

Built of massive blocks of brown stone, it reminded Toman of Barrost.

His voice brimming with excitement, the Steward gave lengthy descriptions of each layer of buildings lining the plaza.

Toman scanned the crowd again. Had someone shouted something about *the children*? What had they meant?

Even though engaging in tone and excited hand gestures, Toman found the Steward difficult to follow.

Too much to absorb when Toman preferred to keep his mind alert for dangers.

"The type of architecture you see here shows the ancient Orrenic preparedness for war. It is believed that this architectural style – if we can call it a true style because it combined designs born in urgency and out of necessity rather than artistic forethought – persisted for the first hundred years after the foundations of the city were laid. All walls and short towers are of a simple, practical angular construction. You will notice that there are few windows on the ground floors. All the openings we now see in the walls were cut through the original protective stonework of The Netherns by the Skylle. The many doors to your left were the entrances to the Skyllian public brothels."

What did he say? Puzzled for a moment, Toman thought he'd misunderstood the Steward. Public establishments, directly on the main plaza, for such private activities? He couldn't imagine a city openly allowing the sale of such sensual gratification, directly on its streets...

...on the other hand, what difference was that to Barrost with all the raw flesh bulging from the tops of sparkling tight dresses? The small of his back suddenly tingled with the memory of the noblewoman's hand sliding down his shoulders and coming to rest on his buttocks. Her green jewels seemed to glare at him again from around her pale delicate-looking neck. Once again, she flaunted her bosom bulging out of her overtight bodice, taunting him to look. The skin across Toman's chest tightened as his heart picked up its pace. He shook his head, struggling to free his mind of the sensations.

The Skylle had done the same thing, just packaged in different wrappings. They must not have even tried to hide their cravings, displaying their ability to gratify them like merchandise at a market.

In a very strange way, Toman found them the more honest of the two.

"The higher elevations of the city once had many more towers. Our Orrenic ancestors, the tribe of Hlimman, kept a constant vigil on the sea." He turned back to face Lady Banah. "Many of the high lookouts have been incorporated into the city we see today."

Lady Banah responded at the end of the Steward's speech. "Lord Loraimen, your country's architects have done a masterful job of blending the different and unique styles into a most beautiful city. Indeed, she sits at the mouth of the Limman Folumpor like a crown on a regal prince."

"Where are our children?" Someone shouted behind them.

Alarm shot through Toman. He scanned the plaza.

Another voice rose, this time from the direction of the river. "What have you done with our children?"

A kidnapping? Placing a hand on his sword, Toman ignited his Eth.

"What children?" Lady Banah looked around nervously.

Lorann's hand flew to her mouth.

The Steward stared anxiously at Palan.

"You promised to send them home!" A woman's voice trembled angrily.

Palan shook his head, frowning. "How dare you speak to us in such a manner?"

Toman quickly faced her. He blinked.

Just an elderly woman.

She shook her walking cane towards them. "You took my son. He has never come home. You promised!"

"Are they even still alive? Or are they slaves in your mansions?" Another voice boomed from the crowd.

"Silence!" The Steward raised a hand. "Silence!"

Toman extended his consciousness, probing the crowd with his mind as quickly as he could.

No detectable weapons. Nothing of metal or any sharp objects.

He withdrew his consciousness.

There seemed to be no real danger.

The crowd kept its distance from the Highborns and the Steward, forming a wide circle around them as Steward Loraimen led them towards the gates of the walled inner city. The looks the crowd gave Palan were difficult to read. Disgust? Hatred?

Physician Wanner's words came back to Toman, 'You'll see.'

Lady Banah stopped for a moment and faced the Steward. "Who are they speaking to in this manner?"

The Steward's dark golden resonance flared orange as he glanced at Palan again. "Please forgive us, Lady Méndrensynn. This was not expected. Please follow me, quickly. I do not feel there is any danger to you and Lord Méndrensynn but let us withdraw immediately."

29

The Shift Continues

Children? What children? Palandred glared in the direction of the voices. And why did the Lord Steward just look at him the way he did?

"I beg your forgiveness for the inconvenience, Your Highness, Highborns." The Steward ushered his dignitaries forward then motioned for the group from Ydassum to follow them. "I repeat, I do not feel there is any true danger. Only old sentiments being aired. But let us withdraw immediately to avoid any further interruptions. This way, please."

Old sentiments? What did children have to do with them?

The paving stones of the plaza began to shake as a

thunderous booming sound reverberated through the air.

The hair on Palandred's arms rose. It was like no sound he'd ever heard.

"An earthquake?" Lady Banah looked at him, seeming to search for an answer in his face.

He nodded. "It must be. But earthquakes sound different." Or at least the few that he'd lived through, where the ground had seemed to moan from deep within. This thunderous din felt somehow more airborne. "We feel occasional tremors on the peninsula of Mendelon City, but they don't usually reach Horróglоryn. And they don't feel like this!" He offered her his arm for support.

She acquiesced, clasping his wrist firmly.

The touch of her hand on his skin sent a wave of warmth through him.

She looked back towards the plaza and called, "Lorann?" She sighed with relief as her servant appeared.

Together they began walking briskly towards the city gate.

Drawing closer to the massive rustic entrance, childhood memories returned... holding his twin sister's hand and walking down the cobbled streets of the Lower Village. Both of them stepping softly behind their mother on their way to the White Garden residence where they had elegant rooms. And the garden itself, with its ornate hedges and particularly colourful plants. It had been like a mythological labyrinth.

The ground quivered more intensely.

"Look! Up in the valley." Toman shouted, running over to them.

A white mist of raging water rose like great plumes of smoke.

Pointing to the high cliff faces of the Limman Folumpor valley, he raised his voice again as large shadowy forms plummeted through the brume towards the river. “Boulders. Falling into the river. They could block the flow.”

The roar of the rushing water began to echo across the plaza.

“Flood waters!” The Steward wrapped his cloak over one arm. “Everyone, everyone, inside the city gate!” His strident alarm had an immediate effect, and people began running towards the shelter of the walled city.

The Steward quickly joined Lady Banah, Druin and Palandred. “As you probably remember from your childhood, Your Highness, the city walls and the Lower Village are sturdy, designed to resist attacks from pirates, storm waves and floods. We will all be safe inside.” Looking back in the direction of the river, he shook his head. “But this is unnatural. We can have occasional flooding during the rainy season. The embankments redirect the water away from the city, past the quay and out into the bay.” He shook his head again. “But we’ve had no rain for days.”

Lady Banah stared at Palandred and spoke barely above a whisper. “The Beckoning. It must be.” She showed no hint fear.

Druin kept looking back over his shoulder towards the growing roar of the river. “Where is the water coming from then?”

“It must be from the Central Highlands, the Marden Morath.” The Steward answered as he hurried them onward. “Word was sent last week that the highland marshes had begun to drain. Over the past few days, the water in the Limman Folumpor began to change in colour. Normally it is a clear, a fresh mountain current.

Shortly before your arrival, a large muddy stream appeared midriver."

The entrance to the city congested quickly with people running for safety. Shoulders bumping shoulders, they joined the throng hurrying under the stout stone arch.

The Steward turned back towards the oncoming stream of people, raising his hands. "Please, everyone, go to your respective homes until order returns. Calmly, please, everyone. No need to be afraid or panic." He stopped abruptly and raised a hand to his ear, closing his eyes tightly. An instant later he opened them again, looking around fearfully. "I think I hear..."

A strident noise began echoing around the buildings.

"Please." The Steward turned to Lady Banah, his voice tightening sharply. "Please enter the first courtyard on your right. It is my town home."

"Thank you, Lord Steward." Lady Banah continued to hold on to Palandred's arm as they quickly approached the house Steward Loraimen indicated.

The sound of rushing waters roared, then the loud cracking of wood splintering. At the top of the embankment the leafy branches of trees and the splintered tips of cracked wooden beams were scraping along the rubble, moving with the raging waters. A massive earth-hued wave, heavy with debris, surged over the congested flotsam and began to flood the lower end of the plaza.

"Danger, from the sky!" Toman shouted.

Palandred and Lady Banah turned towards him at the same time.

Toman shook his head. "No, it's from the mountains!" He shook his head again. "No. I can't tell where it's coming from, but run! There's not much time. Something will be on us soon!".

A few people continued to rush through the gate. The narrow city streets filled with their muffled cries, and the sound of doors and shutters slamming. Then an ear-splitting sound only wild beasts could make, pierced the growing din of the flood waters.

"Here. In here." The Steward pushed open the gate to a small walled area. "Down the path, to the entrance of the house! My servants will be expecting us."

Palandred helped Lady Banah and Druin through, then Lady Banah's handmaiden.

"Your Highness, Your Highness!" A man bellowed from the plaza.

Palandred stopped, placing a hand over Lady Banah's on his wrist.

Dressed in a Mendelonian captain's uniform, the man came running towards Palandred. Panting, he spoke rapidly. "Your Highness, the mines are flooded. We tried to rescue what we could. Production will be delayed for some time."

"Mines? What are you talking about?" Rage flared in him. Was this another venture Fillip was undertaking that Palandred knew nothing about? But mines? What was his brother hiding?

The officer's face began to lose colour. "Oh." He stumbled backwards. "Oh, forgive me, Your Highness." Cold fear shot through his eyes. "I thought you... I assumed you knew..." He turned quickly and ran through the thinning crowds at the city gate and across the plaza towards the river.

The Riddern Chieftains stood motionless in the street, their heads tilted skyward.

Lifting his glowing hands higher, Toman also remained in front of the Steward's gate.

The reflection of his resonance shimmered through the air above them.

Almost as though the wielding of Toman's Eth power triggered the demon within Palandred, a surge of tingling heat rose in him. The nape of his neck burned, and the tips of his fingers began giving off light.

His cursed Eth.

Not now, please not now!

The sudden colour in Palan's fingertips distracted Toman as he struggled to keep his concentration on both the sky and the streets.

An undulating mass was moving quickly towards them.

He couldn't make out what kind of animals they were, but the dark horde of flapping creatures emerging from the forest filled him with alarm.

Something else, a herd of something perhaps, was bearing down on them from the river valley behind the city. There were fewer of them, but much larger in size than the airborne creatures.

"There, above the rooftops!" He spread his Linger over the street, extending the shield to include the Steward's residence.

No need to hide his Linger. His Grace had forewarned him about any public display of his Eth resonance in Barrostania, but he'd never advised him about Limmania. Surely the homeland of his mother's people would not be upset by it.

"Night Flyers!" Someone shouted from a window.

Toman screwed his eyes up towards the dark winged shapes appearing above the buildings. The mass of flapping leathery wings dipped low, entering the street, heading directly for him. Like living shadows from the dead of night, the black winged creatures looked like Flitter Mice from back on Fahtu-Shan, but ten, twenty times larger.

"Night Flyers." Shaking his head, Palan walked up quickly alongside Toman. "Out during the day? It doesn't make sense."

"These animals are not in our forests." Chieftess Beruhn touched Toman's arm. "Keep your shield firm, Gift to the People. I sense the strength of these animals. They could rend you to pieces."

Toman winced as hundreds of the black creatures slammed into his shield.

Clawed wings tried to find a grip on the smooth surface. Body after body thudded against his Linger, scratching and biting blindly before sliding down or taking flight again.

Small splatters of dark warm blood began dripping down his shield. A barrage of impressions assaulted Toman through his link. The sensations of the creatures crashing into his shield almost overpowered him. His eyes filled with blinding fire.

The light! The light burned the Night Flyers' eyes.

Toman must keep his open in order to maintain the strength of his Linger shield. But his eyes burned. The sun, the pain! Through the Eth connection to the creatures, his skin also began to sear. The sunlight scorched every part of his body.

Suddenly, large hairy powerfully-muscled white beasts leapt onto the streets, howling.

"Let them pass through the city!" Someone spoke up from the crowds. "They are normally such peaceful creatures."

Hundreds of Night Flyers continued biting and clawing at Toman's Linger shield.

Their sharp claws were ripping small tears in his skin!

How was that possible?

Was sorcery increasing in power?

He cried out as warm sticky moisture trickled into his burning eyes. The blood began dripping down his cheeks.

Palan coughed hard, almost gagging. "Those beasts smell horrendous!" His red Eth resonance blazed around him.

Chieftess Beruhn touched Toman again on the shoulder then looked at his uplifted arms. "Here." She held up a piece of soft fragrant cloth to his face. "It has been soaked in healing tinctures." A true Master Healer of her race, she wiped the blood gently from his eyes.

"Thank you, Chieftess." Toman looked at Palan. "That smell is not from the animals. It's from the wielding of sorcery."

"Torghyll?" Palan looked around him. "Here?"

Toman nodded. "Or his servants."

"I think so too." Druin appeared back at the gate of the Steward's residence. He looked at the Chieftess wiping Toman's face, and gasped. "Toman! Are you well? By Ber'eth, you're bleeding!"

Druin turned to the Chieftess who reached into the medicine satchel hanging over her shoulder and held out a fresh cloth towards him.

"Thank you, Chieftess." With head bowed, Druin took the cloth and wiped away the globs of thickening blood from Toman's cheeks. New scratches appeared on his skin, and blood trickled afresh down his face.

"Can you hold it?" Druin looked up at the Linger

shield and flinched at the sight. Once more, Flyers tried desperately to claw their way up the barrier.

Toman shouted out again, fresh blood pouring from the growing deep scratches on his forehead.

"I'm so sorry, Toman. It's still too dangerous for you to drop your Linger, but how long can you take this?" Druin exchanged his cloth for another one from the Chieftess and pressed it against the cuts on his forehead.

The fragrance filled Toman's nostrils.

Keeping his eyes open as best he could, he still needed to keep focusing on his Eth to maintain the size of his shield. Luckily, he had also extended it over Steward Loraimen's entire residence and garden after Lady Banah and Lorann had entered.

"Please, let me assist." Lady Banah returned. Her kind voice felt like a soothing ointment.

"Thank you." Druin handed her the medicine cloth and glanced in the direction of the mountains to the back of the city. "The nightmare. It's coming true!" His entire body went rigid.

Palan stared at Druin. "He doesn't seem to be breathing! And his eyes are twitching in their sockets." Sharp anxiety filled Palan's voice.

A gust of cool ocean air blew strongly across the plaza.

Odd. Toman could have sworn that at the exact same moment Palan became upset, the breeze had appeared.

But what had caused Druin's fright? Toman looked in the direction his Highborn's eyes were focused.

A small group of the silvery-white Huddu-Han was moving directly towards the Linger shield. They probably didn't even see the barrier. Their massive shoulder blades seemed to glide over their upper backs as they walked on their knuckles and hind feet. Long snouts and wrinkled faces did make them look like dogs.

They appeared to be inspecting the houses on the street, picking up and sniffing pieces of food and clothing, dropped as people fled. They drew closer to the blood-splattered shield.

Toman braced himself for what would pass through the connection if they touched it or, hopefully not, tried to break it.

A clap of thunder drew everyone's attention to the air above the plaza. A singular dark column of clouds had formed over the Bay of Limman and began moving towards the city.

Jaw clenched, Druin began shivering as though standing alone in an icy current.

Lady Banah put her arm round his shoulders. "Dear Brother, they can't get in. Fyrst Toman's shield is too powerful for them. They can't reach us."

Did Toman see terror in Druin's eyes?

Standing rigidly, the Highborn didn't move, didn't blink, didn't speak. But yes, a trail of tears began to show on his cheek.

What was he going through? Was Druin's fear so great that it could imprison him in his own mind?

Toman wanted to help but couldn't dissolve his Linger to go to him.

Thin tendrils of lightning began shooting down from the column of clouds, searing across the stones. Steam rose wherever they struck.

Was sorcery also the cause of the strange cloud formation and the downpour?

Toman probed the air with his mind. No. It was a strong source of power, but not sorcery. An ancient foreign strength.

The storm clouds began to spin. The swirling gusts gained strength, blowing about pieces of the debris.

Fear rippled through the Linger connection. The windstorm seemed to jolt the Night Flyers out of their mindless frenzy. They stopped their attack, and were swept off the dome of Toman's shield. Those falling and flopping on the cobbles struggled to return to the air.

The herd of white Huddu-Han paced nervously about, seemingly fearful of returning to the mountains, but also fearing the unnatural column of cloud and rain now pelting his Eth barrier.

Chieftains Beruhn and Ruhand approached Lady Banah with a shimmering cloak of feathers and pointed to Druin.

She draped it over his shoulders and held it round him.

Chieftess Beruhn nodded slowly. "He is trapped in his fear. He needs warmth and the touch of friendship, to pull out of it. But he will. He is very strong."

Druin had never shown fear before, only compassion for others.

To be *trapped in fear*... it didn't take much for Toman to imagine the ability of fear to imprison one's mind. He'd always lived with fear, of making mistakes, of failure, and it had bound him on many occasions. But to be completely frozen within it?

Lady Banah's voice was just loud enough to be heard over the sound of rain on his Linger. "The Huddu-Han have been in his worst nightmares. As a small child. visiting the museum, he was terrified by prepared specimens of the Huddu-Han. He was apprehensive knowing that they lived in the Limmanian interior, but he would never have considered making an excursion, let alone an expedition into their territory. He'd hoped their shy nature would have kept them away from the city, but the flood must have driven them towards the mouth of the river."

Toman looked towards the river, muscles still trembling from the weight of all those Night Flyers that had born down on his Linger.

The roar of the flood had grown less.

In fact, it seemed to slowly stop.

Out in the plaza, long shreds of sail cloth, snapped ropes used for rigging, and splintered crates were coming to rest in muddy puddles on the paving stones. Part of the quay was coated in thick river silt and mangled plants.

"The Steward was right." Palan sounded surprised and relieved. "The Lower Village was untouched by the torrent." The intense flaring of his resonance dimmed to his normal red glow.

The cloudburst disappeared almost as quickly as it had come. No trace of its swirling dark clouds remained in the sky as the sun came back brilliantly, lighting up the puddles of debris, plant branches and pieces of cracked wood.

No Huddu-Han could be seen, so Toman released his Linger and the shield disappeared. A few Night Flyer bodies and droplets of dull red blood fell to the ground. The dog-faced apes had scurried up the escarpment and disappeared in the direction of the river gorge.

Lady Banah gasped, pointing at what looked like small glass pebbles strewn over the plaza. "Druin, do you see them?" Smiling, she turned quickly to him, but her face fell.

Her brother still stood almost motionless, sweating and trembling, with his eyes fixed in the direction the group of White Apes had passed.

She kissed his cheek. "Do you see them, Dear Brother?" She waved her hand again towards the beautiful pieces of stone. "What do you think they could be?" She spoke to him as though in an ongoing conversation.

What looked like thousands of blue stars sparkled in the mud.

"Blue-cast diamonds." Druin spoke weakly. "The rarest of jewels."

30

The Sunken Garden

Arden gasped. "It's Caldere, Professor." Not far below, on the avenue leading to their university building! Panic quivered through her. "He has soldiers with him!"

Professor Gwenndon peered out of the window. "My Lady, let's get out the back way." He glanced up at the terrifying image of the Irrshen in the sky and frowned. "Nightmares becoming reality..."

The underbelly of the gargantuan form glowed from the flames in the Lower City. Lightning cracking back and forth between its glassy antlers, the beast raised its terrible head and roared. Its upper body disappeared into the dense smoke from the inferno below.

"We must hurry, My Lady." The Professor's hand shook as he closed his satchel. Pulling the strap up onto his shoulder, he opened his office door.

They set off down the dark hallway.

"Best not to bring a lantern. We could be seen too easily."

Arden nodded, clutching her case even tighter. The parchments in it were also too important to leave behind. "We need to get to the Sunken Garden. There should be another portal there. Crethingan said that there was."

Gwenndon nodded.

How she hoped she understood Crethingan's words correctly, and could find this portal back into the Temmerung, so that they could escape Barrost.

Each time she'd spent reading in the refreshing coolness of the garden, there had been a particular wall, with plain bas-relief arches carved into the smooth surface, that had always drawn her attention.

Typical Barrostanian architecture usually displayed ostentatious swirls and ornamentation. Crethingan structures, however, were known for their simplicity.

The Professor led the way, walking quickly down the unlit corridor. They descended the stairs to the lower level of the building and made their way to the back entrance.

He paused at the door, pulling out his bunch of keys. The sound of his rapid breathing was magnified in the empty passage. He fumbled, dropping the keys.

The clang of metal against the stone floor sent waves of anguish through Arden. "Please, Professor, let me help." She picked up the keys and placed them back in his hand.

Still shaking and breaths becoming shallow and more rapid, he spoke hoarsely. "It's one of these three brass ones." He handed her the keys to the building's entrances. "But I can't seem to find which one." He sounded frustrated.

But Arden still had her wits about her and quickly tried the first key. It didn't turn in the lock. As she tried the second one, the echo of doors slamming above them made Arden recoil. "They're in the building." The words hissed out of her mouth.

The key turned with a soft clicking sound, and the Professor pushed open the door.

Arden closed it quietly behind them and locked it.

She blinked, letting her eyes adjust to the darkness outside. "This way, Professor. We don't have far to go." From all the conversations with Druin and Lord Dalbonn, she had a fairly good idea where to look for the portal Crethingan had mentioned.

They hurried towards the steps of the low-walled garden.

Arden held her case tightly as she led the way down into the Water Atrium within the Sunken Garden. Water splashed softly in channels on each side of the steps, creating a peaceful backdrop of sound. Designed over a century ago, the water feature still beckoned the visitor to repose and meditate in the shade under the trees.

The Professor kept looking back over his shoulder, gasping for air. "I don't see lantern light, nor do I hear them. But they must be close."

They reached the wide paved square in the Water Atrium. Magnified by the deep concave shape of the Sunken Garden itself, the soft sounds of splashing water filled the sheltered space.

Arden hastened to the wall with the simple arch motifs. The story of Prince Lytwon's gardener discovering a portal behind a similar Crethingan design, fuelled her excitement to find them despite the darkness. She ran her hands hurriedly over the stonework.

Trying to recall every detail of what had happened earlier that day in the Temmerung, she knew that something in her bloodline gave her the ability to awaken dead stones within the World of Visions. They had begun to respond to her voice, and she had formed a passageway through the wall in Druin's vision. The opening had simply come into existence as she spoke. And, with Crethingan's help, she had created the domed shield above her, just by speaking it into existence.

She needed to follow the same procedure here. Exiting the World of Visions had been difficult at first, but simple once she'd understood how crucial Forth-telling was within that domain.

Forth-telling. Steeling herself, she spoke the words clearly. "Portal, open." The flagstones beneath her shook, just as they had in the Temmerung!

With growing excitement she repeated her command, careful not to raise her voice. "I require passage... now."

When she'd spoken those words before, she had wanted to find an exit. This time she needed to return. "I require passage for Professor Gwenndon and myself, to safety within the Temmerung."

Continuing her caress of the stonework, she reiterated her command, touching another decorative arch in the wall. "I require passage..." But she stopped short of finishing and smiled.

The glowing outline of an arched passageway took shape on the stones filling the arch. The masonry became like a vapour, then faded from view. Beyond the opening, the breath-taking iridescent luminosity of the

Temmerung appeared, billowing as if moved by a gentle breeze.

Arden wanted to shout for joy. "Quickly, Professor. Please, go first."

The Professor shook his head and waved her forward. "My Lady, please, you -" He exhaled sharply. Or had he coughed?

She nodded and stepped carefully over the wide stone base of the arch.

The Professor entered after her.

Dark shapes moved in her peripheral vision.

She spun around. Caldere?

"No! You cannot enter here!"

"Why not?" He laughed, holding up a small glistening blade. He stood for a moment, mouth open, staring at the multi-coloured lights. From his belt hung one of Lady Banah's red sachets.

"Portal, close!" Arden waved her hand towards the opening. It filled again, stones quickly piling on stones, trapping two of Caldere's soldiers in a narrow space inside the wall.

The muffled crack of bone splintering and a smothered cry of pain made her stomach turn. They were sealed within the walls!

"Oh no! How dreadful." Arden shook her head. "They should never have followed you."

Caldere didn't seem to hear her, or perhaps he just ignored her as he'd always done in their youth. "You had not been given permission to leave the King's presence." The distant coldness in his voice made him sound as though he spoke from another world.

"King?" The Professor held his hand to his stomach as he sat down on a large stone.

"You and Gwenndon are together?" Her brother's

sudden wry smile made Arden's insides twist. "Well, this will be an exquisite tomb for both of you." He slipped his knife into his belt and pulled out a sword, holding it level with the Professor's neck.

"No! You don't." Arden's shout ignited brilliant flashes of light. Confidence grew in her. "I command the stones to confine you."

"How dare you speak to your superior like—"

Boulders began piling up around him, forming a large cylinder with a thick slab closing the top.

"No, no, no you can't!" He tried hitting the stones away from him, but the small boulders flew back into place, stacking in front of him. He cried out in rage. "No, no!" His anguished cries muffled as the Temmerung sealed him inside the chamber.

Arden's heart pounded.

Her brother would have to stay prisoner here.

All of her senses were, once again, heightened by the shimmering atmosphere of the Temmerung.

She could sense movement, and hear things she couldn't see.

Outside, more guards were running up and down into the Water Atrium of the Sunken Garden.

Her half-brother pounded against his prison with furious indignation.

Uncontrollable terror blazed in the minds of the two guards as their minds went silent and the sound of their heartbeats stopped.

How nightmarish!

Intense nausea swelled in her.

She couldn't help any of them. Not now. They were too dangerous. And her own brother wanted to kill her!

She and Professor Gwenndon needed to get to safety immediately.

If she could only talk to Druin. She longed to be back in his arms.

"Can you help me up, My Lady. I seem to have fallen." The Professor's voice sounded raspy.

"Professor! Are you not well?" The stones flickered with light as she spoke. A dark spot showed on the Professor's jacket. "Professor, you are hurt."

"I'm not certain, My Lady." He struggled to his feet. "It could just be the age of these bones of mine." He put his hand inside his jacket and pulled it back out. Blood dripped from his fingers. "Oh. I think you may be right." He sat back down slowly. "I'm so sorry, My Lady. I will only be an encumbrance now. You'll have to leave me here."

"No, no. No, I can't." Sobs caught in her throat. Her voice began to shake as tears streamed down her face. She couldn't lose the Professor. Not him. He had nurtured her gift, listened to her wild tales of an invisible world just beyond reach. He had been like a kind father.

She swallowed then called out again. "Sir Crethingan! Sir Crethingan, can you hear me? Please. We need you. I need you."

Once again, the rocky cavern responded to her, glowing ever brighter.

"Does that happen every time you speak?" The Professor gazed up towards the ceiling, "This is a vast empty cave until you say something. Then the walls, the floor and even the ceiling, glow in response. It's a wondrous sight to behold."

Arden nodded. But at that moment the only thing she wanted to see was Crethingan approaching.

"My Lady, your voice has such power here. How did you acquire this power, this authority over these stones?"

"Sir Crethingan said I was *The Legacy*, the culmination

of all the tribes of Palanth-Orron. In my veins flow the blood of the three different Palanth-Orric tribes."

Professor Gwenndon gasped. "The Legacy? All tribes? That means, that could only mean... also the Bohdne?"

"Yes." She continued. "He said, *Through your veins the blood of all Palanth-Orren flows. Palanshen, Orrenic and Bohdnian. You are the culmination of all the tribes of Palanth-Orron.*"

The Professor's hands trembled even more strongly than before. "My Lady, do you know what you are bringing about? Remember the inscription from Warningen House... the Atonement?" He closed his eyes and slumped backwards.

"Professor!" Her shout ignited blazing colours within the stones. "No. No." She knelt and placed a hand on his chest.

He was still breathing.

But so much blood. He was losing too much.

Hideous laughter filled the air. Impressions assaulted her. Depraved madness. Insatiable hunger. Burning with starvation.

The Greinen!

They had to escape now! Immediately!

Toman's words had been, 'Forth-telling, the power of speaking things into existence.' But he hadn't said anything about how far that could extend.

Could she visualise a destination and demand to go there?

But where would be safe?

"Temmerung, take us to safety, to help!"

The air around became glassy, blurring her vision. The flickering stones faded from sight.

It felt like moments later, but she couldn't be certain how long, the atmosphere cleared again, and she found herself beside a stone wall, kneeling next to the Professor.

"Where are we?"

"You are in my chamber in the Sunken Garden at Warningen House." Crethingan's voice was unmistakable.

Arden turned around as he pushed against the loosely stacked stones of the wall, and they tumbled. "It would be safest for your instructor to stay here, in the care of Prince Lytwon's staff." The inner lights of his crystalline body sparkled. "But we should leave quickly, before they start asking questions." He pointed up flights of steps in the wide garden, where liveried servants had appeared, running towards them. "I will help you to the next portal."

Arden assisted the Professor to sit down outside on some of the fallen masonry. "I'm going to leave you here. We will meet up again soon, I'm sure." She hoped they would. She stepped back over the rubble into the chamber.

"Now, speak again to the Temmerung. Tell it of your need. Command it. Quickly now."

She nodded. "Take me to safety. Take me to Druin."

Her insides felt peculiar, as though she were suddenly falling through air.

Then the sensation stopped.

Through a cave entrance, a forest dripped with mud. A circular portal embedded in the stones around her sparkled intensely then went dark. For a moment, the glowing antlers of a giant elk appeared, then faded.

The Irrshen? She shook her head.

Broken branches hung from the trunks of snapped trees. Huge boulders lay in a river engorged with rushing water.

What a relief. She still had her case!
But where was she?

31

Syngordia

The Meandering Path tavern was already two days behind them, but Lytwon couldn't stop going over and over the conversation with his friend, Petar.

The embarrassment at having to borrow coin to continue this journey still irritated Lytwon. But the gemstones starting to glow? They had shimmered with inner lights, right in his palm!

Since then, every time he'd looked down into his pocket, the faceted stones still gave off a sparkling bluish light.

Doubts and fears riddled Lytwon's mind.

Did the diamonds possess some kind of power? Were

the flickering lights within them an omen of good, or of evil? It would probably endanger his mission to warn his cousin, Richarr, if he showed them to anyone else. But they were the undeniable proof of his message. Palanshen were collaborating with Mendelon against Syngordia! Orren with Palanshen against Orren. Unbelievable.

Staring out of the carriage window, he sighed deeply. So far, the only detectable military activity was that in Norssum along the border. Since then, the landscape had changed from the vast marshes of the Marden Morath to the sylvan hills of Dennelon in northern Syngordia.

Knowing that Warningen House was just a hundred leagues to the north made him homesick for the comfort of his peaceful residence. And for good food, the way Cook Marta always prepared it.

Over the woodlands, dark clouds forming again? Cloudbursts seemed to be coming more often than usual. They needed to take advantage of the present good weather, and keep their steady pace, to reach Lord Blenn Fayren at Hordle House before afternoon. Later everything would certainly be drenched with rain.

Hordle House. Lytwon rubbed his chin. Hopefully Blenn had left behind what had transpired with Verana. A servant back then at Hordle House, she had been from a commoner family, Fera'Genglic.

But she had been anything but common.

Blenn hadn't agreed with him, and the argument that had erupted between them had almost ended in a brawl. But they had been so young, and that was years ago. Time healed, if allowed to.

The years of bliss with Verana were the most beautiful times of Lytwon's life. He had never imagined growing old without her.

The driver tapped on the roof.

Rugger peered out of his window. "We're almost there. I can see a gatehouse just around this curve."

Head leaning against the upholstered carriage wall, Stilsh opened his eyes. "Are you still *Sir Brummel* here? Or can we address you properly with these people? Are they trustable?"

For a moment, Lytwon's mind went blank.

But surely the Fayren family had stayed loyal to the crown. They could lose everything, if found collaborating with Norssum to remove Richarr from the throne. Or… the idea made Lytwon shudder… could they be expecting to gain more land by helping the invaders? Surely not. Despite the grievances with the Double Crown, they had always been faithful Syngordians.

"Yes, I think we will be able to trust them. Blenn will recognise me anyway, so you may return to calling me by my proper name, Fathringen."

Rugger nodded. "Your Highness."

"Prince Fathringen." Stilsh nodded as well.

"Thank you." Lytwon was grateful to Mischul for sending two such good men to accompany him. "The Festival of Ashwond starts tomorrow. To think that a king of Mendelon would have chosen the feast celebrating the unification of the Double Crowns of Syngordia to kill the living symbol of those crowns."

"Or to destabilise the whole of the Northern Horn." Rugger's frown grew deeper. "But he has a son, young Prince Gordyn, as heir. If perchance only King Richarr is killed, the country will still have a reigning monarch. "

Lytwon shuddered at the idea forming in his mind. Would they harm little Gordyn?

Stilsh also looked out of the window, as if searching for something. "I wonder where we can get more information about the troops along the border. I didn't get the impression that they would mobilise immediately, but that they were close."

The rhythmic dull clopping of the horned-beasts' hooves on the earthen road changed, clipping loudly on what must be stone paving.

The sudden smoothness of the carriage ride was soothing to the ache in Lytwon's spine. He felt into his pocket and pulled out the note Petar had written.

Even though he'd read it a few times over the past two days, Lytwon unfolded the note again and studied the elegant wording. Petar was asking Blenn for a personal favour in providing rooms and support for Lytwon to reach the festival on time. He hadn't written the reason for needing to reach Dyndyll Castle before the Ashwond festivities began. Lytwon would have to explain that himself.

But should he mention the whole of the plot he'd discovered?

About the payoffs and the Limmanian diamonds?

Blenn would of course need to know about the troops amassing along the border.

But about the sorcerer?

Sighing deeply, Lytwon carefully closed the note and tucked it back away.

The carriage stopped and the driver spoke for a moment with a gatekeeper. A light tap came on the windowpane and the driver asked Lytwon if he would show his face.

"Prince Fathringen?" The voice sounded familiar, but feebler than Lytwon remembered.

Lytwon opened the window. "Winnt? Is that still you? You still work for Lord Fayren!"

A much older man than the last time he had seen him,

the gatekeeper was now white-haired, and the skin of his wrinkled face had a greyish hue. But his welcoming smile and twinkling eyes were the same as when Lytwon was a lad. His face brought back pleasant memories of carefree youth. Lytwon and Blenn had shared happy times at both his residence at Dyndyll Castle, and at the Hordle House estate.

At least, before Richarr's advisors had Lytwon banished from the court of Dyndyll.

Lywton had been enraged when forced to keep his distance. All his childhood and youth, Dyndyll Castle had hosted the best parties. Pretty girls as well as eligible ladies had always attended. The first sight he had of Warningen House was of a huge angular stone structure, a prison, with too many gardens.

Verana had changed all that for him.

She had even changed him.

"Welcome, Prince Fathringen. Welcome!" Winnt waved towards the area just inside the gates. "Driver, wait here with your carriage, and let me send word to the house."

Lytwon smiled. How pleasant, to be welcomed back in familiar surroundings. And yet it had been so many years since he'd seen Blenn, maybe the quarrel they'd had was still fresh in his mind. It was in Lytwon's.

As a young man, he had dared rescue Verana from the life of a commoner servant.

Even though banished from the Dyndyll court, he'd continued attending parties at Hordle House where Verana's beauty and grace had become the focus of conversation for some young rather unscrupulous noblemen. Unfortunately, one had been Blenn.

"You may proceed." Winnt called out from the gate. "They have signalled from the main house."

"Thank you," Lytwon called from his window as they started down the entrance road. Tension slowly ebbed from his arms and legs. They didn't have time to spend the evening there, but perhaps he would have a comfortable bed later in a tavern. Such simple pleasures had become cherished indulgences on this trip.

The carriage stopped, and the horned-beasts bayed sharply as if frightened.

Rugger and Stilsh flung the door open and leapt down, hands on their swords.

Lytwon looked out of each of the windows. "What is it?"

Unusual shadows passed over Mischul's men and they looked up.

"The Uccell, Your Highness." Rugger pointed skywards then lowered his hand. "But they've flown out of view now."

Somehow the knowledge of the massive lizard-like Firstborn flying overhead gave Lytwon a profound sense of comfort.

He exited the carriage and looked towards the grand house.

Blenn, his wife and what looked like his entire household stood at attention in front of the entrance.

Walking slowly towards them, goosebumps rose on Lytwon's skin. Why would an unannounced visit be greeted with such formality?

Blenn bowed, then his wife, followed by the servants and liveried footmen.

"Welcome, Your Highness. It's good to see you again." His old friend's smile looked genuine and sincere.

Lytwon held out his hand. "Thank you, Blenn, most sincerely. Please forgive this uninvited intrusion."

"No bother, old boy. No bother." Did Lytwon note tension, perhaps fear, in his voice?

"You know my wife, Lady Catrina."

"Yes. Of course. A pleasure, My Lady." Lytwon kissed her outstretched hand.

Lytwon pointed to Rugger and Stilsh. "Blenn, these are two of my most trusted companions. Soldiers from the Lord Protector of Ydassum, Mischul Dalbonn. Rugger, Haydann and Stilsh, Goran."

They bowed and spoke together. "My Lord."

Blenn nodded, then indicated the young man with particularly handsome features to his left. He reminded Lytwon of Toman Foggling. "Let me introduce you to another special guest of ours. This is Lord Danuel Yldshimman, from Horróglоryn."

The young man bowed. "Your Highness."

32

HORDLE HOUSE

"Once again, thank you my old friend, for your hospitality." Relief began to ease the tension in Lytwon's body and, although grateful to Blenn, a slight sense of apprehension nagged in the back of his mind.

Blenn silently nodded his response as they walked down the wide hallway.

The paintings hadn't been moved since the last time Lytwon had been there, over twenty years ago. Blenn's taste had always been particularly exquisite in his collections of farm still-lifes and scenes depicting vast fields of ripening grain. Simple bucolic life possessed an enchanting untamed beauty.

One of the Hordle House liveried footmen pushed open two large doors to a spacious room full of books.

A library. Lytwon couldn't remember ever having been in there.

Blenn pointed at a long table surrounded with heavy chairs, then turned towards Lytwon and Mischul's men. "We can talk freely in here."

Still casual and polite, but the subtle tension in his voice caught Lytwon's attention. Was something amiss?

Servants bustled into the room, quickly pulling out seats for each of them. After setting out a tray with five finely-cut crystal goblets, they placed bottles of what looked like brandy on the table. Bowing, they exited silently, closing the door behind them.

Blenn walked to the head of the table and stood behind a chair. He bade Lytwon take the place to his right, and Lord Danuel the one to his left. He waited for the two of them to be seated. Then, sitting down himself, he nodded for Stilsh and Rugger to be seated as well.

A few moments of strained silence passed. Blenn poured them each a drink as they studied each other.

Their arrival hadn't seemed to surprise Blenn or his guest, Lord Danuel.

Curiosity dissolved Lytwon's sense of decorum. He couldn't keep the obvious question to himself any longer. "Blenn, did you know I was coming?"

Blenn gestured his affirmation with an unreadable face. "But what brings you to Hordle House, Littie. If I may still call you that?"

"Of course." After so many years, hearing his old nickname being used again, first by Petar and now by Blenn, gave Lytwon a pleasant sense of the friendships he'd had in bygone days. "Of course, my old friend. Of course."

Slipping a hand into his pocket, Lytwon cupped the jewels in his fist. They were still slightly warm.

He took a deep breath, steeling himself. He might as well get this over with. No backing out now.

"Blenn, I fear an attempt will be made on Richarr's life, on the occasion of the Festival of Ashwond tomorrow. I found a plot against him." Lytwon paused, studying his friend's face.

Blenn didn't move. He didn't even blink.

Neither did Lord Danuel.

A chill ran up Lytwon's back. "You mean...? You knew already? About King Fillip's plans, and the connection to Barrost?"

Lord Danuel nodded. "Back in Mendelon, Prince Palandred suspected nefarious machinations against the Double Crown because of his brother's long-rooted suspicion that Richarr orchestrated their mother's demise. And, because so many of his brother's activities were tightly guarded secrets, the Prince asked me to investigate. I followed Fillip's men here."

Lytwon shook his head. Brother against brother? A great house divided... history always repeated itself. The dilemma that poor lad Palandred must be living... The last time Lytwon had seen his distant relative was at Richarr and Isabella's wedding celebration. "So, Palandred knows?"

"He suspected." Lord Danuel nodded again, looking from Blenn back to Lytwon. "But he has been kept at a distance, told to mind his own business. All strategies to keep him ignorant of what was going on."

Blenn stared at his clasped hands on the smooth dark table. "We also know about the troops in eastern Norssum, not far from the border, but many details are lacking."

"I... I..." Lytwon couldn't understand why his face suddenly grew hot. "In Barrost, I intercepted a payoff from Mendelon to the Vandrian Kingship, for the placement of troops along the border with Syngordia and, I fear, there is a plot for the ultimate demise of Richarr."

He took a gulp of the brandy, then slipped his hand into his pocket, withdrawing the note that had been passed between Lord Galdyssen and Lord Berlen at the welcoming gala in Barrost. He pressed it open then handed it to Blenn.

Payment hidden in the chapel.
Troops on the northern border.
Awaiting signal from Mendelon.
R will be eliminated at the Festival.

Showing the wrinkled parchment to Lord Danuel, Blenn's hands began to tremble.

Lytwon felt back into his pocket and clasped the stones. "The bribe was in the rarest gems known, blue-cast diamonds." He held out his hand and let the stones tumble onto the wooden tabletop.

Once again, the nonplussed reaction Lytwon expected never came. A shiver ran through him. Were Blenn and Lord Danuel loyal? "You, you aren't working with—"

"Of course not." Blenn's answer was sharp, but his tone sounded more exhausted than angry. "Richarr is an ass, but I don't want him dead."

Lord Danuel shook his head, but a heaviness seemed to push his shoulders down. "No."

Now stern-faced, Blenn reached into his cloak and withdrew a small bloodwood case inlaid with cut shells. He clicked open the lid. Blue-cast diamonds glowed, giving off their unmistakeable sparkling light.

Lytwon and Rugger gasped at the same moment.

Frowning, Stilsh sucked air through his clenched teeth.

"We have also been contacted about the plot." Blenn frowned. "I accepted these to give the impression of compliance. For some strange reason, I feared to oppose the Storryn who brought me the message and *gift.* He was like no other Storryn I've ever met."

"Torghyll!" Rugger pounded a fist into his other open hand.

"Torghyll?" Blenn stared at Rugger.

"My Lord, Torghyll is a sorcerer from Athlonia who disguises himself as a blind Storryn. Long white hair and all."

All colour drained from Blenn's face. "Athlonia? Are you certain?" His voice grew weak as he closed the box and replaced it inside his cloak. "Athlonia? Old women's fables coming true? How? When?"

Lytwon stood from his chair. "Did he touch you? Come in contact with your skin?"

Shaking his head, Blenn began to exude anxiety. "No. But he had strange powers... Of persuasion. His voice seemed to penetrate deep into the mind." Blenn touched the side of his head. "Definitely evil, but I couldn't describe to you exactly how or what his powers were, but they made us all afraid."

"Good that you weren't touched!" Lytwon exhaled in relief. "The sorcerer has also been recruiting others by means of very dark powers. Your visitor could have been one of them. But you are probably safe from their curse." He hated to continue recounting the living nightmares, but they needed to know more. "I'm not certain how long Torghyll and his cohorts have infiltrated the Northern Horn, but they have been here for a while. They look almost identical to our gentle Storryn, but their eyes are not pure white like all Storryn's. They're like the foggy blue eyes of a dead animal." He paused, glancing from the pale face of Blenn to Lord Danuel's scowl.

"They are using an ancient Skyllian curse called the Beàl'Toht, that is transmitted by touch, but the scar it leaves isn't the Scarab Wasp of the Alldai, rather, it looks like the antlers of the Athlonian Irrshen. A young lad from Landsend on board one of the Highborns' barges from Ydassum succumbed to the curse, and attempted to murder the young Lord Druin Méndrensynn." Lytwon shuddered at the memory.

For an instant, his emotions threatened to get the better of him. A tear formed in his eye. How he missed Banah and Druin, those precious children.

"The lad had been hired in Turicum, so I assume that Torghyll, or I fear some other hellacious Athlonian being of his ilk, had been in the capital city for some time."

Lord Danuel rubbed his face with his hands. "And they look like Storryn?" His chest began to rise and fall with rapid breaths. "I haven't seen a Storryn in Mendelon since I was a child. I thought they'd all passed away."

"Bless a Storryn to receive a blessing." Rugger quoted the old proverb. His gruff voice seemed to rumble through the room. "In Turicum they are rare, but still around. When one is in the city, they are usually near the docks where a lot of travellers and merchants pass. They are generally treated with the greatest respect."

Anger bristled in Lytwon. "That's probably why Torghyll chose the guise of a Storryn. It would give him free and unchecked movement in all our lands."

Lord Danuel also stood from the table and began pacing in front of the bookshelves. "Prince Palandred asked me to keep an eye open in Mendelon City. I became aware of a small band of King Fillip's men and followed them here. Four of them. They were cloaked as merchant travellers and kept their swords hidden. I overheard their arrival date. The inauguration of the festival tomorrow."

Something about the young man was definitely familiar. Had Lytwon met him before? He had more than a passing resemblance to Fyrst Toman. But other things were more pressing. "Blenn, can you help us? Dyndyll Castle is, what, four or five hours from here?"

"Yes of course. But I don't have any troops at Hordle House that I could send to accompany you."

"I won't need troops, thank you. They could trigger an alarm to enemies of the crown. If I can get to the grounds safely, I will be able to talk to my cousin and warn him. But the urgency of our mission is paramount, and we should leave today before sunset. We should have a few hours of daylight."

Lord Danuel stopped pacing. "May I accompany you? We could leave immediately."

Lytwon blinked in surprise. He recognised Danuel. "Lord Danuel, you attended the wedding feast of Isabella and Richarr, with Palandred, didn't you?"

Lord Danuel's face fell and he closed his eyes, turning his head. He seemed to struggle for an instant but regained composure and nodded. "Yes. Yes, I did." He looked back to Lytwon, then Blenn. "If My Lord Fayren would allow us fresh steeds, we could depart shortly."

Quickly draining their goblets, Rugger and Stilsh also stood and pushed their chairs back under the table.

Loud knocks came at the door.

Blenn looked up. "Enter."

The door swung open slightly. The head of one of

his footmen appeared. "My Lord!" He gulped for air. "Creatures from legends! Three of them in front of the house!"

Lytwon gathered up the diamonds he'd displayed on the table and put them back in his pocket.

They all hurried through the hallway to the entrance and walked out under the arches of the portico.

"Menne Gootay." Rugger looked at Stilsh.

"The Uccell!" Lytwon smiled and inclined his head. "Welcome, Lords G'nallun, B'noru and B'h'rants."

Flanked by his fellow Uran Draigana, Lord G'nallun nodded, extending a clawed fist.

A fist? Why his closed hand?

Then the Uccell Lord opened his hand, offering Lytwon a small scroll.

He opened it quickly. "It's from the Highborn, Druin Méndrensynn!"

Lytwon scanned the script. "Oh my."

Blenn and Lord Danuel stared at him.

Lytwon sighed. "Barrost has fallen. Lady Sofian murdered her husband and has declared herself King of Barrostania."

33

The Blessing

What had happened out in the street? Gently folding the Riddern's glistening feather cape and handing it to the Chieftess, Druin couldn't understand his own reaction, and why his heart was still beating erratically. Never had he expected to encounter the Huddu-Han in the city!

He stopped for a moment in the Steward's courtyard, letting Banah and Palan walk ahead.

Why had all his muscles become painfully stiff, practically immovable?

Fear did very strange things to the mind.

But he'd been in many frightening circumstances before and not frozen.

The scene from within Toman's Linger flashed before his eyes...

The Night Flyers crashing against the transparent Eth shield, screeching and clawing.

White Apes coming straight at him!

Scenes from the nightmares in his childhood had seemed to become reality. Encountering the dreaded Huddu-Han, then drowning in a terrifying flood.

Terror had exploded in him.

He'd thought the frantic pounding of his heart would break his ribs.

His memory failed him from that point.

His vision had blurred. Not blindness, but not seeing.

Strange voices had echoed around him.

Time stood still.

Then someone touched his face.

His beloved sister had called out to him from somewhere. Her voice had seemed close by.

His sight had then returned and he could speak again.

He sighed with relief. Thankfully, it was over and hopefully wouldn't happen again. He proceeded quickly across the courtyard.

Banah, Maiden Lorann and Palan were already at the Steward's door.

Steward Loraimen was still standing at the gate, instructing a few of his servants about collecting the gems outside in the plaza. "Clear up those broken crates but bring the stones to me here once you've washed and dried them."

They bowed and hurried back into the street.

The Steward smiled at Druin. "Please." He pointed towards the residence. "Please, come in. Welcome!"

Toman and the Riddern joined the group at his door.

They followed the Steward into his grand house, and up two flights of stairs. At the top, the landing led to a luxurious meeting room, with several young manservants standing to attention. Facing the plaza was a semi-circular wall of large, mullioned windows. In the middle stood doors opening onto a wide balcony. "My Lady, My Lords," the Steward opened the tall glass-panelled doors and invited them to follow him outside. "We can view the plaza from here."

A gentle breeze wafted across the room. The peculiar, earthy odour of river mud reminded Druin of alluvial valleys in the Cloud Forests of Auyana.

He stepped out onto the balcony and smiled. Indeed, the view from there was excellent.

The wide-open space of the plaza below was still majestic even though devoid of statuary or fountains. Behind it, the Bay of Limman sparkled with the reflected sun.

On the other side of the bay, the outer rim of craggy outcrops formed a protective barrier for the harbour. Rugged. Tranquil. Beautiful.

In this setting, the crippling ordeal from earlier dissipated and peace settled back into his body.

Steward Loraimen turned his back to the plaza and faced them. "As you can see, the city was spared the flood. The embankment constructed by the first Orrenic settlers has stood the test of centuries in protecting us. They first built defences in fear of Athlonian invasions, then Limmania built for elegance and beauty. The savage architecture left by the blood-thirsty Skylle has mostly been dismantled, and the materials used elsewhere in the beautification of the city." Steward Loraimen beamed with pride. "The Skylle however loved their gardens. You will see traces of their style, and plants from the Alldai on our tour together."

Druin's interest was aroused. Plants from the southern desert regions of the Great Continent so far north?

"The upper portion of the plaza was completely spared so the celebration of your visit will continue unhindered. Tomorrow evening a concert will be held in your honour. And the day after, a true Limmanian feast in the city's banquet hall."

Lorann grinned at Banah.

"Thank you, Steward Loraimen." Were his sister's cheeks turning pink? "But the flood, and the clean-up? Surely we should cancel some events. I wouldn't want to inconvenience you."

He waved his hand through the air. "Nothing of it, My Lady. No imposition, just a few hours of swilling and sweeping and all our preparations can continue."

"Your rooms are ready, if you would like to have your luggage brought from the Sindrea Isabella, my manservants will show you to your suites just down the hallway. They all face the bay."

"Steward?" Palan's voice seemed to startle the Steward.

"Yes, Your Highness?" He bowed then lifted his head, his chin jutting out slightly.

"Who are these 'children' people were shouting about?"

The Steward blinked rapidly, his face losing colour. "Your Highness?" He shook his head gently. "You are asking me? Begging your pardon, Your Highness, but wouldn't it be more appropriate if I were to ask you that question?"

Palan frowned. "I have no idea what you are talking

about." Irritation simmered in his voice. "I asked you a question that merits a clear answer."

Druin triggered his Eth. His blue spectrum would help him sense whether the Steward was being truthful.

Toman looked at him for an instant, then nodded his head slightly. He turned back towards the bay, and continued staring in the direction of Palan's ship at the end of the quay.

"Pardon, Your Highness. Please, pardon me." Steward Loraimen bowed low. When he straightened again, his hands were shaking. "Your Highness, they are referring to the children recruited into your special schools for the gifted in Eth. Most have never returned home. The few that did return told us that they were sent back because they demonstrated no further potential and their clear Lingers had begun to show colour." The Steward's eyes glazed over with a hardness. "They didn't know what happened to the others."

"Clear Lingers?" Toman appeared visibly shaken.

"What?" The intensity of Palan's outburst made Druin's stomach tighten.

Banah gasped.

Lorann put a hand on her Lady's arm.

"What are you talking about!" Palan seethed. "I have never heard of such a school, nor recruitment of the gifted! Where has this preposterous idea come from?"

The Steward flinched. "From Mendelon. King Fillip sends recruiters every year to test our children's Eth resonances. Those with clear Lingers are taken to special schools."

Banah looked nervously from Palan to Steward Loraimen. "Please, Steward, would you explain?" Her peaceful tone had an immediate calming effect on the growing tension.

"You didn't know..." Muttering to himself, the Steward kept shaking his head. He faced Palan, the subtle wrinkles around his eyes looked taut. "Your Highness, since the reign of your mother, Mendelon City has sent Akkoren to read our children's Eth colours. All are tested. At first, it was considered the highest honour, because the request was directly from the monarch. But over the years, many families began to hide their children, because rarely did their sons and daughters ever return from these schools." The Steward looked genuinely upset now. "King Fillip makes the request each year. Your Highness, please forgive me. I was convinced you knew all this."

"I believe you." Druin looked at Palan. "I believe he is speaking in earnest."

"Fillip!" Palan scowled, talking in a hoarse whisper. "And my mother!" He rubbed his face then pushed his hair back. His breaths came erratically. "Incredible! I can't believe my brother and my mother have been doing this!" The anguish in his friend's voice pierced Druin. Palan obviously accepted the Steward's words as the truth.

"Where do you think the children are?" Once again, Banah's gentle voice flowed over them like a soothing ointment. "Is there any way to find out where they are, and bring them home?"

The Steward's eyelids began to twitch, and a tear ran down his cheek. He shook his head slowly. "We are never given an address of the school. Never allowed to visit the children—"

"Do you have any brandy?" Palan strode through the open balcony doors, back into the meeting room.

The Steward hurried after him.

Banah, Lorann and Toman followed them inside.

Druin remained on the balcony with the Riddern Chieftains and leant against the balustrade.

Chieftess Beruhn turned slowly towards Druin.

He quickly lowered his eyes.

"Highborn, the Emerald Spiders we procured in Barrost were taken from our quarters. They are dangerous." The Chieftain's arm tattoos rippled agitatedly as both he and his female turned and walked back into the meeting room.

Druin sighed. "Hopefully Prince Palandred will be able to make some enquiries when back on board." A weariness was settling into his arms and legs, as the experience with the White Apes grew more distant. He filled his lungs with the salty air. Salty ocean breezes refreshed in a different way from those off the Great Inner Sea at Turicum.

Below, the long and splintered boards of what must have been part of a boat hull, plus all the broken pieces of crates, had already been stacked in piles at the side of the plaza.

People were now gathering the hundreds of blue-cast gems. Others followed, throwing buckets of water on the muddy paving stones, and brushing away the thin layer of sticky river sludge.

Druin shook his head. He'd never seen so many uncut diamonds before!

Out in the bay, just beyond the long quay protecting Palan's ship, an island of wreckage floated slowly in the dull brown stream of the river. Off to the right, a small group of Mendelonian soldiers were making their way down from the river gorge.

He walked back inside.

Banah was engaging the Steward in conversation. "It would only take a few moments. I would really like to."

She focused on Druin. “Dear Brother, I would like us to bless the ancient shipbuilding ruins, for complete restoration.”

“And so would I.” Toman added.

Something about his sister’s sudden smile gave Druin the impression that Toman’s offer to join her was all a part of her intention. It was understandable. She would certainly also want to tap into Toman’s powerful Gebayt Bithen.

As he lowered his brandy glass, Palan’s mouth stayed open slightly.

“I would gladly join you.” Druin looked at her in amazement. What an example she was, always encouraging and uplifting others.

The Steward started counting on his fingers, mumbling to himself. “We could work it into the scheduled festivities before the concert.”

“Please forgive me, Steward Loraimen, but I would prefer that we pray privately over the shipyards. Not as an official act of the next Lanfothe of Ydassum, but as Banah Méndrensynn.”

Her modesty struck Druin. The depth of her humbleness never ceased to astonish and inspire.

Standing in silence, the Steward appeared bewildered at first. Then he nodded. “Of course, My Lady.”

“I didn’t see a bridge from the Lower Village over to the ancient shipyards, so I would like to go to the embankment to pray.”

The Steward looked slightly flushed at first, then a smile appeared on his face. “Of course, My Lady. Thank you. Let me organise some men to clear a path to the wall.”

“I am grateful.” Banah bowed.

It didn’t take the Steward long to have a way cleared.

First, near his residence, a few carcasses of Night Flyers were carried away. But once they were back out of the city gate and walking towards the embankment, it became apparent that the floodwaters hadn't even come near the Lower Village. There was no debris. And the flagstones were already dry again after the cloudburst.

Walking alongside her male, Chieftess Beruhn pointed to the massive stone embankment wall. Her deep guttural speech held a tone of interest. Chieftain Ruhand nodded back to her.

Palan paused for an instant, staring at the Steward's men still gathering the gemstones from the plaza.

Drawing closer to the wall, it became apparent that the wide steps and a walkway had been cut directly out of the huge stones. The path on top led back towards the steep valley of the Limman Folumpor.

The Steward stopped at the base of the steps and looked up along the embankment. "Good, the guards are gone." He spoke in a low voice. A slight smile appeared on his face. He pointed towards the top of the wall and continued. "Just a few paces and you should find a flat area appropriate for speaking your prayers."

"Thank you." This time Toman spoke first. The tips of his fingers already glowed with the power of Eth.

Banah inclined her head. "Our appreciation, Steward Loraimen. Would you like to join us?"

He blinked, then nodded. "It would be my pleasure."

They climbed the steps of the embankment to a pathway along the top. The view across the Limman Folumpor revealed piles of broken branches and the splintered hulls of cargo ships. But it seemed as though the force of the river had pushed most of the debris towards the mouth of the river already. The remaining flotsam reminded Druin of rotted, tattered tent canvas.

A chill ran through him. Were there also Mendelonian uniforms in the wreckage?

"Here we are." Steward Loraimen pointed to a paved area a short distance along the wall.

It looked like the old foundations of a demolished structure, perhaps some sort of a pavilion overlooking the river, but the walls and roof no longer existed. Druin looked around. Even in the state of abandoned disrepair, it was obvious that the shipyards across the river, together with the Lower Village and plaza, had once been part of an exceptionally beautiful city.

Further along the opposite bank, there seemed to be a perfectly formed circle of carefully-hewn stones. Definitely of more modern style and not a part of the ruins around them, it reminded Druin of a pit for the sport of fighters.

"May I, My Lady?" Toman raised his glowing hands.

Banah nodded, smiling.

"Dear Father, I pronounce restoration here, of hearts and histories, of commerce and prosperity." A massive wave of shimmering lights ignited around them. Toman's Gebayt Bithen. It was huge, and magnificent. The wave began to spin around them like a curtain of glistening liquid light. A gentle wind blew.

Each going down on one knee, the Riddern Chieftains bowed low, then raised their hands. Their colourful feather capes whipped back and forth in the air currents.

Druin also lifted his hands in blessing. His sister and Lorann did the same.

Palan stood stiffly and looked down.

Switching his weight from one foot to another, the Steward muttered under his breath. "Oh dear, oh dear. What will Mendelon say?"

Toman's voice began to echo strongly around them.

He was extending his Linger over the shipyards, the plaza, and the entire Lower Village! The vast curtain of sparkling light began to shimmer with iridescence.

Shouts came from the city, joyous sounds of wonderment. People began pouring back out into the plaza, looking up and pointing at the phenomenon.

Druin looked around the area. A sense of change permeated the air.

Someone appeared further down the embankment pathway.

A woman was walking towards them. Her dress was smeared knee-high with mud.

Her red-blonde hair glowed in the sun.

Peculiar, though... she was carrying a scarlet case pressed to her chest.

That case looked like the one Arden had in the Temmerung!

Druin's heart felt as if it would explode with joy.

"Banah! It's Arden! She's here! Here in Limmania!"

34

Festival of Ashwond

"Oh my, oh my." Lytwon frowned at Druin's fine script on the small piece of parchment.

It was difficult to even grasp its full meaning. A shiver ran up his spine and he read aloud.

"Barrost has fallen. Lady Sofian murdered her husband, and has declared herself King of Barrostania"

Lytwon rubbed the stubble on his chin. Things were changing faster than he had ever expected. "But I see there is a smaller comment scribbled at the bottom." Squinting, he tried to focus on the second message.

"The sign of the Irrshen is over the city."

Rugger recoiled. "Over the city, Your Highness?" The veins in his neck bulged. "We were there just days ago."

"Terrible news. Terrible." Stilsh pounded a fist against his leg. "How long until it invades the whole continent?"

"The Irrshen?" Sir Danuel stared at the note in Lytwon's hands then looked up at Mischul's men. "What does this mean? Irrshen?"

Handing the scroll to Blenn, Lytwon couldn't stop his hands from shaking. "It's an ancient Athlonian symbol, The Stag of Death. A terrible omen of utter annihilation. The Lord Protector spoke of it as 'a manifestation of the evil will of the Great Sorcerer Lords of Athlonia.' It takes on a form resembling the Great Maned Elk."

"Athlonia!" Blenn gasped as he pressed open the parchment. He shook his head, and his chest seemed to sag. "Nightmares coming true. Barrost must be in complete chaos. It won't be long until the troops along our border are given orders to march! Our few soldiers won't stand a chance, outnumbered as they are." He passed the note to Sir Danuel. "We need to get Prince Lytwon on the road right away. Richarr must be informed of these developments. Perhaps then he will get off his lazy backside and protect his country, instead of enriching the coffers of every brothel and ale house in Syngordia!" Scowling, he called for his footmen.

"Lord Blenn, I will be accompanying him." The sternness in Sir Danuel's voice gave Lytwon a sense of comfort. One more able-bodied man at his side would be an advantage in this perilous undertaking.

So much to do in so little time. Lytwon shook his head. "That poor girl, Isabella, and the boy Gordyn... We need to get them out of Syngordia immediately. Perhaps anonymous asylum in Immen? The Abbaths should be able to offer them refuge." Surely they could get her and the child out, if unhindered by Richarr.

Sir Danuel stared at Lytwon. "Yes. In Immen they should be safe from this brewing storm. We should depart immediately."

"Yes, of course." Blenn turned to an approaching footman. "Transfer their luggage to my carriage and bring it around here. And tell cook to give them something for their trip. Bread, cheese, a bottle of wine."

The man bowed then hurried away.

Blenn looked at Lytwon unblinking. "If Lady Soffian rules now in Barrost, surely she had to invoke the council of the other Quaterni. We heard nothing of the gathering to select a new Vandrian head of state." He shook his head. "And she should have observed the obligatory period of mourning after the death of the Steward."

"Neither have I heard of any assembly of the Kingship to vote on a new Steward." Lytwon shook his head. "King. She declared herself *king*!

Blenn's face lost all expression. "King? Not Steward?" He sighed deeply, staring at the rows of columnar trees lining his driveway. "Her shift of styling...it's an ominous sign." He sighed again." You're a good man, Lyttie, to risk your life like this."

The clipping of hooves on the paving stones signalled the approach of their carriage. From around the side of the great house, four harnessed steeds appeared, pulling a shiny dark brown coach trimmed in black wood.

Blenn stepped back and bowed, raising his voice slightly. "Speed and protection on your way, Your Highness."

All the members of his household bowed and a woman in a white apron stepped forward with a covered basket.

"Thank you." Stilsh nodded and took the basket.

Opening the carriage door, Rugger offered Lytwon his arm.

"Thank you." He accepted Rugger's assistance and climbed in.

Lytwon indicated that Rugger should take the seat next to him.

"Please." Sir Danuel motioned for Stilsh to enter before him.

Stilsh bowed to Blenn then sat down across from Rugger, placing the basket next to him on the seat.

"My sincerest gratitude for your hospitality, Lord Blenn. I hope we may meet again, soon." Sir Danuel nodded then also climbed into the carriage and closed the door. He seated himself opposite Lytwon.

Lytwon tapped on the roof and the driver responded, calling out, "Onward!"

The coach lurched gently into motion.

Sir Danuel appeared to scrutinise Rugger and Stilsh. He seemed to assess them, looking at their attire and sinewy frames. After a moment, he gave a slight nod and leaned back in his seat. He pulled out a small dagger from his boot and turned the blade over slowly in his hands. "The men I saw travelling north made no attempt to hide their identities. I'm assuming they feel the festival will bring in many strangers from different parts of the country as well as from distant lands, and that they won't be noticed in the crowds. But they bore Mendelonian colours and shouldn't be difficult to pick out again. There was something odd about their cloaks – the linings were black, not gold like merchants' garb."

Something about Danuel's sombre countenance and the persistent heaviness in his tone... His sallow skin and the fine downturned wrinkles around his eyes seemed to be those of a much older man, worn by years of frivolity and drink. But also of sorrow.

Lytwon wanted to put his arm round Danuel's shoulder and tell him all would be well.

They passed countless fields and farms glowing with the early evening light. An otherworldly beauty. Lytwon could understand why so many landscape painters tried to capture the ethereal luminescence of dusk over the heartlands of Syngordia.

He sighed with gratitude. Everything had worked out so well with Blenn. And the subject of Verana hadn't even come up. But then, she had been the centre of Lytwon's world, not Blenn's. Maybe his old friend could forget her. Lytwon never would.

Despite his plans going smoothly, apprehension still nagged in the back of his thoughts.

What would happen once he arrived at his old home? Would Richarr welcome him? Or would he consider him a threat to the Crown, an unwanted intrusion, as Richarr's advisors had felt years ago? Richarr had a healthy son, so the throne was secure. They should no longer have concerns regarding Lytwon's intentions.

But dark thoughts kept creeping through his mind.

What if Fillip intended to have both Richarr *and* the heir to the throne killed?

It was too terrible to contemplate.

Lytwon studied Danuel's face. "Danuel? If I may call you by your first name?"

"Yes, of course, Your Highness." Danuel's thin smile didn't reach his eyes.

"Do you think that King Fillip intends to have Richarr's heir and wife assassinated as well?"

Danuel pursed his lips as his expression hardened. "I don't know." He looked down at his hands clasped together on his lap. "Your Highness, I have no idea what he is capable of. I hope not. I surely hope not. That would be unthinkable! They wouldn't deserve his wrath." Danuel wiped a tear from his cheek.

"I'm so sorry. You were close to her, weren't you?"

Danuel nodded slowly. He turned away and rubbed at his eyes.

Rugger's weathered face seemed to soften.

Stilsh stared at the floor.

It wasn't right to embarrass the young man with further questions. He obviously had some kind of emotional connection to Isabella. Lytwon leaned back and looked out of the window.

Village after village, the festive decorations increased. Yellow and white flowers festooned every tavern window and fence post. Bright yellow, blue and green ribbons, the traditional colours of the Double Crowned Kingdom, hung from eaves, streetlamps, and the boughs of trees.

The Festival of Ashwond. The national celebration of the unification of the two crowns of Syngordia... His childhood memories of the festival were filled with celebrations, music, dance, and feasts. Such pleasant recollections of halcyon days. That was, however, before Richarr was crowned and Lytwon was banished to the northern province of Lowarthen.

"Rugger, will you keep an eye open for a suitable tavern to spend the night?" Without waiting for a response, Lytwon rested his head against the cushion and let his eyelids close. The ride was bumpy, but perhaps he could get a few moments of rest despite that.

"Of course, Your Highness." Rugger's gruff voice seemed distant as Lytwon slipped immediately into what felt like an ongoing story.

"Lyttie, would you like some cordial?" Laughing, Verana held up a large blue lace parasol. Her long gloves matched her parasol. She reached inside a picnic basket and withdrew two glasses.

Why not? Lytwon tapped on his belly. He wasn't getting any younger or thinner, but he was content. He looked around and smiled. It was nice to see the Sunken Garden of Warningen House looking so pristine. All the fountains flowed. The hedges were clipped. The topiaries perfectly trimmed. The decorative bas-relief arches had been scrubbed and bleached. Jonatan Prach was an excellent Head Gardener. He paid attention to every detail. The whole Prach family had been a part of the groundskeeping team for many years before Lytwon took up residence there. Such faithful workers.

Lytwon smiled again. How fortunate he was.

The ground shook violently.

Verana didn't seem to notice. "Cook Marta made us some sandwiches. And some spice fritters." She pulled out a double-tiered tray covered in small triangles of cut bread.

The retaining walls behind the pool cracked. The stones filling one of the decorative arches toppled and fell forward.

The Crystalline Man stepped through the opening and approached them.

Verana didn't look up, but continued setting out the food. "Today turned out to be such a nice day for a picnic, don't you think, Lyttie?"

"Yes, of course, my dear." Lytwon couldn't take his eyes off the Crystalline Man. Why was he there? Lytwon stood up and faced him. "Sir? What is your business here?"

"The remnant of the Firstborn rejoices. They take new flight over the Great Continent. Their voices burst into thunderous jubilation for the first time in countless ages.

Many Orren, Palanshen and Bohdne recognise the changes

in the flow of Eth, as waking dreams and night visions begin to open their minds to ancient portals to Ber'eth's will.

The Urborn are sensing the Shift in power but remain unhearing as the Beckoning continues to flow through earth, water and wind. Descendants of Limman, held in thraldom by the Urbonnic Skylle, sense the flowing forces of the Beckoning and ponder their escape.

Athlonia declares war.

The Spectrals are uniting.

The Wailing One stirs from her confinement, having found cracks in her prison.

She seeks to destroy all.

The Legacy walks among us, bringing restoration as the ancient dead stones quiver with renewed life. The Temmerung pulses with iridescence and the Legacy rises."

"Your Highness." Rugger's rough calloused palm rested on the back of Lytwon's hand. "We've stopped for the night."

"Pardon? Oh yes, of course." He pushed himself back up on the seat. "Stilsh, can you find me a piece of paper? I just had a night vision. I need to write it down!"

35

Your Majesty

The night in the tavern seemed to have passed quickly. Lytwon couldn't remember any further dreams.

As he sat down with Danuel and Mischul's men for some eggs and cold meats, he tried once again to recall the elements of his night vision in the carriage. He'd filled the piece of parchment Stilsh had procured for him, back and front, with the words of the Crystalline Man. Lytwon hadn't wanted to miss a word.

Their voices burst into thunderous jubilation for the first time in countless ages.

Many Orren, Palanshen and Bohdne recognise the changes

in the flow of Eth, as waking dreams and night visions begin to open their minds to ancient portals to Ber'eth's will.

The Urborn are sensing the Shift in power but remain unhearing as the Beckoning continues to flow through earth, water and wind. Descendants of Limman, held in thraldom by the Urbonnic Skylle, sense the flowing forces of the Beckoning and ponder their escape.

Athlonia declares war.

The Spectrals are uniting.

The Wailing One stirs from her confinement, having found cracks in her prison. She seeks to destroy all.

The Legacy walks among us, bringing restoration as the ancient dead stones quiver with renewed life.

The Temmerung pulses with iridescence and the Legacy rises."

Lytwon folded the piece of parchment then finished his eggs.

"Your Highness," the owner of the inn came to their table and bowed. "Thank you so much for stopping at our establishment on your way to Ashwond." What looked like his wife, and three young women, perhaps his daughters by their resemblance to the portly red-haired man, all curtsied behind the innkeeper.

"The weather should be beautiful for today's inauguration celebrations." His wife's voice was high-pitched and excited.

Their daughters nodded vigorously.

"Thank you." Lytwon stood and motioned to his companions. "We need to depart now." He looked at Stilsh, "Please settle our account with this good man."

"Oh no, Your Highness!" The innkeeper's wife spoke up. "It is our gift." She reached back and put her arm over her eldest daughter's shoulders. "Our gift to the

House of Fathringen on such an occasion. Thank you, once again, for choosing our establishment."

Lytwon nodded and smiled. For a few moments, the cheerful reception back in his homeland counterbalanced the growing anxiety.

"Before we leave," Lytwon turned back to the owner. "Could you have a message sent to King Richarr? A sure-footed steed will reach the castle some time before our carriage. I would like him to know of my arrival beforehand."

"Yes, of course, Your Highness. Of course. I will find someone immediately." The innkeeper bowed again and hurried away.

Rugger moved towards the door. "We still have about an hour before we reach Dyndyll Castle Park where King Richarr will inaugurate the festivities. We should arrive just as the festival begins."

Arriving *just* in time? But would it be in enough time to warn Richarr?

Danuel helped pack their few pieces of luggage on top of Blenn's carriage then opened the door for Lytwon to enter before him.

Stilsh and Rugger then climbed in and settled across from Lytwon and Danuel.

"Lord Yldshimman." Rugger tapped on the roof but kept his eyes on Danuel. "If I may ask. Are you also in the military in Mendelon?"

Danuel blinked as though waking up. "No. My office is 'Companion' to Prince Palandred. But not as his secretary. I serve him as his friend."

"His family also has large plantations under Watergrass cultivation, just north of Horróglоryn." Adjusting the thin seat cushion, Lytwon smiled at

Danuel. "Landed gentry. We have something in common."

Danuel seemed uncomfortable with the attention, but continued nevertheless. "My surname, Yldshimman, is the name of the third and most northern province of Mendelon. My family's Welsordian-Orrenic ancestors found deposits of golden crystal sands there and started the Vlachonian glassworks."

"Vlachonian amber glass comes from your family?" Lytwon couldn't hide his surprise. "Such an exquisite product! I have your wares throughout Warningen House." Lytwon looked at Stilsh and Rugger. "It is a very successful industry on the Horn. All the noble houses have Vlachonian amber glass from Yldshimman. It must bring in great wealth to your family."

Danuel's face darkened. "It should." He nodded. "But royal excises on amber glass exports are exorbitant. Mendelon takes fifty percent. My family receives the rest."

Stilsh frowned, shaking his head silently.

The trip passed in relative silence, and more quickly than Lytwon had expected. Soon they drew close to the high brick wall surrounding the Royal Garden of Dyndyll Castle. The peaks of numerous pavilion tents peered above the walls, and sounds of merriment began to fill the air. All along the wall, thin tapering banners rippled at the tops of long poles.

Rugger opened his window.

Pointing to the garden entrance, Lytwon leaned forward. "Tell the driver to pull up close."

Rugger nodded. "Yes sir."

Well, it was time.

They were almost there.

Lytwon's heart throbbed in the veins of his temples.

"Richarr might already be in the royal marquee. He should have received word of my arrival by now, so I will go there immediately."

"We will be at your side." Rugger nodded to Stilsh.

"So will I, Your Highness." The heavy melancholy was suddenly gone from Danuel's voice. He opened the door and leapt from the carriage. Turning back quickly, he offered Lytwon an arm to stabilise his descent.

"Thank you." Lytwon stepped out of the carriage and adjusted his belt. His clothes were beginning to hang loosely on his body. "Danuel, please inform me of anyone you recognise. We must hurry."

Danuel nodded, walking quickly beside him.

Lytwon waved Rugger and Stilsh in front of them. Both of Mischul's guards gripped the handles of the swords strapped at their sides and began gently parting a way through the throngs, towards the royal marquee. Their heads turned back and forth as they looked over the crowds.

Danuel leaned closer to Lytwon and whispered. "The men I saw wearing Mendelonian colours were of average height and build, but their capes had black linings." He shook his head.

Richarr had spared no expense. The festival was beyond opulent. His love of ostentation could rival even the Vandrian Baronholds. Musicians and dancers were everywhere. Sinewy bare-chested wrestlers grappled on raised platforms, performing breath-taking moves for gasping onlookers. Acrobats walked on taut ropes high above anxious crowds. The enticing aromas of roast lambling and mulled wine filled the air.

Lytwon's cousin had truly spared no expense.

Danuel slowed his pace, then stopped. With one hand he formed a tight fist.

"Do you see them?" Fear curdled Lytwon's blood. Were the assassins already there?

Danuel nodded. "We need to move quickly. They're at the entrance of the marquee."

Rugger and Stilsh pushed forward with Danuel.

Lytwon tried to keep up with them, but congestion at the entrance impeded him.

Strange, or perhaps typical of Richarr, no guards stood at the marquee. In fact, Lytwon had only seen a few positioned at the entrance to the garden.

"Rugger, you may announce me. I can no longer hide my identity here."

Nodding, Mischul's man turned towards the open window and shouted. "Make way for the King's cousin!"

The loud announcement had an immediate effect and a pathway opened through the crowd.

"Prince Lytwon?" Voices called out.

Lytwon smiled to himself. It had been so many years ago, but somehow people still recognised him, and none of them sounded angry. He had expected resistance or resentment if the citizens of the Double Crown Kingdom had completely lost their allegiance to Richarr.

Stilsh and Rugger moved aside and let Lytwon enter next to Danuel.

Lytwon studied Danuel's face as the young lord scanned the crowds. Danuel blinked and glanced back at him.

A shiver ran through Lytwon. "Where?"

"To my right. All four men."

Lytwon looked around for the royal family.

They had not entered the marquee, not yet.

Tables and chairs had been set up on the clipped grass of the lawn. Towards the back of the venue, richly coloured carpets were spread under a line of the most ornate tables. At the centre table, three chairs were draped in deep red velvet cloths.

Obviously for the King, the Queen, and the Heir Apparent.

With the crowds pressing in from all sides, Lytwon needed to maintain his focus on that area.

Sudden horn blasts near a side entrance jarred him. Anxiety blistered in his mind. It became difficult to take in normal breaths. He looked at Danuel and all his thoughts froze.

Fear in his eyes, Danuel was shaking his head nervously. "They've gone, Your Highness. When the trumpets sounded, they disappeared into the crowd. Now I can't locate them anywhere."

"Tell Rugger and Stilsh." Lytwon felt sick.

Danuel casually beckoned Mischul's men to come closer.

"Your Highness?" Rugger looked at Danuel then Lytwon.

"The men from Mendelon." Danuel spoke with urgency. "They've disappeared."

Rugger and Stilsh spun around, looking anxiously over the crowd.

"Their Majesties, the Double Crown King and Queen of Syngordia!" Someone shouted from the side entrance as horns blared once again.

As soon as the royal family appeared, Lytwon waved and began moving towards them through the crowd of Syngordian nobility.

Richarr looked up and smiled, also raising a hand in greeting. His cousin seemed genuinely glad to see him.

A black-cloaked man sprang from behind a flap of the huge tent, a short curved blade in his hand. He knocked the king's delicate tiara off his head and grabbed a fistful of his hair.

Isabella screamed.

The man plunged the knife into Richarr's neck and dragged it across his throat, shouting. "For the murder of Queen Sindrea!"

Isabella leapt forward, falling to her knees and shielding little Gordyn, wrapping her arms around him.

Another assassin shouted and moved towards mother and son. "And the heir to the murderer shall die with his father!"

"No!" Isabella shouted. "He is not the heir!" Sobbing open-mouthed, she struggled to breathe.

For an instant her proclamation appeared to distract Fillip's henchmen.

Rugger lunged forward, plunging his sword up to the hilt into the first assailant.

"Get away from them!" Stilsh shouted.

Gordyn's would-be killer glanced at him.

Just enough time for Danuel to throw his knife into the man's chest.

Guards rushed in from the entrances.

"Look behind the flaps of the royal pavilion," Lytwon instructed. "Behind the curtains! There were four of them!"

Weeping, Isabella pressed her son's head against her chest, and began rocking him in her embrace. "All is well now, my son. You are safe."

Lytwon's heart ached as he watched poor Isabella and Gordyn holding tightly to each other.

A nightmare had become reality.

Lytwon had hoped to avoid it, but it had happened anyway. He had done the best he could. His cousin's life should never have ended in such a horrible way. And his poor widow...

Danuel walked unsteadily towards her. His chest rose and fell rapidly. Tears filled the young man's eyes.

A shocked expression on her face, Isabella stared at him.

"Danuel?" She smiled, then looked at Gordyn. The tension in her face smoothed. She touched little Gordyn's cheek.

Danuel fell to his knees in front of her and the boy.

A rush of emotions flooded Lytwon. He wiped his eyes with his sleeve. He couldn't help noticing how many of the boy's features were identical to Danuel's.

Isabella glanced at Lytwon.

Did he see apprehension in her eyes?

Of all the rumours about the Double Crown Kingdom that had reached Warningen House, most were about Richarr's tavern indulgences and inclinations – nothing regarding Queen Isabella's connection to the House of Yldshimman, even though suspicions had been circulating ever since little Gordyn was born.

Lytwon looked around the pavilion. The gentry present from Gelondria and Dennelonia huddled together in a corner of the pavilion.

Others were running back and forth in total chaos.

From the cries of fear and anger outside, the tumult was rapidly spreading from the marquee into the garden.

A few guards now stood next to their Queen. Others entered with the last two of the assassins in shackles.

Where had these guards been when Richarr needed them? Had they also been bought off like so many others? Anger seethed in Lytwon. His cousin shouldn't have died, not with the information that had been intercepted! Why, why, why did all of this need to happen after the forewarning they'd received?

Shaking, Isabella stood and shouted over the noise. "Long live the King."

Confusion seemed to cause a hush through the pavilion.

She repeated, "Long live the Double Crown King of Syngordia, King Lytwon Fathringen!"

All Lytwon's blood seemed to drain out of him. A chill ran through him.

"Your Majesty." Danuel bowed.

"Your Majesty." Lords and Ladies went down on one knee, lowering their heads.

Isabella knelt and held little Gordyn tightly again. Then she lifted the small crown from her son's thick curly hair. She bowed her head and held out the gold circlet towards Lytwon.

36

THE DOUBLE CROWN KING

Staring at the small gold crown in Isabella's hands, Lytwon's mouth fell open.

'*Your Majesty*' seemed to echo from everywhere.

He tried to grasp the sudden change of events.

Looking around the vast pavilion, he bowed gently towards Isabella and the gathered Dennelonian and Ghelondren nobles.

This couldn't be happening!

His head throbbed.

King of Syngordia? The weight of the responsibility pressed heavily against his chest.

Isabella raised her head and walked towards him, still

holding out Gordyn's gold circlet. "Your Majesty." She made a deep bow. "As former queen, please allow me to present this to you. My son has no blood claim to your throne."

No blood claim?

Lytwon nodded sceptically.

But what was the correct protocol? Surely the present queen publicly declaring him monarch couldn't be challenged. Not ethically. Not when denying the crown for herself and her son, and proclaiming him successor in front of so many high-ranking witnesses.

An official ceremony would have to be held later. Too many pressing matters were at hand, things that needed his immediate attention.

Isabella bowed again, then grasped little Gordyn's hand and stepped backwards into the crowd.

Joining her, Danuel reached for her other hand.

Looking at the three of them, a sense of sorrow rose in Lytwon. Verana wouldn't have liked the change of role, but she would have followed him anyway and done her best to adapt to court.

He steeled himself for the task at hand. Now was not the time for nostalgic dreaming!

"I will need to meet with the captains of the guard, all heads of the military, and message carriers. Immediately. All the nobility of Dennelon and Gelondria must join forces to protect Syngordia. Join me in the preparation for war."

"War?" Anxious gasps rippled through the pavilion, then tense angry murmurs.

They needed to know more.

Lytwon took a deep breath and spoke loudly, hoping to be heard throughout the pavilion. This announcement would shake the lives of many present.

"Norssum soldiers have been gathering on our northern border with the Marden Morath for weeks now, under the leadership of an Athlonian sorcerer. The Vandrian Steward of Barrost is dead. We believe murdered. His wife has declared herself King of Barrostania. Her consort is Duke Borinbranth's son, Caldere. The Irrshen has been seen over Barrost."

He stopped as complete silence fell.

"Yes, that's right. The creature of nightmares, harbinger of doom and destruction, the Irrshen from our ancient homeland of Palanth-Orron."

His heart pounded painfully in his chest. He needed them to believe everything he said. It would determine whether the legacy of Syngordia would remain intact for future generations.

He lowered his voice slightly. "Fellow citizens and subjects faithful to the Double Crown, Syngordia is in dire peril. We must defend the Double Crown Kingdom together, unite to save our homeland. Please do not be dismayed. We still have time, but I fear not much." It was important that they all understood the urgency, but it was equally important for them not to lose heart.

Lytwon nodded to Stilsh and Rugger, then Danuel. "Men would you please join me." All three men hastened towards him.

Lytwon exited the royal pavilion and started towards the castle's side entrance.

The path was the same one he'd taken hundreds of times as a youth. Back then he'd dreamt of ruling as Syngordia's monarch and residing in this, his ancestors' palatial residence. But those childhood ideas had long been buried, especially after his removal to Lowarthen and then meeting his gentle-hearted Verana.

But here he was, crossing the foyer and climbing the same long stairs, but to a very unexpected reality.

He paused on the landing and grasped the handrail. So many steps!

How ironic that, once again, Richarr had the power to change Lytwon's life path. What a pity, though – Lytwon would have loved to speak to his cousin. The image of Richarr's smile when seeing him enter the royal pavilion still lingered in his mind.

Taking a few gasps of air, he became aware of the tumult in the palace.

"King Richarr, dead?"

Voices echoed from the upper floors.

"Prince Lytwon is here, and Queen Isabella has declared him king!"

A small group of soldiers marched into the foyer just below Lytwon. They stopped and looked up and down, in the direction of the shouts.

One of them called out. "Where is the new King? We have a message of some urgency for him."

"I am here." Lytwon looked down over the balustrade and beckoned for them to join him. He turned towards his three men. "A library should still be on this floor, the first doorway on the right." He pointed to double doors framed in ornate goldwork.

Rugger opened the doors and bowed.

"Thank you." Lytwon entered and looked around. It was indeed the old library, but few books were left. The room was filled with beautifully-carved white marble busts of fierce-looking men of fables, and statues of nude warriors in battle.

Rugger, Stilsh and Danuel stood to attention, hands on their swords.

Lytwon turned back as the soldiers appeared in the

doorway and bowed. They spoke almost in unison. "Your Majesty. Long live the king."

Lytwon raised his hand. "Just one of you enter." He looked quickly from Rugger to Danuel and Stilsh.

Nodding, an officer took one step into the room. "Your Highness, we must report very strange activity along our northern border. A gargantuan apparition passed there, just two days ago."

Lytwon nodded. "The Irrshen."

The officer seemed to be taken aback with Lytwon's quick response. "Yes, Your Highness."

"Please proceed."

"Our lookouts noted that the ghostly creature was following the course of the Great River along our northern border near the Marden Morath, and then through Lowarthen. They also noted what looked like ships in an unnatural fog beneath it, and what appeared to be glowing white sages, men with white garments and long white hair, on their decks".

Lytwon's lack of surprise seemed to unsettle the officer.

"You knew, Your Highness?"

"Yes, but only recently. We need to get word to the commanders of the army. War is about to break out along our borders with Norssum."

The officer clicked his heels together and nodded sharply. "And, if I may add." Tension seemed to pull the skin around his eyes in taut wrinkles. "The apparition, the Irrshen and the strange, glowing men, they were bypassing the regions of Dennelon and Gelondria, heading towards Geholiogarth in Edendor."

37

Lady Arden

Druin ran towards Arden.

His heart pounded as though he'd just climbed an alpine cliff.

She set her case down at her feet and opened her arms towards him.

He embraced her.

Pulling her in close, he kissed her. Soft and warm, her lips sent a shiver through him.

He gently cupped her face in his hands and continued kissing her, her forehead, her eyes, her cheeks.

The salty taste of her tears lingered on his mouth.

Cradling her in his arms, he cherished the sensation of her body against his chest.

He never wanted to let go.

Never again.

"How are you here in Limmania?" His own tears welled in his eyes. He leant back and stared at her face. "My dear Arden, I am overjoyed to see you. So grateful that you have been returned to me." He ran his hands over her sleeves. She was real, so very real. He embraced her again, pressing her tighter against his body. "I was so afraid for you. But how did you get here from Barrost?"

"A Temmerung portal." She responded, hugging back. Then she looked up at him. "We have much to talk about."

He nodded.

"Druin, Professor Gwenndon helped me escape. He was attacked." Her blue-green eyes glistened like the rarest of jewels.

"How?"

"He was stabbed by my brother, Caldere."

"Oh no! Arden, I'm so sorry." Druin brushed away tears from her cheeks.

In the Temmerung she had mentioned her half-brother and Lady Soffian resorting to violent actions, but…. "Why Professor Gwenndon?"

"I think the knife was meant for me, and the Professor was in his way."

He suppressed the rage searing through him.

Closing his eyes, he rested his cheek on Arden's head. Her light sweet perfume was mingled with the murky smell of the floodwaters. "But…?" Druin leant back again, studying her. It was hard to grasp that she was actually there.

She lowered her arms from his shoulders. Her eyes

lingered on his for a moment. "I found the Temmerung portal in the Sunken Gardens at the university. I thought we could escape Caldere and his soldiers, but he and two of his guards leapt through the portal before I could close it."

Druin's insides twisted seeing the tormented expression on Arden 's face.

She looked so pale, so fragile.

He kissed her cheeks again. "What you have gone through..."

"The Temmerung took us to a chamber at Warningen House. Crethingan was there." She spoke quickly. Her shallow breaths sounded hoarse. "He pushed down a wall of loose stones. The base of a long flight of steps appeared. Another Sunken Garden! Then I heard servants or guards shouting. The Professor was too weak to continue with me. Crethingan advised me to leave him there, for them to tend to his wound. Then the Temmerung brought me here."

Druin held her hand up to his lips. "You did well. The trip would surely have been too much for him.

"I've done a terrible thing though." Her tone suddenly dropped. Her lower lip quivered. "But it couldn't be avoided."

"Whatever it is, it must have been justified."

"I commanded the Temmerung to imprison Caldere and his guards within the stones of the World of Visions." She covered her mouth with her hands as she began to sob. "Terrible. Horrible. I could sense their fear and anguish before the two guards perished. Caldere remains entrapped in his prison of boulders."

Shaking his head, Druin wrapped his arms around her. "Dear Arden, you are so brave. What you did was fully warranted. They were trying to kill you."

The warmth of her against his chest was heavenly.

"You not only saved your own life, but probably the lives of hundreds, perhaps thousands of others. He'd become a madman."

She nodded slowly.

"Dear Arden, I can hardly believe you are actually here. I am so thankful."

"So am I." She smiled up at him.

Toman drew slowly closer. Sadness veiled his face. He looked at Arden and bowed, then his expression lightened. "It's good to see you again."

Banah approached with Maiden Lorann and Palan.

The Chieftains were a few steps behind them.

"Lady Arden!" Banah held her arms open wide. "I am so relieved you are safe! But how did you escape Barrost?"

"A Temmerung portal." She leaned over and picked up her case. She patted its worn red leather. "And in here are maps where I feel certain we will find others." The case slipped in her hand, falling to her feet. The latch sprang open. A small sparkling stone vase rolled out of many sheets of notes and yellowed scrolls of aged vellum.

Druin, Toman and Maiden Lorann all knelt at the same time to lend assistance in gathering her documents.

Picking up the small vase, Druin marvelled at its smooth crystalline form, then handed it to Arden

"Thank you. It was a gift from my father." As she touched the vase, a brilliance ignited from within the stone, flashing thin beams of light around them.

She gasped. "Well, I never!" She looked mystified, staring from Druin to Toman. "This must be from the Temmerung! The stones have begun to react to my voice and my touch. But how did my father come by this?"

She stopped suddenly and her eyes grew larger. She whispered something that sounded like *'Bohdnian?'*.

Shouts came from across the plaza. "The gems! Look at the stones!"

The servants Steward Loraimen had sent to gather the blue-cast diamonds held up boxes of the small gemstones. A bright iridescent blue light now glowed from each container!

Druin looked back at Arden.

She held up her vase in the sunlight.

Once again, thin shafts of piercing white light erupted from its crystalline depths, shooting out in all directions.

Palan gasped and grabbed at the back of his head.

His eyes filled with horror.

His fingers began to glow brightly, like Toman's when he channelled his Eth!

"Those lights! I've seen them before." Palan's breaths came in shallow, rapid gasps. "The day my mother was killed. The day I released the demon within the Rubinstone."

"Demon?" Banah's body stiffened.

Dark clouds began to gather over the plaza. Gusts blew in from the Bay, carrying a mist of fine rain.

Palan kept his eyes on his glowing hands. His nostrils flaring, he calmed his breathing but didn't answer Banah's question.

"Look up!" Someone called out from the plaza.

Cries of alarm echoed off the city walls.

Familiar winged shapes appeared in the clouds above them.

"The Uccell Lords." Returning already? Druin had hoped for good news, but something serious must have happened if they were returning so soon.

Chieftess Beruhn and Chieftain Ruhand knelt and raised their hands towards the Firstborn.

Landing in front of Druin, Lord G'nallun folded his massive wings and bowed, then beckoned him to approach. "My Lord." The Uccell's deep resonant utterances always sent shivers through him. It sounded as though three voices spoke at once. "Lord Druin, a message from King Lytwon Fathringen."

"King?" Druin's legs felt weak. King? What had happened?

Lord G'nallun opened his large taloned hand.

"Thank you, My Lord." Druin took the note, unrolled it and read aloud.

'*Dearest Druin.*

Many things are changing. I have been declared king of the Double Crown Kingdom at the death of my cousin, Richarr. His wife, Isabella, and her son, Gordyn, were spared and sent away from court with a nobleman of the Yldshimman tribe.'

Druin sighed in relief at the news his friend's dear sister and nephew were safe.

Visibly shaken by the news, Palan didn't look up from staring at his hands, and mumbled a name. Danuel.

'*I also wanted to share with you a very strange dream that I think will have some significance for you, Banah and Lord Dalbonn.*'

Sadly, Uncle Lytwon didn't know about the Lord Protector's current very fragile state of health. That information would need to be a part of the next message the Uccell carried for him.

"*The Marden Morath is draining. Ancient streets and waterways, giant sculptures of the Firstborn, are being exposed by the receding waters.*

The Crystalline Man appeared to me in a dream, and recounted this message:

The remnant of the Firstborn rejoices. They take new flight over the Great Continent. Their voices burst into thunderous jubilation for the first time in countless ages.

Many Orren, Palanshen and Bohdne recognise the changes in the flow of Eth, as waking dreams and night visions begin to open their minds to ancient portals to Ber'eth's will.

The Urborn are sensing the Shift in power but remain unhearing as the Beckoning continues to flow through earth, water and wind. Descendants of Limman, held in thraldom by the Urbonnic Skylle, sense the flowing forces of the Beckoning and ponder their escape.

Athlonia declares war.

The Spectrals are uniting.

The Wailing One stirs in her confinement, having found cracks in her prison.

She seeks to destroy all.

The Legacy walks among us, bringing restoration as the ancient dead stones quiver with renewed life. The Temmerung pulses with iridescence and the Legacy rises."

Druin rolled up the note and slipped the scroll into his pocket. "So much is changing that we need to discuss. This is remarkable information."

"Yes. The Shift is altering history already." Banah pointed towards the entrance to the city. "We all need to reassemble back at Steward Loraimen's residence." She looked up as Toman walked closer to her and bowed.

"Lady Banah, if I may...? I would first like to check on my master's condition. I would join you straight afterwards."

"Of course, Fyrst Toman. Of course. We shall await your return." Banah paused, looking intently at Arden. "My Lady? Are you well?"

Arden's face had flushed dark pink. "Lord

Crethingan..." The vase flickered again in her hands. "...told me that I am *the Legacy* of which he speaks."

38

I Believe in You

Toman bowed to Lady Banah and began walking toward Palan's ship.

The masts of the impressive Sindrea Isabella stood tall in the calm waters of the Bay. She was such a luxurious masterpiece of a warship, her gilt trim glaring in the sun. She looked proud even with her sails lowered.

Glancing around the plaza, Toman's Ber'eth Lobe tingled with subtle warmth. The power of Eth was everywhere, swirling around him, surging in torrents just out of sight. Occasional glints sparkled in the clouds and from shadows cast on the water. He couldn't be certain, but the forces moving through the Great Shift seemed to be powerfully drawn to the city of Limman. He had the impression that the glistening, undulating curtain of his Gebayt Bithen was still lingering at the edge of his vision.

The morning had been exhausting.

So many bewildering things happening, one after another. The short but violent flood... Night Flyers during the daytime... Druin becoming paralysed with the sight of the White Apes... Crates of diamonds burst open in the plaza... The unbelievable power that had emerged during his last Gebayt Bithen...

And then Lady Arden's appearance and her explaining about a Temmerung portal.

A physical portal!

And the stones that had responded to her voice!

They needed to carefully examine all of these recent occurrences. Something about them was both tantalising and frightening. But he couldn't put his finger on what exactly made him feel afraid. However, it was there, the fear, like a grey speck of mould on bread, ready to spread across the loaf.

Toman studied Palan's ship, motionless in the water.

Many things could have happened onboard the Sindrea Isabella in the few hours since they'd disembarked. But Yannu hadn't sent news of any improvements or any worsening in the Lord Protector's condition.

Thinking back to Lady Banah, his conscience pricked him slightly. He had asked her to first see his master before going to the meeting she'd called. He'd never deferred any request from her before.

Nevertheless, he cherished the opportunity to have a moment alone with His Grace. Especially now, in his fragile condition.

If Toman could use his Linger connection directly on

His Grace's skin, surely the link would once again reveal his master's mind. Hopefully a healing process was taking place in his body, perhaps unseen and undetected by Physician Wanner.

The now familiar sadness ached in Toman's chest.

He shook off the anguish piercing his heart. No, his master wouldn't die. He *had* to get better.

Toman needed him. Ydassum needed him.

The plaza was still bustling with workers clearing off the last of the debris left after the flash flood.

Toman glanced back towards the river gorge. What had caused so much water to come down from the highlands so rapidly?

Prince Lytwon's letter said that the Marden Morath was draining.

From what Toman could remember of their trip down the Suyan Folumpor, the vast marshland was just southwest of Prince Lytwon's estates in Lowarthen. And hadn't Druin mentioned something about the trees around there? Something about them seeming to be in straight lines as though planted that way long ago? The Uccell had also said that an ancient civilisation of *Great Builders* had once worked alongside the Firstborn in what was later a part of Upper Syngordia.

Toman climbed the short ramp up to the massive stone quay and paused. He looked around and smiled. Not a crack or loose slab anywhere. And the shape of the quay had guided the overflow of the river cleanly out towards the Bay.

Here in Limmania, as well as in every city constructed by the Orren that he'd seen, the builders had excelled. The Orrenic cities of Limman, Turicum and the Lower City in Barrost – they all showed superb masonry work.

Still smiling, he enjoyed the sense of pride in his ancestors tingling through his chest.

"Hoi, Tomi!" Yannu's joyful voice welcomed him as he walked across the gangway to the ship's deck.

Toman had the urge to hug his friend but didn't. Men didn't hug.

Yannu walked towards him, quickly grabbed him and squeezed Toman to his chest. He let go immediately and stared at Toman's face. "What happened to you? Are you alright?" He frowned slightly. "You scared the grunt out of me."

"What?"

"From here on the ship I couldn't tell where you were." He pointed in the direction of the embankment. "A huge wave of watery mud smashed into the wall over there, then hit the quay. It was full of tree branches and long broken planks. And the noise! It roared like thunder, with wood cracking like lightning. But here behind the quay, the ship was sheltered. It only rocked in the water a bit." He raised his eyebrows slightly, sighing as if exhausted. "And then there were those big flapping black Flitter Mice."

"Night Flyers." Toman couldn't stop from smiling at his mate's intensity.

"And then you did your thing, you know, your Gebayt Bithen. Menne-Gootay, Tomi! It was huge. It filled the whole plaza and sparkled right over the ship. It covered the whole city!"

"Really?" Toman blinked. He hadn't seen how far it had spread.

"Everywhere!" Yannu waved his arms about. "I'm telling you. As far as I could see, it even went beyond the city and rippled up the mountains!"

Toman shook his head in disbelief. How was that even possible?

"But how is His Grace?"

His question seemed to deflate his friend.

Yannu blinked then started studying Toman's boots. "Not so good, Tomi. Not so good. The Limmanian physician came but couldn't do anything. He just agreed with Wanner's treatment." Yannu bit his lip. "I'll take you to the infirmary."

Toman struggled against the lump forming in his throat. "I know the way."

His friend stepped aside for him to pass first.

They climbed the steps in silence.

Pausing for a moment, Toman looked back over the embankment to the ruins of the shipyard. People were already over on the other side of the river, hauling off branches and piles of thick stringy moss.

Yannu opened the door and let Toman enter the corridor first.

One look at his friend's face, and Toman knew the situation must have become even more grave.

Why had he even left the boat? He should have stayed at his master's side.

"What has happened with His Grace since I left this morning?" Toman's voice quivered with a mixture of apprehension and shame.

"Nothing much on the outside, but he's been mumbling."

"Mumbling? That is great news. That means that he could soon be awake and speaking again!"

Yannu nodded then knocked on the infirmary door.

"Enter." Physician Wanner responded immediately.

Walking into the low-ceilinged room, the familiar sting of salts and alcohol assaulted Toman's throat. He coughed. "Could we open a window in here? The air—" He coughed again.

Wanner shook his head. "Draughts can close the lungs."

Nodding, Toman moved to his master's bedside.

Yannu stood in the doorway, watching silently.

His Grace was still taking slow but normal breaths.

Toman touched his hand.

It wasn't cold. Neither was it of normal warmth.

The physician stared at Toman's face. "Do you need treatment for those scratches?"

"No. But thank you." His Grace's health was more important right then. His wounds were small and would heal.

Wanner nodded.

"Physician, may I again?" Toman pointed to his master's crisp white shirt. "I can hear his thoughts."

"Yes, I know." Wanner's normally sharp tone sounded dull and resigned. "You may proceed."

"Thank you, Good Sir." Toman knelt next to the wooden bedframe and ignited his Eth. He watched as the light in his bones spread from his fingertips to his whole hand.

He unbuttoned the top of his master's shirt.

His Grace stirred suddenly, clenching his teeth and making guttural sounds as if he was trying to clear his throat. He moved his head. The pillow was damp with sweat.

"He has grown ever more restless." Wanner stood from his desk and applied a clean moist cloth to His Grace's forehead. "Especially after the phenomenon that happens when you pray."

"My Gebayt Bithen? But does the Lord Protector's restlessness mean he's healing? Sometimes muscles tend to crave movement when reknitting and growing back together."

The Physician nodded. "That is my impression of the Lord's condition as well. But I don't understand his symptoms sufficiently to be able to deduce a diagnosis." Wanner shook his head slowly and went back to his desk.

Summoning his Linger, Toman closed his eyes and gently rested his hand on His Grace's bruised chest, careful to not put weight on it.

Nothing came at first.

Nothing understandable.

Just impressions of early life, echoes of distant memories. Children laughing. Then children weeping.

The muscles in Toman's arms tensed.

Reliving his childhood traumas, his master seemed to be searching for his homeland. A haven, a refuge, for his thoughts and feelings?

The impressions shifted and different images emerged from his master's foggy consciousness.

He stood at a funeral pyre. A smooth white box lay open. Surrounded by masses of white flowers, a man lay in it. His hands crossed over a sword on his chest, his garb was identical to His Grace's official uniform.

Toman's stomach lurched as his master's body shook suddenly.

Comfortless sorrow twisted in him. Regret. Shame.

His Grace touched the rim of the coffin.

Lanfoth Steffen put a hand on his shoulder then whispered something to him.

The scene changed again.

His master stood just inside the entrance of the Barefoot Monk, watching Toman.

Then His Grace stood in the shadows, just outside the glow of the streetlamp, watching him.

Such a mixture of emotions.

Amazement. Astonishment. Disbelief… but also…

A shiver ran up Toman's spine.

Love?

The love of a father?

The scene quickly faded and new impressions tumbled through his mind, then were replaced instantly by others.

His Grace stood in front of Lady Banah and Druin. "Toman, even though powerful and matured by grief and hardship, is still a boy with a strong belief in the bonds of friendship. He risked his position because he felt his only companion could have died."

Once again, a strong sense of fatherhood enveloped Toman.

His master's memories had become a multi-coloured tapestry. Too intricate to disentangle.

His Grace stirred on his cot again.

Toman opened his eyes.

His master raised a hand slightly.

Wanner rushed to his side and pulled his hand down. "I think that is enough now." Once again, the absence of the Physician's typical harsh tone made his words sound like a suggestion rather than an order.

"I will leave. But I need a few more moments." Toman concentrated harder, sending a question through his Linger connection to His Grace's consciousness. "What happened in the brig? Who injured you?"

His master groaned slightly and began to tremble as vivid images flashed through Toman's connection.

Trend bound to the massive beam. His chains glistening with fresh blood.

The terrifying image of the Greinen's wing-like forms spreading out behind her.

Then, suddenly, a familiar voice whispering into His Grace's mind. She called to him, just like she had done to Toman. She slithered up and down his skin, seeking entrance into his soul.

His Grace resisted.

Then searing pain shot through his master's chest.

Or was it through his own chest?

The bones in his fingers began to burn. Toman gasped and looked down.

"Tomi! Look at your hands!" Yannu stared in horror.

The normally bright orange light was darkening from his fingertips towards his palms, as though his Eth was being pulled from him and consumed! But he hadn't released his hold on Eth. His Linger always held on until he released it! What could absorb his Eth against his will?

His Grace's body convulsed violently. He coughed hard and tiny droplets of blood splattered over his mouth.

"Your Highness, please leave. Now." Voice still low and controlled, Physician Wanner's face twisted with irritation, and he pointed to the door.

Toman stumbled into the corridor.

Death couldn't be approaching His Grace. No, not now.

The burning sensation in his hands began to recede. But the image of his master's blood-stained mouth was seared into his vision.

A weight seemed to crash onto his shoulders.

Losing his master, losing his mother... was his life supposed to be riddled with the deaths of the people most precious to him?

"Tomi, you all right?"

The sound of Yannu's kind voice shattered the dam that held back Toman's anguish and fears. "I can't lose him, Yannu." Tears welled in Toman's eyes then began streaming down his face. "I just can't." He began to weep uncontrollably. "It's too early for him to pass from this life. He can't leave me, too..." He lost the energy to continue speaking.

Yannu stared at him, a slight frown creasing his forehead. He put his hand on Toman's shoulder. "Tomi, are you forgetting who you are?"

Toman rubbed tears away with the back of his hand, but his body continued to shake with silent sobs.

"You are a great man, Tomi. You know what to do. And if you don't now, you will. Look at what you've done so far." Yannu put his other hand on Toman's shoulder and looked straight at him. "I believe in you, Prince of Ydassum."

39

Meeting Room

Banah accompanied the others of her party to the Steward's brightly-lit meeting room. She smiled and walked out onto the balcony with Lorann. The sunset over the Bay of Limman was brilliant. "Something about this place makes me happy." Leaning against the balustrade, she pointed beyond the plaza to the placid blue waters of the Bay of Limman. "Isn't it lovely?"

Lorann joined her at the parapet. "Yes, it really is."

"And the safe return of Lady Arden. I couldn't be more pleased." Banah glanced back through the mullioned windows of the meeting room. Such joy glowed on the faces of her brother and Lady Arden. Slight confusion in Palandred's expression.

"I see that the Steward has returned with a group of servants." Banah opened the door and stepped back inside.

She bowed to the Steward. "Lord Loraimen."

"My Lady." The Steward smiled, bowing in return.

"I wanted to thank you, Lord Loraimen, for your generous hospitality. Also, my gratitude for your attendance at our blessing of the shipyards. Your participation and support are highly valued."

He blinked, his cheeks flushing slightly.

She continued, "Ber'eth is changing the course of history, and I feel certain that many good things are in store for Limmania, and that you will play a crucial role in its restoration to glory."

He blinked again, his face reddening even more. "You honour me, Highborn." His typical excited pitch had softened to a gentle tenor. He walked to a chair, looking pensively around the room.

Banah's words seemed to have moved him. She was pleased. He deserved far greater honours for his years of dedicated service to his people.

The Steward shook his head slightly as though waking, then made a sweeping gesture towards the chairs around the conference table. "Please, be seated. And allow me to have some refreshments brought before we commence discussions. All of you must be famished, and exhausted, after today's ordeals."

He laid a hand on the shoulder of one of his manservants. "Bring up the chilled sweet wines first, then the light soups. The rest of the meal will come later. We will need our privacy, so make yourselves scarce thereafter, unless called." He waved towards the door.

"Of course, My Lord." The elegant young man inclined his head. Walking towards the door, he stopped suddenly in front of the Riddern Chieftains, seemingly taken aback by their presence. He quickly looked at the floor. The manservant obviously knew the protocol regarding not looking the Chieftess in the eyes. Waving for the other young serving men to follow, he hastened off on his errand.

Lady Arden and Druin approached the table.

He carried her red case in one hand. With his other, he held one of hers.

How lovely, the sight of the two of them together. Banah couldn't be happier for her brother. Lady Arden would make a splendid kinswoman.

Lorann came in from the balcony, gently closing the doors. She looked back through the windows. "From up here, it appears that all the diamonds have been gathered." Amazement tinged her voice. "So many rare blue gems..."

Lady Arden looked over to Lorann.

Subtle melancholy clouded the beautiful child-like eyes of the noblewoman from Borinbranth.

What a burden she must be carrying. Sir Crethingan had called her *the Legacy*.

But what did that mean?

The stones in the plaza and Lady Arden's vase itself had all responded when she'd spoken.

Banah had never heard of a form of Eth that had such an effect on stone.

And how had the Temmerung transported her from Barrost to Limmania?

A sense of awe tingled in Banah's chest. Lady Arden must have powers beyond anything the chronicles of Eth Lore had described. Her abilities were astounding. As with Fyrst Toman, Banah was certain she would play a pivotal role in Ber'eth's designs.

Druin placed Lady Arden's weathered case on the table.

"Please, do take a seat." The Steward made another flourishing gesture.

A perfunctory knock came at the door and Steward Loraimen's manservants entered with trays of plates and glasses.

If only the Lord Protector could have been with them for this important discussion.

"My Lady." Fyrst Toman appeared in the doorway. His countenance had completely fallen. After bowing in respect, he kept his head down and his eyes lowered, looking at his hands.

Something must have happened.

An unpleasant feeling spread in Banah's stomach. "Fyrst Toman? How is the Lord Protector?" She pointed to a chair at the table. "Please, join us."

"Thank you, My Lady." He bowed again. "Physician Wanner is content that my master has begun to stir in his sleep." His words lacked his normal optimistic conviction.

"And *your* impressions?" Druin looked from the Fyrst to Banah. "What is your assessment?"

Fyrst Toman sat slowly onto his chair, then rested his palms on the tabletop. Slowly opening and closing his hands, he looked at Druin. "Something has changed. But I can't tell if it's for the better or for the worse. Yes, His Grace is breathing more freely, but unexplainable things are happening in his consciousness." With a strained expression the Fyrst lowered his hands to his lap. "But... may we speak of it later?"

"Yes, of course." Banah responded quickly. "Please

forgive us." It was obvious that they had made him uncomfortable with their questions. He was always a man of few words. She and Druin should not press him further.

"Thank you. My Lady." Toman looked intently at the Steward. "My Lord, may I ask why there were Mendelonian guards on the embankment?"

The Steward sat up in his chair and grasped the armrests tightly. "They are here to make sure we don't break their laws. Limmania is still under Mendelonian overlordship. Even though we govern our city and the southern regions of our country, the interior is strictly forbidden to anyone other than approved individuals from Mendelon City." He looked at Prince Palandred. "Part of the secrecy of Mendelonian activities in our interior may be explained by the crates of jewels flushed out onto the plaza today. Rumours have always circulated that our mountains held the rarest of diamonds, but only historical jewels were ever cited. The Luminous Water Diamond and the gem in the Limman Staff are the two most noted examples."

Prince Palandred frowned slightly. "It's all beginning to make sense. My brother's lies... He portrayed this country as an impoverished province of—" He looked apologetically at the Steward, then at Banah. "—a lethargic people who weren't capable of self-betterment and were not willing to work." His face grew red. "I am so sorry. Things will change when I get back, of that I am certain."

Banah smiled. She sincerely hoped his good intentions would come to fruition.

The Steward appeared to study the tabletop. "Thank you, Prince Elstundreth-Fathringen."

Lady Arden placed a hand on Druin's arm. "The blue-cast stones I saw in the plaza today... I feel certain they were once a part of the Temmerung, perhaps a portal. They responded to my voice, just as the stones in the Temmerung do." She sighed as though exhausted.

Druin grasped her hand on his arm.

Between her brother and herself, he had always been the more sensitive, but the pure and intense emotion in his eyes moved Banah deeply. He must be experiencing true affection, perhaps even love.

A deep longing sprang up within her.

Would she ever feel that way herself ?

Lady Arden continued her explanation. "I do not understand what this term, *the Legacy,* entails, but the Temmerung conducted me and Professor Gwenndon from the Upper City in Barrost to Warningen House, then brought me here, to just outside Limman. I exited the World of Visions in the mouth of a cave just above the river."

The Steward emitted a high-pitched gasp then covered his mouth. "My Lady, do you mean the old quarry caves? Just up the gorge?"

"Yes, My Lord, I think so. I came through a portal at the mouth of a cave in the gorge."

Steward Loraimen pushed his chair back from the table and stood. "My Lady, legends have always had it that those caves were magical. And that our ancestors were supposed to have found blue-cast diamonds in them. But since the Edict of Mendelon, which banned shipbuilding and free trade from or to Limmania, no Limmanian has been allowed to go near them. For more than a hundred and fifty years now, the ban has prohibited access under penalty of imprisonment or death."

Lady Arden frowned and reached for her case.

Druin slid it closer to her, and she unlatched it.

The familiar sparkling lights filled the room as Arden picked up the smooth vase. She set it on the table in front of them and stood, unrolling a few of her documents. "I think this map is of importance to us." She pressed open one of the old scrolls and placed the vase on a tattered edge to keep the parchment from rolling up again.

The ancient drawing looked distinctly like the map of the Northern Horn in Banah's Glortrom vision back in Barrost. But that one had appeared to be freshly drawn.

"Look at these markings." The vase flickered even brighter with her every word. "Professor Gwenndon and I felt that they are representations of other portals to the Temmerung, created by the royal architect, Sir Han Crethingan." She pointed to groups of triple dots next to Barrost, Limmania, and Lowarthen approximately where Warningen House was situated. "We also know that he is the Crystalline Man who first appeared at Warningen House." She glanced up at the vase. "Somehow, I was able to awaken a portal in the university Sunken Garden, and a passage. Physically inside the Temmerung, I found I could exit at Warningen House, then here, after entering the portal in Barrost."

Prince Palandred looked nervously at Lady Arden. "So, you think that the diamonds in the Luminous Water Crown and on the Limman Staff are pieces of the Temmerung?"

Lady Arden stiffened slightly but nodded. "Yes, Your Highness, I would conjecture that they are. Based on your descriptions and their historical provenance in Limmania, I feel that they were also dug from one of the collapsed ancient passages of the Temmerung."

Even though the Riddern Chieftains' faces remained

placid, their unblinking gaze somehow emitted joy as she spoke.

Palandred leaned forward slightly in his chair. "But how could that explain the behaviour of the Luminous Water Diamond? I saw it attack the Scarab Wasp within the Rubinstone."

A restless silence enveloped the table for a few moments, then Lady Arden's eyes widened. "The Wayfarers! Canthalida, the Greinen, must have some bearing on all this. She was captured by the Skylle and imprisoned in the Temmerung." She stopped suddenly and shook her head. "But..." Her sudden enthusiasm deflated. "I'm sorry. It doesn't make sense. Not yet. I cannot finish my hypothesis without knowing more. It needs further research. But I feel there is a link between the Luminous Water Diamond and the Rubinstone. One jewel, a piece of the Temmerung itself, was a part of her prison. The other must also be connected somehow."

Prince Palandred's face darkened. He rubbed his cheeks then pushed hair behind his ears.

Fyrst Toman raised his hand to speak.

Banah smiled. His polite gesture reminded her of her school days and asking a governess permission to speak in class. "Please proceed, Fyrst Toman."

"Thank you." He turned and faced Steward Loraimen. "My Lord, during my Gebayt Bithen, I got the impression from something you said, that Mendelon does not approve of Eth Wielders? Is it like Barrost here? Wielding Eth being frowned upon?"

Steward Loraimen's sudden mischievous smile was unexpected. He started to chuckle. "Please forgive me, Fyrst of Ydassum. I didn't mean to show disrespect for your prayer." His smile grew to a grin. "But your impression would be correct. Mendelon discourages the use of Eth here in Limmania, especially the wielding of any form of transparent corporeal Linger." He chuckled again. "But you could not have known that obscure rule." The Steward leaned back in his chair. "For which I am thankful."

Baffled at his amused response, Banah shook her head. "Thankful, My Lord?"

"Yes, My Lady. Mendelon may not want us to use our Eth abilities, but all of Limmania would. And I will not enforce an obscure law, designed to suppress our own people, on visiting dignitaries. Fyrst Toman's actions will have ramifications far beyond your visit. Of that, I'm sure. But I welcome them in advance."

"If that is a law from Mendelon, Fillip will have heads for the open defiance." Prince Palandred rested his fist on the table and stared at the Steward. "He is ruthless. You need to be careful."

"Would he behead the Fyrst of Ydassum for a prayer of blessing over the city? Or for protecting the next Lanfothe of his country from maddened flying beasts by raising a shield?" The Steward continued chuckling darkly. "What the Fyrst did was to encourage our nation to be Limmanians again."

The Steward stood and walked over to the windows. "Many with the ability to wield Eth have been hidden from the examiners. I am certain, even though I do not have numbers to back up my impression, that Limmania still has hundreds, perhaps thousands, who are capable of wielding clear corporeal Lingers."

There could be thousands? Pride swelled in Banah for a nation she had long adopted in her heart. The popularised, oversimplified image of Limmanians being a folk of weak constitution had been grossly misrepresented. There was incredible power stored here, a potential powder keg that perhaps just needed someone or something to light the fuse.

Toman's eyebrows were arched high on his forehead and the hint of a smile was on his face.

Prince Palandred frowned. "We must consider that my brother is still very dangerous. As we've just heard, his planned assassination of King Richarr must have met with success. From what I know of my brother, he will gloat for a while." Prince Palandred's calm impressed Banah. No sign of his initially insecure tone, nor his frequent seizures back in Barrost. "His glee over avenging our mother's death will leave him besotted with his own magnificence. At least for now."

Druin caressed Lady Arden's fingers. "And Prince Lytwon is a different man from Richarr. Things will change in Syngordia."

"Uncle Lytwon." Banah sighed. "King of Syngordia. Somehow, I think he was born for this. His integrity will be held in high regard."

"Yes, and he will do great things for the House of Fathringen in the Double Crown Kingdom." Druin smiled and lifted Lady Arden's hand to his face. He kissed the back of her hand then looked at the others. "We need to continue our study of Arden's maps and explore more of the passage she created. These portals could change our history."

Lady Arden nodded. "But we mustn't forget that the Greinen is imprisoned somewhere in the Temmerung. And she is still very dangerous."

The Riddern responded in unison. "The Beckoning does not sleep. The Great Shift does not repose. We must keep constant guard because dark things move along the same roads as we take."

Banah shivered at their words.

"Frightening." Lorann looked anxiously at Banah. "But hopeful, don't you think?"

"Yes, I do." Banah acknowledged her question, but noticed that Fyrst Toman had lifted his hand again. She motioned for him to speak.

His jaw tightened. "I think I should tell you something."

Druin released Lady Arden's hand and gestured to Toman. "Please, speak freely."

"When I visited Lord Dalbonn..." He exhaled slowly, opening and closing his hands again. "As most of you know I can connect to the subconscious mind with the touch of my Linger. I visited my master's last memories as he was struck. I relived his fear and shock, his torment at the Greinen's strike against him. As I felt his pain, the glow of Eth in my hands was drained from me. My fingers began to burn with bitter cold and darken against my will."

Lorann gasped.

"It was as though she could drain my Eth through my master's mind." Toman lowered his head onto his open palms.

A sharp knock came at the door, and it swung open. Lord Loraimen's manservants flowed back into the room. They moved quickly around the table proffering golden wines.

Banah kept her eyes on the Fyrst. His posture denoted unbearable weight on his shoulders. "Fyrst Toman, if you would like to adjourn for the evening, I will inform you of our further discussions here. I am sure you would prefer to be closer to your master."

"Thank you, My Lady." Fyrst Toman lifted his head and smiled, pushed his chair away from the table, and stood up straight. "I think it would be best if I slept on the Sindrea Isabella tonight." He looked at the Steward. "However, thank you for your hospitality, My Lord."

Banah was touched by his bearing and confidence.

"I feel certain that something may happen to my master soon. Maybe he will awaken." The Fyrst bowed. "My Lady, I will inform you of any change."

"Yes, of course." Banah smiled again. He was sounding and acting more like his master every day.

40

Sweet Mead and Confessions

"Thank you." Toman nodded to the Steward's footman as he opened the door to the residence.

Walking out into the courtyard garden, the salty air off the bay filled his lungs. He paused for a moment and looked up. The stars were beginning to twinkle in the darkening sky.

Out of instinct, he sent his consciousness into the air, probing for anything unusual.

He half expected to feel the presence of the Uccell Lords circling out of sight, continuing their vigilance over Lady Banah and the group from Ydassum.

The fact that Druin was in contact with the Firstborn,

speaking to them, was still hard to believe. But it was a cherished blessing. Even Arden had found Druin's personal connection to the Firstborn historically unique.

Toman sent his consciousness higher.

Nothing brushed against his mind.

The air currents were gentle, steady, and much warmer than what Toman was used to. Even in Barrost there had been cool air currents winding through the warmth of the Northern Horn's coastal regions.

In Norssum he had assumed the much cooler air was due to the increasing strength of the Greinen. The memory of that sensation, the bitterly cold black frost spreading across his Linger dome, still sent shivers through him.

However, looking back on Barrost now... could it also have been the oncoming Athlonians with their sorcery and the Irrshen?

Toman probed higher.

All calm.

Relief.

Here in Limmania, there didn't seem to be even hints of such currents. Only gentle ocean breezes.

Two guards at the entrance to the Steward's courtyard stood at attention. "Evening, Your Highness." One opened the iron gate and bowed.

"Evening, men. Thank you." Toman stepped out into the lamplit street. He looked up and down at the darkened windows of the closed shops on each side.

But a sweet gentle melody echoed from an open window two stories up. Humming, a woman moved the curtains apart and leant out, pulling her slatted shutters closed.

She began to sing. To a child, perhaps? Her song

sounded like a nursery rhyme. Her Limmanian accent was melodic and rich.

A muscle in Toman's cheek twitched involuntarily.

Wait. He *knew* the song.

Iig ghöre es Glöggli, das lüüted so nett.
De Tag isch vergange, jetzt gagni is Bett.
Im Bett tueni bäte und schlafe dänn ii.
De lieb Gott im Himmel, wird au bi mir sii.

Alyena had always sung it to him, Odilia and Rueddan when putting them to bed! He could almost hear her...

A little bell's a'ringing, 'tis time now for bed.
The day has now left us, so lay down your head.
In bed speak your prayers and then go to sleep.
Ber'eth, Father of Heaven, shall with you be.

Powerful homesickness washed over him. Alyena's smiling face appeared in his mind, leaning over his bed, singing him to sleep.

He reached into his shirt pocket and gently touched the leaf from his mother's herb plant, now rather brittle and dry. He patted his pocket softly. "I'll make you proud, Ma. We'll meet again one day."

As he turned towards the city gates to make his way to Palan's ship, someone was shouting in the tavern in front of him.

What? No. It wasn't possible.

Not here in Limmania.

But Toman knew that voice all too well!

He quickly walked over to the entrance.

The tavern sign was of finely hammered brass. The Silver Zephyr.

He pulled the heavy wooden door open, and the sound of raucous laughter poured out. The wonderful smells of broiled meats, malted beer and honey mead wafted over him as he entered the bustling tavern.

Narrowing his eyes, he searched through the smoky atmosphere for the person that voice belonged to.

The tavern had an unusual layout.

In the centre of the square room, instead of a raised platform, there was a large circular lower area with seated customers.

Back in Turicum, taverns often had a raised area for musicians to perform.

But this looked like some kind of pit, full of tables and chairs. The scuffed wooden floor was blotched with odd dark stains. Many spilled beers? Or stews? The floor needed a deep scrubbing with lye and some sand. From one of the tables, a pleasant-looking young girl waved to him. Dressed in a green and white dress, she motioned for him to come down and sit in the chair next to her.

He smiled but shook his head and continued looking.

A rotund tavern keeper appeared behind a long counter. His crisp white apron was strapped around his belly. He nodded to Toman and shouted across to him. "Evenin' My Lord Sir. The name is Mas', Mas' Denelan. Welcome to my establishment."

"Thank you." Toman inclined his head. "Evening, Good Sir." It was odd that it no longer bothered him being addressed as royalty.

But where was the voice he'd heard from the street?

Slowly scanning the upper level near the counter, a chill crept up his spine.

"You should 'ave seen me, Ladies." The familiar loud voice slurred. "I knocked him out with my little finger!"

Toman spun around.

A pair of bloodshot eyes met his. A bedraggled young man sat at a table on the other side of the pit, each of his arms wrapped around the shoulders of a young woman. One on his left, and one on his right.

"Shann?" Toman whispered hoarsely.

He walked closer, studying him more carefully.

Was it his old friend?

The crusted gash running from his left cheek to his forehead and the livid bruises under his eyes looked as if he'd had a recent rather savage brawl. His eyes were hollow and spent. His filthy white shirt was unbuttoned to his stomach. His dark hair hung matted and limp onto his chest. Grime sullied his face.

Heart pounding in his ears, Toman stood motionless.

It *was* Shann.

Uri's twin was almost unrecognizable.

His old friend glowered at him.

Slowly pulling his hands from the tops of the women's bodices, he attempted to stand up. His uncoordinated, wobbly movements filled Toman with pity, mingled with disgust.

The Landsender was obviously drunk again.

He needed help.

Toman couldn't judge him. The pain of losing someone so close had obviously been too great. Impressions came back of him and his twin together, bounding surefootedly over the decks.

They had been remarkably lithe and agile, confident in their skills, and good workers.

Shann's face darkened. "You!" His deep growl blistered with hatred.

Customers near his table stopped eating and drinking and looked up.

The sound of his old friend's voice, so full of loathing, hit Toman like a fist to the heart.

"You!" Repeating himself, Shann slurred, but his tone was deadly. Beer dripped from his stubble beard.

He stumbled back, away from his table, knocking his chair over.

The two young women at his sides quickly pulled their bodices back up. Grabbing a few coins from the table, they scuttled off.

"You!" Spittle flew from Shann's mouth as he raised both fists to his chest.

His furious tone made Toman's sense of guilt sear.

Staring at his friend's clenched hands, Toman sighed deeply. "Yes, Shann, it's me." The Landsender looked haggard and weak. But was he dangerous? Triggering his invisible Linger to bind his old friend wouldn't be right here. Better to wait and see what he would do next.

"Of all people, *you* walk in here!" Shann knocked over his mug of beer.

Denelan, the tavern owner, moaned. "Hey, watch the spills! I just cleaned in here!" He frowned at the small cascade of beer splashing onto the worn floorboards.

Shaking a fist, Shann seemed to quiver with rage. Tears formed in his blood-shot eyes. "Traitor!"

Once again, his words pummelled Toman's heart.

Feelings of betrayal had indeed stewed in the back of his mind, ever since accepting his promotion with Lord Dalbonn, ever since killing Uri.

Toman had often wondered if this day would ever come, a day of reckoning when he'd have to face Uri's twin. But now that it was here, he didn't feel prepared for it at all.

"Shann, please, can we talk?" Toman's voice shook under the weight of unbearable remorse. He had killed Shann's twin. But His Grace hadn't allowed him to confess to Shann what he'd done.

"Talk? With You?" Raising his fists, Shann staggered down into the pit.

Many of those on the lower level stood up quickly, dragging their tables to the side, clearing an area in the middle. Arranging their chairs to face the centre, they all sat back down. A young, bearded man laughed as he pulled his bowl towards him and dug his spoon into the stew. "This'll be a fight we don't even have to pay to watch!"

Toman shook his head. Fight? Not if he could avoid it. He glanced toward the tavern keeper.

What? The robust man was chuckling to himself.

Shaking his head, a grey-haired customer, after glancing at Toman, stared at Shann. "Drink'll give you boldness, Sonny, but it won't be a'handin' out muscles, or brains." He returned to his meal on the table in front of him. "Stupid kid, you're going to get your eggshell cracked tonight".

Once again, Toman looked for Master Denelan's reaction. Why wasn't he doing something?

"This isn't going to end well for the scrawny northerner." Another of the tavern guests shook his head. "But I'm up for watchin' the scrap!"

The tavern keeper called out to Toman from the bar. "My Lord, if this miscreant is botherin' you..."

"No, Sir. He is a friend."

"But he's just boat refuse. Been around for a few days. He's a nobody. I'll have him thrown out."

Toman raised his hand. "Please, don't. He *is* my friend." Toman walked down a set of steps into the pit and held a hand out towards Shann.

"Friend?" The portly owner smirked, then a grin appeared on his plump face, and he laughed. "As you say then, My Lord. I've never seen a Lord scrap before."

Someone shouted as Shann lunged forward with a sudden burst of energy. He began swinging ham-fistedly.

"No." Toman held his hands up to block any blows and stepped back. "Stop, Shann!"

The Landsender stumbled again, this time falling to his hands and knees. He propped his body up with one hand and jabbed a finger towards Toman. The dark veins in his eyes seemed to grow thicker. "My brother is dead because of you!"

"I am very sorry about Uri. Shann, please believe me." Toman moved towards him, offering to help him stand up again.

Surprisingly, his old friend accepted Toman's hand. Shann pulled himself up from the stained floor in jerky movements.

Once standing, he took a swing at Toman's face.

Toman quickly grabbed Shann's wrists and squeezed.

Shann gasped. With a dumbfounded look, he made another attempt to hit Toman. He winced, grunting in pain as Toman squeezed even more tightly.

"Stop, Shann. We need to talk. But not here." Keeping his voice low, Toman nodded towards the upper level.

"No. You Méndrensynn dogs killed Uri!"

Gasps hissed around the room.

Toman's blood turned to ice. There was no way that Shann could have known that. Toman hadn't broken his promise to His Grace. He had told no one that he had pierced Uri's heart.

Face turning dark red, Shann struggled to free his hands. With the strained effort, the fresh cut on his forehead opened and a thin stream of blood began to flow.

Toman pulled up on Shann's arms to keep his friend from falling again.

"Let go of me!" Shann twisted his wrists in Toman's grip.

His hands were paling. The circulation was being cut off.

Sadness began to overwhelm Toman.

It was shameful to use his strength against a weakened friend.

"Please, Shann." Toman widened his stance to improve his balance.

"You lot murdered my brother!" Shann barked, bringing a knee up toward Toman's groin.

Toman blocked his strike with his own knee, hitting Shann in the thigh.

Shann groaned sharply in pain.

"Please, stop, Shann." Toman pleaded, keeping his voice low. "Please, let's talk."

"I won't talk to murderers!" Shann hissed.

Nervous murmurs arose from those sitting around and watching the action.

Toman's face flared with shame. He *had* killed Uri, but he hadn't *murdered* him.

"Get off, get off!" wailed Shann as he struggled more fiercely.

Toman blocked more strike attempts from Shann's legs and knees. "Please, stop! Shann, stop! We need to talk."

"Why should I talk to a leashed dog of the House of Méndrensynn?" Blood now dripped from Shann's chin.

The sight of his friend's blood-smeared face, and his once mischievous blue eyes now ringed in dark shadows, chilled Toman to the bone.

"My brother... He was my twin brother!" His body thrashed pitifully as his efforts to free himself grew weaker. Gasping for air, Shann grimaced. Tears began to flow down his cheeks. "My hands!" The blood pouring from his now wide-open wound poured in rivulets through the filth on his face. "Let me go! Please let me go." His hands were now white from the lack of blood flow.

Toman's insides twisted. The wretched misery that was crippling his old shipmate was difficult to watch. "Then just stop, Shann. Please. We *have* to talk."

Tension left Shann's body and he nodded, lowered his head, then sagged to his knees. Speaking in a hoarse whisper, he said "Please let my hands go, Toman. I can't feel them any more." He shivered.

Toman released him.

Shann covered his face and began rocking back and forth on his knees.

His pitiful sobs were distressing.

"Pathetic!" A man shoved his chair back from the table and stood. "Nothin' happenin' here."

Muttering slobbery words, Shann spoke barely above a whisper. "My brother... my brother... Uri. gone... gone. What will I do without him?"

Toman found tears welling in his own eyes. "I am so sorry, Shann. I am truly, so very sorry." He helped his friend back to his feet.

Toman waved to Denelan and tilted his head towards Shann. "Do you have a room where the two of us could talk?"

"Yes, follow me." With a huge sigh of relief, the tavern keeper started walking towards a door at the side of the room. "But I'm warnin' you two – don't you break out in a fight in there. That room is clean."

"That won't happen." Toman assured him. "But could I have a bowl of warm water and a couple of towels? May I also ask, sir, if you would make a tisane blended of nettle and mint. My friend here needs to drink something other than ale for a while." Toman wrapped an arm around Shann's back to stabilise his wobbly gait. They climbed the steps back to the ground level of the tavern.

"Yes, of course." Denelan frowned at Shann then smiled at Toman. "And I'll bring your Lordship some of my mead. It's the best in Limman. Follow me." Pushing chairs and a table out of the way, he made a path for them to the side room.

"Thank you."

Opening the door, and waving Toman and Shann in, a nervous look passed across the tavern keeper's face. He lifted two tall, fragile-looking porcelain vases off a low cabinet near the door and tucked them under his arm as he slipped back out of the room.

Toman helped Shann onto a chair beside a large wooden table.

He needed a bath, badly.

Shann folded his lanky arms on the smooth table top then buried his face in his sleeves. His shoulders shook as he breathed noisily.

With a heavy heart Toman waited, silently watching his friend. How raw-boned Shann had become. How long had it been since he'd had some solid food and not just drink?

The innkeeper's words back in Barrost came vividly back to mind...'*He already looked like a dead man. It's like a half of his own soul shrivelled and died with his brother. And the other half of him doesn't know how to live without him.*'

...didn't know how to live without him... Toman swallowed hard.

Master Denelan bustled back into the room, a wide bowl of steaming water in his hands, and two thick towels over his shoulder. "'E's been in 'ere every night this week." He handed Toman the towels then patted him awkwardly on the shoulder as he started to leave again.

"Good Sir, would you be able to locate a clean shirt for my mate? I'll pay you for it."

The tavern keeper smiled and nodded, then quietly closed the door behind him.

Toman dipped half of a towel in the hot water, wrung it out, and held it towards Shann.

Shann ignored it.

So Toman placed it next to him on the table, then wet the corner of the second towel and began rubbing the clots of blood off Shann's clothes. "Were you aware that Ensign Eckel had persuaded Uri to join his ring?"

Shann started breathing more deeply. "Yes." He raised his head and stared at the wall as if trying to focus on something.

"Did he tell you why?" asked Toman carefully.

"Yes!" Shann snarled through clenched teeth. "I mean..." His shoulders slumped. "No! He never made it clear what Eckel was having him do."

Shann seemed to just notice the towel next to him, but he dropped his head back onto his folded arms. His wrists were now ringed with welts from where Toman had held them.

"No, he didn't tell me what he was doing." His head still on his arms, Shann took a deep breath and spoke more calmly. "He just showed up with coin, good coin. He needed it to marry Sere Shorann back home, because he'd lost his purse to... to..." He swallowed hard as though trying not to weep again.

"To the woman in the tavern. I remember."

Shann nodded, mumbling to himself. "A life wasted. A life for nothing."

Toman picked up the wet towel again and put it closer to Shann's hands. "Not long after we'd signed up and were on board the ship in Mirshod, Eckel was already secretly asking new deckhands if they wanted to earn some extra money after hours. I had said yes at first, but he never told me what work I would have done. His Grace recruited me before Eckel even had the first job for me."

Shann looked up. He seemed to finally be listening. "So Eckel approached you, too?"

A loud knock came at the door, and it opened before Toman could respond.

In one hand Master Denelan balanced a small tray with a cup of tisane and a large frothing tankard. And held a clean folded shirt in the other. "Here you go, My Lord."

"Thank you, Good Sir." Toman stood and took the tray, placing it on the table.

The tavern keeper laid the shirt out then walked quickly back through the door.

Shann seemed to finally notice the moist towel next to him. He picked it up and began wiping his face. "Me and Uri... Me and my brother..." Shann paused. "Toman I haven't talked to nobody about this." He sucked in a ragged breath. His body quivered as though fighting back sobs. "Me and Uri had fought. I mean, we *always* fought, but I love my brother."

He grimaced. "I *loved* my brother." He reached for the cup and swallowed the tea in two gulps. Tears dripped from his eyes, but he regained composure quickly. "But, but the last few weeks before he... he..." Shann struggled to finish his sentence. "...was killed..."

Sometimes actually saying that a person is dead makes their death seem more real, too heavy to bear.

"I cannot fathom what drove him. He had become so dark, I didn't know him anymore." Shann glanced at the dirty smudge now on his towel and dipped it back into the bowl then wrung it out. The old familiar blue of his now tired eyes stared out from his filthy face. "You know that Eckel hated you, right? That was obvious."

"Yes, I became aware of that." Toman didn't want the conversation drawn towards himself, so he guided the subject in a different direction. "Eckel had offered coin, gold coin. Gold has a powerful effect on many people's minds. They think very differently when gold flashes in front of them."

"But, dead for a few more coins?" Shann spat, twisting the towel between his hands. "My brother is dead, and for what?" He looked pleadingly into Toman's eyes, "Why, Toman, why?!"

"Did you know Uri had fallen under a sorcerer's power?"

Shann's mouth fell open. "What?" He frowned. "Uri had changed a lot. I didn't know him any more." He repeated the words sadly. "He'd turned violent. I was afraid he'd end up dead."

"Uri was under the power of a terrible sorcerer, under a terrible spell called the Beàl'Toht. I don't think he could resist the evil. It commanded him."

"Eckel!" Shann gritted his teeth together.

"No, Eckel was actually under *Uri's* power!"

"What? How? I don't understand."

"Neither do we. But His Grace found notes that were addressed to Uri as the leader of a group. It seemed that Uri's connection with the sorcerer named Torghyll went all the way back to our time before we left Turicum."

Shann frowned at the floor. "That's about the time he

started acting strange, too. Uri changed so much, Toman. So much, I didn't understand him any more."

Toman was not supposed to tell anyone the whole story, what had happened in those final minutes of Uri's life. Those terrifying sensations of Uri's last heartbeats as he died...

But what would His Grace say about it now?

Toman shuddered.

His master would understand. Things had changed. It wasn't right to withhold this anymore.

Toman would take the responsibility for disobeying his master because if Shann was ever to trust him again, Toman needed to be honest and tell him. Right then.

Courage filled him.

"My life is so empty without that stupid fish-brained moron." Shann's voice was muffled by the wet towel he dragged over his face. "We were twins, Toman. Together since birth."

Toman couldn't imagine losing a twin brother, a constant companion from the day he took his first breath. "Shann, uh..." The muscles in his throat tightened. His stomach trembled. "Uh..." The moment of courage to tell Shann the truth passed as quickly as it had come. "We missed you on board in Barrost."

Shann frowned and stared at him blankly. He ignored Toman's attempt to change the subject. "Even if Uri had gone off the deep end, no-one had any right to kill him."

"Shann." His tongue suddenly felt like a dried slug in his mouth. Where was the courage from a moment before? Toman steeled himself. Courage or not, he had to tell his friend. "Uri was just about to kill Lord Druin." Toman tried again to swallow. "It was my Linger sword that stopped him. I am the one who killed him."

Shann continued to stare. His expression didn't

change. He didn't even blink. No anger. Nothing. "I know." He said flatly.

Toman finally flopped onto a chair. "What? You *knew?*"

"I knew he'd died because of you… I just didn't know why." Unblinking eyes still fixed on Toman, Shann finished unbuttoning his filthy shirt. "We were twins, Toman. Twins are connected to each other." He tugged the shirt off and crumpled it into a ball. Dipping his towel back in the basin, he began rubbing under his arms. Below Shann's protruding ribs, the sides of his body were covered in large dark purple and black blotches.

Toman winced. Goosebumps rose on his arms.

What a beating Shann must have taken!

Grabbing the tankard of mead, Toman finished it in three quick gulps. He distractedly smiled in surprise. It didn't need any honey. Sweetened already to perfection.

"Please forgive me, Shann."

Shann stared at him.

He swallowed.

More tears formed in his friend's eyes. The dullness seemed to clear and life seemed to come back into them. He mumbled. "You don't have to ask me for forgiveness. I know Uri deserved what he got. I just miss him. A lot."

The weight on Toman's chest lightened slightly. "Listen, Shann, come back with me. You need a home again… with people you know. I'll give you back your old job." Toman would explain to His Grace as soon as his master woke up.

Moaning a 'yes', Shann gingerly slipped into the clean shirt. He stopped half way and looked at Toman. "Wait. What did you just say? *You* will give me my job back? What happened to—"

"I'll tell you about it on our way back to the Sindrea Isabella."

"The Sindrea Isabella?"

"Prince Elstundreth-Fathringen's warship."

41

SHONIN

Toman was glad to see the light of Yannu's torch on the upper deck.

His friend was waiting for him to return. Such diligence. Yannu was going to be a remarkable man one day. Such a vigilant man would be an excellent guardian to the Highborns.

"So, you say that Uri could have been innocent, that this Trend could also be?" Shann sounded bewildered.

"Yes, and these evil beings, the sorcerer Torghyll from Athlonia, and the Greinen from the Temmerung, are growing in strength. And they are connected somehow."

Shann's body seemed to stiffen as he walked.

Toman looked up as the flickering light of Yannu's torch appeared down on the gangway.

"Hoi." Yannu waved from the railing, then started walking towards them. In the torch light, his deeply creased frown looked like black lines on his forehead.

Yannu walked up to Shann and began scrutinising his face. "Wait a minute. You were at the fights earlier this evening, weren't you?"

Toman blinked. What?

"I didn't recognise you there. You got the grunt beat out of you!" Yannu looked down at Shann's dirty trousers. "Doof en Donder, Shann! What were you doing in a pit fight?"

Toman raised an eyebrow. And what was *Yannu* doing at a pit fight?

Shann shrugged, looking disheartened. "They pay. I needed to eat."

"Yea?" Yannu's normal friendly smile was missing from his face. "And what are you doing *here* in Limmania? And not on your way back to Turicum?"

Toman frowned now. "Come on, Yannu, be gentle. Our old friend has had a hard time. He needs some food." Alarm rang in him. "Ah, but the kitchens? Did they find out what caused the bad pastries?" Surely it hadn't been an intentional poisoning earlier that morning.

Yannu shook his head. "I dunno. Cook Marta thought it was most likely the sweet meats had gone bad, and the kitchen staff hadn't realised it before serving them?"

"Good." Toman adjusted the cuffs of his jacket. "I'm bringing Shann back on board."

Yannu stared at Toman, then Shann, then Toman again. "Ok, but are you sure he's not under the—?"

"I'm sure." He waved towards Shann. "No white hair, and no scalded mark on the chest."

Shann's eyes widened. "Wha—?"

"I'll explain later." Toman clapped Shann on the back then looked at Yannu. "Would you show him the way to the kitchens and see that he gets his fill? He needs a few good meals. And a bath."

Yannu sniffed, wrinkled his nose then nodded.

A surprised look passed over Shann's face. "You still listening to him like he's your boss?"

Yannu snorted a laugh. "Oh mate, he's *definitely* my boss. And yours now, too." He bowed. "Let me catch you up." He waved towards Toman, and spoke with some sort of awkward-sounding lofty accent. "He's a 'Fyrst of Ydassum', you know. That means he's nobility now, a prince, if you didn't know. Like a Highborn. And I'm manservant to his Lordship."

Shann's open mouth snapped shut. "You're joking. No?"

Toman laughed. "Meet you later in my quarters, Yannu. I'm going to see His Grace now."

A hint of a smile twitched at the corners of Yannu's mouth. "You do that."

Toman frowned. "Yannu? What's been happening?"

"See you later, Your Lordship." His friend's mischievous smile returned, and he bowed low again.

"What are you trying to say?" Excitement tingled in Toman. "It's His Grace, isn't it! Yannu? Is he well?"

"Go and see for yourself, Your Lordship." Not turning back, Yannu waved at Toman as he placed his other hand on Shann's shoulder. "The kitchens and our sleeping quarters are this way, aft, belowdecks."

Heart beginning to beat wildly, Toman bolted to the stairway leading to the infirmary. Taking the steps two and three at a time, he reached the landing. He ran down the corridor. Heart throbbing, he stopped in front of the sick bay door. He tried not to knock too loudly.

"Enter." Physician Wanner's immediate response filled him with hope.

Opening the door, Toman gasped. "Your Grace!"

His master was propped up with pillows, looking blankly towards Toman. A weak smile appeared.

"Your Grace!" Toman knelt at his bed. "I'm so glad to see you awake!"

No greeting? Nothing more than the hint of a smile?

Something was strange about his master.

"Your Grace?" Concern gripped Toman.

He looked at Physician Wanner.

"He hasn't spoken, Your Highness. But I am very pleased with this new development. With the help of some pillows, he can sit up, which is remarkable. And even though his breathing is still shallow, it is regular." Wanner's eyes seemed to smile. "We have hope."

Toman reached for his master's hands and gently squeezed them. "Welcome back, Your Grace. Welcome back." Toman stood slowly and uttered a prayer. "Be well, Lord Protector, please be well."

His Grace slowly tilted his head as though trying to focus on Toman's height.

"Your Highness, I think it best not to disturb him further tonight and allow his convalescence to continue without interruption." Wanner stood next to Toman. "I hope you can rest as well. Your master's health is improving.

"I will leave my master to rest now." A weight seemed to dissolve and fall from Toman's shoulders. For the first time since His Grace's injury in the brig, peace began to soothe the tension in Toman's entire body. Then exhaustion pulled on his arms and chest.

He hadn't realised how tired he was.

"Thank you most sincerely, Physician Wanner." Toman leaned over and placed his palm on his master's folded hands. "Good night, Your Grace. I shall come back in the morning."

Wanner bowed and opened the door for him "Your Highness.".

"Thank you."

Toman walked slowly down the corridor and past Palan's rooms.

A strange sensation filled his chest. Hope.

Hope was strangely both light and heavy at the same time. Hope lifted dreariness but filled the mind with dreams. Plans to be fulfilled.

He reached the landing to his corridor. "Evening." He saluted the guards standing at the glass-panelled door.

"Your Highness." They bowed, opening the door, then stepped aside.

Nodding his thanks, he walked down the lamp-lit hallway and entered his cabin.

Closing the door behind him, he quickly unlatched and opened the windows.

The air felt strangely warm, but refreshing at the same time.

Pulling his boots off, he pushed them under the suspended bed. He quickly undressed, then pulled his nightshirt over his head and chuckled to himself, remembering Yannu calling him 'Your Heininess'.

Climbing up onto the bed, the ropes attached to the four corners of the bedframe creaked slightly under his weight. He stretched out on the feather mattress and sighed with pleasure. A strange invention to sleep on, suspended in the air, but comfortable both in choppy seas and in a still harbour.

Yannu should soon arrive.

There were a few things he wanted to talk to his best friend about before sleep overtook him.

Toman let his body relax and closed his eyes for a moment. Just for a moment.

An image passed through Toman's mind... His Grace sitting, propped up on his pillows.

Once again, Toman's chest filled with a pleasant weightiness, but not the heaviness of worry. The feeling tingled with a sense of joy, like in his Gebayt-Bithen.

He slowly filled his lungs.

His Grace would live!

The fact that he wasn't speaking yet was just a small hurdle his master would have to overcome. But The Lord Protector was strong. He'd make it.

Toman smiled again and slipped quickly into a deep sleep.

"Shonin, I think we need to take our places." One of her two older, fellow Hlimmanian companions nervously urged her forward.

The young woman with the pale golden hair began walking in front of the other two.

Toman's skin prickled with chills. This young woman, Shonin – she'd been in his dreams before. He was once again in some part of the strange dream that had started back on Fahtu-Shan. But this was different.

A short distance away, in the heart of the city, the culmination of the consecrated fast would take place and the beginning of the holiest ceremony of the year – the Invoking of the Blessing for the sowing of the seeds would begin. The population of the region had already poured into the streets of Rubinoug, the Glowing Jewel of the Desert, bringing seeds and tubers to be blessed, in hopes of abundant harvests.

Her thoughts were filling Toman's mind as though she

had touched his Linger. He instinctively looked for things that had been in his last vision of her. Where was her little son? No blood dripped from her hands this time.

At the massive arches spanning the entrance to the fortified city, the thirty lesser priests of the High Temple stood up. Their superiors, the three high priests of the Triate Santonin, gestured towards them.

The thirty lifted sacred Eornum-horn trumpets to their lips. Multiple piercing blasts rent the air, echoing off the high stucco facades of the Inner City.

Innumerable human voices responded in jubilation. Their joyous cries resounded through the city, flowing out and over the vast plaza of the holy temple grounds like the froth-capped ocean waves on a beach.

Then thunderous booms from cannons, aimed at the cloudless sky, reverberated above the city.

The ground underfoot trembled in response.

The sacred procession began lumbering forward.

The booms of the cannons shook Toman. He kept his eyes closed. He didn't want to miss any part of this strange night vision.

Shonin lowered her head for one of the Santonin high priests to place the chained collar around her neck. Again this year, she would lead the Hlimmanen in the Skyllian procession through the streets of Rubinoug.

Shonin's companions, Tymea and Heicha, walked just behind her, to her right and left.

Both were strong in Ber'eth's power.

They were interlinked with her through the markings on the nape of their necks, inked into their skin with the dark crafts of the Santonin's sorcery.

The collared chains around their necks were powerless in comparison.

Despite being older, this was the first time the other two would participate in the procession and the tight lines around their eyes showed their obvious apprehensions. Like her, their hoods were drawn back, and their hair pulled up on their heads to display the Santonin mark of ownership – the intricate tattoo of the Scarab Wasp at the base of the skull.

Four mighty beasts, Eornum from the Eastern Alldai, shuffled up to at the head of the procession. The Eornum were coaxed forward with barbed poles. Their massive hooves churned the dusty earth as they came to a halt.

"Slaves, here!" the eldest of the high priests growled.

Four men scuttled forward with a black spider silk awning held aloft on poles, then took their places alongside the Eornum and stretched the shade cloth over Shonin and her fellow Hlimmanen.

"We wouldn't want their pasty skin to burn before they've served their purpose," hissed the second of the Triate priesthood. He pushed Heicha forward. "Disgusting night rats!"

Shonin glanced down at her exposed hands.

The Skylle's skin, the colour of a starless night, could withstand the radiance of the desert sun. Indeed, the Hlimmanian pallid complexion scorched in its brilliance. She glanced up at the shimmering black threads of the spider silks in the canopy. When on display for the Santonin's purposes, the Special Ones of her race had to be shaded.

Shonin had been taught that those of her ilk, the accursed Hlimmanian descendants of Orren, were unclean and the unclean had no right to live free. Only to serve. As trophies of war over a century ago, their only duty was to obey. Or be slaughtered. Their blood would provide the libations for the high ceremonies of the Santonin.

But those sacrifices... Shonin's stomach knotted as she

squeezed her eyelids shut. The image of the bound and hooded people being led from her compound again this year tormented her.

Rather than participate in the annual ceremony and witness their massacre, she would have preferred to be the sacrifice herself, if it wasn't for her precious son.

As Heicha and Tymea stepped forward with her in the procession, the crowds shrank back, hissing and spitting on the ground in front of them. The Skylle called their hair dead and colourless like parched grass. Their pale blue eyes were compared to those of the ashen sightless creatures that crept in deep wet caverns.

But Shonin knew Ber'eth had a purpose for them. He had not forsaken them. Something pulled on her heart, a rush of emotion she hadn't known before. Its course in her veins felt foreign, but also powerful. Almost like hope.

The Novice of the Triate raised his hand to the musicians and dancers.

Silence fell over the procession.

Acrobats climbed the massive legs of the sluggish Eornum, taking their positions on platforms mounted on the backs of the gargantuan beasts.

Their breath-taking size struck fear in Shonin, but she found them strangely beautiful. With their polished horns, deeply crackled hide, and the jewel-encrusted gold plates attached to their bony heads, they moved like adorned walls of living stone.

A long thunderous wave of sound now came from the sacred Eornum-horn trumpets, announcing the official start of the procession.

Innumerable human voices responded to the clamorous instruments as the throngs lining the streets danced in jubilation. Above Shonin, the acrobats leapt through the air, somersaulting from one platform to another. Their svelte torsos were painted dull maroon, stippled with chalky white. Their narrow eyes and full lips were outlined in deep orange.

The Day of Invoking, such a grand and terrifying spectacle, was underway. How could any race take joy in such an elaborate display celebrating death, subjugation, and thraldom?

On this, the holiest day of the year to the Skylle, the Santonin would draw the menacing primordial forces, called the Pletoran, from the depths below the city and wrest them under their control to bring moisture to the whole Alldai. The need for the rains was great. And the subsequent harvests were the lifeline not only for the pitiful farmers that had poured into the city from the surrounding Vastans, but everyone. Everyone wanted to survive.

But at what cost?

She had only known anxiety and fear. Dread had always been instilled into her, as well as all the Hlimmanen imprisoned within the compound. They were told that one transgression could end all their lives.

Heicha glanced in her direction, the corners of her mouth curved down and quivering.

Shonin tried to give her a reassuring smile.

The Santonin wielded fear as a weapon even on their own kind. Fear of starvation, of imprisonment, of torture and death. The torment of incessant fear... No need for the torturers to slowly stop their hearts because fear quenched lives much quicker. And hope died in fear. Life without hope might as well be living death.

She looked around at the gaunt petitioners bearing their baskets.

How much of their own crops were they allowed to eat?

A sense of awe at Ber'eth's mysterious kindness, swept over her. She was fed well. Heicha and Tymea, too. Their eyes were not sunken into hollow sockets like so many of those in the throngs gathered. Shonin lowered her head in shame, and pity.

The peasants had come seeking assurance that the Santonin would invoke the annual blessing on their crops, calling the distant rains inland. Their gazes were fixed on the Triate Priesthood as they strode three paces ahead of her.

The Triate Priests had told her she was special, and her young son, Dhomon, could be as well. Her Linger was powerful. "The most powerful ever born to the accursed Hlimmanen". Not that it did her much good. Their control over her kind was absolute. In early childhood, all Hlimmanen were stung with inks on the nape of their necks with the sign of the Santon–n – designs into which the Triate wove spells of imprisonment and subjugation. If a Hlimman manifested Eth abilities later, they could not wield their Eth without the consent of the Triate. Or else they would feel the searing pain of insubordination stabbing through their skulls.

But she didn't want to be special.

The little privileges she had been given, special meals, walks in the garden... they only caused jealousy and doubts among her people. And what use was having any power if it was only subjugated to someone else's will?

She feared that her son, little Dhomon, would one day demonstrate Eth powers and also be enslaved with their sorcerous inks, bound by the same forbidden arcane spells.

Toman sat up in bed, his heart racing. The smell of the dry sandy soil filled his nostrils.

Dhomon, her child's name was Dhomon.

He blinked and blinked again to clear the vision from his sight.

But it wouldn't go away.

The dream was cast on the walls of his cabin! The heads of the giant horned-beasts walking alongside the three women seemed to pierce through his ceiling. The inky skinned guards were the same Toman had always seen in these dreams... but this time it was almost as though he could reach out and touch them!

The woman's thoughts rushed back into Toman's mind...

Creaking just behind them, the cage of a wizened Uran-Draigana rocked back and forth on a cart. The last of its kind, another trophy of a long-ago war. Its wings had been bound and its beak muzzled with iron. Shonin couldn't bear to look at the now-pitiful creature. He must have once been proud and fierce.

The procession entered the sprawling Temple Plaza.

The ornately decorated building the Skylle revered as their Sacred Temple stood in the centre of the wide-open paved area.

In front of the temple, the wings of the colossal statue of the vanquished Uran-Draigana cast a wide shadow over the altar at its base. Beneath the gilt effigy was the aperture to the subterranean realms of the Pletoran.

To one side of the temple, the Lord Successor's raised golden throne glimmered in the shade of a silk canopy.

Surrounded by sombre brown facades, the Temple Plaza filled with dazzling colour, sound, and movement. The musicians filled the air with the pounding of drums and the shrill strain of flutes. The dancers fanned out, spinning, and leaping, their deep scarlet gossamer clothing swirling in the air around them.

The sun blazed above as all took their places around the altar in front of the temple.

Trumpets pierced the air, announcing the arrival of the Lord Successor, High Ruler of Rubinoug and the southern deserts of the Alldai.

Appearing near the steps to the dais, his crown sparkled fiercely in the intense sunlight. His long, braided chin-beard was worn over his left shoulder in the fashion of Skyllian rulers of old. He climbed the steps, then turned and sat on the throne, facing the statue and the aperture.

Attendants stepped up to the Lord Successor, placing his pet in his arms. The indigo and yellow desert reptile bumped its head against its master's hand. Its collar sparkled with a strand of diamonds.

The Successor nodded to the Triate.

They didn't acknowledge his presence as they took their places before the temple.

Rumours had reached even the Hlimmanen that the Lord Successor was a puppet dancing to the Triate's will.

The sun reached its zenith in the sky.

Shonin, Tymea and Heicha were not allowed to speak to each other, but once they formed the shield, the three of them would have means of communication. By linking their Lingers, they could sense each other's feelings and receive mental impressions. Sometimes images or even words flitted back and forth. The forbidden communication was kept a guarded secret from the Santonin.

The Elder Priest raised a hand. His deep blue fingernails glistened in the blazing sunlight.

The drums stopped. The dancers' tiny bells fell silent as they prostrated themselves before the altar.

The air soon filled with the piercing cry of the Blood Song of the Innocents.

Shonin shuddered.

The Temple Plaza shook under her sandals as the power of the sacrifice reverberated up from the ground and through her body.

She choked back bile.

Black fog filled her sight, threatening to darken her vision completely. She locked her knees. She could not faint. Not here, not now. She would be severely punished if she did. She blinked the tears out of her eyes. Surely they could not punish her for crying.

Porcelain vessels needed for the Drawing-Forth incantation, each filled with the sacrifice of the Innocents, were brought to the Triate. They poured the libation out and the altar glistened with the sacred hue as rivulets flowed down the stone, filling the circular trough around the aperture to the Pletoran's realm.

The Triate Santonin pronounced ancient spells, terrible words of the Drawing-Forth and subjugation. The thick crimson liquid around the aperture began to quicken. At first rippling on the surface, bright red droplets rose slowly, forming a towering cylinder of glistening beads.

Closing their eyes, the Triate lifted their faces, hideous grins unfurling on their lips. "Come! That which was bequeathed by the Ancients." The Elder Priest's raspy voice sent shivers down Shonin's spine. "From all four Vastans, we command the power of the Rubinstones, come!"

"Tomi! What's happening here?" Yannu stepped into the room, his mouth agape. "What are these people, these animals?"

"You can see them too?" Tension filled Toman's body. He tried to swallow. Were Glortroms now for more than one person?

42

Apprentice

Toman gasped as the Glortrom faded. His whole body shivered with goosebumps.

"We need to tell the others!" Yannu still stood by the door, his palm resting on the handle.

"Yes, of course." Toman stumbled out of the hanging bed. "Druin and Lady Banah need to know of this Glortrom, and of the mysterious woman that keeps appearing in my dreams. This *Shonin*." Toman sat back down on his cot. "But it's very late. Perhaps first thing in the morning?"

Yannu narrowed his eyes. "You've dreamt of this woman before?"

"Yes. A few times, but never as clearly as tonight." Toman wiped the sweat off his forehead. "We both have to try and remember every detail of this one for when we meet tomorrow at morning tea."

Yannu seemed to become lost in thought.

"Would you stay here again tonight?" Toman pointed to the divan that Yannu had already used once as a bed. "I'd like to talk a bit before hitting the pillow."

"Sure, mate. I don't know about you, but I think we need some ale first, eh?"

Toman grinned. "I think you're right."

"I'll be back in two shakes." His friend hurried out into the corridor, closing the door behind him.

The last dream Toman had of this Shonin, she had been with two other women, but also a small child, who must have been Dhomon. Toman could recall the dream almost as though he'd had it the previous night.

Three very fair-skinned women with white-blonde hair had walked in a procession. They wore long dark green cloaks.

Their garments had stood out in sharp contrast to the throngs of people around them.

Their hair had been braided and fixed in tight rolls at the back of their heads.

They'd had an image of beetle-like wasps tattooed in dark red at the base of their skulls.

Shonin, the youngest-looking, had held the hand of a small child at her side.

Even though the window was still open, his nightshirt began to stick to his chest with perspiration.

What could all of this mean?

Of all the night visions before, he'd never had a Glortrom. And how could Yannu see and hear it all as well?

Listening for Yannu's footsteps in the corridor, the only sound he could pick up on was his own quickly beating heart.

He was beginning to sweat profusely. Pulling his thin night shirt up over his head, he folded it carefully and placed it near the pillow, then laid back down on the mattress.

Rapid soft footfall in the corridor signalled Yannu's return.

Toman quickly arranged the thin sheet to cover himself.

A moment later his friend entered the cabin with four large, stoppered bottles, and held two out to him.

Toman sat up. "Just one, thanks. The last time I drank with you on an empty stomach, I forgot most of what happened that evening."

Handing him a bottle, Yannu chuckled. "Ye, you got pretty slurred that night."

"Yannu, what exactly did you see and hear tonight?"

Taking a long gulp of the ale, his friend sat slowly onto the divan. "It was like I could hear a woman's thoughts. As though they were coming directly into my mind."

"The same thing happened to me."

Yannu nodded then closed his eyes tightly. "I saw a very old Uccell, bound like a prisoner, and on display on the back of a cart. People were walking in rows as if in a parade." He took another long swig. "It looked like they were coming up to a huge plaza with a temple in the centre. It was hot, hotter than anything I'd ever felt before. I could smell dry dust in the air. There were also gigantic horned-beasts with thick grey hide." He opened his eyes. "And dancers with blood red dresses, spinning and jumping."

Toman nodded again. "Yes, that's what I saw and felt as well."

"What does it mean, Tomi?"

Toman shook his head. "I don't know, I don't understand how you could have seen my vision... I thought Glortroms only appeared to one person at a time. But surely the Highborns will understand more. Tomorrow."

He finished his bottle and started to lay his head on the pillow but stopped. "Yannu?" Toman sat back up again. "What is this about you being at a fight where Shann was?"

His friend laughed through his nose then finished his second bottle. "Tomi, your mother's people here..." He pointed towards the door. "They are some leather-hided blokes that love a good round of fisticuffs. They even have rings set up in some of the taverns, and one over in the shipbuilding yard. That's the one I went to."

From the embankment, Toman had seen the large stones arranged in a ring in the old shipyard. "How did you get over there? There's no bridge."

Yannu chuckled. "Small ferry boats. Back and forth all evening. The place was packed." His friend seemed to swell. "There was an amazing fight tonight. These two really big blokes slammed into each other like rams in the rut."

The glee in his voice was unmistakable. But there was something else about Yannu. Something very special. A fierceness and gentleness at the same time. And an alertness to detail, and keen ears.

"They were massive, Tomi. Arms as big as my legs." He slapped his thighs. "They ploughed into each other. At first, heads planted on each other's shoulders, they just kept on swinging over their heads. Fists flying everywhere."

Yannu pummelled the air.

"Incredible! They started poundin' on each other like blacksmith hammers on anvils! It didn't take long before they were both covered in blood. But they didn't stop."

Pausing, Yannu chuckled again and shook his head. "None of them stop, not until one or the other gets the mugs rattled in his cupboard... You know what I mean." He tapped on his skull and continued, "Knocked out flat. Legs crossed at the ankles, hands shakin' in the air like they were holding a pillow, their eyes twitching."

A pensive look passed over his friend's eyes. "But you know what, Tomi?" Yannu opened the third bottle.

Toman shook his head. Such violence.

"After every fight they brought the winners a bowl of water, a towel, and some ointments. They then knelt and washed their opponents' wounds." Yannu stared at his knuckles and shook his head. "No wonder the one poor bloke lost, Tomi. Once the blood was washed away, you could see his eyes were completely swollen shut. He couldn't see anything anymore."

Yannu paused again as a wide grin split his face. "But, Menne-Gootay, what great fights!" He swung his fists through the air again. "You know, when you enter the ring, it's like coming alive."

"You? In the ring?" Yannu was beginning to baffle him. He'd only caught glimpses of his friend's willingness to fight but had never actually seen him fight.

"Where do you think I got this little trophy." Grinning, Yannu pointed to the scar under his eye.

Toman laughed. His friend was not only very observant, but fearless. "Yannu?"

"Hmm?" Yannu looked up as he began pulling his boots off.

Should Toman ask him without first talking to His Grace? A sense of certainty overcame Toman, and he posed the question that had been in his mind for a while. "Would you ever consider becoming my Apprentice? To protect the Highborns? I'd have to ask them first of course, but I'm sure they'd agree."

Sock-footed and chuckling, Yannu stood.

Toman stared at him unblinking.

"Seriously?" Yannu's mouth slowly fell open. Exhaling sharply, he flopped back onto the divan.

43

Glortroms

After a peaceful night's rest, Druin made his way down the corridor. He straightened his jacket and pulled his cuffs neatly below his wrists then entered Steward Loraimen's meeting room.

Such a beautiful architectural space! The curved wall full of mullioned windows seemed to invite the spectacular view of the bay into the room itself.

The early morning light reflecting off the water possessed a pristine brilliance he'd never observed back in Ydassum. With no rising morning mists filtering the luminosity, the dawn's colours were exceptionally vibrant.

"Good morning, dear Brother." Banah walked in behind him, side by side with Lorann and Arden.

"Good morning, My Ladies." Druin bowed.

Arden's presence made his heart skip a beat.

He suddenly found it difficult to keep breathing at a normal pace. She was beautiful. No, she was more than simply beautiful, she was breathtaking. The warm golden light of the dawn brought out glistening reddish strands in her long blonde hair.

And her eyes... her eyes, a bright blue-green like the waters of the bay, sparkled exceptionally this morning.

He walked over to her and clasped her hand. "You look lovely." His smile was beginning to hurt his cheeks.

She smiled back.

The sunlight seemed to suddenly lose its golden hues, shining clearer and brighter.

"Good morning." Palan joined them. He appeared better rested this morning than in the past week.

"Good morning all. I hope you slept well." Steward Loraimen bustled through the landing entrance and waved a small group of his manservants past him. "Go ahead and set the table for morning tea, then we must not be disturbed." One of them nodded. "Yes, Your Grace."

The young men flowed around the large circular table, quickly arranging each setting with measured precision.

Toman and Master Elden walked into the doorway. Both looked slightly ill at ease.

"Good morning." Toman bowed then glanced nervously at his manservant. "Please forgive me, My Lady. May I have Master Yannu Elden join us today?"

Toman had never brought him to an official meeting before. However, Banah had begun to include Maiden Lorann in their meetings, so there shouldn't be any reason why not.

Banah smiled. "If you desire it, yes. Of course, Fryst Toman."

"Thank you, My Lady." Toman approached a chair, then indicated for Master Elden to stand next to him as the Steward's servants finished bringing beverages and platters of food, then left the room.

Toman seemed to stare at Banah. He moved his head as though responding to a question, then spoke in a solemn monotone. "My Lady, I had a Glortrom last night."

"A Glortrom? Here in Limmania?" The Steward's brow creased slightly then he began walking around the chairs, double-checking the table settings. His deep red velvet robes dragged slightly on the floor behind him. "Your Highness, I await with great anticipation to hear its message."

Druin wasn't certain if Steward Loraimen's response was humorous or just uncertain.

The Steward fixed his eyes on Banah and spoke in a confident tone. "The Great Shift awakens the Continent. Ber'eth beckons us toward our fates."

"You are aware of the Great Shift?" Banah smiled. "I am relieved."

She looked quickly towards the landing.

The tall, elegant headdresses of Chieftess Beruhn and Chieftain Ruhand swayed into sight.

"Chieftains, welcome." Banah spread out her arms. "Please, come and join us at the table."

"Master Elden," Druin whispered to Toman's manservant. "Remember, refrain from ever looking the Riddern Chieftess in the eyes."

"Or it could mean your death." Toman finished his statement.

Master Elden flinched. "Yes, My Lord."

The Riddern Chieftains glided towards the table. Their magnificent colourful feather cloaks shimmered like burnished metal.

Toman whispered to his manservant. "Yannu, please fill in anything I forget."

He nodded in response.

The Steward made a sweeping elegant gesture towards the chairs. "Now, my guests, please be seated." He made a second expansive gesture, but towards the food. "In Limmania we like to eat while we talk, so meals are included when conducting meetings." He smiled. "Please forgive the lack of servants, but I've asked my staff to give us privacy. We have much to discuss this morning. I also need to inform you about the concert in your honour later today, and the dinner tomorrow."

Druin pulled out a chair for Arden. Then one for himself and they sat down.

Banah lifted her hand towards Toman. "Steward Loraimen, if Fyrst Foggling could begin by telling us of his Glortrom?"

"Yes, of course." Like a grand majordomo, the Steward began passing platters of food and pots of tea. His attention to detail was exquisite.

The Chieftains ignored the food as the rest of the group started eating and drinking.

"My Lady, I've had night visions for some time, but not Glortroms. For more than a year. Perhaps longer. They started before leaving Fahtu-Shan. Many have been about what I now know are Skyllian fleets. Most have been focused on a specific woman named Shonin."

"You know her name?" Druin stuttered.

Toman and Master Elden glanced at each other, then Toman motioned to his manservant. "Yannu, please tell them what you saw and heard."

He raised his head calmly and said, "She revealed her name in the Glortrom."

Banah gasped. "Master Elden? You heard what transpired in Fyrst Toman's vision?"

He nodded. "And saw, My Lady."

"You heard and saw the same thing Toman did?" Arden sat up tensely in her chair. She stared at Druin. "That has never been heard of."

Palan pursed his lips. "It happened to me as well. Rather, to Toman. He heard the voices in my Glortrom."

"Prince, you had one as well? It had completely slipped my mind." Banah's surprised tone was suffused with embarrassment. Her voice sounded anxious. She paused, frowning slightly.

Perhaps the lingering effects of the Queen Summerbird dust still clouding her recollection?

Palan's face was unreadable, but his voice was steady. "I thought it was a message for me personally."

"But Fyrst Foggling heard it?" Banah's eyebrows rose. "May I ask what was contained in that one as well?"

Palan inclined his head. "Yes, of course. But let's first hear more about the Glortrom Toman and his manservant had. Master Elden, if you would continue?"

Banah blinked at Palan as her slight frown disappeared.

Master Elden looked questioningly at Toman, who indicated his approval, then continued. "We heard cannons but not like for a war. More like for a parade. And there were gigantic horned-beasts, as big as small barns. Grey crackly hides as thick as tree bark. I could smell the dusty sand as they walked!"

"Eornum?" Druin couldn't contain his surprise. "You saw Eornum?" He shook his head, looking around the table. "They are indigenous to the southernmost deserts of the Alldai."

Toman's manservant nodded then lowered his eyes in silence.

Banah turned to Toman. "Fyrst? Is there more?"

Toman spoke without intonation. "Shonin is a young mother. Her son is called Dhomon. She wields a clear Linger, like me. So do others where she is. She, and others of her kind, are enslaved by a group of three priests she referred to in her thoughts as 'the Santonin' or 'Triate Santonin'. They were preparing for some immense ritual. She kept thinking of herself and her comrades as 'Hlimmanen'—"

The Steward's hands flew to his mouth. "Oh my! Hlimmanen?" His eyes were wide open in surprise. "Hlimmanen is our ancient historical name. We were called Hlimmanen before the desolation brought about by the Skylle."

"My Lady." Toman's face was taut. The veins in his temples stood out. "Shonin's thoughts... I realise now that she has been sending messages for a long time. Maybe years. She is desperate to break free from her slavery. I understood that she is the most powerful Eth Wielder the Skylle have ever enslaved, and she is bound to them through an inked design on the nape of her neck, the Scarab Wasp..." He placed his palm on the back of his skull. "...where our Eth Lobes are. Forbidden crafts have bound her to the will of these Santonin. But..." Toman paused for an instant, shaking his head. "I cannot tell if these visions are glimpses of the past, present or future, but I can't help but feel that they are somehow upon us now."

"Are you sure these weren't just vivid nightmares, really bad dreams?" The Steward asked half-heartedly.

Lorann stirred slightly in her chair.

"Maiden Lorann, would you share what you know about the subject?" Druin had previously marvelled at her knowledge of Glortrom histories. She had first spoken about them and their relevance to the Orrenic races back on the trip to Baron and Baroness Armgolt's in Barrost.

Keeping her head lowered, Lorann spoke clearly, but in the direction of the Riddern. "Glortroms are mentioned often in Old Orrenic writings."

"They are extremely important messages. They were what Ber'eth used to convince our ancestors to make the dangerous trip that led them to the Great Continent. Glortroms also led tribes to migrate to the safety of the Cloud Kingdoms of Ydassum and Edendor before the Skyllian invasions. Glortroms are a part of our shared Orrenic histories."

A loud knock at the door startled Druin. Weren't the servants commanded not to disturb?

The Steward rose quickly and opened the door.

Cook Marta's flushed face appeared, Captain Westrum and two guards standing behind her. Steward Loraimen spun around towards Banah. "Is she a part of your entourage?"

"Yes, yes." Banah's voice sounded strained. She stood. "Cook Marta? What is the matter?"

Uncle Lytwon's cook remained in the doorway wringing her hands. "My Lady." She swallowed. "We found ze man who poisoned ze Prince's pastry."

"Poisoned?" Banah's eyes turned sharply to Druin. "Did you know of this?"

Druin shook his head. But was there perhaps a connection to the venomous Emerald Spiders the

Riddern had recently reported stolen? The ones they'd procured from the Bazaar Districts in Barrost.

"Please forgive me, My Lady." Toman leaned forward. "So much has happened. As we left the ship, Yannu told me that two kitchen servants had died after eating pastries from our morning tea."

"Only ze food on ze Prince Palandred's plate had zis evil in it. But we found him." Cook Marta's voice trembled with emotion. "He is Mendelonian and in chains in ze brig. His name is Bithard, a common deckhand."

"Where did this man come from?" Palan's voice shook with controlled rage.

"Zey sinks he came onboard in Barrost. My kitchen crew did not recognise him."

"He will pay dearly for this. He risked not only my life but also all of yours." Palan focused on Banah.

"Another attempt to destabilise a royal house by killing off a member of its ruling family." Toman scowled in the direction of the wall. "Cook Marta, was there anything else...?

She shook her head. "Not zat I heard. But he was such a young lad to have so much white hair."

Toman gulped and looked nervously at Druin then Banah. He mouthed silently, 'the Beàl'Toht again?'

Druin nodded. "That would be another piece of a pattern we are slowly recognising."

"Then, thank you." Palan waved dismissively towards the door. "That will be all."

Cook Marta bowed and backed out onto the landing to the awaiting guards.

Closing the door again, the Steward addressed Palan. "Your Highness, do we need to send soldiers to your ship?"

Palan shook his head. "I have Captain Westrum. He will investigate thoroughly and deal with him when he gets back to the Sindrea Isabella." Staring pensively towards the windows, Palan kept shaking his head. "Since there haven't been any other instances of poisoning on my ship, I think we can assume his actions were personal and focused on me."

"We can investigate further once back on board." Toman's piercing glare now seemed directed at his plate. "This is inexcusable.'

"I agree with you." Palan sighed deeply. "But Westrum will report to me if my presence is needed. I believe we have more urgent matters at hand here." He tapped on the table, then stood and walked to the windows. "Referring back to the Glortroms." He pushed his hair back behind his ears. "Mine had elements from the terrible day my mother passed away. These Santonin, as Toman called them, are searching for me and the birthright they feel I stole."

Banah joined Palan at the windows. "Palandred, what birthright of theirs do they think you have?"

His eyes met hers and he whispered, "You called me Palandred." A brilliant smile replaced his worried expression. He looked down at his hands as the tension returned to his face. Opening and closing them slowly, Druin's old friend somehow reminded him of Toman.

"I don't know how I did it, but that day I overpowered the scarab demon that was released from the Rubinstone. It entered my body through my palms."

Banah covered a gasp with her hand. "But surely, it wasn't a demon, Palandred."

Palan grasped her other hand in his. "I hope not."

"Were there any other Glortroms?" Arden looked quickly from Palan to Druin. "Are there any other elements to consider? These messages from Ber'eth are trying to tell us something."

"I was visited by one as well." Banah walked back to the table and looked at Steward Loraimen. "But my Glortrom, I feel, has already come to pass. It was of the Athlonian attack, and the arrival of the Irrshen. And the maps of Barrost which we now know were connected to the student Dobbesser in Prince Palandred's brig." She sat back down next to Lorann. "Then there was the Glortrom reported from Landsend that also contained information about the attack on the Northern Horn. It seems that one was the first of many."

"Yes." Arden stared towards the windows. "I heard of the account from Landsend. But what do the visions of the Skylle mean? Toman, did you perceive anything else from the connection to this Shonin? What we should do, or where we should go?"

He shook his head. "I'm sorry. That was all."

"Except the sacrifices they were making. It was huge." Master Elden looked worriedly at Toman. "I had the impression that they were sacrificing innocent people for something. It felt terrible."

Palan walked back to the table and sat next to Banah.

She rested her hand on his arm.

Although silent and showing no reactions, the Riddern Chieftains seemed to be listening attentively to everything.

"Many mysterious and sad things..." The Steward's countenance fell. His smile disappeared completely. "Lady Banah, I understand the sense of urgency, and the need to continue your journey..."

Heaviness permeated his words.

Banah's deep sigh added to the weightiness of the atmosphere.

Druin looked from the Steward to Palan who seemed deep in thought.

"But, My Lord..." Unblinking, Palan regarded Steward Loraimen. "We should not disregard the importance of the celebration you've planned for the Highborns. It is indeed an historic event that will surely be commemorated for generations."

"Forth-telling?" Banah whispered. Surprise lit up her eyes and she smiled at Palan. "I agree, Lord Loraimen."

Druin smiled at them both. They were getting along well.

Tension in the Steward's face seemed to ebb. He bowed low. "My appreciation, Your Highness, My Lady." His own benign expression returned.

Another knock on the door jarred the pleasant atmosphere.

Steward Loraimen once again hurried to the door and opened it with a jerk. A note was handed to him. Thanking the messenger, he closed the door again. He faced Palan and announced stiffly. "Your Highness, the gems collected in the plaza are washed and packed for your journey."

Palan blinked, frowning. "My Lord Loraimen. Those belong to your country. Accept them as my gift back to their proper owners."

Steward Loraimen's face softened like warm wax. "Your Highness." He swallowed then said breathily, "Thank you. Thank you most sincerely." With joyful tears in his eyes, he beamed at the group around the table. "Please, everyone, enjoy your meal. Then we have much to do before the concert this evening."

44

Death to the Orren

Shonin tried not to let the disgust show on her face, as the Triate Santonin pronounced their ancient spells of Drawing-Forth and oppression. The thick crimson libation flowing around the aperture quivered at their words. At first rippling only on the surface, it then formed bright red droplets that rose slowly, forming a wide cylinder of glistening beads.

With their Lingers, she and her Hlimmanian landsmen were to form a Barrier of protection around the blood to shield the terrified priests.

"Come! That which was bequeathed to us by the

Ancients, come!" The Elder Priest's raspy voice sent shivers down Shonin's spine.

She stared at him as he continued the traditional rite of summoning with lifted arms. "From all four Vastans, we command the power of all the Rubinstones, come to our aid!"

Closing their eyes, the three members of the Triate Priesthood lifted their faces as hideous grins curled on their lips. "You have been summoned!"

The Elder Priest lowered his arms.

The deep red Rubinstone pendants, adorning their bare chests, flickered with subtle lights. Then, from within their crystalline depths, the jewels radiated an eerie crimson sheen onto the dark skin of the Skyllian priests.

Suddenly, from across the vast Temple Plaza, thin bright darts of reddish light began to streak towards the Triate.

The numerous strands of luminescence converged and circled around them.

An anxious silence spread over the masses as the Elder Priest concluded his summoning, and the Rubinstones began to pulsate.

After the loss of the Great Rubinstone during the Expansion Period in the north, the lesser Rubinstones had been entrusted to the Land Princes of the four desert Vastans of the Alldai.

The Santonin could pull on the primordial powers trapped within the gems by the ancient Wayfarers, even when leagues away.

Standing now in swirling crimson light, the three high priests nodded towards Shonin and her Hlimmanian companions, then released the block on their ability to wield Eth.

The accursed tattoo on the back of Shonin's skull tingled, then a cool sensation spread across the nape of her neck.

That was the signal.

Shonin grasped Heicha and Tymea's hands, lifting theirs in her own.

The bones of their fingers began to glow in unison as they drew on their Eth abilities.

Shonin released their hands.

The tingling of Shonin's Eth blossomed from her nape, rippling powerfully out across her shoulders and through her arms.

In the air in front of the three Hlimmanian Eth Wielders, familiar transparent disks shimmered. Like the thinnest glass, their corporeal Lingers sliced through the air, flowing toward the dreadful cylindrical form of rising blood droplets.

Shonin kept her voice low but steady. "First spread your Lingers like a cloth. Then raise them like an upright shield. Now overlap the disks to form a vertical casing around the rising sacrificial blood. And now, seal the Lingers together."

Her companions followed her lead.

Their Lingers were much stronger than Shonin had remembered. She smiled.

Together they were able to form an impenetrable barrier.

The Triate Santonin continued to call forth the Pletoran from under the ground.

Heicha's sudden trepidation, as well as Tymea's profound hatred of the Santonin and desperate longing for freedom, flickered into Shonin's mind.

She had spoken to them about the overpowering impact that the Pletoran would have on their minds.

Hopefully, they had prepared themselves. As best they could.

Concentrating on their link, Shonin sent thoughts of comfort to her Hlimmanian sisters. Ber'eth had made both of them strong. They would survive this test. They would do well.

The ground began to quiver.

The great Drawing-Forth was having its effect.

The Pletoran must have begun to move.

Shonin would attempt to pull the brunt of the Pletoran's might toward herself, away from Heicha and Tymea.

Impulses of fearful gratitude fluttered back through their Linger connection.

The ground shuddered as a sound like low grinding thunder emanated from beneath the city.

Whimpers and muffled cries spread through the plebian throngs. All awaited the appearance of the terrifying primordial forces.

The Santonin's sudden screams of pain made Shonin cringe.

Gasping for breath, they dropped the libation vessels. The remaining offerings splashed over the steps as their ornate decanters shattered.

The Priests twisted with spasms.

Shonin held back a sneer. The so-called invincible Triate stumbled on the steps of the dais like common drunkards. Clutching their throats, they coughed and gagged.

Terror rippled through the masses at the confusing sight.

Baskets fell to the ground, seeds and tubers were strewn over the dusty paving of the plaza.

The lights within the Santonin's Rubinstone amulets flickered like spluttering candle flames.

In her peripheral vision, Shonin saw the Lord Successor stagger to his feet. Handing his sleeping reptilian pet to an attendant, he groped for his sword with heavily bejewelled fingers.

Guards ran up the steps to his throne, flanking him with shields raised to their chests.

The skin on Shonin's forehead crawled. The Pletoran were approaching.

Her companions' fear whipped back and forth like thin willow branches within their connection.

Shonin projected her own thoughts.

Do not fear. It will turn out well.

Shaking, the Elder Priest cried out in rage. His eyes bulged and his face contorted as he clawed at the air.

The Novice Priest doubled over in spasms, struggling to complete the spell of Invoking.

Tears of anguish melted the paint around the Middle Priest's eyes, gold streaks trickling down his dark cheeks.

The Triate remained relentless in their incantation, the reddish glow flickering around them like living flames.

Heicha cried out in terror as the Pletoran began to appear. Dense wisps of indigo smoke crept up from the aperture like the sinuous appendages of a deadly squid. Spiralling upward within the towering cylinder of glistening drops of blood, its tentacles flushed violet then deep red.

Steady! We must remain steady. Shonin glanced quickly at the other two.

Tymea's eyes were tightly shut.

Heicha looked on, her mouth and eyes wide open.

Something had changed. Shonin sent her

consciousness toward the Pletoran, probing. A weakening of the primordial strength? Or a weakening of the power of the Santonin over it?

The tendrils of smoke seemed to search for prey as they coalesced, and a behemoth form rose from the entrance to its subterranean realm. Trapped within the rising veil of blood drops, it looked like a titan serpent gliding out from its underground lair.

"Something... is terribly wrong!" Speaking to the Novice Priest, the eldest Santonin's raspy voice was full of fear, shattering his normal composure.

The Pletoran's presence seared through Shonin's consciousness as countless voices collided within her skull. Her Eth Lobe burned. A single voice formed, erupting through her throat and mouth. "Your power over us is waning!" The words, suddenly magnified a thousand times, thundered through the Temple Plaza, echoing off the surrounding facades.

Everyone fell suddenly silent. Some fainted in fear.

Shonin's skull pounded as though it would burst.

The Pletoran was many minds, many powers, but they continued to speak with one voice through her.

This had never happened before!

"Soon will we be free of your kind." Their message roared out through her throat, bearing down on the Triate Santonin. "We will soon no longer be beholden to you. Your authority fails!"

The Santonin lurched as the force of the Pletoran's voice assaulted them. But they refused to back down from the altar.

'Your authority fails. Your authority fails.' The Pletoran's foreboding proclamation seemed to rebound even more powerfully off the temple walls.

Thousands cried out in crippling fear. Countless

supplicants ran from the temple grounds. The Priests tottered, shouting the conclusion of their incantation. They invoked the power within the libation of the sacrificed ones. The power of the Blood Song.

Touching the rising droplets of blood surrounding it, the Pletoran twisted in defiance.

Shonin roared in searing pain.

Compelled to speak once again for the Pletoran, their voices boomed again from her throat. "The Child of Orren, who has been impeding your authority over the Great Rubin, soon becomes a man. He is a powerful Spectral, foretold in ancient lore. The Wayfarers' power you coveted, and used to trap us, diminishes in you and now grows strong in him."

Shonin frowned.

Child of Orren? We Hlimmanen are also descendants of Orren!

But she could sense that the Pletoran's teeming thoughts were not focused on her and her tribe.

The many minds of the Pletoran were travelling northward, toward a city by the sea. For an instant, unclear images appeared... A young boy, standing before a queen covered in jewels, then the same boy again, but as a young man, standing next to a queen without a crown. The images faded as quickly as they had come.

The Triate shook their heads, their mouths agape.

The Elder Priest raised his fists to the colossal Pletoran. "Bless the sowing! We command you to bring the rains and bless the harvest also!"

For an instant Shonin felt something like the touch of cold iron fettering the Pletoran's will. Bars of an invisible prison, forcing them into submission.

The Novice Priest now lifted his arms and added his

voice. "We invoke the power of the Blood Song over you!"

As though from an invisible firebrand, heat burned Shonin's consciousness.

The Pletoran writhed in torment. Beneath the surface of their smoky form, the tendrils shook with violent agitation. The hideous entity extended its body into the air above the cylinder of blood droplets. Its upper form spread out widely, taking on the terrifying semblance of the Hooded Serpent of the deserts. Arching high above the Triate as if to deliver a fatal blow, it bellowed in pain.

All the Santonin extended their shaking arms towards the Pletoran. With strident voices they shouted their command again.

A sense of strangulation enveloped Shonin, and she coughed.

Then violent rage exploded in the Pletoran, penetrating her mind as well.

The Triate's spells were drawing power from the Blood Song of the sacrifice, compelling the primordial beings to rise from their hidden realms and submit to their will.

Shonin could sense the Pletoran's manifold consciousness extending far beyond the city, swelling out over the plains, the sea, the mountains.

Unfathomable invisible powers reluctantly shifted. Forces were released from deep underground and the paving stones resonated with tremors.

The Pletoran's mind delved deeply. Hidden subterranean rivers began to move far below. Their mind then went forth into the sky. Thin clouds began gathering, swirling high above the city and casting light shadows over the landscape. A cool, fresh breeze swept in from far out at sea.

The Elder Priest heaved a sigh. "The movements of the

air signify the blessing has been procured, but it has been weakened."

"Pletoran, you are released! Return to the abyss!" The Triate's unison voices were now weak and breathless.

Shonin felt their iron-like grip loosen on the arcane being.

"I am compelled by the Blood to obey you now, but your dominion wanes and will soon be no more!" The Pletoran roared once again through Shonin's throat. Defiant anger. Vindictive rage. "Our brethren who you imprisoned in the shards of the Holy Temmerung will soon be free, and we shall be reunited."

The vast form spiralled downward. Its deep red shape unravelled into the writhing crimson tendrils, then back into indigo plumes, before vanishing back into its obscure subterranean realm.

The veil of suspended blood droplets collapsed, splattering around the aperture.

For the span of a heartbeat, silence reigned.

Then the Santonin doubled over, gasping for air.

A hushed wave of curses and questions swept over the masses.

Shonin lowered her arms. She swallowed. A sense of amazement came over her. After the force of the Pletoran's words raging through her throat, she felt no soreness.

Tymea and Heicha followed her lead and also lowered their arms.

Hundreds fell on their faces before the Triate Santonin, crying out in adoration. "Oh terrible and powerful ones!"

Still linked through their Lingers, Shonin's companions glanced at her. The tension in their eyes told her that they had felt the change too. She allowed herself a hint of a smile and nodded to them.

Something significant had changed! Something very significant.

Once again, not all the Rubinstones had yielded to their summons. For many years now, the Great Rubinstone had continued its silence.

The Priests called out desperately to the people, "Do not fear! We have procured the blessing!"

But had they?

"This thief, this child of Orren shall die! We will find him and avenge ourselves, recapture our birthright!" Intense hatred erupted in the Novice Santonin's throat. "Death to the Orren!" His voice was no more than a hoarse whisper.

Shonin shivered. Hlimmanen were Orrenic as well! How many Hlimmanen would they include in their revenge?

She would not die. Neither would her son!

They must find a way to escape, soon.

45

HEALING

Palandred accompanied Banah through the Steward's entrance doors and out into the atrium garden.

The midday sun had already passed, and late afternoon shadows lay across the courtyard. The day had gone by quickly, with the discussions about the different Glortroms and the recognisable signs of the Great Shift.

"The concert stage is being constructed in the plaza. The performers will soon be making their way through the streets of the city to the venue." As he spoke, the Steward's voice filled with a palpable sense of joy. "The planned trips to our city's ancient gardens have been postponed." His broad smile disappeared for a moment.

"But things being the way they are, I'm overjoyed that the concert in honour of Ydassum will still take place, as well as our banquet tomorrow. And I can at least show you the gardens of the residence here."

The Steward paused in the centre of the atrium and waited for the group to assemble. "This way." He smiled and started down a narrow pathway between the enclosing wall of the garden and his residence.

Druin and Lady Arden walked ahead, talking quietly together.

There was something about Lady Arden's knowledgeable interpretations and analytical thought that brought a certain reassurance.

And despite the growing trepidation in the atmosphere, Druin had also brought a sense of peace in the turmoil. His dear friend had faith that the Firstborn's messages were true, and that everything would work out well in the end.

Palandred shivered at the idea that Druin had been communicating with the Firstborn.

But their words did transmit great comfort...

Even though they were travelling within the eye of a storm, they should stay on course and continue with Banah's planned State Visit.

A growing sense of order was undeniable, despite what felt like the overwhelming chaos in the world.

Somehow, if Palandred kept his thoughts on the fact that so many seemed to be guided by Ber'eth, and that the creator was intervening in their lives through Glortroms and dreams, the whole situation felt calmer. More orderly. Less fearful, even though their situation wasn't resolved. All the signs and messages kept pointing to a singular benevolence. But Palandred still had some difficulty accepting that concept.

Ber'eth was not good.

He had cursed Palandred with Eth powers. ...or that's what he had been telling himself for so long. It was difficult to comprehend Eth any differently.

But why was it that no one else seemed cursed in the same way?

Was he set apart to be the recipient of Ber'eth's wrath?

Or was the Skyllian demon inside him the cause of his torment?

Palandred looked at his palms again.

Banah touched his sleeve. "Whatever is distressing you..." she spoke at a whisper. "...we will find out, and free you of it. You are not under the control of a demon." The sincere gentility in her voice pierced Palandred like a sharp blade.

Self-loathing filled him. He wanted to remove her hand from his arm. Push her away. But, at the same time, he wanted to throw his arms around her and pull her close.

"Now, if you would follow me to the back of the residence, I would like to draw your attention to the flora here in the garden." Smiling, the Steward flourished an elegant hand gesture towards a row of plants that looked more like upright dusty green daggers than leaves. "Many of our most unusual plants in the city are actually from the coastal Alldai." He frowned. "Left behind by the Skylle."

Palandred paused and turned toward Lady Arden.

"My Lady?" Palandred still had many questions about Glortroms. "Do you think my Glortrom means that the Skylle are coming physically? Or could it be understood that they simply wish to find the Rubinstone." As far as he was concerned, they could take the dark jewel encased above Fillip's throne. Palandred detested the gem and resented Fillip keeping it on display.

Lady Arden blinked, but her face was implacable. "Your Highness, my personal impression..." She stopped, blinking more nervously. "Following the precedent of the prophetic visions of Lady Banah and of the Landsender, my opinion is, yes – the downfall of the city you witnessed and the intent of the Santonin to reclaim their hereditary power, shall come to pass. The time frame, however, is very unclear."

The blunt clarity of Lady Arden's response sent chills through him.

"We will work together. Ber'eth will guide us." Once again, Banah's calm had the surprising power to counterpoise anxiety. She didn't have the answers he sought, but her simple faith gave a strong sense of assuredness.

The Steward led them further through the back of his residence. The garden was much larger than it first seemed, and the Steward had an uncanny memory regarding the provenance and specific cultivation of every plant within it.

Druin seemed enraptured.

Palandred longed desperately for some silence.

"Well now..." Still beaming, Steward Loraimen turned and faced them but looked directly at Palandred. The Steward seemed different, more relaxed now, and always smiling.

"Shall we return to the courtyard and then proceed to the plaza?" As he spoke, a piercing sound filled the sky. "Please, everyone under the canopy of the trees!" The sudden imperative tone of the Steward's voice sent disquiet through the group and everyone hurried to an adjacent tree.

Palandred clasped Banah's hand to keep her from tripping over the paving stones, then looked up through the broad leaves above them.

An instant later the sky, then the entire garden, plummeted into half-darkness. Shrill screeching filled the air. White Sojourners?

The unnatural twilight quickly turned to the deep gloom of a moonless night.

A splattering of what sounded like rain hit all around them.

The Steward spoke over the din. "This has been happening for weeks now. But one time they are flying north, then the next time south, as though confused."

Palandred's skin prickled. The flock was immense. The noise deafening. But it didn't take long. The light returned as the birds continued their erratic flight.

"Watch your step!" The Steward moved out from under the trees and pointed to the stone pavers. "Guano." He waved to the group. "This way. The concert will begin soon!"

"Just like back on Fahtu-Shann." Toman looked at his manservant. "These White Sojourners were following strange air currents. Despite their huge numbers, they are basically harmless and afraid. So were the herds of domestic beasts crossing the countryside back in Ydassum, and the black geese over the barges on the Suyan Folumpor." He paused, frowning. "But the Night Flyers were driven by sorcery. It's odd that nothing about these events has been revealed in the Glortroms."

Glortroms... Palandred had one last question for Lady Arden. "My Lady, why do you think Ber'eth is showing Glortroms to more than one person at a time?"

Druin answered. "I think it's because he is revealing

more of the effects of the Great Shift, to prepare us. The prophesied Atonement is almost upon us."

Lady Arden nodded in agreement.

Palandred's stomach lurched with anxiety. He stopped walking.

"You carry a heavy weight." Banah patted his arm gently then lowered her hand. "But I am certain Ber'eth will help you with your task if you ask him. I am interceding for you and for your role in the story of this land. Look at the changes already happening because of your presence." She nodded toward the Steward. "Your honour towards him is healing a painful part of the history of Limmania. Your kind words are already releasing him to fulfil his mission."

Healing history?

What was she saying?

He couldn't grasp what she fully intended with her words. But emotions began to surge within him.

He breathed in deeply, bracing himself for a dreaded seizure.

But the distressing trembling in his arms and legs... didn't come.

Not even the blurring of his sight.

46

In Her Honour

"All these migrating animals..." Toman shook his head, studying the frown on Yannu's face.

"Tomi, it seems that disaster multiplies wherever we go!" His friend shrugged. "How is it that we're actually getting used to all this?"

Good question. But Toman felt he had an answer, however vague it may seem. "I think because we're all awaiting what these signs are leading to... the fulfilment of the Beckoning, the Atonement, the 'restoration of the once dead stones' that was written on the inscription in Prince Lytwon's garden..."

Yannu stared at him. "If it weren't for the Uccell's

words, I don't know how I would feel about all this. It's all pretty frightening."

"It would be, without their encouraging words." Toman stopped for a moment. "Even with their encouraging words, it's hard to think it all through. Impossible to fully understand."

Yannu nodded.

Following the Steward back to the gate, Toman and Yannu walked with the others through the courtyard and out onto the street.

Serene as usual, the Chieftains looked especially noble in their glistening feather capes. The long plumes of their headdresses whipped back and forth in the sea breeze like dark green and blue reeds.

"And now, back to the plaza." The Steward waved theatrically towards the gates of the city. "Where preparations will be well underway for this evening."

Toman looked at Yannu. His friend had never given him a clear response to his proposal. "So? What is your answer? Apprentice or not?"

Yannu grinned then winked. "What do you think?"

"Of course, I have an idea." Toman frowned. "A pretty good idea, I think. But you need to say it yourself, for it to be official."

Yannu's grin disappeared, and he bowed his head slightly. He spoke in a hoarse whisper. "I would love it, Tomi. Thank you."

Toman clapped him on the shoulder. "You'll be a great Apprentice. But who's going to lay out my clothes in the mornings now?" Out of the corner of his eye, he caught sight of Lady Banah smiling at him. "Shann?" He shrugged.

A mischievous grin sprouted on Yannu's face again. "Ye, right!" He beamed. "Shann washing and ironing your clothes?" He laughed. "I think I'll continue. It helps me keep an eye on you anyway."

Toman smiled. "I'd like that."

"And here we are!" The Steward raised his voice over the growing noise of people talking excitedly.

Walking through the city gates, the wide-open plaza teemed with activity.

The air hummed with voices. People bustled in every direction, carrying large bouquets of flowers, banners on top of long poles, and various musical instruments.

To Toman's left, near the city wall, a large wooden platform had already been erected and draped with shimmering cloths in the colours of Ydassum – blue and white. The three semi-circular rows of chairs on the raised area were obviously for the musicians. People were placing the bundles of flowers in vases arranged all around the edge of the platform.

"I have special seats for all of you near the stage." The Steward turned towards them. "Please, if you would, remain here until I call you forward as our honoured guests." His voice trembled with joy.

Something pricked Toman's conscience. "Yannu, could you check on Lord Dalbonn for me, then come right back? I'll save you a place next to me."

"Of course." Yannu looked at him quizzically then hurried off towards the quay.

More people began pouring onto the plaza. Their excited voices echoed off the massive city wall, creating a wave of sound around him. The effect was exceptional, making the volume of their voices seem much louder.

Cradling instruments in their arms, musicians began climbing the steps to the platform. Toman recognised a few of the stringed instruments, but most of the drums, horns and flutes were very different from anything he'd seen before. The drums had very short and thick batons. The horns were made both from animal horn and of hammered metal.

The dancers appeared out of the crowd and seemed to float towards the stage then glide up the steps. Tall and slender-bodied, the men and the women both wore the green and gold of Limmania.

The back of Toman's skull tingled suddenly.

He looked down at his hands.

No light shone in the bones of his fingers, but the sensation that Eth was surging was undeniable.

Looking over the plaza, the flickering mosaic of Eth resonances seemed to increase greatly in colour. Goosebumps rose over Toman's entire body. The colourful lights resembled the iridescent shimmer in his Gebayt Bithen as well as the sparkling lights in Arden's vase made of Temmerung stone. It was almost as though the iridescence of Ber'eth's power had surfaced and was flowing through the plaza.

"This way, please." The Steward pointed to the neatly arranged chairs in front of the stage.

Lady Banah nodded, then she and Palan started walking to their places.

Druin and Arden followed.

Then the Riddern.

Toman waited a moment, looking back towards the quay in case Yannu was already returning.

Shaking his head, Toman joined the procession behind the Chieftains.

Hundreds of smiling eyes greeted them as they made their way to their seats. So many had come in honour of Lady Banah, holding the House of Méndrensynn in high esteem.

The Steward climbed the steps to the platform then

walked to the centre and raised his hands for silence. "My fellow citizens of Limmania, today marks the historical convergence of three great Orrenic countries. We have the immense honour of hosting two prominent houses today. The House of Méndrensynn with the future Lanfothe of Ydassum, Lady Banah—"

The crowd burst into applause before the Steward finished his announcement.

Smiling, he motioned for silence again. "I would like to welcome the Prince of the House of Elstundreth-Fathringen, His Highness Prince Palandred!"

Toman leaned back in his seat. What a surprise. The difference in the Steward's tone towards Palan was huge.

"May I ask you, My Lady and Your Highness, if you would join me on the stage, and address the assembly?"

Seated an arm's length in front of Toman, Palan stiffened visibly. He looked at Lady Banah. "This is your moment, not mine. You have won their hearts, not I."

She smiled. "Would you accompany me if I were to invite you?"

The shock on his face was apparent.

His hesitation seemed to be a polite way of saying 'no', but then he nodded.

"Then I do. Please accompany me." Serene-looking as always, Lady Banah stood slowly to thunderous applause.

Druin and Arden both clapped.

Slightly red in the face, Palan also stood, then walked alongside Lady Banah to the base of the steps.

The Steward's smile grew even wider. He waited for Lady Banah and Palan to climb up onto the platform, then opened his arms wide. "Welcome, My Lady. Welcome Your Highness!"

People cheered.

But Toman thought he heard a subtle hiss right behind him. He hoped Palan wouldn't pick up on it from the stage.

Lady Banah waved to the crowd.

The Steward raised his hands again and the crowd went silent. He motioned to the Highborn

She bowed, then turned to Palan. "Would you like to speak first?"

Toman couldn't read the expression that passed over Palan's face, but he seemed to shudder just before he stepped forward.

Questioning murmurs and a strange sense of nervous tension seemed to spread.

Palan cleared his throat. "Beloved Limmania."

The silence returned.

"I would like to apologise."

Hands clasped together, Lady Banah lowered her head slightly. Toman had the impression that she wanted to smile.

"I would like to offer my apologies to you as a nation, for the abuses inflicted upon you. And for the injustice dealt you in our shared histories."

The silence between Palan's statements seemed to deepen, leaving only the gentle swishing of the ocean breeze through the legs of the chairs.

"The great inequities shown to Limmania will cease. I do not know how, but they will cease."

To Toman's left, Lorann gasped. Holding her hand to her mouth, she appeared to sob.

"We are told that Ber'eth has sent forth his Beckoning. The Great Shift has brought Glortroms to help lead us, as they have done in times of old."

Toman held back his own gasp as Palan's resonance

altered once again. It had changed on the voyage to Limmania, and now blazed an intense pure red.

Lady Banah raised her head, her own yellow resonance shone more intensely than Toman could ever remember. Tears were running down her cheeks, ...but the subtle knowing smile on her face?

Had she already known what Palan was going to say?

No, that wasn't possible.

Palan bowed to the Steward then held out his hand towards Lady Banah.

She pulled out a handkerchief from her sleeve. "My beloved Limmania. I have dreamt of this day." She dabbed at her cheeks then quickly tucked the cloth back away. She raised her chin and continued speaking. "I have dreamt of the day when your magnificent legacy would be restored, and you would be free to pursue your livelihood with impunity."

The eruption of cheers and applause once again seemed to bounce off the city wall and return louder and stronger. The sound was deafening.

"Tomi!" A hushed voice startled him.

"Yannu?" Toman looked around quickly.

His friend moved to the empty seat next to him. He seemed troubled.

"Problems?"

Yannu sighed. "The Lord Protector is talking."

Toman's pulse started to race. "That is excellent news!" But Yannu's frown left him with a sickening sense of foreboding.

His friend glanced towards the stage. "I'll have to tell you later." He lowered his voice even more as the applause died down. "But the Lord Protector is not the same any more."

The cheers seemed to regain strength. “Long live the House of Méndrensynn!”

The Steward joined in the tribute, cupping his hands on the sides of his mouth and shouting. Then he gestured for silence. “Today a new chapter begins! A new era!”

Lady Banah and Palan made their way back to their chairs.

“We shall celebrate this day with song and dance!” The Steward waved his arms again, this time towards the orchestra behind him, then also stepped down from the platform.

Flutes started first, filling the air with light notes like birds chirping. Then the earthy sounds of beating drums and deep horns blowing reverberated in Toman’s stomach. The music seemed to penetrate his skull, igniting his Eth Lobe. The bones in his fingers glowed with bright orange light.

Bliss filled his mind.

But then his conscience pricked him, and anxiety returned.

What was the matter with His Grace?

Most likely his master was exhausted and needed more rest before interacting with people. Maybe they were overtaxing His Grace, provoking him with too much attention before he felt well again?

Dancers began leaping across the stage. Their shoes made loud clicking sounds as if their soles were tipped in metal.

Drums began pounding a quick-paced rhythm. Flutes matched the repeating sound.

Singers stood behind the musicians and the blend of sounds they made took Toman’s breath away. Like some kind of magical forest of sound, harmonies grew and increased in complexity, spreading out over them.

The singers' voices seemed to penetrate Toman's skin, flow t hrough h is b lood, p ierce h is h eart. T he b ack of his skull seared with intense heat. His fingers now flared even brighter orange.

Looking around the audience, Toman tensed. Many hands were beginning to glow with the same light.

The music stopped suddenly.

As the sunset started to blaze in the sky and torches were lit, a single voice rose light and clear.

"I am a voice..."

A woman clad in long flowing fabrics walked through the choir towards the front of the stage and continued her song.

'I am a voice.
I am a voice,
Calling, calling...
I am a voice, I am a voice,
Calling you home,
Mothers of Limmania, rejoice!I
am a voice, I am a voice,
Calling, calling
I am a voice, I am a voice, O
weary souls,
Fathers of Limmania, rejoice!
Your homeland,
Beckons you home.
Your homeland
Welcomes you home.

The orchestra started back up, softly at first, with stringed instruments, then with low horns.

On white ships of glass
Fair lad, fair lass,

Come home,
Come home."

"Sh... Ships of glass?" Toman stuttered. His dreams, starting from the night before leaving Fahtu-Shann! How were they connected to this Limmanian folksong?

Lady Banah turned around. "Fyrst?"

"I dreamt about this song, My Lady." He kept his voice as low as he could and still be heard. "It had to do with the Skylle and an attack on a city with many slender white towers."

Palan turned around now, his brows raised.

"Yes." Toman stared at him. "The dark slant-eyed men were in the dream as well."

People began singing with the woman. The entire plaza began to resonate with the chorus.

"Your homeland,
Beckons you home.
Your homeland
Welcomes you home.
On white ships of glass
Fair lad, fair lass,
Come home,
Come home."

Sadness pressed against Toman. An aching loneliness. Deepest longing for family.

Lady Banah kept her eyes on him, studying his face. She spoke softly. "Fyrst, it's a song about their children."

"Your homeland,
Beckons you home.
Your homeland
Welcomes you home."

Their overwhelming longing for their lost ones... A longing Toman was all too familiar with.

The words of the song, and the melancholic tone of

the music, seemed to permeate his bones. A gentle heaviness tingled on his skin, a presence he knew from his Gebayt Bithen.

He began singing the chorus with the others, then stood and raised his arms.

"Your homeland,
Beckons you home.
Your homeland
Welcomes you home."

Moved with compassion, he focused a prayer on their lost children and spoke under his breath. "Dear Father of Heaven, let them find their loved ones. Let them find their sons and daughters." He envisioned families reunited, parents embracing their children. He willed his Gebayt Bithen into the unseen world then released his intercession. "Let it be so."

A massive wave of lights shimmered around the edge of the plaza.

Shouts of anxious joy spread quickly through the crowd as the wave began to spin. Slowly at first, it moved with ever increasing speed.

His Gebayt-Bithen glistened like a vast sheet of liquid lights.

47

Leave Me

Palandred peered into the glistening curtain of lights flowing around them. Subtle illusions undulated just beyond Toman's Gebayt Bithen.

Another salty gust blew across the plaza, lifting the cloth decorations on the stage. But an eerie sound of violent howling wind seemed to come from everywhere.

The whole plaza was standing now. But no one seemed to be leaving in fear.

The reflective surface of the Gebayt Bithen seemed to thin and dull. The light brown walls of a city appeared. Around it, a sea of sand dunes stretched in all directions.

Palandred shuddered.

A Glortrom? But it was enormous!

Fearful shouts told him that others could see it as well!

The gentle air currents of Toman's Gebayt Bithen began to increase, teasing cloaks and the hems of dresses this way and that.

Standing close to him and Banah, Druin and Arden huddled together.

They all looked aghast at the immense apparition that began encircling the plaza.

On a sandy horizon, tall dark men with narrow eyes painted in bright gold, marched behind Eornum in a procession Toman had described earlier.

"The Skylle!" Someone shouted, and anxiety spread rapidly through the crowds.

Toman gently nudged Palandred with his elbow. "Please come with me, quickly. Up on the stage."

Palandred stood immediately and hurried behind him.

"Steward Loraimen?" Toman got his attention as well. "Would you join us? Quickly now. We must tell everyone that it is a message from Ber'eth and not to be afraid."

They quickly climbed the steps to the stage as the sound of the wind began to roar all around the now windless plaza.

"Please, everyone. Please listen to me!" Toman shouted at the top of his voice.

Palandred held his arms out towards the crowd. His Eth resonance blazed around him like a red furnace. "Do not fear. What you are seeing is a message from Ber'eth. He is good and will surely reveal something for us to heed!"

"Ber'eth is *good?*" Mouth slightly agape, Toman blinked questioningly at him.

Palandred's Eth flared more intensely.

The scene around them expanded and soon the entire plaza seemed to be both a desert settlement and a city by the sea.

"I know this scene!" Toman shouted. "I've had this vision before!"

A procession of the Skylle made its way through the streets of a city of light brown stucco buildings, some three and four stories high.

Three women appeared, walking slowly under the black silk canopy.

He pointed then looked quickly at Palandred. "Those women are Shonin, Heicha and Tymea. I've seen them before."

The air filled with fine pale brown dust. Horns blared powerful long notes. Dancers ran and leapt, their thin deep-red garments flowing around them.

The scene changed.

Three Skyllian priests climbed the steps of the temple and poured out vases of deep red liquid.

The scene changed again.

A strange classroom appeared. The windows were tall and elegant. The shiny white granite floors and walls shone. Children stood in front of a teacher dressed in Mendelonian garb. But something told Palandred that they were not Mendelonian. Their hair was too fair. Their skin too pale.

Heart-wrenching cries ripped through the air.

"That's my son!" Someone screamed at Palandred.

"That's my daughter, too!"

One by one, the children were divided into two groups.

Coins exchanged hands, and one group was led to a side door where tall, dark-skinned men placed black cloth bags over their heads. The other group was bound with chains. Both were led away.

"The Skylle!" Many shouted with rage.

The vision blurred, shifting the scene again.

Weeping broke out. "Those were our children! Our children!"

The white walls of the classroom disappeared, and transparent waves began to swell over the paving stones of the plaza. The water began to roil around the crowds, and a fleet of many ships appeared. High above, a dense red cloud swirled in an invisible prison.

A thunderous roar boomed across the night sky.

Toman shuddered visibly as the next scene appeared. "This is my dream, my nightmare from back in Fahtu-Shann all over again!"

People shouted, recoiling.

Slender white towers of a familiar-looking city exploded. Waves swelled high as broad streets engorged with seawater.

Mendelon!

It was Palandred's home under siege!

Countless voices both in the vision and in the plaza cried out in anguish and fear.

The vision faded.

For a moment, restless quiet spread over the plaza.

Then bitter weeping spread through the crowds.

The main singer shouted and raised her hand, pointing to the quay. "Look!"

Toman spun around.

Soldiers in Mendelonian uniforms were running

towards them. "Prince Elstundreth-Fathringen? We must speak to His Highness!"

"Let them through!" Palandred stepped down from the stage.

"Your Highness." The officer panted for breath. "Our spies report a fleet of Skyllian vessels just south of Mendelon. Two days away at maximum. Your presence is requested immediately, and any troops left after the devastation of the flood."

"King Fillip already knows about the flood?" Mumbling, Toman shook his head. "The Ferend Service? Or sorcery?"

"Such unnatural speed..." Palandred groaned deep within his throat. "Sorcery must be involved again." He stiffened to attention and addressed the officer and his men. "The Sindrea Isabella is already armed for war. I would ask your assistance to provision her for immediate departure."

He clenched his teeth. He couldn't stop the shaking in his arms and legs. Had his visions foretold the demise of Mendelon? What was he to return to, the ruins of a once great city?

"Ber'eth!"

Sinking to his knees, his thoughts became a vicious battle between debilitating fear and resolute faith.

Courage then cowardice.

Boldness then timidity.

It was as though the demon inside him was writhing in duress. But it seemed afraid of Palandred himself.

This demon had to go, had to leave his body at once! Palandred would no longer tolerate its presence. He shouted, "Ber'eth, please, help me!"

Orange light in Palandred's fingers spread to his hand and arms, then up his neck and into his jaw.

Tentacles of brilliant red smoke began to seep from his palms.

"Speak into existence what you desire and release it to Ber'eth." Toman encouraged him. "It's the essence of the Gebayt Bithen. And Forth-Telling.

Palandred raised his hands skyward.

"Demon, leave my body. In the name of Ber'eth, get out!"

The smoke flowing from his hands suddenly swirled, billowing and twisting around him like a serpentine tornado.

The plaza erupted in screams of terror.

Lady Banah ran to him.

The red cloud moved over them both, spiralling and recoiling like a serpent. Its hooded neck and head reared, as if ready to strike.

A flood of fear and trepidation deluged Palandred's mind, then the creature spoke.

"We are Pletoran."

Its voice boomed through Palandred's throat like echoing thunder.

48

Linked Lingers

Toman shuddered as the huge Pletoran bent over Palan and Lady Banah. He could almost see the multiple beings of the creature writhing within its smoky form.

A tentacle of its body snaked slowly towards the two of them. Then it stopped and moved back and forth slightly as though somehow considering them both.

The movement reminded Toman strangely of a child poking a stick at a dead fish on the shore, to see if it would move.

He reignited his Eth power and formed a Shield, ready to thrust it at the creature.

Palan jumped back to his feet, raising his glowing fists towards the Pletoran.

Brilliant red light roared around Palan's body. "You will not touch us!"

The exact shade of the Pletoran itself, the purity of Palan's colour was startling. "Stay back!" His Linger washed the smoky entity with brilliant red light.

The Pletoran recoiled its tentacle and seemed to cower away from him.

Toman gulped as an idea, an unbelievable idea, came to him.

An encasement!

Shonin had been able to encase the Pletoran of the Alldai in her Linger. Why couldn't he? She had done it with Heicha and Tymea...

He didn't have time to think it through, immediate action was necessary!

"I need help!" Toman drew deeply on his Eth power, and launched his Linger towards the Pletoran, shouting, "Can anyone here help me make an encasement barrier?"

As he spoke, the noise of hundreds of frightened voices in the plaza calmed slightly. He shouted again. "Can anyone here wield a clear Linger?"

Then an unknown force slammed into him – an immense power. Many ancient minds.

Like rapidly flipping through the pages of an illustrated book, ancient histories of vast populations passed before his mind's eye. The thoughts and impressions of the Pletoran engulfed him.

Lands sinking into the depths of an ocean.

Other lands rising up from the ocean floor.

Mountains exploding with liquid fire.

A boy, one of the formidable Spectrals foretold in Palanth-Orric lore, standing in a blazing reddish light.

The young man commanding the Pletoran to come forth, and then them suddenly being ripped from the crystalline prison of the Rubinstone.

Now they were trapped within the innocent blood of the boy.

Toman moaned under the tremendous weight, struggling to find his own thoughts in the storm bearing down on his mind. The source of Palan's distress... What he must have gone through all those years!

His Grace had mentioned something about linked corporeal Lingers. Shonin's example had shown it.

He had never linked with anyone before. But there was no time now to study other possibilities. "Please! I need help!" Toman's throat burned as he forced out the words with all the strength of his lungs.

"I can!" A young man started walking towards Toman.

"I also!" Someone else raised their voice.

"Good!" Toman shouted instructions to the two Limmanians who'd responded. "Cast your Lingers towards mine! Quickly! I will try and bond us together."

Transparent disks flew through the air towards his barrier.

The two other minds connected with his.

The strength of his shield suddenly doubled, then tripled.

The increased power was intimidating and yet exhilarating.

But terror shot through the connection. Then crippling fear and nausea... loss of bladder control. Searing shame.

"Don't stop!" He tried to encourage them. "We can do this together! Don't stop.

The Pletoran's mind felt perplexed and strangely calm as though it were studying Toman.

Toman could sense its mind probing his.

A profound sense of calm came over him, too.

Focusing on the two other Eth Wielders, Toman tried to share his mental image of the encasement in the last Glortrom... how Shonin and the other Hlimmanian women captured the Pletoran the Triate had summoned.

Reactions of surprise came back to him.

Then agreement.

Good, they understood.

The youngest in the link wrapped his Linger around Toman's.

A surge of power flowed into Toman's Eth resonance, and he wove the second Linger into his.

Then another surge of Eth, much stronger than the first, entered the connection.

Toman wove it into the growing barrier as well.

He willed the linked Lingers to seal around the Pletoran.

They did.

Confusion and fear now filtered through the link.

Words echoed, *Never again to be imprisoned!*

Imprisoned?

What did the Pletoran mean?

And why was it afraid?

Toman took the chance to look at the two who were helping. His heart sank.

A lad, barely a man by the thin stubble on his chin, wept but kept his arms held upright. The front of his trousers was wet.

Glancing around for the second Wielder, Toman's mouth dropped open. He closed it quickly.

"Steward Loraimen?"

49

To Mendelon

The deluge of impressions continued as Toman struggled with the weight of the Pletoran's minds. The creature's vast consciousness bore down on him.

Other sensations came through the Eth link... the Steward's lack of fear was impressive, but was he hiding something?

The young man's mind, however, was full of torment.

Toman sent reassuring thoughts. "It will be all right."

"But what is this thing?" The young man's sharp response came back clearly.

"I don't know." Toman had seen the apparition in his dreams, but never understood what it was.

"We are Pletoran. We are the force of wind, the heat of fire, the power of water." The words burst from Toman's mouth, ringing like an explosion.

"We are the forces birthed with the Great Continent. We are also children of Ber'eth."

Covering his ears, Palan staggered. He braced himself against Toman. "We must depart for Mendelon. Now." He looked fearfully at the Pletoran.

Anxiety shuddered through Toman as the Pletoran spoke again through his own mouth. "We will accompany you. You will have need of us."

The Pletoran's words seemed to reverberate in Toman's bones.

But... the total lack of animosity?

And the absence of any anger or hostility...?

They had completely misunderstood the Pletoran.

He looked at the Steward and the boy helping with the encasement. "Release them."

"Pardon?" The Steward gaped.

"Release the Pletoran." Toman nodded towards their linked encasement.

Palan's face contorted in horror. "No! Please no!"

MAIN GLOSSARY

A

Abbh: one of the governing clergymen of Immen in Edendor.

Ahnya Seynor Méndrensynn, Lady: wife and Lanfothe-

Consort of Lanfoth Steffen Méndrensynn; co-ruler presiding over Ydassum; *see also Méndrensynn of Daerumor, the House of.*

Akkoren: a 'Reader of Colours' in archaic eastern Orrenic dialects; an individual of Palanth-Orric descent with the inborn ability to read the chromatic resonances of Eth, an ability often attributed to those with green Eth resonances.

Alldai, the: a vast arid region of the southern Great Continent; homeland of the Skylle; country of origin of the Urbonnic Riddern and Stagriders.

Alyena Foggling (*maiden name:* Kunic)**:** Toman Foggling's deceased mother; adopted as a child, one of many orphans resulting from conflicts of the Bnornum-Welsordia civil wars spreading to the province of Honstan in Ydassum; *see also Foggling family.*

Amber Tendril: a climbing shrub or woody vine found in areas with moist peaty soil; the source of Amber Tea; *see also in the Botanical Glossary.*

Anders Armgolt, Baron: member of the Quaterni of the

Vandrian Kingship, resident in the Armgolt Baronhold; *see also Baronhold.*

Ando: one of the young boys in Ensign Eckel's crew.

Andur Burrli: a shoemaker in Landsend, present at the Shantab where Mannu Sundermun tells of his Glortrom.

Arden Shannorn of Borinbranth, Lady: only daughter of Duke Edwythe Shannorn and Duchess Ghoda Thiess Shannorn of Borinbranth; residing in the Galdyssen Baronhold during her studies in Barrost; student of Eth Lore and ancient Orrenic languages; half-sister to Lord Caldere Shannorn; *see also Shannorn of Borinbranth, Ducal House of.*

Arzat, Physician: the Ydassumer court physician on board the Solyssia during the Highborns' trip to Barrost and the Summit on Trade.

Ashwond Festival: a feast celebrating the unification of the Double Crowns of Syngordia.

Athal: the innkeeper of the Blue-Eyed Ram in Turicum.

Athlonia: the folkloric name for the northern archipelago of Palanth-Orron, a term used by the banished Orrenic and Palanshen tribes living on the Great Continent.

Athlonians: the fabled last surviving race of the once numerous peoples of the northern archipelago of Palanth-Orron; historically, the race of overlords who banished all other indigenous races from their island homelands.

Aura: the Light of Life or Lifelight; a luminescence emitted by all living beings, seen only by the Riddern and those Orren with green resonances, who have the Eth ability of an Akkoren or 'Reader'.

Auyana: the mostly unexplored reaches of remote eastern Ydassum and the vast highlands of the

Thousand Rivers District that border Ydassum; *see map of Ydassum.*

Avye-Sonther: the 'Set Apart', the 'Sanctified'; the school of thought teaching that the Power of Ber'eth is exclusively for the spiritually pure and those extensively schooled according to the Holy Writings of Geholiogarth; a doctrine insisting that Eth powers should never be used or studied outside the clergy's authority – an interpretation strictly enforced by the ruling Abbaths of Immen in Edendor.

B

Balbrun: a town in Ydassum on the eastern shore of the Great Inner Sea, opposite the islands of Fahtu-Shan, Maureshaan and Plankaan; *see map of Fahtu-Shan.*

Banah Méndrensynn, Lady: daughter and firstborn of Lanfoth Steffen and Lanfothe-Consort Ahnya of Ydassum; Heir Apparent to the Lanfoth Seat of the House of Méndrensynn; *see also Méndrensynn of Daerumor, the House of.*

Banecraft: the ancient Stagriders' Poison Lore; the study and administration of elixirs, venoms, toxins, tinctures, extracts, essences and distillates from plants, animals and minerals, used by the Stagriders to take life.

Banecraft, Accursed: toxins and venoms that penetrate the bone marrow, the effects becoming hereditary (blindness, barrenness, early death, over-sensitivity to light and the occurrence of bleeders.).

Bardur: Prince Lytwon Fathringen's valet, formerly a footman at Warningen House.

Barefoot Monk, the: an alehouse in the waterfront

district of Turicum, frequented by workers living in the nearby barracks.

Baronhold: the name of each of the four landmark baronial structures in the city of Barrost which house the Quaterni, the ruling families of the Vandrian Kingship:

- **Armgolt Baronhold:** the residence of Baron Anders Armgolt, his second wife, Baroness Damantra Armgolt, and the Baron's children from his first marriage.
- **Freymuot Baronhold:** the residence of Baron Haynts Freymuot, Baroness Margit Freymuot and their four children.
- **Galdyssen Baronhold:** the residence of the Vandrian Steward, Baron Lornz-Ullen Galdyssen, Baroness Soffian Galdyssen Vandran and their two children.
- **Vandran Baronhold:** the residence of Baron Mertten Vandran, Baroness Thenea Vandran and their three children.

Barrost: the capital of Norssum; the port at the mouth of the river Suyan Folumpor, on the southern coast of the Northern Horn; previously called Noèsh, the foundations of the present city lie in the Early Orrenic Migration Period; latest research reveals evidence that the city may go as far back as the Bohdnian Period; *see also Noèsh, and map of the Northern Horn.*

Barrostania: a term given by the Four Great Houses of the Vandrian Kingship to the territory around the city of Barrost; a name later also used of the entire country of Norssum; *see map of the Northern Horn.*

Barrùs: the legendary Palanshen founder of the Four Great Houses of Barrost, the ruling Vandrian Kingship of Norssum; the leader of the third and last

Palanth-Orric migration that arrived on the Northern Horn of the Great Continent.

Barsch, Miss: one of Toman's grade school teachers on Fahtu-Shan.

Bazaar Districts: the extensive market districts of Barrost.

Beàl'Toht: a malevolent arcane Urbonnic spell wielded by the sorcerer caste of the Santonin priesthood of the Skylle; in an ancient Urbonnic language: 'of the bone marrow'; also known as 'The Curse of the Santonin'.

Beckoning: the increasingly potent draw and call within the Shift in Eth power, to return to Ber'eth and his ways.

Ber'eth: the Creator of the World; Mother-Father of All Nations; the name can also be interpreted as 'the Breath of Mother-Father of All'; sometimes called Father of Heaven.

Ber'eth Appendage: the projection of the lower brain stem, inherent in peoples of Palanth-Orric descent, that conducts the Power of Eth flowing through all creation; also known as the 'Ber'eth Lobe' or 'Eth Lobe'.

Ber'eth Lobe: see Ber'eth Appendage.

Berlen Galdyssen, Lord: brother to Steward Baron Lornz-Ullen Galdyssen.

Beruhn, Chieftess: Riddern co-ruler of the Forest Riddern of Ydassum; a master of Urbonnic Healing Lore; the female of Chieftain Ruhand.

B'h'rants, Lord: one of the three Uccell Lords who accepted Lady Banah Méndrensynn's invitation to accompany her on her State Visit.

Bite of the Beast: a sword fighting move made by swinging the blade overhead, bringing the tip down at an angle directed at the base of the neck or the heart.

Bithard, Lord: a penniless deposed noble, a Mendelonian

stowaway on Prince Palandred's warship, the Isabella Sindrea.

Black Goose: a species of large waterfowl native to the highland marshes of the Laggol Palaath, bordering the Great Inner Sea; *see also in the Zoological Glossary.*

Black Lion: a species of large feline, from the Alldai on the southern plains of the Great Continent; so named because of its dark brown fur and black mane; *see also in the Zoological Glossary.*

Black Swan: a constellation of stars in the northern winter sky; a folkloric symbol of freedom and independence, based on a species of waterfowl believed to be extinct; *see also in the Zoological Glossary.*

Blenn Fayren, Lord: a Syngordian Lord sympathetic to the Double Crown; a friend of Petar Rothringan; resident at Hordle House.

Bligger: a manservant in the Galdyssen Baronhold.

Blue-Eyed Ram, the: an alehouse in the Grocers' District of Turicum.

Bnorni: 'of or pertaining to Bnornum'; the Orrenic tribe who founded the autonomous region of Bnornum, which later became a part of Welsordia; historically, one of the banished Palanth-Orric tribes of the collective group called the Orren, that arrived on the Great Continent during the Second Migration Period.

Bnornum: once an autonomous region on the northern coast of the Great Continent, founded by the Bnorni; in a war for independence after being annexed by Welsordia.

B'noru, Lord: one of the three Uccell Lords who accepted Lady Banah Méndrensynn's invitation to accompany her on her State Visit.

Boaddan: the support barge accompanying the Highborn's boat, the Solyssia, on the Ydassumer

Highborn State Visit; equipped with stables, larders, storage and basic sleeping quarters for crew and workers.

Bohdne: the legendary mystic beings thought to have founded Geholiogarth, 'the Holy Enclosure', around which the city of Immen arose; the first wave of immigrants to the Great Continent from Palanth-Orron; referred to in Riddern lore as The Great Ones.

Borinbranth, the Duchy of: the hereditary lands of the House of Shannorn in Norssum, ruled by Duke Edwythe Shannorn under the auspices of the Vandrian Kingship of Barrost; *see map of the Northern Horn.*

Bosom of Ber'eth: *death; the permanent ethereal slumber after death.*

Botts-two'sik: in Fahtu-Shanner dialect, an exclamation of unpleasant surprise.

Brandr Nemming: a school friend of Toman Foggling.

Brewesh Ge'on: 'The Novice Priest'; the youngest of the three head priests of the sect of the Santonin of the Alldai.

Brewesh Nonum: 'The Elder Priest'; the head priest of the sect of the Santonin of the Alldai.

Brewesh Mithe: 'The Middle Priest'; a senior priest of the sect of the Santonin of the Alldai.

Brummel, Sir: Prince Lytwon's incognito name on his journey to Syngordia; *see also* ***Lytwon Dor-Tanumm Fathringen, Prince.***

Brun Foggling: father of Toman Foggling; farmer and shepherd at Upland Farm on the island of Fahtu-Shan in the Great Inner Sea; *see also Foggling family.*

Byr: a genus of woody shrubs and trees of the Northern Horn, characterised by small highly reflective silvery under-leaves and narrow upright branching; *see also in the Botanical Glossary.*

Byrud Sundermun: Mannu and Sonna Sundermun's young grandson; son of Marna and Jos Sundermun; *see also Sundermun Family.*

C

Caldere Shannorn of Borinbranth, Lord: the son of Duke Edwythe Shannorn of Borinbranth and the late Elida Galdyssen; half-brother to Lady Arden Shannorn; *see also Shannorn of Borinbranth, Ducal House of.*

Canthalida: synonym for 'The Wailing One', the 'Greinen'; *see Greinen.*

Catrina Fayren, Lady: the wife of Lord Blenn Fayren of Hordle House, Northern Syngordia.

Child of Orren, the: a term used by the Santonin for Prince Palandred Elstundreth-Fathringen, who they consider the thief of the Rubinstone in the Fire Brooch of Edendor.

Cloud Forests of Auyana: the dense and mostly unexplored rainforests of eastern Ydassum, bordering the Thousand Rivers District, perennially covered in clouds; *see map of Ydassum.*

Cloud Kingdom, the: an alternative name for Ydassum, in reference to the cloud-covered forests of the country.

Cloud Kingdoms, the: an older name for the combined territories of Ydassum and Edendor. historically both Edendor and Ydassum; in present day Ydassum is referred to as The Cloud Kingdom.

Clustor, Abbath: a ruling monk of the High Council of Immen.

Constellations:

- in the Northern Winter sky: Black Swan, Triple-Horned Ram.
- in the Southern Winter sky: Winter Scorpion with a high arching string of stars.

Costanza Degardine Armgolt, Lady: participant in the Debutante Gala at the Galdyssen Baronhold.

Crethingan, Sir Han: a Syngordian court architect of international renown, a man of devout piety, best known as a designer of intimate spaces such a chapels and small gardens, Warningen House being the exception.

Crethingan Structures, surviving:

- **Warningen House** (Lowarthen, northern Syngordia)
- **Sunken Garden Features** (University Gardens, Warningen House)
- **The White Garden Chapel** (The White Garden, Limmania)
- **The Inner Chapel** (within the Galdyssen Baronhold)
- **Dadringen Palace** (southeast Syngordia),
- **Moorcastle** (Drengul Borinbranth),
- **Passageway** (The Garden of Meditation)

Crimson Scarab Wasp: the flaw within the Rubinstone of the Fire Brooch of Edendor, resembling a Scarab Wasp.

Crown of Horróglоryn: a part of the regalia of the House of Elstundreth, a gold circlet worn in official processions by only unmarried men of the immediate royal family.

Curse of the Santonin: the Beàl'Toht; a malevolent

arcane Urbonnic spell wielded by the sorcerer caste of the Santonin priesthood of the Skylle.

D

Daeruma: Lord Druin Méndrensynn's valet.

Daerumor: the ancestral home of the House of Méndrensynn; also the name of the province where Turicum, the capital of Ydassum, was established; in Old Orrenic: 'of stone' or 'carved of stone'.

Dalbonn, Lord Protector: the chief advisor to the House of Méndrensynn whose responsibility is to protect their interests and their lives; mentor to Toman Foggling; *see also Mischul Dalbonn.*

Damantra Armgolt, Baroness: second wife of Baron Anders Armgolt.

Danuel of Yldshimman, Lord: the best friend of Prince Palandred Elstundreth, of the noble House of Yldshimman whose origins go back to the Colonisation Period of Welsor-Mendelon.

Davies Farthering: an elderly citizen of Landsend, present at the Shantab where Mannu Sundermun tells of his Glortrom.

Deadman's Needle: the mountain on South Head Island near Landsend.

Dennelon: a region of western central Syngordia; once an autonomous Orrenic kingdom founded by the Dyndyll, who gave their name to the main river of the area; *see map of the Northern Horn.*

Dennelonian: of or pertaining to the ancient House of Dyndyll, founders of the defunct Kingdom of Dennelon; one of the two kingdoms that formed Syngordia, The Double Crown Kingdom; the western province of Syngordia.

Dennelonian Crown, the: the defunct kingdom once south of the Dyndyll River in present Syngordia that merged with the Ghelondrian Crown to form the Double Crown Kingdom of Syngordia.

Doloons of Borinbranth: a landmark grey granite massif of unusual rounded peaks, with sheer rock cliffs marking the sudden rise of the terrain from the extensive grain-belt of the Northern Plain of Lofwardan to the highlands of the Hohn Fennsor South and the Duchy of Borinbranth in Norssum; *see map of the Northern Horn.*

Doof en Donder!: in Fahtu-Shanner dialect, an expletive of sudden surprise or embarrassment; Good grief! How stupid of me!

Double Crown: the emblem of the ruling monarch of Syngordia.

Double Crown Kingdom: the united crowns of the former Kingdoms of Dennelon and Ghelondria; also known as Syngordia; *see map of the Northern Horn.*

Dreym: Prince Palandred Elstundreth-Fathringen's valet.

Druin Méndrensynn, Lord: son and second born of Lanfoth Steffen and Lanfothe-Consort Ahnya of Ydassum; *see also Méndrensynn of Daerumor, the House of.*

Drusian Vandran Russ, Lady: the widowed sister of Baroness Soffian Vandran Galdyssen; residing in the Galdyssen family Baronhold.

Dune Ginger: *Ivernmentis ferbodins*, a member of the Sand Ginger family, a monocot with grass-like foliage and swollen underground stems, often used in curative tinctures and tisanes; *see also in the Botanical Glossary.*

Dwardian Case: a transport crate for plants, made of glass and wood, specially designed by Lord Druin

Méndrensynn for his most recent expedition to the Cloud Forests of Auyana.

Dyndyll: historically, one of the banished Palanth-Orric tribes of the collective group called the Orren, that arrived on the Great Continent during the Second Migration Period; the inhabitants of the Region of Dennelon in western central Syngordia; *see map of the Northern Horn.*

Dyndyll Castle: historically, the residence of the Dennelonian kings along the Dyndyll River.

Dyndyll, River: a main river flowing south-southwest through Syngordia named after the Palanth-Orric tribe of the Second Migration; *see map of the Northern Horn.*

E

Eckel, Haftinger, Ensign: the ensign of the maintenance crew for the ships of Turicum harbour, employed by His Grace Mischul Dalbonn.

Edèndi: 'of or pertaining to Edendor'; the Orrenic tribe who founded Edendor; historically, one of the banished Palanth-Orric tribes of the collective group called the Orren, that arrived on the Great Continent during the Second Migration Period.

Edendor: one of the two landlocked countries formerly referred to as The Cloud Kingdoms of the Northern Horn; the homeland of the Orrenic tribe of the Edèndi; country of which the capital city, Immen, is revered as a repository of Orrenic and Bohdnian cultures and languages; *see map of the Northern Horn.*

Edwythe Shannorn of Borinbranth, Duke: hereditary ruler of the Duchy of Borinbranth in Norssum, governing under the auspices of the Vandrian

Kingship of Barrost; father of Lord Caldere Shannorn with his deceased wife, Lady Elida Galdyssen, and of Lady Arden Shannorn, with his second wife Duchess Ghoda Shannorn; *see also Shannorn of Borinbranth, Ducal House of, and map of the Northern Horn.*

Ehningen, Lady: the first Lady-in-Waiting to Lady Banah Méndrensynn; from a noble Turicum family of dye merchants.

Elsornaum: 'The White Isles'; archipelago off the coast of Landsend at the north-western tip of the Great Continent; *see map of Landsend.*

Elstundreth: the ruling house of Mendelon from the Late Colonisation Period of Welsor-Mendelon until the late Queen Sindrea Isabella Elstundreth; her children bear the combined surname Elstundreth-Fathringen.

Elstundreth-Fathringen: the present Royal House of Mendelon:

- **King Fillip Wendron Elstundreth-Fathringen:** eldest son of the late Queen Sindrea and Prince Consort Wendrynn; ruling king of Mendelon; wife Queen Halin Dwennora; sons Allric Fillip Wenron, heir apparent, and Harolt Dwennr
- **Prince Palandred Worbroth Elstundreth-Fathringen:** son of the late Queen Sindrea and Prince Consort Wendrynn
- **Queen Isabella Forwynna Fathringen of Syngordia** (*born* Elstundreth-Fathringen): daughter of the late Queen Sindrea and Prince Consort Wendrynn, wife of King Richarr Fathringen of Syngordia
- **Queen Reyna Welsorthum** (*born* Elstundreth-Fathringen): daughter of the late Queen

Sindrea and Prince Consort Wendrynn; married to King Ans Ulric of Welsordia

•Princess Leahn Elstundreth-Fathringen: daughter of the late Queen Sindrea and Prince Consort Wendrynn; currently a novice at Immen

Ember Lily: a scaled-bulb lily usually with reddish flowers but variations of ochre, yellow and white are known; emblem of the ruling House of Mendelon; *see also in the Botanical Glossary.*

Emd: the second cut of fragrant hay; root of the month name Emded 'the time of Emd'.

Eornum: a species of horned-beast from the deserts of the Alldai in the far south of the Great Continent.

Estuary of Barrost: the large estuary mouth of the River Suyan Folumpor.

Eth: the Power of Ber'eth flowing through the world.

Eth Linger: the colour residue or resonance of Eth; also known as a 'Linger'.

Eth Lobe: the appendage below the back of the brain, inherent in peoples of Palanth-Orric descent, that has the ability to conduct the Power of Eth; also known as the 'Ber'eth Lobe' or the 'Ber'eth Appendage'.

Ewe's Parsley: a woody perennial shrub native to bogs and alluvial plains near river systems; a herb traditionally used by farmers for its calming effect on newly birthing or nervous horned-beasts; *see also in the Botanical Glossary.*

Expulsion Wars: a series of wars to eradicate the Skyllian overlordship from the Horn; a period of great social upheaval that coincided with the arrival of the Palanshen on the Great Continent; the wars culminated in the Siege of Limman, and the signing of the treatise of Mendelon.

F

Fadron, Hussar: the young Riddern attendant to the Chieftains' steeds.

Fahtu-Shan: the main island in the Great Inner Sea, near the eastern shore; *see map of Fahtu-Shan.*

Fathringen of Syngordia, Royal House of the Double Crown Kingdom:

- the late **Prince Consort Wendrynn Fathringen of Mendelon,** Prince Consort to Queen Sindrea Isabella Elstundreth
- **King Richarr Worbroth Fathringen II:** the Double Crowned ruler of Syngordia, married to Queen Isabella Forwynna Fathringen; father of Crown Prince Gordyn Cynnelm Fathringen
- **Queen Isabella Forwynna Elstundreth Fathringen:** (*born:* Elstundreth-Fathringen) wife of King Richarr Worbroth Fathringen and mother of the Syngordian Crown Prince
- Gordyn Cynnelm Fathringen.
  Crown-Prince Gordyn Cynnelm Fathringen: Son of King Richarr Worbroth Fathringen and Queen Isabella Forwynna Elstundreth Fathringen.

Faydann: the trusted foreman and friend of the Highborn Druin Méndrensynn.

Feldling, Family: a family of Landsend.

Fennsor Borinbranth, the Duchy of: an area of central Norssum; ancestral homeland of the Dukes of Shannorn; *see map of the Northern Horn.*

Fennsordia: the northern mountain ranges of the Hohn Fennsor that create a barrier against the gales off the

Great Northern Ocean, and form the boundary to the province of the same name in Norssum.

Ferend Service: Western Coast Postal System with small ships sailing between Mendelon, Vlachonia and Barrost.

Fideran, Major-domo: head butler of Warningen House.

Fire Brooch of Edendor: a piece of jewellery consisting of a single massive ruby set in silver; believed to have been taken from the Skyllian Vastans by the ruling Abbots of Edendor during the late Expulsion Period. The brooch was later presented to Queen Sindrea Elstundreth by the Double Crowned King Richarr of Syngordia to secure a marriage to her daughter Princess Isabella.

Firstborn of the Continent: the Firstborn of Ber'eth's Children, winged reptilian beings to whom he endowed access to his thoughts and tangible presence, plus the Great Continent, as their heritage; the only native race of the Great Continent; also known as the Uccell or by the archaic name: 'Uran-Draigana'.

Firstborn's Touch: an act of great honour conferred by the Uccell, in which they reveal their distant past to someone they consider chosen by Ber'eth; the experience of the ancient Uran-Draigana massacre, transmitted in a two-part rite: upon request by the Firstborn, the recipient places their face on the Uccell's open palms, then the Uccell places his face in the recipient's open palms.

Firstlings: first time attendees at a Maidens and Masters Dance, unmarried and usually just turning eighteen years of age.

Fisherman's Sedge: a grass-like plant with triangular stems and inconspicuous flowers, growing typically in marshes or near watercourses; fragrant when crushed; *see also in the Botanical Glossary.*

Flughol: East Orrenic dialect based on Old Orrenic, "wings" or "winged".

Foggling family:

- **Brun Foggling:** father to Odilia, Rueddan andToman Foggling
- **Alyena Foggling** (*born* Kunic)**:** Brun Foggling's deceased wife
- **Odilia Rupp** (*born* Foggling)**:** daughter and eldest child of Brun and Alyena Foggling
- **Rueddan Foggling:** son and second child of Brun and Alyena Foggling
- **Toman Foggling:** son and youngest child of Brun and Alyena Foggling
- **Metsch Rupp:** husband of Odilia Foggling

Folumpor: the main river flowing east to west on the Northern Horn; *see also the Great River* and *the Suyan Folumpor.*

Forth-telling: *Forth-tell, Forth-told*; speaking a wish or desire, expressed to cause the wish or desire to become reality; associated often with foretelling, but distinctively different and not necessarily prophetic in scope.

Fram: a servant of the Galdyssen Baronhold, responsible for the transport of fresh goods to the kitchens; the person who helps Lady Arden Shannorn escape the Baronhold.

Freymuot, Haynts Baron: a member of one of the Quaterni families of Barrost, resident in the Freymuot Baronhold with his wife Baroness Margit Freymuot and their four children; *see also Baronhold.*

Friar: an honorific title within the Abbathcy of Immen.

Frinden Imner: a Vahlen fisherman from Landsend,

present at the Shantab where Mannu Sundermun tells of his Glortrom.

Fyrst: an Old Orrenic word meaning 'principle', 'the beginning'; formerly a title of a Land Prince.

Fyrst of Ydassum: title conferred upon Toman Foggling by Highborn Lady Banah Méndrensynn.

G

Gahdan: *Granary* in Old Orrenic; one of the island cluster at the mouth of the Bay of Limman

Gahoin: a large genus of predominantly ground dwelling fowl; different species are distinguished by size, call, and the length, pattern and colour of feather; the name is derived from the Old Orrenic word 'to cry out'; *see also in the Zoological Glossary.*

Galdyssen, House of the Steward Baron:

- **Baron Lornz-Ullen Galdyssen:** current Steward of Barrost, living in the Galdyssen Baronhold; his title inherited after the tragic accidental death of the previous Baron Galdyssen; son Lornz, and daughter Yrmel.
- **Baroness** Soffian **Galdyssen** (*born* Vandran): wife of Baron Lornz-Ullen and mother of Lornz and Yrmel.

Games played on the Northern Horn:

- **Cobbles:** played, in one form or another, by many peoples of Orrenic descent. In Mendelon, the Game of Cobbles is also called Trophies.
- **Steckees:** a game where the lead player waits while the rest of the players hide then, at given moment, the lead must go and find the

hiding players.

- **Schellen:** a card game played in different forms, by most Orrenic peoples.
- **Tambur:** a ball game played with a hand-held paddle of leather stretched over a wooden circle.
- **Yassen:** popular card game in Ydassum.
- **Gebayt Bithen:** to ask or plead for oneself or on someone else's behalf.

Geholiogarth: a vast temple complex in the city of Immen, founded in the latter Early Migration Period, as guardian of the culture and faith of the Orrenic people; thought to have been built on an area venerated by the Riddern and Uccell; also known as 'The Holy Enclosure' or 'The Great Temple'; *see map of the Northern Horn.*

Gelondria: the southern territory of Syngordia bordering on Edendor, Vlachonia and the province of Yldshimman in Mendelon; once the Kingdom of Ghelondria; *see map of the Northern Horn.*

Geshan al Mansh: 'Gift to the People'; the school of thought that teaches that all manifestations of Eth are intended for the service of everyone and are not a sign of rank or prestige in society.

Ghelondren: the inhabitants of the Region of Gelondria in eastern central Syngordia; historically, one of the banished Palanth-Orric tribes of the collective group called the Orren, that arrived on the Great Continent during the Second Migration Period; *see map of the Northern Horn.*

Ghelondrian Crown, the: the historic kingdom north of the Ghelòthry River in present Syngordia that merged with the Dennelonian Crown to form the Double Crown Kingdom of Syngordia.

Ghelòthry, River: the main river flowing south-southwest through Syngordia, named after the Ghelondren, a Palanth-Orric tribe of the Second Migration; *see map of the Northern Horn.*

Ghoda Thiess Shannorn, Duchess: second wife of Duke Edwythe of Borinbranth, mother of Lady Arden Shannorn; *see also Shannorn of Borinbranth, Ducal House of.*

Gift to the People: individuals of Orrenic descent with special gifts who are called to serve their countrymen with their increased abilities.

Gladys Sagoma: daughter of Baron and Baroness Sagoma of Castle Vandronbol; a participant in the Debutante Gala at the Galdyssen Baronhold.

Glortrom: a lucid dream, triggered by the increasing flow of Eth, becoming waking visions that reveal consequences of the Beckoning reverberating through the world.

G'nallun, Lord: the principal lord of the three Uccell Lords who accepted Lady Banah Méndrensynn's invitation to accompany her on her State Visit; Lord Druin Méndrensynn's personal contact among the Firstborn.

Golden Scales: the pollen scales of several Summerbird orchid species native to the high elevations of the massive eastern Ydassum mountain ranges, used in the production of spices.

Gordyn Fathringen, Crown Prince: Son of King Richarr Fathringen and Queen Isabella Elstundreth Fathringen; *see also Fathringen of Syngordia, Royal House of.*

Gor Shorann: the owner of Under the Cliffs inn in Landsend; father to Sere Shorann.

Goyt: *Protected Hold* in Old Orrenic, one of the island cluster at the mouth of the Bay of Limman.

Granary of the North: one of the historic Orrenic names for Lowarthen; in Palanshen dialects referred to as 'Lofwardan'; *see map of the Northern Horn.*

Great Builders: an ancient, fabled race of beings who worked alongside the Uccell in what was later called Lowarthen.

Great Continent: the immense island homeland of the Uccell, surrounded by the Olmish Mechen and Aved Oceans; the third and largest of three island continents created by Ber'eth, also populated by descendants of peoples from Palanth-Orron and Urborn.

Great Grey Swan: a species of Grey Swan native to vast lakes of Daerumor and Edendor; *see also in the Zoological Glossary.*

Great Inner Sea: one of the two high altitude, glacially-fed and land-locked seas of Ydassum; *see map of Ydassum.*

Great Maned Elk: the largest species of highland elk known on the Great Continent; its territory is believed to extend from the glacial highlands of Ydassum eastward through to Auyana and the Thousand Rivers District; *see also in the Zoological Glossary.*

Great Northern Ocean: *see Olmish Aved.*

Great River, the: the main river flowing east to west on the Northern Horn; *see also Suyan Folumpor and map of the Northern Horn.*

Great Sorcerer Lords (of Athlonia): the sovereign rulers of ancient Palanth-Orron, the ancestral home of all Orrenic, Palanshen and Bohdnian tribes extant on the Great Continent, believed to have harnessed forbidden powers by which they dominated the wills of their subjects.

Great Western Ocean: *see Olmish Mechen.*

Green River Drake: a species of waterfowl with deep green plumage, a broad blunt bill, short legs, webbed feet, and a waddling gait; domesticate strains exist.

Greggor Boatan: the Landsender blacksmith known for the quality of his harpoons and hooks; father of Malric Boatan; present at the Shantab where Mannu Sundermun tells of his Glortrom.

Greinen: an ancient succubus spirit, a fallen Wayfarer leader, sealed in a collapsed branch of the ancient Temmerung; also known as 'The Wailing One' and 'Canthalida'.

Grenn, Family: a family of Landsend.

Grey Heron: a large fish-eating wading bird with long legs, a long S-shaped neck, and a long, pointed bill; the grey colour form of Stalker waterbirds; *see also in the Zoological Glossary.*

H

Heavens Worshippers: a large family of predatory insects with slender bodies and sharply triangular heads, capturing its prey by stealth, raising large forelegs like hands in prayer; *see also in the Zoological Glossary.*

Heicha: one of the three Special Ones, members of the Hlimman in captivity, selected due to the strength of their clear Eth Lingers used to create The Encasement in sacred processions; *see also Special Ones, Shonin and Tymea.*

Heidl Hanster: an elderly woman from Landsend present

at the Shantab where Mannu Sundermun tells of his Glortrom.

Heiri Huabber: a Landsender Vahlen hunter who rendered a year's harvest of Vahlen blubber for the preparations against the Athlonian attack.

Highborn: an honorary form of address for noble Ydassumer families not of dynastic Orrenic lineage.

High Council: governing body within the Abbaths of Immen.

High Seat of Barrost: the position of ruling Steward within the Vandrian Kingship.

Hlimman/Hlimmanen, Hlimmanian: Old Orrenic for Limman, Limmanian.

Hohn Fennsor North: the mountain range and highlands to the north of Barrost, extending from the western tip of the Northern Horn of the Great Continent at Landsend to the Arid Strand bordering the Duchy of Borinbranth; *see map of the Northern Horn.*

Hohn Fennsor South: the highlands to the south of Barrost, extending from the western coast of Norssum to the southern reaches of the Duchy of Borinbranth; *see map of the Northern Horn.*

Holy City, The: Immen, capital city of Edendor; *see map of the Northern Horn.*

Holy Enclosure, The: the Great Temple of Immen; also known as 'Geholiogarth'.

Honstan: the province where Toman's mother Alyena Kunic-Foggling and Lord Mischul Dalbonn spent their childhood as Limmanian orphans; *see map of the Northern Horn.*

Hordle House: residence of Lord Blenn Fayren, situated in the north-west of Syngordia.

Horn, The: a geographical area which encompasses the nine north-western countries of the Great Continent:

Welsordia, Bnornum, Ydassum, Syngordia, Limmania, Norssum (Barrostania), Mendelon, Edendor and Vlachonia; *see map of the Northern Horn.*

Horned-beast: a large genus of horned animals native to the Great Continent; both feral and domesticated species exist; *see also in the Zoological Glossary.*

Horróglоryn, North and South: the twin cities at the mouth of the Great Firth of Mendelon.

Huddu-Han: *Huddun hanen;* the Dog-faced Ape; a long-snouted white ape native to the dense forests of Inner Limmania, and throughout the Cloud Forests of Edendor, Ydassum and Auyana; *see also in the Zoological Glossary.*

Hussar: a Riddern servant of the Chieftains, caring for their steeds.

I

Idassium Mekkumenor: ancient name for Ydassum, 'the Realms of/in the Clouds'.

Immen: the capital city of Edendor, the foundation of which is attributed to the Bohdne; later developed and extended by the Orrenic tribes of the Edèndi; the seat of the theocratic rulers of Edendor and the Abbaths of Geholiogarth, a name that in some ancient texts refers to the city itself; *see also Holy City; and map of the Northern Horn.*

Imner, Frinden: Landsender present at the emergency Shantab.

Irrshen: the terrifying Stag of Death from Palanth-Orric legend and fable; an apparition, conjured by the united wills of the Great Lords of Athlonia, taking the form of a Great Maned Elk; *see also Stag of Death.*

Isabella Forwynna Fathringen of Syngordia, Queen (*born*

Elstundreth-Fathringen): wife of Double Crowned King Richarr Fathringen of Syngordia, mother to Crown Prince Gordyn Fathringen; sister of Prince Palandred Elstundreth-Fathringen of Mendelon; *see also Fathringen of Syngordia, Royal House of.*

J

Jon: one of the kitchen servants in the Galdyssen Baronhold.

Jonatan Prach: Head Gardener at Warningen House.

Jos Sundermun: Sonna and Mannu Sundermun's eldest son; present at the Shantab where Mannu Sundermun tells of his Glortrom; wife, Marna, son Byrud; *see also Sundermun family.*

K

Kenddan, Master: Lord Druin Méndrensynn's chief porter during his last expedition to Auyana.

Keniss, Master: tavern keeper in Limmania.

L

Laggol Palaath: the wide flat wetland valley leading from the south-eastern coast of the Great Inner Sea to the plains of Lowarthen; *see map of Ydassum.*

Landsend: a village in a province of the same name, at the north-western tip of the Norssum coast, formerly called Dur-Vangod; *see map of the Northern Horn.*

Lanfoth(e): an Old Orrenic title, once an elected position, but later an hereditary role as ruler of the ancient Cloud Kingdom, known as the Confederation of Ydassum; the status and term of address for heads of the ruling family of Ydassum, to indicate non-royal but still noble position in the country's government.

Lath Courts: elaborate shadehouses, designed by craftsmen of the House of Méndrensynn, specifically to cultivate diverse high-altitude Summerbird orchids as well as other spice orchid species; a circular structure with massive stone walls, shaded only by timber slats to reproduce the light shade of the cool mountainous growing conditions the orchids need.

Letters School: in Ydassum, the first five years of schooling open to children from ages five to ten years old.

L'Ida: a dialect of Orrenic derivation spoken in the area of Daerumor on the west shore of the Great Inner Sea in Daerumor Mekkumenor. Dialect used in the city of Turicum.

Lieutenant Protector: an officer-in-training to the Lord Protector; Toman Foggling was elevated to this rank after his promotion; *see also Lord Protector.*

Life Light: aura or the Light of Life; a luminescence emitted by all living beings, seen only by the Riddern and those Orren who have the Eth ability of an Akkoren or 'Reader'.

Light Between Worlds: believed by many to be a metaphorical place of spiritual intimacy with Ber'eth; Lady Arden Shannorn, student of Eth Lore at Barrost, revived the Old High Orrenic name Temmerung for this phenomenon; *see also the World of Visions.*

Lily Farnham: Chambermaid to Lady Arden Shannorn of Borinbranth.

Limman: the capital city of Limmania; *see map of the Northern Horn.*

Limmanen: the people of Limmania; the ancient name is written as 'Hlimmanen' when in reference to

Limmanian citizens imprisoned in the Alldai; historically, one of the banished Palanth-Orric tribes of the collective group called the Orren, that arrived on the Great Continent during the Second Migration Period.

Limmania, Lower: historically, the southern territory of a once greater Limmania; after the Edict of Mendelon, the area became the country known simply as Limmania; *see map of the Northern Horn.*

Limmania, Upper: the southernmost province of Norssum; once the northern province of Greater Limmania, ceded to Norssum with the Edict of Mendelon; *see map of the Northern Horn.*

Limmanian: 'of or pertaining to Limmania'; dialect of Limmania.

Limman Staff: a part of the regalia of the ruling House of Mendelon, a symbol of the Elstundreth Dynasty; the large blue-cast diamond set on the top of the sceptre was seized as penalty from Limmania at the end of the Expulsion Wars.

Limmorn: tribes of ancient Limmornia (now Limmania) descent: Darumdendi, Andrandi and Bnorni, now blended.

Linden: *Duftana lindeninsis,* a medium-growing hardwood tree; *see also in the Botanical Glossary.*

Linger: the colour resonance or luminescent residue of Eth, the power of Ber'eth, sometimes seen as hints of colour in shadows and reflections.

Lofwardan: the rich grain belt of eastern Norssum bordering on the Syngordian province of Lowarthen to the east and the Duchy of Borinbranth to the west; these productive flatlands, as well as the greater region of Lowarthen, are also known as 'The Land of the

Loaves' and 'The Granary of the North'; *see map of the Northern Horn.*

Loorwood: *Eberholtiana gigantea;* a tall-growing majestic hardwood seed-bearing tree of the Cloud Forests; a key component of the high canopy abode of many types of bird, particularly the large-beaked Swordbill family; *see also in the Botanical Glossary.*

Loraimen, Lord: Steward of Limmania, descendant of an ancient Orrenic house of appointed overseers of the country, under the direct authority of the dynastic rulers of Mendelon.

Lorann Illurend: Maiden-in-Waiting to Lady Banah Méndrensynn, from a mercantile family of Turicum; part of the Highborns' entourage on the State Visit.

Lor-beren: the evergreen form of Highland Blue Cherry, cultivated mostly as a fragrant herb for cooking; *see also in the Botanical Glossary.*

Lord Protector: the title given to the chief advisor to the members of the House of Méndrensynn whose responsibility is to protect their interests and their lives; post held by Lord Mischul Dalbonn.

Lornz-Ullen Galdyssen, Steward Baron: the present elected Steward of the Vandrian Kingship of Barrost, resident in the Galdyssen Baronhold; *see also Baronhold* and *Galdyssen, House of the Steward Baron.*

Lowarth: Old Orrenic for 'a loaf of bread'; an ancient symbol of wealth and prosperity.

Lowarthen: also known as 'the Land of the Loaves', and 'the Granary of the North'; an autonomous region of northern Syngordia; according to Riddern legend, once the centre of two ancient cultures where the Great Builders worked alongside the Holy Uran-Draigana; *see map of the Northern Horn.*

Lower City, the: formerly Noèsh, the older part of

modern Barrost, founded by Orrenic settlers in the Second Migration Period.

Luminous Water Diamond: the large blue-cast diamond in the royal crown of Mendelon; considered to be the twin of the stone in the Limman Staff.

Lyrana Armgolt, Lady: the young daughter of Baron Armgolt and deceased Lady Marlan Armgolt-Freymuot, a participant at the Debutante Ball at the Galdyssen Baronhold.

Lyttie: an adolescent nickname for Prince Lytwon Fathringen, given by Petar Rothringan, an old school friend of the Lofwardan prince; *see also Lytwon Dor-Tanumm Fathringen, Prince.*

Lytwon Dor-Tanumm Fathringen, Prince: the second cousin to the present King of Syngordia, His Majesty Richarr Fathringen; widower of Princess Verana Fera'Genglic Fathringen; lifelong friend of Lanfoth Steffen Méndrensynn, referred to as 'uncle' by the Lanfoth's children, Lady Banah and Lord Druin.

M

Maidens and Masters Dance: the dance during Wintersong festivities which many young people attend in the hope of finding a mate.

Maiden's Song: a robust member of the diminutive violet family, producing large pure white flowers; *see also in the Botanical Glossary.*

Malmo: one of the young boys in Ensign Eckel's crew.

Malric Boatan: a young fisherman, son of blacksmith Greggor Boatan; childhood friend of Uri and Shann Sundermun, present at the Shantab where Mannu Sundermun tells of his Glortrom; travels to Barrost to deliver the warnings given in Mannu's vision.

Mandrenn (also Mandrann): the 'Men of the Clouds'; surnames in the ancestry of the Ydassum Méndrensynn family; *see also Méndrensynn of Daerumor, the House of.*

Mannu Sundermun: a Landsender fisherman who had a Glortrom vision; husband of Sonna Sundermun with whom he had five children; *see also Sundermun family.*

Marden Morath: the High Flooded Plain, bordered by the highlands of Mardoènia to the south, the Hon Fennsor South to the west and the Drengul Borinbranth to the north; *see map of the Northern Horn.*

Mardoènia: a region in the Limmanian Highlands; a vast marshland through which the ancient course of the Suyan Folumpor passed on its way through Limmania to the Olmish Mechen, the Great Western Ocean; *see map of the Northern Horn.*

Marna Sundermun: wife of Jos Sundermun, mother of Byrud; present at the Landsend Shantab when the attack from Athlonia was expected.

Marta: Prince Lytwon Fathringen's cook.

Marta Gressing: a woman from Landsend present at the Shantab where Mannu Sundermun tells of his Glortrom.

Mas' Denelan: tavern owner and keeper in the city of Limman in Limmania.

Master Healers: the famed Riddern practitioners trained in making and using curative tinctures, tisanes and medicines; *see also Riddern.*

Maylin Méndrensynn: daughter and third born of Lanfoth Steffen and Lanfothe-Consort Ahnya of Ydassum; *see also Méndrensynn of Daerumor, the House of.*

Meandering Path, the: an inn located in Syngordia near

the Norssum border and the Marden Morath; *see Marden Morath.*

Mendelon: the southernmost country on the Horn of the Great Continent, comprised of the three provinces Yldshimman, Dórumbor and Ethyndùl; historically, the only Orrenic territory never conquered by the Skylle; *see map of the Northern Horn.*

Mendelon City: also called The Triple City, being divided into three distinct water-front municipalities: the Twin Cities of Horróglоryn, and Mendelon City, each occupying important strategic locations on the great Folùm Estuary; home of the dynastic houses of Fathringen and Elstundreth; *see map of the Northern Horn.*

Mendeloni: 'of or pertaining to Mendelon'; historically, one of the banished Palanth-Orric tribes of the collective group called the Orren, that arrived on the Great Continent during the Second Migration Period; the tribe that, together with the Welsordi, first settled the western coastal areas of the Northern Horn, an area once called Welsor-Mendelon.

Mendelonian Maritime Court: the post Expulsion War court initiated during the Reformation after the Skyllian Vastan leaders were driven from the Horn.

Mendelon, Treaty of: laws and ordinances passed by the Orrenic Alliance, authored by King Wintar Elstundreth of Mendelon, heavily favouring Barrostanian and Mendelonian interests, and penalising those of Limmania after their presumed role in the escape of the Skyllian Vastan overlords. *See also: Expulsion Wars* and *Siege and Fall of Limmania.*

Méndrensynn of Daerumor, the House of: later also called The House of Ydassum:

- **Lanfoth Steffen Ghindred Méndrensynn:** the presiding ruler of Ydassum.
- **Lanfothe-Consort Lady Ahnya Eleor Seynor Méndrensynn:** wife of Lanfoth Steffen and co-ruler presiding over Ydassum.
- **Lady Banah Ahnya Eleor Méndrensynn:** daughter and firstborn of Lanfoth Steffen and Lanfothe-Consort Ahnya of Ydassum.
- **Lord Druin Adwynn Méndrensynn:** son and second born of Lanfoth Steffen and Lanfothe-Consort Ahnya of Ydassum.
- **Lady Maylin Theda Ahnya Méndrensynn:** daughter and third born of Lanfoth Steffen and Lanfothe-Consort Ahnya of Ydassum.

Menne-Gootay: in Fahtu-Shanner dialect, an expression of surprise; Goodness gracious! My goodness!

Migration Periods (First, Second and Third):

- **First Migration:** the Banishing of the fabled Bohdne, estimated landfall on the Great Continent somewhere before 4190
- **Second Migration:** a period of gradual migration of Palanth-Orric tribes, collectively called the Orren, occurring between the years 4580 and 4680
- **Third Migration:** the arrival on the Northern Horn of a single Palanth-Orric tribe, the Palanshen, led by their commander Barrùs, in the year 5169

Mirshod: the northernmost town on the island of Fahtu-Shan in the Great Inner Sea of Ydassum; *see map of Fahtu-Shan.*

Mischul Dalbonn, Lord: His Grace, the Lord Protector;

appointed to the House of Méndrensynn to defend the Highborns and their interests.

Modwynn, Lady: Lady Banah's second Lady-in-Waiting, pregnant and unable to travel at the time of the State Visit.

Molkey: a small building on older Orrenic farmsteads, dedicated to cheese making, built around a cold water spring.

Months of the year (and celebrations) in the common speech of Ydassum:

- Yaned
- Febred
- Merret – (Spring Equinox)
- Avred
- Emded
- Somned – (21st – 22nd Celebration of White, Summer Solstice)
- Somersh
- Augsh
- Erved – (Autumn Equinox) (Autumn Equinox)
- Herved
- Novred
- Wintred – (21st – 22nd Wintersong, Winter Solstice)

Morenia Galdyssen: participant in the Debutante Ball at the Galdyssen Baronhold.

Myrnish Channel, the: the narrow channel of water between Landsend and The White Isles.

N

Netherns, the: in Limman, the lower level of the city, also called 'the Lower Village'; a heavily fortified area of the city facing the Bay of Limman, dating back to the original Welsordian culture in the Orrenic settlement period.

Noèsh: the ancient Orrenic city upon which Palanshen Barrost was later built; the downfall of Noèsh followed sieges by the Skylle and a virulent plague that wiped out its entire population.

Northern Horn: the north-western lands of the Great Continent; the first area settled by the peoples of the second Great Migration from Palanth-Orren, collectively known as the Orren; *see map of the Northern Horn.*

Lands of the Northern Horn:

- Bnornum (an autonomous region of Welsordia, once an independent confederation of Bnorni tribes)
- Edenendor (theocracy ruled by the Abbots of Immen)
- Limmania (the later name given to the territory of Lower Limmania)
- Mendelon (comprised of the provinces of Yldshimman, Ethyndùl and Dórumbor)
- Norssum (comprised of Barrostania, Landsend, the Duchy of Borinbranth, Upper Limmania, Lofwardan, Tothbory and Tendumen)
- Ydassum (confederation of autonomous provinces)
- Syngordia (the territory of the "Double Crowns" of Dennelon and Gelondria, as well as the autonomous region of Lowarthen)
- Welsordia (the northern coastal territory above Ydassum, settled by the Welsordi.)
- Vlachonia (vassal state of Mendelon, governed by an official appointed by the court of Mendelon)

North Isle: the largest island of a small archipelago off the coast of Landsend; Widow's peak is the landmark mountain on North Isle; *see map of Landsend.*

O

Odilia Foggling Rupp: daughter and eldest child of Brun and Alyena Foggling; *see also Foggling family.*

Old High Orrenic: the ancestral language of the Palanth-Orren; a mostly literary or scholarly written language extant in holy texts and ecclesiastic writings; an archaic form of High Orrenic spoken only among the Abbots and clergy of Edendor.

Old Mendelonian Trade Law: a system of taxation established at the end of the Expulsion Wars in which Mendelonian excises were levied on precious goods such as oils, perfumes, amber glass ingots, spices, fragrant woods and rose salts.

Old Orren(ic): an archaic Palanth-Orric language spoken at the time of the First and Second Migrations; the ancient root language from which modern Orrenic languages stem.

Olmish Aved: the Great Northern Ocean; *see map of the Northern Horn.*

Olmish Mechen: the Great Western Ocean, The Endless Seas; *see map of the Northern Horn.*

Ornden, Mayor: the elected mayor of Landsend at the time of Mannu Sundermun's Glortrom; has the honorary title: Protector of Dur-Vangod (Old Orrenic for Landsend).

Orren: the collective name for the group of Palanth-

Orric immigrants of the Second Migration, who settled mostly on the western coastal lands of the Great Continent that later became known as the Northern Horn.

The Historical Tribes of Orren, and the lands those tribes settled and named:

- Bnorni (Bnornum, an autonomous region of Welsordia)
- Eastern Edèndi (Edendor)
- Hlimman (Limmania, Upper and Lower)
- Welsordi-Mendeloni – the amalgamated tribe later known as the Mendeloni – (the western coastal area from Landsend to present-day Mendelon)
- Welsordi(Welsordia)
- Tendumen (Lowarthen, northern Syngordia and eastern Norssum)
- Ghelondren and Dyndyll (central Syngordia)
- Yldsh and Southernern Edèndi: (the Mendelonian provinces of Yldshimman and Ethyndùl.)

Orrenic: 'of or pertaining to the Orren'; the collective name for the diverse Palanth-Orric tribes of the Second Migration; also the language and varying dialects of those peoples.

Orrenic Alliance: the group of Palanth-Orric countries on the Great Continent, united to drive the Skyllian overlords from the Northern Horn; later used to describe the loose political alliance of countries of Orrenic origin; also used in reference to a group of laws created during the Orrenic Migration Period, still in force on the Northern Horn.

Ous'Gweld: Old Orrenic for 'the Selected' or 'the Chosen'; the school of thought teaching that mastering higher levels of the Power of Ber'eth shows an elite status in political and cultural spheres of society; adherents to the school of Ous'Gweld believe the use of Eth to be a sign of a spiritually royal pedigree.

Ous'Vall: in Fahtu-Shanner dialect, 'that which has been chosen'.

P

Palandred Worbroth Elstundreth-Fathringen, Prince: second son of Queen Sindrea Isabella Elstundreth and Prince Consort Wendrynn Fathringen of Syngordia; *see also Elstundreth-Fathringen.*

Palanshen: the tribe of the Third Migration from the Palanth-Orric archipelago to the Northern Horn of the Great Continent, led by Barrùs.

Palanth-Orron: the remote archipelago to the north of the Olmish Aved; ancestral home of all Palanth-Orric tribes residing on the Great Continent.

Petar Rothringan: an old school friend of Prince Lytwon Fathringen; a Syngordian nobleman loyal to the Double Crown.

Plague: a virulent disease characterised by death of living tissue and heavy bleeding; annihilated the population of Noèsh and spread to the surrounding countryside towards the Duchy of Borinbranth.

Pocker and Fish Guts!: a Turicum exclamatory expression; Good grief!

Poison Lore: the ancient Stagriders' Banecraft; the study and administration of elixirs, venoms, toxins, tinctures, extracts, essences and distillates from plants, animals and minerals, used to take life.

Professor Gwenndon: an instructor at the School of Eth

Lore, University of Barrost. Former teacher at the College of Eth Studies in Immen.

Professor Yohn: an instructor at the School of Eth Lore, University of Barrost.

Q

Quaterni: "Four in One"; the four ruling families of the Vandrian Kingship who reside in the Baronholds of Barrost; *see also Baronhold.*

Queen Summerbird: the most recent Summerbird orchid discovery; the only known specimen of the species was collected from the wild by Lord Druin Méndrensynn and cultivated in his sister Lady Banah's private Lath Court; *see also in the Botanical Glossary.*

R

Rand: one of the young boys in Ensign Eckel's crew.

Reader: the name given to an individual of Palanth-Orric descent with the inborn ability to read the chromatic resonances of Eth, an ability often attributed to those with green Eth resonances; also known also as 'Akkoren' in archaic eastern Orrenic dialects.

Realm of Lights: a term Sir Han Crethingan used for the Temmerung.

Red Honey: honey from bees that draw nectar from the Red Spider Orchid, noted for its sleep-inducing properties.

Red Summerbird: a diminutive form of the Summerbird orchid genus found mostly on exposed rock in the Cloud Forest of Ydassum; *see also in the Botanical Glossary.*

Reformation: period of reorganisation on the Northern Horn after the fall of the last Skyllian Vastan and the Treatise of Mendelon penalising Limmania for treason.

Regula Mutig: a woman from Landsend, present at the Shantab where Mannu Sundermun tells of his Glortrom, reluctant to donate her silverware for the defence of the village.

Rethshepp: diverse breeds of sleek-bodied horned beasts; its name is derived from the Old Orrenic words for 'wrath' and 'fury', due to their power and strong temperament.

Rethshepp, Southern: a breed of Rethshepp horned beasts developed exclusively for the royal family in Mendelon, the only colour known in the breed is black.

Richarr Fathringen II, King: the firstborn son of deceased King Landwynn Dor-Tanumm Fathringen; husband to Queen Isabella Elstundreth Fathringen; father to Crown-Prince Gordyn Fathringen; *see also Fathringen of Syngordia, Royal House of.*

Riddern: the converted tribes of the Urbonnic Stagriders, or pertaining to those tribes; renowned practitioners of Healing Lore.

Ridge Road: the road running east to west across northern Syngordia, just south of the Marden Morath; *see map of the Northern Horn.*

Riparian League: a network of excise collection stations along the great northern waterway, the Suyan Folumpor, established by the Vandrian Kingship of Barrost; some stations are equipped with officiaries, jails and gallows to carry out swift punishments for perceived infractions of Barrostanian taxation laws.

Rissons: the high glacial barrier ranges of eastern Edendor.

River Limmorn / Marden Folumpor: The main river flowing through Limmania; *see map of the Northern Horn.*

River Pup, the: small Norssum tavern west of Borinbranth on the River Folumpor.

Robban Fingerling: schoolmate of Toman Foggling, caught stealing from the blacksmith and made to work the streets of Mirshod as punishment.

Robbeth, Friar: advisor to Lanfoth Steffen, who was defrocked as a member of the High Council of Immen.

Rock Daisy: a small perennial daisy which blooms at the peak of the day; *see also in the Botanical Glossary.*

Rorclay: the porter in charge of maps during Lord Druin Méndrensynn's last expedition.

Rubinstone, the Great: the largest ruby and most sacred of many Rubinstones venerated by the Skylle; the jewel in the Fire Brooch of Edendor with a crystalline flaw resembling a Scarab Wasp.

Rud: Master Baker in Mirshod, on Fahtu-Shan.

Rueddan Foggling: second child of Brun and Alyena Foggling; *see also Foggling family.*

Rugger, Haydann: one of Captain Vachter's men, accompanying Prince Lytwon Fathringen on his journey to Syngordia.

Ruhand, Chieftain: the male Riddern co-ruler of the Urbonnic Forest Riddern of Ydassum, a master of Urbonnic Healing Lore; the male of Chieftess Beruhn.

Rus Raykmut: a man from Landsend present at the Shantab where Mannu Sundermun tells of his Glortrom.

Ruthiana Galdyssen: participant in the Debutante Ball at the Galdyssen Baronhold.

S

Sacred Portion: one tenth of produce or income, given annually to the Abbaths of Immen.

Sagoma, the House of:

- **Baron Perter Sagoma:** one of the Vandrian Kingship families of Barrost, resident of Castle Vandronbol,
- **Baroness Nyrrna Sagoma:** wife of Baron Perter Sagoma
- **Lady Gladys Sagoma:** daughter of Baron and Baroness Sagoma of Castle Vandronbol; participant in the Debutante Ball at the Galdyssen Baronhold.

Samual: one of the household guards of the Galdyssen Baronhold.

Sand Jasmine: *Shlafrueta sempervirens*, a coastal plant and component of the dune flora of most of the coast of the Northern Horn, cherished as a component of deep sleep and healing tisanes; *see also in the Botanical Glossary*.

Santonin: the high priest sect of the Skylle of the Alldai.

Sara Minder: Toman Foggling's former desk mate in grade school on Fahtu-Shan, currently married to Yeral Fayris.

Scarab-Wasp: the sacred emblem of the Santonin Skylle of the Alldai.

Schellen: a card game played in different forms by most Orrenic peoples.

Schlamp: Barrost dialect for prostitute, whore, woman of ill repute.

Schofsgrind!: in Turicum dialect, an exclamatory expression; You idiot! You forgetful person!

School of Eth Lore: a special programme within the College of Ancient Languages at the University of Barrost.

Schools of Thought regarding Eth:

- **Avye-Sonther:** 'the Sanctified'
- **Geshan al Mansh:** 'the Gift to the People'
- **Ous'Gweld:** 'The Chosen'

Scribbners: an obscure order of monks in Immen committed to faithfully copying all ancient texts about Ber'eth and spreading them throughout the Orrenic world; believed to have evolved from the ancient order of Bohdnian monks.

Sea Hawk: a small raptor species native to the marshlands and shores of the Great Inner Sea; *see also in the Zoological Glossary.*

Season out of Season, Harbinger of Ruin: an Old Orrenic proverb regarding the delicate balance of nature; an ancient proverbial foretelling of doom.

Second Beckoning: the calling out to Ber'eth's children, resounding in the flow of Eth through the world.

Sere Shorann: the daughter of Gor Shorann, owner of Under the Cliffs inn near the docks of Landsend.

Servant of Geholiogarth: a layman of the faith who feels called to dedicate their life to service in Immen, leaving all their belongings and family ties behind in the pursuit of sincere servitude to Ber'eth.

Servant of Immen: An honorary status given by the Priesthood of Geholiogarth (Immen) to select scholars of Orrenic Lore.

Shannorn of Borinbranth, Ducal House of:

- Duke Edwythe Shannorn: hereditary ruler of the Duchy of Borinbranth in Norssum.
- Duchess Elida Galdyssen: first wife, deceased, of Duke Edwythe of Borinbranth.

- Duchhess Ghoda Thiess Shannorn: current wife of Duke Edwythe of Borinbranth.

- Lord Caldere Shannorn: first-born son and heir to Duke Edwythe Shannorn of Borinbranth and the late Elida Galdyssen Shannorn.

- Lady Arden Shannorn: second-born and only daughter of Duke Edwythe Shannorn and Duchess Ghoda Thiess Shannorn

Shann Sundermun: the firstborn of Sonna and Mannu's twin sons who left Landsend for work on the Great River; *see also Sundermun family.*

Shalder: a witch or sorcerer; any person assumed to practice forbidden arts.

Shantab: a traditional Orrenic family or community meeting in which the head of the household or the village mayor leads discussions regarding important decisions; the gatherings often end in a vote, with the majority decision being carried.

Shellen: Mannu Sundermun's horned-beast of burden.

Shift, The: a recent increase in the flow of Eth throughout the world; the source of power causing the Beckoning.

Shonin: the strongest Eth Wielder of the three Special Ones, Hlimmanian members in Skyllian captivity, selected due to the strength of their clear Eth Lingers used to create The Encasement in sacred processions; *see also Special Ones, Heicha and Tymea.*

Siege and Fall of Limmania: the last battle, and conclusion, of the Expulsion Wars often referred to in Limmanian folklore; the historical kidnapping of shipwrights and captains, along with their families, by the Skyllian Vastan rulers, to navigate a retreat to the Alldai of the south; the captains are believed to have run the ships of the last escaping Skylle against the craggy reef perimeter of the Bay of Limman, thereby killing all on board.

Silk Spider: several spider species, both venomous and non-venomous, native to the southern coastal regions of the Great Continent; the domesticated species used in the textile industries of Mendelon and Vlachonia was left behind by the Skyllian invaders; *see also in the Zoological Glossary.*

Silver Duck: diverse species of waterfowl indigenous to the northern coast of Norssum; *see also in the Zoological Glossary.*

Silverling: a small fish native to the cold currents of the Olmish Aved, found in large shoals near Landsend; *see also in the Zoological Glossary.*

Silver Zephyr, The: tavern in the city of Limman in Limmania.

Sindrea Isabella, the: one of the royal armed ships of the Mendelonian fleet; the ship Prince Palandred Elstundreth-Fathringen uses to travel north to Barrost.

Skylle: the Urbonnic peoples who crossed the newly formed land bridge to the Great Continent after the cataclysmic World Forming and settled on the arid southern plains of the Alldai.

Skyllian Supremacy: the period of Skyllian overlordship on the Northern Horn when the Skylle ruled over most of the Great Continent, approximately 150 years before the present time.

Skyllian Wars: the period of Skyllian attacks and conquests on the Great Continent, approximately 250 years before the present time.

Soffian Galdyssen-Vandran, Baroness: wife of Baron Lornz-Ullen Galdyssen, Steward of Barrost; *see also Galdyssen, House of the Steward Baron.*

Solyssia: the Méndrensynn luxury barge used on the Ydassumer Highborns' State Visit, equipped with dining hall, private apartments, guards' and kitchens.

Sondervay: the ship on which Toman Foggling and Yannu Elden travel, to reach Turicum.

Sonna Sundermun: the wife of Landsender fisherman Mannu Sundermun, mother to Uri and Shann, present at the Shantab where her husband tells of his Glortrom; *see also Sundermun family.*

Special Ones, the: Hlimmanen held in captivity by the Skylle of the Alldai, selected due to the strength of their clear Eth Lingers used to create The Encasement in sacred processions; *see Shonin, Heicha and Tymea.*

Spectrals: Eth chromatic resonances with the clarity of the primary colours: red, blue or yellow.

Spicewood: various fragrant woods from the semi-desert and desert areas of the Great Continent; *see also in the Botanical Glossary.*

Spider Silk: the cloths woven from the web silk of the domesticated species of silk spider brought from the arid Alldai by the Skyllian invaders.

Stag of Death / Destruction: the Irrshen; a manifestation of the evil will of the Great Lords of Athlonia; an apparition that takes on a form resembling the Great Maned Elk; *see also Irrshen.*

Stagriders: the Urbonnic tribe from which the Riddern arose, noted for their highly developed Poison Lore.

Stalker: a large fish-eating wading bird with long legs, a long S-shaped neck, and a long pointed bill; *see also Grey Heron, and the Botanical Glossary.*

Steckees: also called 'Ferbor'ghena'; a children's game where all the players hide, except one who must then try to find the others.

Steffen Ghindred Méndrensynn, Lanfoth: the presiding ruler of The Confederation of Ydassum, husband of co-ruling Lanfothe-Consort Lady Ahnya Eleor Seynor Méndrensynn; *see also Méndrensynn of Daerumor, the House of.*

Stilsh, Goran: one of Captain Vachter's men, accompanying Prince Lytwon Fathringen on his journey to Syngordia.

Storryn: a person of Orrenic descent with a rare form of hereditary blindness in which the hair, the skin and the sightless eyes are pure white; it is considered good luck to give them alms.

Summerbird: a genus of orchid species native to the high elevations of the eastern Ydassum mountain ranges, distinguishable by their massive leathery leaves and year-round bloom; *see also in the Botanical Glossary.*

Sundermun family:

- Mannu **Sundermun**, father
- Sonna Sun**dermun**, mother
- J os **Sundermun:** eldest son (wife Marna, son Byrud)
- **Timea Sundermun:** eldest daughter
- Layna **Sundermun:** youngest daughter
- Shann **&** **Uri Sundermun:** identical twin sons, the youngest of their children

Sunken Garden: along with Secret Garden and Room Within a Room, a landscape feature designed by the legendary architect Sir Han Crethingan.

Suyan Folumpor: the Great River; the largest river of the Northern Horn, flowing from east to west through Norssum, starting in the Palaath Region of Daerumor in Ydassum, passing through Lowarthen and Lofwardan, the Duchy of Borinbranth, the Plain of Fennsor and ending at the estuary and port of Barrost;

the main watercourse for shipping and travel from the landlocked countries of the Horn; *see map of the Northern Horn.*

Syngordia: the central kingdom of the Northern Horn, comprised of Dennelon and Ghelondria; *see map of the Northern Horn.*

Swordbill: one of three species of large-billed birds of the high canopy of the Cloud Forests of Ydassum and Edendor; *see also in the Zoological Glossary.*

T

Tambur: a sport in which a piece of leather is stretched over a ring of wood and used as a paddle to hit a leather ball against a wall.

Temmerung: an ancient Old High Orrenic term, reintroduced by Lady Arden Shannorn of the School of Eth Lore at Barrost, for 'The Light Between Worlds'; a phenomenon occurring in conjunction with the powerful Shift in Eth and the release of the second Beckoning.

Temple Plaza, the: the vast paved area surrounding the Skyllian temple at Rubinoug in the southern Alldai.

Tendumen: a northern province of the Autonomous Region of Lowarthen; *see map of the Northern Horn.*

Tennumen: 'of or pertaining to the ancient Orrenic culture of Tendumen'; historically, one of the banished Palanth-Orric tribes that arrived on the Great Continent during the Second Migration Period and settled in the area north of Lofwardan and the Syngordian region of Lowarthen; *see map of the Northern Horn.*

Tennum Vandriana: from Old Orrenic, the 'Valley of

Kingly Passage', a north-running valley above the city of Barrost; *see map of the Northern Horn.*

Thousand Rivers District: the unexplored territories to the east of Ydassum, also called Auyana.

Thunderweather!: a Fahtu-Shanner expression used to show surprise or sudden fright.

Tickory: an evergreen tap-rooted herbaceous plant mostly used for its stimulant properties; *see also in the Botanical Glossary.*

Toman Foggling: horned-beast breeder and youngest child of Brun and Alyena Foggling of Upland farm, Fahtu-Shan; left home for work in Turicum, initially in the employ of the House of Méndrensynn under Ensign Eckel and later under Lord Dalbonn; *see also Foggling family.*

Torghyll: the white-haired, Storryn-like sorcerer, presumed Athlonian.

Trade Summit: the gathering of representatives invited to coordinate legislation and taxation of merchandise transported on the River Suyan Folumpor; called by the Vandrian Kingship of Barrost.

Treaty of Mendelon: laws and ordinances passed by the Orrenic Alliance after the Expulsion Wars; heavily favoured Barrostanian and Mendelonian interests, and penalised Limmania for their supposed part in the escape of the governmental heads of the Skyllian Vastans; *see also The Expulsion Wars* and *The Siege and Fall of Limmania.*

Trend, Dobbesser: the Barrostanian student who participated in the Eth study group formed by professors Gwenndon and Yohn to delve into etymologies of Old Orrenic and their relation to the assumed Shift and Second Beckoning; the student of

Eth Lore awarded a scholarship to carry out research in the Méndrensynn archives in Turicum.

Triate Priesthood, the: the three head priests of the Skyllian Santonin sect.

Trivium: the study of the three-fold balance between Grammar, Logic and Rhetoric, concentrating on the formulation of concrete concepts from abstract thought.

Trumpet Flowers: *Taddura magnifica;* a small-growing flowering tree, sometimes herbaceous shrub, of the warmer regions of the lower Cloud Forests, often grown for the ornamental value of their huge trumpet-like flowers; *see also in the Botanical Glossary.*

Tunfluh: *Refuge* in Old Orrenic, one of the cluster of islands at the mouth of the Bay of Limman.

Turicum: the capital city of Ydassum on the western shore of the Great Inner Sea; founded during the eastward movement of the Orrenic tribes of the Second Migration; *see map of Ydassum.*

Twin Firths, the: the firths in Mendelon separating Horróglоryn North and Horróglоryn South from Mendelon City; *see map of the Northern Horn.*

Tymea: one of the three Special Ones, members of the Hlimman in captivity, selected due to the strength of their clear Eth Lingers used to create The Encasement in sacred processions; *see also see also Special Ones, Shonin and Heicha.*

U

Uccell: the Firstborn of the Great Continent, also known as the 'Uran-Draigana' or the 'Holy Uran-Draigana' by the Riddern; the undying race created by Ber'eth from the soil of the Great Continent; rather lizard-like in appearance, but walking upright on powerful legs and possessing strong leathery wings; the three Uccell Lords accompanying the Ydassum Highborns to the Summit on Trade were:

- G'nallun
- B'noru
- B'h'rants

Ullen, Family: a family of Landsend.

Under the Cliffs: a tavern near the docks in Landsend, run by Gor Shorann and his daughter Sere.

Upland: the name of the Foggling family farmstead on Fahtu-Shan.

Upper Limmania: the southern province of Norssum; former northern province of Greater Limmania before the Treaty of Mendelon; *see Treaty of Mendelon.*

Urandi: the race of beings created from the soil of Urborn, the southernmost landmass in the Olmish Mechen; the ancestors of the Skylle, Stagriders and Riddern.

Uran-Draigana: great winged beings, the Firstborn of the Great Continent; also known as the 'Uccell'; the Riddern refer to them as the 'Holy Uran-Draigana'; *see also Uccell.*

Uran-Draigana Ivory: the harvested talons, claws or bones of the Uran-Draigana. The only Uran-Draigana Ivory jewellery ever found was of the southern Uran-Draigana massacred by the Urandi in the Alldai.

Urbonnic: 'of or pertaining to the Urandi' whose homeland was the former island continent of Urborn

Urborn: originally the Southern Island Continent; after the World Forming, it became connected to the southernmost landmass of the Great Continent by the Isthmus of Androcaì.

Uri Sundermun: the second born of Sonna and Mannu's

twin sons who left Landsend for work on the Great Rive; *see also Sundermun family.*

V

Vachter, Captain: the captain of the Highborns' barges, in charge of security for Highborn Lady Banah's State Visit, under the command of the Lord Protector Mischul Dalbonn.

Vah: in Turicum dialect, an expression of disgust.

Vahlen: a group of four known species of air-breathing fish-like sea creatures native to the colder currents of the Olmish Aved and Olmish Mechen; source of Vahlenskin leather, Vahlenbone and Vahlen oil; *see also in the Zoological Glossary.*

Vahlenbone: the precious ivory-like bone of the Vahlen used to make small carved decorative items such as jewellery, buttons, hair ornaments and combs, as well as inlays in fine wood furniture.

Vahlen oil: the rendered blubber of Vahlen, highly prized in the production of perfumes.

Vahlenskin: the thick, weather-resistant leather made from Vahlen hide.

Vandran, House of: Baron Mertten Vandran of the Quaterni, and his family, living in the Vandran Baronhold; *see also Baronhold.*

Vandrian Kingship: the collective group of rulers of Barrostania, descendants of the Four Houses of Barrùs, the Palanshen leader of the last migration from Palanth-Orron.

Vandronbol: a large domed castle in Barrost, built during the Second Migration Period; first-hand accounts, by the Palanshen immigrants arriving at the castle, reveal the devastating effect of the Plague on the Orrenic population of Noèsh: "*...dried edible foods and drinkable wine were found in the cellars, plates with remnants of food were found on decked tables, but the inhabitants were only piles of bleached bones still clothed in stained garments, haunting reminders of a terrible great pestilence...*"

Vastans of Kalaq and Konsuul: the territories on the Northern Horn of the Great Continent, conquered by Skyllian overlords; comprised of lands from present day Norssum, Limmania and Syngordia to Yldshimman in the south.

Verana Fera'Genglic Fathringen, Princess: born a commoner, the late wife of Lytwon Dor-Tanumm Fathringen; death unexplained.

Villi: one of the young boys in Ensign Eckel's crew.

Viper's Strike, the: a sword fighting move made by jabbing the blade toward the torso, aiming at the heart.

Vlachonia: a vassal state of Mendelon, originally a coastal province of the Double Crown Kingdom of Ghelondria and Dennelon, governed by an official appointed by the court of Mendelon; large deposits of rare amber sand gave rise to the country's famed glass flagon industry, from which the territory derived its name; *see map of the Northern Horn.*

W

Wailing One, the: synonym for 'Canthalida' and the 'Greinen'; *see Greinen.*

Warningen House: a large palatial mansion in Lowarthen, northern Syngordia, designed by the famed royal architect, Sir Han Crethingan; the origin of the name is uncertain; ancient references to the location hint at a much greater antiquity than generally believed by historians at the university of Barrost.

Warring Period: the period of Skyllian invasions.

Wasp Nest of the North: Ydassumer and Lowarthen nickname for Barrost.

Wayfarers: a small legendary sect of the ancient Palanth-Orric tribe, the Bohdne, cast out of their archipelago homeland due to the rebellions against the Athlonian Overlords incited by their leader, Canthalida; *see also Greinen, and the Wailing One.*

Welshlar, Forwenda: student associate of Professor Gwenndon at the School of Eth Studies, University of Barrost.

Welsor: the ancient Orrenic culture of the Welsordi on the Great Continent; later amalgamated with that of the Mendeloni; *see also Orren.*

Welsordi: 'of or pertaining to the ancient Orrenic culture of Welsor"; 'of or pertaining to the people or country of Welsordia'; historically, one of the banished Palanth-Orric tribes that arrived on the Great Continent during the Second Migration Period; the tribe that, together with the Mendeloni, first settled the western coastal areas of the Northern Horn, founding a territory once called "Welsor-Mendelon"; later moved to the northern coast of the Horn, forming 'Welsordia'.

Welsordia: the alliance of two realms, Welsordia and Bnornum, on the northern coast of the Great Continent, dating back to the Orrenic Migration Period; *see map of the Northern Horn.*

Welsor-Mendelon, Royal Houses of: a term referring to the clans formed following the Orrenic Migrations from Palanth-Orron, from which rose the House of Mendelon, the House of Welsordia and Bnornum, plus the defunct Houses of Limman and Noèsh, and the Méndrensynn family of Ydassum.

Westrum, Captain: captain of the Sindrea Isabella, Prince Palandred Elstundreth's ship.

White Isles, the: Elsornaum; the archipelago at the north-western tip of the Great Continent that includes the guano islands; *see map of Landsend.*

White One, the: Athlonian sorcerer known also as 'Torghyll'.

White Sojourner: a small species of white tern that migrates to the Great Continent in late winter; *see also in the Zoological Glossary.*

White Sorcerers: the legendary evil sorcerers from Athlonia, seen in Glortroms and visions.

Whitewall: the cottage of the Sundermun family, on the slopes above the town of Landsend on the north-western tip of Norssum.

Widow's Peak: the highest peak on the North Isle near Landsend, Norssum.

Winnt: the elderly gate keeper of Hordle House in northern Syngordia.

Wintar Elstundreth: the Mendelonian dynast who authored the Treatise of Mendelon.

Winter Palace, the: main residence of the ruling Elstundreth family of Mendelon

Winter Scorpion: a constellation that appears in the late autumn and winter sky; a cluster of stars resembling a scorpion, the tail of which points due south.

Wintersong: a winter festival of lights, candles and flowers celebrated in different forms and versions throughout the Orrenic cultural continuum.

World Forming: according to Riddern Lore, the fabled cataclysmic event that caused the three landmasses of Palanth-Orron, Urborn and the Great Continent to move, creating catastrophic tidal waves, earthquakes, fissures in the land and volcanoes; the event that moved the landmass of Urborn towards the Great Continent, eventually joining the Alldai through the Isthmus of Androcaì.

World of Visions: a term given by Lord Druin Méndrensynn to the Temmerung; *see also the Temmerung* and *the Realm of Lights*.

Wyerson, Master: Head Gardener of Lady Banah Méndrensynn's private Lath Court in Turicum.

Wyssmaur – *White Beacon*, one of the island cluster at the mouth of the Bay of Limman

Y

Yannu Elden: the young man from Balbrun on the eastern shore of the Great Inner Sea who became Toman Foggling's best friend.

Ydassum, the Confederation of: the political alliance of Orrenic, Urbonnic and Uccelic races under the Lanfoth-Shantab system of rule; *see map of the Confederation of Ydassum.*

Ysbal: Head Cook in the Galdyssen Baronhold.

51

BOTANICAL GLOSSARY

Amber Tendril: *Aurana tendrilensis*; variable species of climbing shrub or woody vine found in moist peaty soil at lower elevations of Edendor and Lower Limmania, often near the coast; the tender vine tips and leaves are dried and used to produce Amber Tea.

Beauty-for-a-Day Lilies: *Snellferbensis cintrina*; a member of the *Sparagaceae* family of monocots that grow from a system of roots emerging from a crown instead of a bulb; flowers are similar to a true lily, but last only a day or a night.

Byr Tree: *Byr silbranus edenorani;* the Edendor Byr; a tall deciduous tree, native to northern Edendor, that typically has rough serrated drab grey-green leaves with a highly-reflective silvery bloom on the undersides; often used in formal garden design due to its highly ornamental stately presence at full maturity.

Ember Lily: *Perpetum mendelonia,* a member of the *Perpetum* group native to higher regions of the southern Northern Horn; a scaled-bulb lily usually with reddish flowers, but variations of ochre, yellow and white are known; emblem of the ruling House of Mendelon.

Ewe's Parsley: *Selinonensis pecoranum*; a woody perennial shrub native to bogs and alluvial plains near river systems throughout the Northern Horn; a traditional herb used by farmers for its calming effect on newly birthing or nervous horned-beasts.

Fisherman's Sedge: *Carex secgunum;* a grass-like plant with triangular stems and inconspicuous flowers; typically grows in marshy areas or near watercourses of Edendor and Ydassum, and throughout eastern Lowarthen; fragrant when crushed.

Golden Bellflower: *Campanadora dorata*; a variable genus that includes over 50 species and subspecies, and includes annual and perennial forms ranging in habit from dwarf coastal types to large open grassland and woodland species.

Kuddun (fibres): a collective name for the tough fibre-producing *linum* species used in the production of resilient supple cloths.

Leatherleaf: *Brendana argentosa,* a tall-growing tree with a distinctive silver grey bloom to the leaves; used ornamentally where their cultivation requirement of dry warmth is achieved.

Lor-beren: *Lorberan comunala;* an evergreen form of a woody perennial shrub, the Highland Blue Cherry; native to Honstan, growing mostly on shale soil; widely cultivated as a fragrant herb for cooking.

Maiden's Song: *Veilinena wyssanensis*; a robust evergreen member of the diminutive violet family, with a multi-branched inflorescence of large pure white flowers; native to sunny pastures and to chalky or stony soils.

Night Violet: *Veilinena fragrans;* a compact herbaceous plant of the understory of deciduous forests growing at moderate to higher elevations on the Horn, typically possessing purple, deep violet, or white five-petalled flowers; blooms both diurnally and nocturnally but its powerful sweet fragrance is released only in the still-dark early morning hours.

Northern Watergrass: *Uhcrauda acquatica*; an edible watergrass species used in the production of watergrass seed and oil; native to bogs and wet riverbanks along the river systems of Norssum, Edendor and Syngordia.

Rock Daisy: *Bellis saxumensis*; a small perennial grassland plant which has diurnally blooming flowers with a chartreuse disc and bluish white rays.

Spicewood: *Bonnumdrema, various species*; a group of trees with fragrant wood, native to the southern semi-desert and desert areas of the Great Continent.

Summerbird: *Sumrfurgheli*; a large genus of orchid species native to the mist-shrouded high elevations of the eastern Ydassum mountain ranges; distinguishable by their massive foliar growth and tendency to produce year-round blooms; flower colours range from deep indigo through pale blue to dusky pale red and ivory; the source of Golden Scale pollens used in spice production.

- **Queen Summerbird:** *Sumrfurgheli banahensis*; a unique and intensely fragrant form of the genus; possesses long graceful branched inflorescences with ivory-rose flowers and thick leathery leaves; discovered in the Cloud Forest of Auyana, the only specimen known is under cultivation in the private Lath Court of Lady Banah Méndrensynn within the Méndrensynn Palace grounds.
- Red **Summerbird:** *Sumrfurgheli rodlichana*; a diminutive form of the Summerbird genus, found mostly on exposed rock in the Cloud

Forests of Ydassum; often used in the hybridisation of spice orchid strains of *Sumrfurgheli*.

Swordlily: *Juccalgum pericolosum, veroxum and spicherensis;* a variable genus typically with tall inflorescences; includes three main species, ranging in habitat from scrub-forest coastal areas of the southern Horn, to open woodland types, each species forming rigid spiky leaves that arise from a woody base.

Tickory: *Ligrum ihmellensis*; a small herbaceous evergreen perennial, usually blue-flowered and possessing wrinkled rugose leaves; common to sand banks above alluvial plains throughout the Northern Horn; a tap-rooted herb used mostly for its stimulant properties.

52

Black Goose: *Gregos eorpum;* a non-migratory species of waterfowl, indigenous to the highland marshes bordering the Great Inner Sea; a watergrass seed grazer, the species shows a preference for nesting in the Laggol Palaath to the east of Turicum.

Lesser Black Goose: *Gregos eorpum minor*; a subspecies, inhabits the wetlands within the steep canyon waterways of Inner Limmania.

Black Lion: *Leonaum eorpum;* the largest member of the genus of felines from the Alldai, the arid southern plains of the Great Continent; the name derives from the thick black mane that drapes from the shoulders to the ground; the overall colour is a shiny dark brown, almost black; still found in some animal parks of remote castles on the Northern Horn, survivors of private animal collections of the Skyllian Vastans.

Black Swan: a genus of waterfowl once inhabiting the landlocked seas and highland lakes of Edendor and Ydassum; believed to have been hunted to extinction during the Skyllian overlordship on the Northern Horn due to the demand for their white oily flesh.

Blue Mourner: small blue-breasted songbird native to Lofwardan.

Elk: one of three species of the genus *Cornumen.*

Great Maned Elk: *Cornumen giganteus;* the largest highland species of elk known on the Great Continent;

has massive wide-spreading palmate antlers and long hair on its neck and upper back; its territory is believed to extend from the glacial highlands of Ydassum eastward through to Auyana.

Forest Elk: *Cornumen minor*; diminutive species native to the high-elevation temperate forests of Bnornum, Welsordia and the Honstan province of Ydassum.

Lowland Elk: *Cornumen paludensis*; native to the northern coastal region of Norssum, slightly smaller than the highland Great Maned Elk, distinguished by its smooth coat and slender antlers.

Fughol: a single-species genus of scaleless, very wide-bodied, chiefly oceanic fish with a cartilaginous skeleton; bony protrusions from their tail tips are used for self-protection and territorial battles.

Gahoin: a large genus of predominantly ground dwelling long-bodied fowl; different species are distinguished by size, call, and the length, pattern and colour of their ornamental feathers; diverse forms exist, some with luxuriantly long neck hackles and/or trains of feathers flowing off the upper back; most species and subspecies also have colourful bony protuberances on the head; the name is derived from the Old Orrenic word 'to cry out'.

Great Gahoin: *Gahoinen giganteus*; the largest of the genus, standing taller than a man, native to the dense ravines of Central Limmania.

Highland Gahoin: *Gahoinen spettaculus*; a large species found in the mountainous regions of the northern Great Continent.

Rock Gahoin: *Gahoinen felsensis*; often found on farmsteads in the Cloud Kingdoms of Ydassum and Edendor; many domesticated forms exist, bred for both their large blue eggs and meat.

Green River Drake: a species of waterfowl with deep green plumage, a broad blunt bill, short legs, webbed feet, and a waddling gait; domesticated strains exist.

Great Grey Swan: a species of Grey Swan native to vast lakes of Daerumor and Edendor.

Grey Heron: a large fish-eating wading bird with long legs, a long S-shaped neck, and a long pointed bill; the grey colour form of Stalker waterbirds.

Heavens Worshippers: a large family of predatory insects with slender bodies and sharply triangular heads, capturing its prey by stealth, raising large forelegs like hands in prayer.

Horned-beast: *Gadincum sps.*; a vast genus of hooved grazing animals found on the Great Continent; attributes common to all species are twisting or back-curling horns, cloven hooves, and either short hair or wool; some so-called species are actually feral groups released by early Palanth-Orric settlers; many domesticated forms exist.

Huddu-Han: *Huddun hanen;* the Dog-faced Ape; the White Ape; a long-snouted silver-white ape native to the dense forests of Inner Limmania, and throughout the Cloud Forests of Edendor, Ydassum and Auyana; fierce and territorial, it lives in small colonies near rivers, main diet consisting of fish, small mammals, fruit and leaves.

Red-Fin: a species of large fish that swims in shoals in the cold currents of the Olmish Mechen; a delicacy in Barrostanian cuisine.

Sea Hawk: *Fealconens paludastris*; a small raptor native to the marshlands and shores of the Great Inner Sea; has blue-grey feathers, bright yellow legs, black talons and eyes with white irises.

Silk Spider: *Gangewifrum godwebensis;* a domesticated form of a non-poisonous spider species, used in the production of silk for the textile industry; native to the Alldai in the far south of the Great Continent; venomous species of silk-producing spiders of this genus include G. *godwebensis var. atorum* and G. *godwebensis gelsterum*.

Silver Duck: diverse species of waterfowl indigenous to the northern coast of Norssum.

Silverling: *Smeltum communalis;* a small fish native to the cold currents of the Olmish Aved, found in large shoals near Landsend.

Stalker: a large fish-eating wading bird with long legs, a long S-shaped neck, and a long pointed bill; *see also Grey Heron*.

Swordbill: one of three species of large-billed birds of the high canopy of the Cloud Forests of Ydassum and Edendor.

Vahlen: a group of four known species of air breathing fish-like sea creatures native to the colder currents of the Olmish Aved and Olmish Mechen; source of Vahlenskin leather, Vahlenbone and Vahlen oil.

Greater Vahlen: *Vahlensis avediana;* native to the Olmish Aved, the largest of the known *Vahlen* species; solid blue-grey in colour, with a relatively small dorsal fin and wide pectoral and tail fins, often found in large family herds; hunted for their valuable blubber, bone and skin, as well as the fatty flesh which is preserved in seasoned brine.

Great Seas Vahlen: *Vahlensis olmechiana;* native to the Olmish Mechen, a species similar to *Vahlensis avediana* but having a larger, white-tipped dorsal fin and subtle light grey stripes down the body; also hunted for their blubber.

Mannach Vahlen: *Vahlensis mannachan;* found in coastal waters from the Bay of Barrost to the Bay of

Limmania; presumed to be albino due to their pink-white skin, the species has the typical small dorsal fin and wide pectoral fins of the genus.

Mourning Vahlen: *Vahlensis reddinlachana;* found only in the Bay of Limman, and living specimens have only ever been sighted at a distance; the rare diminutive species possesses short dorsal and pectoral fins and a wide tail, but reportedly grows only to the length of a man's height; the sound of its call at night has been compared to a sorrowful song; often featured in Limmanian folklore, each supposedly being the soul of one the shipwrights, captains and their families, who perished in the Bay of Limman during the Expulsion Wars.

White Sojourner: *Swinsturmen mendelonensis*; a small gregarious white species of tern that migrates to the Great Continent in deep winter; thought to originate on the remote northern archipelago of Palanth-Orron; winter breeding grounds are along the coast of Mendelon.

White Squid: *Sepiana calweralba;* a small elongated, rapidly swimming shell-less mollusc with eight tentacles; a delicacy in Barrostanian cuisine.

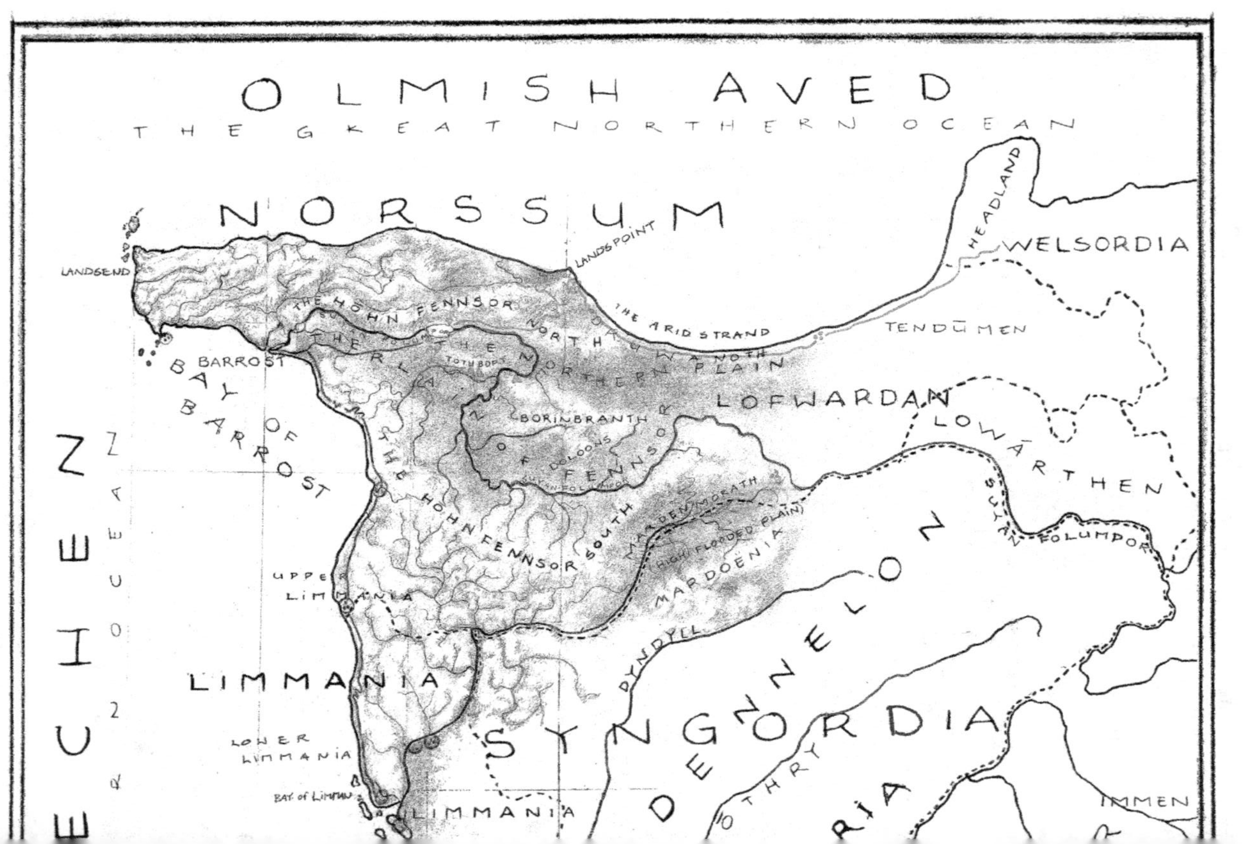
OLMISH AVED
THE GREAT NORTHERN OCEAN
NORSSUM
LANDSEND
LANDSPOINT
HEADLAND
WELSORDIA
THE ARID STRAND
TENDŪMEN
THE HOHN FENNSOR
NORTHERN PLAIN
LOFWARDAN
LOWĀRTHEN
BORINBRANTH
BARROST
BAY OF BARROST
THE HOHN FENNSOR SOUTH
MARDOENIA
SUYAN FOLUMPOR
DYNDYLL
NENELON
UPPER LIMMANIA
LIMMANIA
LOWER LIMMANIA
BAY of LIMPAU
SYNGORDIA
IMMEN
ECHEN

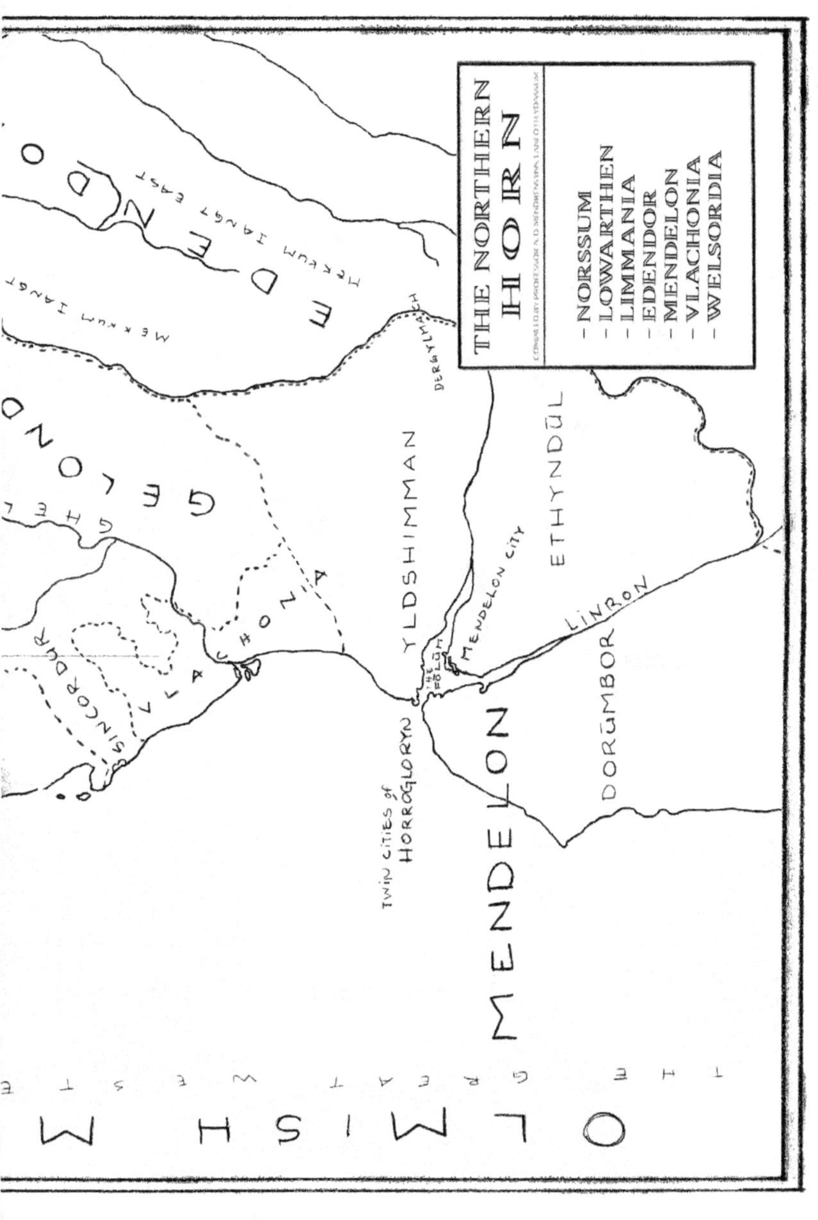
THE NORTHERN HORN
– NORSSUM
– LOWARTHEN
– LIMMANIA
– EDENDOR
– MENDELON
– VLACHONIA
– WELSORDIA
DERGYLMACH
YLDSHIMMAN
ETHYNDŪL
MENDELON CITY
LINRON
DORŪMBOR
THE FOLŪM
TWIN CITIES of HORROGLORYN
VLACHONIA
SINCORDUR
MENDELON

EDENDOR
- IMMEN
- GEHCLIOGARTH
- SHIMMANIA
- DORUM

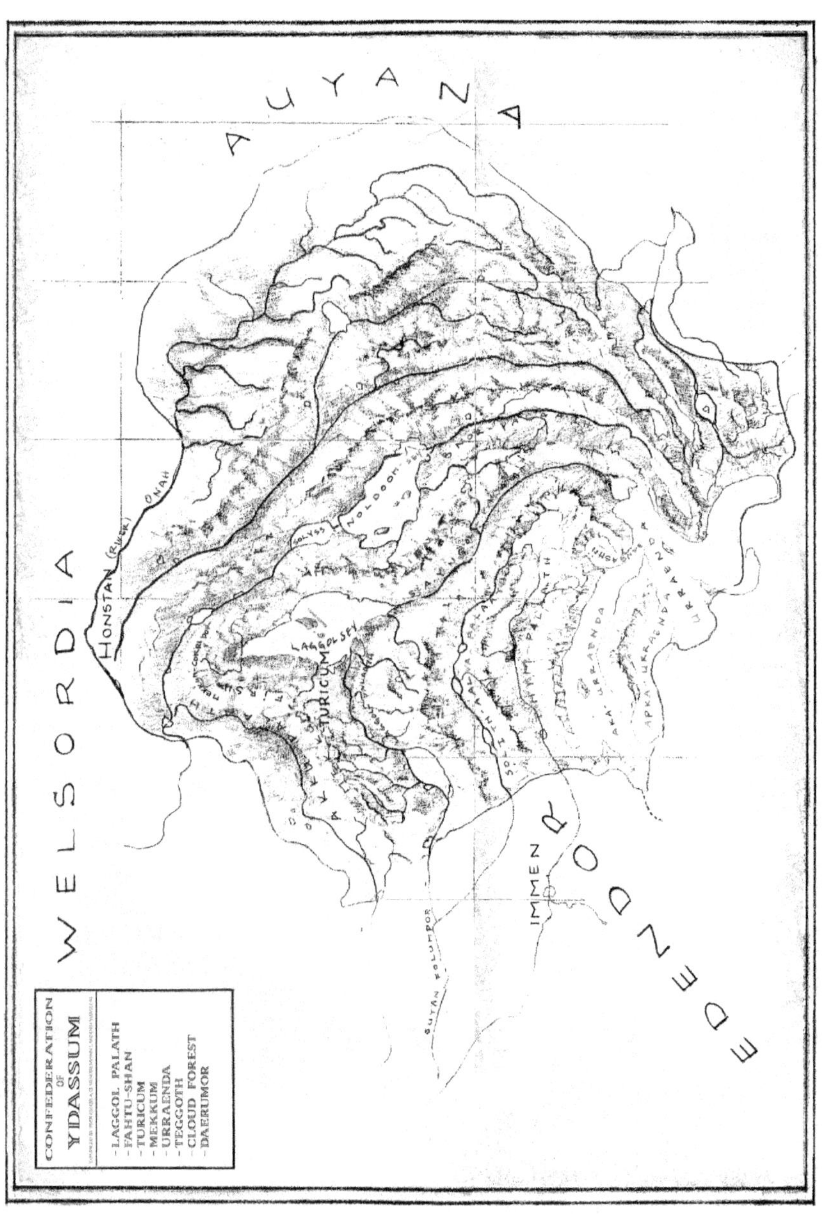
AUYANA
WELSORDIA
EDENDOR
IMMEN
HONSTAN (RIVER)
ONAH
NOLDOOM SEY
LAGGOL SEY
TURICUM
SUTAN FOLUMPOR
CONFEDERATION OF YDASSUM
- LAGGOL PALATH
- FAHTU-SHAN
- TURICUM
- MEKKUM
- URRAENDA
- TEGGOTH
- CLOUD FOREST
- DAERUMOR

MAPS OF THE NORTHERN HORN: **MENDELON**

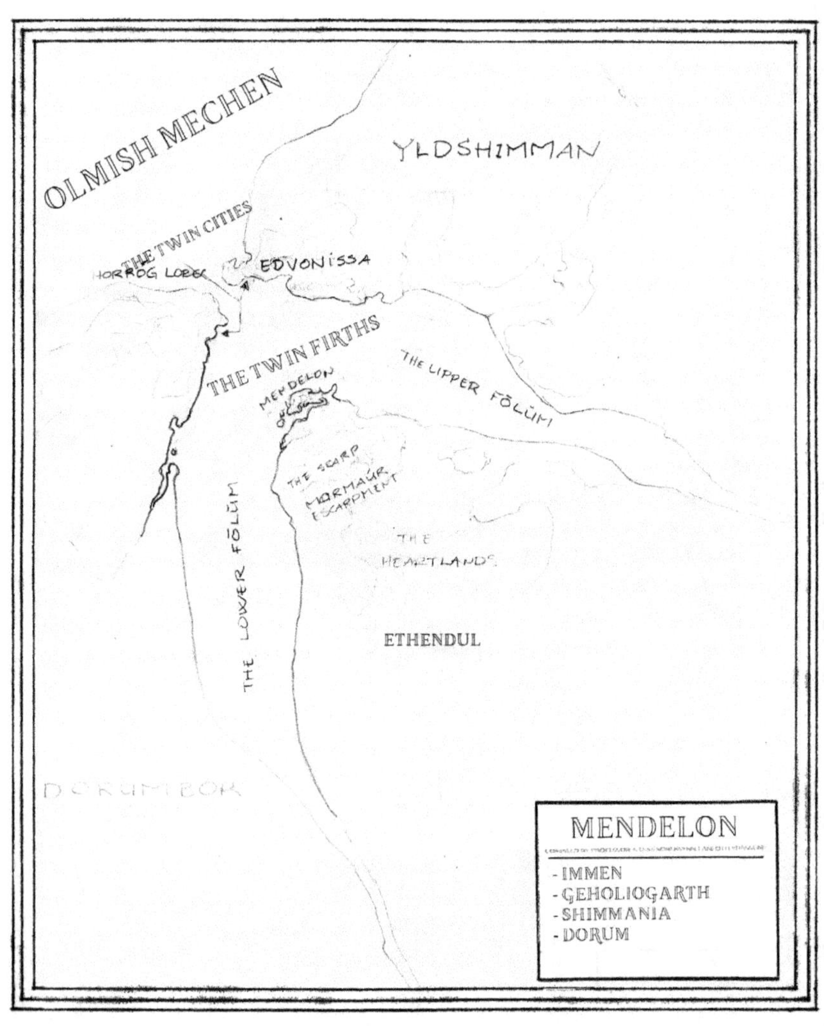

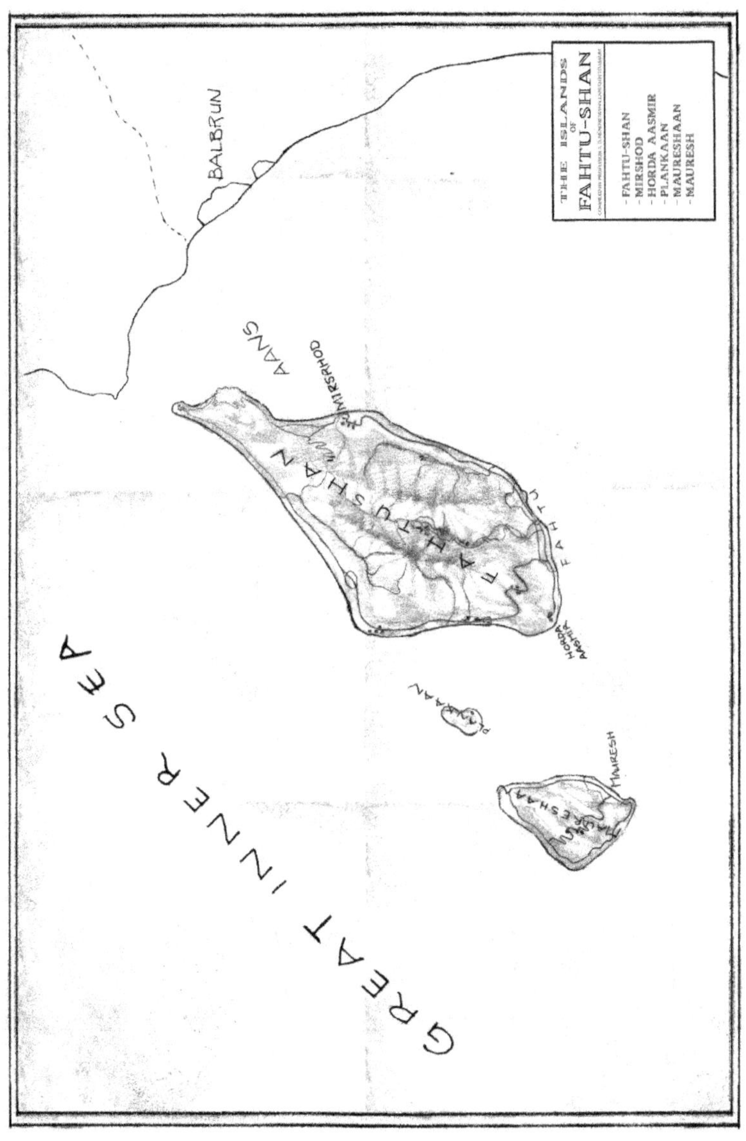
THE ISLANDS
OF
FAHTU-SHAN
- FAHTU-SHAN
- MIRSHOD
- HORDA AASMIR
- PLANKAAN
- MAURESHAAN
- MAURESH
BALBRUN
GREAT INNER SEA
MAURESH

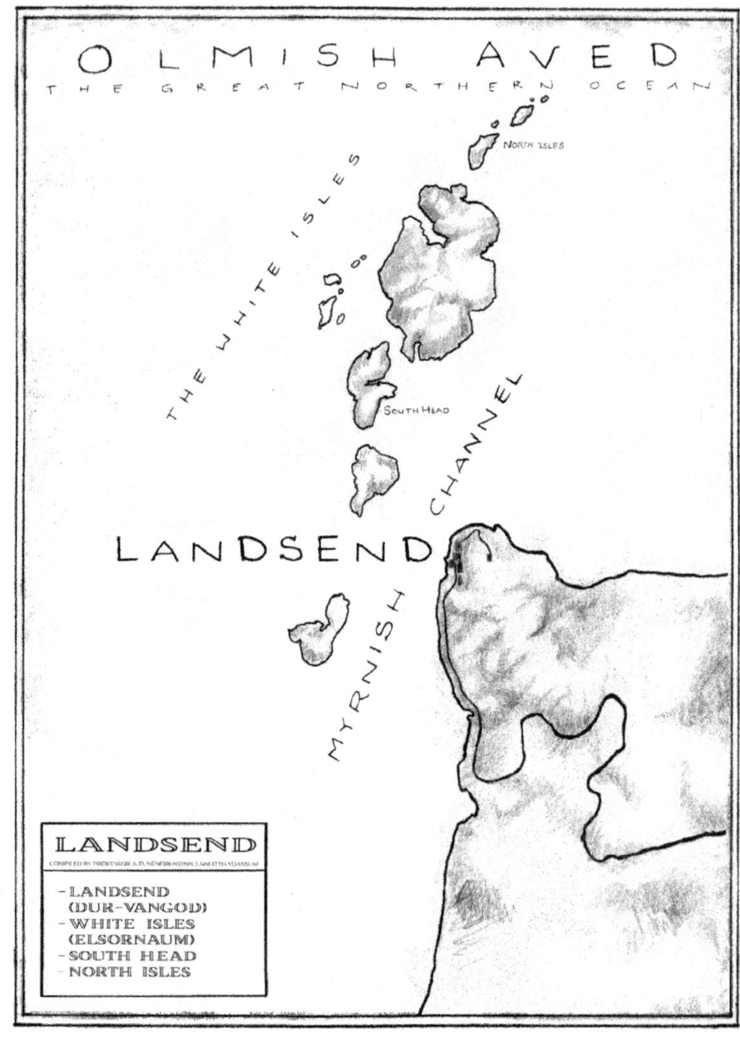
OLMISH AVED
THE GREAT NORTHERN OCEAN
NORTH ISLES
THE WHITE ISLES
SOUTH HEAD
MYRNISH CHANNEL
LANDSEND
LANDSEND
- LANDSEND
(DUR-VANGOD)
- WHITE ISLES
(ELSORNAUM)
- SOUTH HEAD
- NORTH ISLES

ABOUT THE AUTHOR

All of American-born William Chancellor's interests and strengths are brought together in the fantasy world he has created.

His passion for art, languages, and Medieval Literature led him to complete a BFA in stained glass design. He then went on to work towards a Masters, combining an in-depth study of Swiss German dialects, German, and English as a Foreign Language. He is fluent in them all as well as in Italian.

There are many of his stained-glass works throughout Europe. He designed and constructed a three-storey work which is the largest, non-sacred, stained-glass installation in Switzerland.

The natural world also plays a big part in his life. He has been recognised for his work with Hemerocallis, the Daylily, having developed over forty-five new cultivars. He was also instrumental in the development of the Japanese poultry breed Minohiki in Europe, as well as in the origination of the Toyger cat, producing the specific coat colours required in the Toyger and Bengal breeds.

Palanshia first came into being while he was still at university in the USA. Working in a pizzeria one stormy night, he started to sketch on the back of a menu, and the world of the Great Continent began to flow from his pen.

That was over 40 years ago, and since then he has moved to Italy, and become a husband, father and grandfather. But Palanshia has been part of his life all that time.

And what a story teller he is! The fantasy world he has created is made completely believable through detailed and brilliantly crafted descriptions both of vast continents and also the minutiae of everyday lives.

The reader is taken into the minds of the characters. We see what they see, hear what they hear, and feel what they feel. We care what happens to them and constantly wonder what next will unfold in this amazing place.

This epic tale he has crafted is real, gripping and totally immersive. A wonderful story and experience.